PRAISE FOR *THE OCCULT PERSUASION AND THE ANARCHIST'S SOLUTION*

Lisa de Nikolits sets readers on a rollercoaster ride of clever twists and unexpected turns. *The Occult Persuasion and the Anarchist's Solution* is a lot of fun and filled with believable, yet zany characters. It bounces between the viewpoints of Lyndon and Margaux, a retired couple whose marriage speeds steadily downhill after Lyndon decides to call it quits and runs off. It's the ultimate story of marriage meltdown told in a style all Lisa de Nikolits's own, and this one should be on everybody's must-read list."
—DIETRICH KALTEIS, author of *Zero Avenue*

The Occult Persuasion and the Anarchist's Solution is a very adult *Alice in Wonderland* with a dash of *The Conjuring*: readers will be smiling one moment and breaking out in goose bumps the next. As one character succinctly points out, "Things come to light in the darkness." Warm, witty, wildly imaginative and inspiring, *The Occult Persuasion and the Anarchist's Solution* puts the "joy" in joyride! Lisa de Nikolits is one of the most exciting authors in CanLit today and this funny, fearless new novel will not disappoint her fans.
—HEATHER BABCOCK, author of the forthcoming *Filthy Sugar*

Lisa de Nikolits has penned a taut, tight thriller involving domestic disputes, death, and a wonderfully jarring book title. Along the way there's a stolen cat, a suspicious boating accident in Sydney Harbour, Australia, assorted crimes, and a slew of quirky, compelling characters that will keep you reading. If you're a fan of off-beat mysteries with a dash of dark humour, this novel is for you."
—NATE HENDLEY, author of *The Boy on the Bicycle: A Forgotten Case of Wrongful Conviction in Toronto*

Her creative powers at a peak, in *The Occult Persuasion and the Anarchist's Solution,* Lisa de Nikolits, a sage wrapped in a cloak of language, offers us a crystal ball to gaze upon ourselves. With Lisa de Nikolits's brand of camp and mysticism, the story zig zags, spirals with vortices, depths and explosive happenings as she weaves a story of magnitude—a disappearance and a demonic spirit to a punk rock tattoo parlour and a protest of such vision it plays on the world's stage. You come to love the characters, you want to remain in the book, which seems to read the reader on the inside. We become part of its structure. *The Occult Persuasion and the Anarchist's Solution* will haunt and guide you long after you finish it. Lisa de Nikolits has written a masterpiece that firmly places her as one of the best Canadian writers of our time.

—BRENDA CLEWS, author of *A Fugue in Green*

Lisa de Nikolits takes you on a wild ride through the disintegrating lives of a husband and wife who are lost, figuratively and literally, in Sydney, Australia. Told from the alternating points of view of Margaux and Lyndon, the narrative rolls out in a kind of stream-of-consciousness that grabs at your heart. On their volatile journeys, they each encounter people who change their lives. Lyndon meets an aging anarchist who tries to save the world; a woman's tortured soul reaches out to Margaux in repeated visions. In this unique novel, de Nikolits explores the lives of desperate people struggling to find meaning in the modern world.

—SYLVIA MAULTASH WARSH, author of *The Queen of Unforgetting*

Lisa de Nikolits has written another page turner—this time a novel of transformation—with especially captivating secondary characters, including a large affectionate Maine Coon cat. Addictive—and a joy to read.

—ELIZABETH GREENE, author of *A Season Among Psychics*

Lisa de Nikolits' imagination has a seemingly unlimited cast of colourful characters and she uses several of them to full effect in this, her latest look into her wonderous mind. Like rows of dolls on a shelf, Ms. de Nikolits picks a few at random, dresses them up, and builds a fantastic story around them. Less rotten than *Rotten Peaches*, less furious than *No Fury Like That*, *The Occult Persuasion and the Anarchist's Solution* has more fun than *No Fury Like That*, but has its serious, introspective moments as well. An Oakville couple having a mid-life crisis in Australia is the stepping off point of another of Ms. de Nikolits's imaginative adventures, full of colourful characters and witty, but realistic dialogues about life, anarchy, capitalism and tattoos.

—JAMES FISHER, *The Miramichi Reader*

Prepare for a wild and wondrous ride! *The Occult Persuasion and the Anarchist's Solution* is a page-turner like only Lisa de Nikolits can deliver. Featuring a cast of memorable characters—including a functionally dysfunctional family of four; a Maine Coon cat named Queenie; a former punk-hacker-turned-anarchist barber; an olive-eyed cross-dresser; and the malevolent ghost of a former psychiatric nurse—and set in the picturesque (and sometimes seedy) Australian cityscape, *The Occult Persuasion and the Anarchist's Solution* gives fans something to truly sink their teeth into, from start to surprising ending. Mark my words: After reading de Nikolits' latest *tour de force*, you'll never look at familial relationships the same way again."

—RUTH ZUCHTER, author of *The Mother Suite*

This cathartic and ultimately healing book conjures paranormal horror from historic events our collective consciousness would seek to gloss over, punk rock and rolling readers into a tumble of lapsed and bizarre behaviour that breaks a conventional marriage in two. As both players swirl into deep self-discovery, a supporting cast of eccentrics, gurus, bikers and a spirit medium guide the unceremoniously separated pair toward an intense crescendo where the forces of witchery are called into battle and freedom-loving values are jerryrigged to outlive life.

—SK DYMENT, author of *Steel Animals*

Be Your Own Revolution and steal back your world! Live your life to the fullest and be the person you want to be, not what others want! *The Occult Persuasion and the Anarchist's Solution* offers characters

that are realistic, flawed and yet have redeeming qualities as, once again, author Lisa de Nikolits gives us a novel that is unique, has many powerful messages and makes everyone wonder which way would they align? Filled with suspense, action, intrigue, deceptions, betrayals, unknown answers, family love, discord and change, plus an anarchist's occult beliefs, [this is a] perfect blend and recipe for a noir novel, a serio-comic thriller with five-star flavour.
—FRAN LEWIS, *Just Reviews*

Lisa de Nikolits's *The Occult Persuasion and the Anarchist's Solution* gallops off to a frantic start with a drowning off Sydney Harbour and a jeep and cat theft in Kirribilli. Margaux and Lyndon, a previously happy bourgeois couple from Oakville, Toronto, have embarked on an "Around-the-World-For-However-Long-We-Want" trip but Lyndon's mid-life crisis derails their plans. A collision of accidental meetings brings more excitement into these two retirees' lives than either could have reasonably imagined. They encounter anarchists, white witches, demon ghosts, tarot readers, tattoo artists, and more. De Nikolits grabs the reader by the scruff of their neck and pulls them along, willingly, for a wild, unexpected, and zany ride.
—MYNA WALLIN, author of *Anatomy of an Injury*

What a fabulous, gripping story *The Occult Persuasion and the Anarchist's Solution* is. A hugely consequential and restorative story, written with an unerring ability to draw the reader so completely into its riveting landscape. We bond with this band of humans we grow to care deeply about. The characters' startling mutiny is at times unnerving—a full-tilt unravelling—mutating into magnificently odd odysseys, driven by catalysts that cut to the core. I revelled in this saga's spirited and gutsy guides and gurus, who pop up and prop up, soothe, support, smooth, unravel, and disconcert, and who present challenges and offer expanding perspectives, teeming with unanticipated and suspense-filled consequences.
—SHIRLEY MCDANIEL, artist

THE OCCULT PERSUASION
AND THE ANARCHIST'S SOLUTION

Canada Council for the Arts   Conseil des Arts du Canada    ONTARIO ARTS COUNCIL CONSEIL DES ARTS DE L'ONTARIO an Ontario government agency un organisme du gouvernement de l'Ontario   Canada

We gratefully acknowledge the support of the Canada Council for the Arts and the Ontario Arts Council for our publishing program. We also acknowledge the financial support of the Government of Canada.

Cover art: Glenn Larkby/Shuttershock
Cover design: Colin Frings

The Occult Persuasion and the Anarchist's Solution is a work of fiction. All the characters and situations portrayed in this book are fictitious and any resemblance to persons living or dead is purely coincidental.

Brief quotes from *The Dispossessed* by Ursula K. Le Guin are used with permission of HarperCollins Publishers. Copyright © 1974 by Ursula K. Le Guin, renewed copyright © 2002.

Library and Archives Canada Cataloguing in Publication
Title: The occult persuasion and the anarchist's solution : a novel / Lisa de Nikolits.
Names: De Nikolits, Lisa, author.
Series: Inanna poetry & fiction series.
Description: Series statement: Inanna poetry & fiction series
Identifiers: Canadiana (print) 20190147180 | Canadiana (ebook) 20190147202 | ISBN 9781771336499 (softcover) | ISBN 9781771336505 (epub) | ISBN 9781771336512 (Kindle) | ISBN 9781771336529 (pdf)
Classification: LCC PS8607.E63 O33 2019 | DDC C813/.6—dc23

Printed and bound in Canada

Inanna Publications and Education Inc.
210 Founders College, York University
4700 Keele Street, Toronto, Ontario, Canada M3J 1P3
Telephone: (416) 736-5356 Fax: (416) 736-5765
Email: inanna.publications@inanna.ca   Website: www.inanna.ca

FSC
www.fsc.org
MIX
Paper from responsible sources
FSC® C004071

THE OCCULT PERSUASION
AND THE ANARCHIST'S SOLUTION

A NOVEL BY

LISA DE NIKOLITS

inanna poetry & fiction series

INANNA PUBLICATIONS AND EDUCATION INC.
TORONTO, CANADA

ALSO BY LISA DE NIKOLITS:

Rotten Peaches
No Fury Like That
The Nearly Girl
Between The Cracks She Fell
The Witchdoctor's Bones
A Glittering Chaos
West of Wawa
The Hungry Mirror

To Bradford Dunlop.
And the mystical place where stories come from.

1. MARGAUX

"MY HUSBAND HAS FALLEN OVERBOARD." I kept repeating that to anyone to who would listen, but everyone looked at me as though I were deranged. I was certain he had fallen into the black sea of the Sydney Harbour. Panic stopped my breath as if a cork had been shoved down my throat. I ran from one side of the ferry to the other and back, but, just like the last time I checked, he was not there.

It was close to midnight and the Sydney Harbour was a tar pit of roiling waves, churning and chopping. I leaned over the railing, trying to see him in the water, searching for an outstretched arm, but the ferry was moving too quickly. Half a dozen people onboard looked at me curiously, and I could see them thinking, *Nuts, she's nuts, don't make eye contact.* I started panting like a dog, making horrible sounds.

I grabbed the deckhand by the arm. I tried to form words but I could hardly talk. All I could say was, "Husband. Gone. Must have fallen overboard." I pointed to the water, thick like molasses.

The deckhand was kind. He didn't call me a raving lunatic. He helped me check the ferry from stern to bow, starboard to port, not once but twice. He asked for my husband's cellphone number, and he dialled it on speaker. It went straight to voicemail. I had already tried, with the same response. *Hiya. Lyndon here. Do the necessary or forever hold your peace.*

"He's fallen overboard," I said. "We have to find him."

2. LYNDON

I SIDLED AROUND THE CAR, opened the door, and shot into the driver's seat, quickly pulling the door closed. The air con was an arctic blast, and I was chilled in seconds. Where was the off switch? But more importantly, I had to get the hell out of Dodge.

I pulled out into the traffic, bracing for sirens, flashing lights, and my imminent arrest, but there was just the usual Sydney gridlock. I threaded in-between the cars, glancing in the rear-view mirror, and looking for a furious blonde in hot pursuit, shaking her fist and probably dialling 0-0-0 to call the cops, but there was no sign of her. What kind of idiot left a brand-new Jeep running while she went to get a coffee? I was standing there, about to sip my skinny flat white, when this rich suburban ditz came along, parked right in front of me, leapt out, and rushed into the coffee shop. It wasn't like I was looking for a car to steal. Of course not.

I fumbled with the car's buttons and levers, driving with one hand, and I managed to turn the air con off. I opened my window and let the warm summer wind blast into the car, washing it clean of the cold, burnt air.

But where was I going? A quick decision was necessary. I called up a map of Australia in my mind. While I'd had no interest in the adventure Margaux was so excited about, I'd studied a map of Australia for hours, losing myself in the tongue-twisting Aboriginal names like Woollabra, Woolloomooloo, and

Wollongong, wishing I didn't have to go at all. But here I was, and I had to make a choice. I could go northeast or southwest. But the Gold Coast to the north sounded cheap and nasty, so Melbourne won the mental coin toss.

I was about to take the turnoff for the Hume Highway when I realized that highways might have cameras, whereas the smaller roads would not, so I decided to navigate by the compass on the dashboard and stay off the radar as much as possible. I had the sudden worry that the car might have a tracker, but I figured that if it did, there wasn't much I could do about it. I felt strangely free and yet resigned at the same time.

I checked the gas tank. Full. I didn't have to worry about that. In fact, for the first time in ages, I didn't have to worry about anything at all. I was free. Free from all the societal and familial shackles and manacles. I pounded the steering wheel with my fist and I grinned a Jack Nicholson crazy-man smile—yes, I was doing the Jack-man proud! I had been bowed and beaten and nearly broken but not for one second longer! I had finally taken control.

I released all the windows in the car to get the full volume of the sweet-scented, hot Australian summer, and I leaned back in my luxurious seat to savour my moment of triumph. I hadn't let the bastards grind me down!

I reached for my skinny flat white and took a satisfying gulp. As I took another slug, thinking it was possible that the Australians made the greatest coffee in the world, a scream pierced my eardrums and my scrotum clenched so far back in my body I was convinced I'd lost my balls for life. I choked down the mouthful of coffee and shoved the cup into the holder.

Another ungodly ear-piercing howl filled the air, and I nearly swerved off the road. I white-knuckled the car into submission and tried to steady my heart, which was pounding so hard my eyeballs popped like a cartoon character given a wedgie. What in God's name was that? Was there a demon in the car? Was it a baby? Please don't tell me it was a baby. I had stolen a car with a baby in it, hadn't I? I glanced into the back, fully expecting to see an infant staring at me with accusing eyes. It was one thing to be a car thief—which, I'll have you know I am not—but a kidnapper? My insides sloshed back and forth as if I'd swallowed a litre of the green mush that Margaux made me eat in lieu of breakfast, hoping to help me shed my unwanted pounds. I had that same bitter taste in my mouth now as I prepared to meet the gaze of the stolen baby strapped into its car seat, pursing its little Chucky-doll monster mouth and winding up its batting arm to let loose another Stephen King-inspired scream. But there was no baby. There was no car seat. No Chucky. Relief washed over me and my balls un-gripped a millimetre. At least I was not a child thief. I breathed again. Thank God. There was, however, a large grey box on the back seat. A cat box.

I took my eyes off the road for a moment and swung around to look at the box. I had kidnapped a cat. I had catnapped. I was a sixty-year-old cat-thieving felon. One did not steal cats. Top of the range Jeeps, yes, that was somewhat acceptable, although of course, I was not a car thief by profession or nature. Deep down, though, I supposed I must be one since I appropriated the car with such ease. But I was not, nor would ever be, a cat thief.

Thoughts filled my mind like dust devils, and I forced my eyes back to the road. I needed to focus. Self-recriminations and internal philosophical debates were of little use to me at that point. But another eardrum-destroying howl filled the car, as if a hundred geese were being mauled by a pack of wild dogs. It was all I could do to keep the car moving in a straight line. My hands were shaking and sweat poured off me, and I was stuck to the leather seat I had been admiring only moments before. What in the blazers was in that box? Was a cat even capable of making sounds like that? I needed to pull over and dump the box. Nothing in the world should make a noise like that, not even Lizzie Borden's family as they succumbed to her axe-wielding little hand. And why was the cat suddenly so distraught when it had been utterly silent when I took the car? Why was it howling now, a good half an hour later?

I scrambled for solutions, which was pretty hard to do when devilish sounds were turning the mushy insides of my bowels to ice despite the summer heat flooding the car. I remembered the air con—how the car had been like a butcher's storage locker when I took it—and it struck me. Could it be that the creature wanted the air conditioning back on?

Another yowl filled the cabin, and again I wanted to pull over and ditch the box at the side of the road, but I was flanked by cars and couldn't stop. Where had all this traffic come from? Stopping was not an option.

I fumbled with the buttons on the steering wheel and managed to close the windows. I punched the air con up to the max, full blast. The cat was still squealing and hissing, and I pounded the steering wheel with my fist.

"Shut up, shut up, shut up, cat," I shouted into the back of the car. I gave a low growling moan, trying to quell the beast into submission. I couldn't count the years since I'd raised my voice. I'd never raised my voice to my children, or my wife, and certainly not to my staff. But now I did. "Shut up! Shut up!"

I increased the volume of my chant, and my growl turned into a scream that sounded rusty at first, a bit squeaky, but I was certainly no match for the cat who was still putting me to shame. "Shut up! Stop it, *eyyyyyyy yayyyyy!*" I put some force behind it, and soon I was reaching down into my lungs and my gut, and it felt fantastic. I was screaming like a toddler having a tantrum and grinning like maniacal Jack. It took me a while to notice that the cat had gone quiet and the only sound in the car was coming from me. Feeling remarkably stupid, I stopped shouting and all I could hear was the frigid air blasting into the confines of the vehicle. I was covered in goosebumps, teeth nearly chattering, but the cat was silent. My detecting skills had proven sound. The cat loved the air con.

I cleared my throat and readjusted my body in the seat and tried to reorganize my thoughts and myself after my unexpectedly exhilarating screamfest. I wondered if I should carry on screaming just for the fun of it but I had lost momentum. The car was as cold as a mortuary's freezer. That was why the woman had left the car running when she went to get her coffee. To keep the cat happy. That must be some cat.

I knew I would need to address the cat situation at some point, but I decided not to think about it right at that moment. That was how I'd managed to navigate most of my life, by not thinking about things for the moment, and generally things had worked out fine. Well, up to a certain point, I supposed.

But I was so fricking cold. I poked around with the controls, trying to see if I could get the air con to blow into the back of the car and not the front, but it didn't seem to work. I finally settled for turning on my seat warmer. The back of my thighs and my back got blissfully warm, but my hands were like icicle claws in rigor mortis on the steering wheel.

I wondered what kind of search was taking place for me. Margaux would have been freaked out by my sudden absence—to put it mildly—and I wondered what she would make of my disappearance. But I couldn't think about that either right then. I did wonder if there was an alert out for the car and I turned on the radio, trying to find a news channel. But I couldn't find anything about me or the car and every station seemed to be playing that scourge of the earth, Taylor Swift, singing her vapid songs, and I flicked the radio off.

I had turned my cellphone off the moment I stepped off the ferry, so there was no way Margaux could find me via that. I patted my jacket pocket. Yes, the phone was still there.

Thoughts of Margaux refused to leave my mind, so I turned my attention to the cat. Anything rather than think about Margaux. The cat needed water. I needed water. I would think about these things, not about my wife of thirty-five years who I unceremoniously ditched in the middle of the night on the edge of the Sydney Harbour. She would be hysterical with fear and worry. The cat needed water. I needed water.

I had been driving for just over an hour and the signs for Wollongong were becoming insistent so I decided to stop there. The scenery was spectacular, with the aqua Pacific Ocean on my left and rugged bluffs to my right, but it was hard to think about how pretty it all was when I was waiting for sirens and policemen to jump out at me and arrest me.

I wondered if I could change the license plates of the Jeep with a set from another car, but I figured that was something people only did in movies. It would hardly look inconspicuous to be kneeling down in broad daylight, unscrewing someone's license. No, when it came to license plates, I would have to hope for the best.

And what about the cat? Would it start howling as soon as the car was turned off and normal air temperatures resumed? I would have to be speedy if I left the car. Perhaps I shouldn't stop at all and let the thing die of thirst. But what about me? I didn't want to die of thirst. I knew that a few hours without water was hardly life-threatening, and I had polished off half that skinny flat white. I was being overly dramatic. But I was hungry too. I hadn't had breakfast, and my stomach was a growling echoing cavern.

I pulled into a parking lot with a gas station and turned around to talk to the cat I had yet to see.

"Listen to me, you little beast," I said, although the box opening was facing the car doors and not me, and I had no idea who or what I was really talking to. "Shut up, do you hear me? Do not whine or yowl or scream, do you hear me?"

There was silence. "I am not telling you again," I said firmly although there was a quaver to my voice. "One squeak out of you and you're toast on the side of the road."

I turned off the engine with a flourish of bravado I did not feel and slipped out of the car, eying it uneasily. I wished I had a baseball cap to hide my head just in case there was some kind of alert out for me. I hailed from Canada where we watched shows like *The First 48* and *CSI* and *Forensic Files,* and there were cameras spying at you from every angle, able to identify everybody. I had no idea how realistic those things were in Australia, but I was sure that Big Brother was at the ready a lot more than we cared to know.

I checked the time and was startled to find that it was only a quarter to nine in the morning. I felt as if I'd been up for days, escaping, a fugitive from justice, cat in tow.

I did some calculations and I figured I must have taken the cat and the car around seven-thirty a.m.

Many of the stores in the strip mall weren't open and the parking lot was empty for the most part. I glanced back at the Jeep, which I had parked in the furthermost corner. There were acres separating it from the next car, a rusty old sedan that looked as if it had been abandoned some years back.

There was a dollar store, the Hot Dollar, and I ducked inside, telling myself that walking like a criminal was not what I should be doing. I needed to be casual and cavalier. I straightened up and grabbed a basket. I loaded it up with chips and pop and chocolates and a few bottles of water. I stood in the pet aisle and I was about to buy a cat bowl when I realized this might look suspicious. A cat had gone missing in Sydney and some guy was seen buying a bowl in Wollongong? I told myself I was overthinking but I took a dog's bowl instead, along with a few dog toys and a tiny dog's leash. I was fairly certain, without ever having met this cat, that it would need restraining when I let it out of the box.

The baseball cap selection was pitiful. They all had "Wollongong" on them or the Australian flag, which would hardly be worn by a native, so I settled on an ivy-green floppy fishing hat. I was going to buy a pair of sunglasses, but I tallied my purchases and told myself to be circumspect. I returned the dog toys to their shelf.

The cashier was on the phone when she rang up my lot. She

was arguing with her mother about her lout of a boyfriend who was camping out, uninvited, at the mother's homestead. I thought the conversation was great—she wasn't concentrating on me at all. I took my bag and left the store bracing myself for a Bonnie and Clyde showdown, fully expecting the police to be outside en masse, guns held high, lights flashing, and bravado shouts of, "Hands up! On the ground, NOW!'

But the parking lot was empty, and the Jeep was stationed in silence. I approached it cautiously and unlocked the car. I opened the back door, pushed the cat box to the left, slid in, and shut the door.

I took a deep breath. It was time to face the demon feline. I leaned down and peered into the cat box, and the next thing I knew, I fell in love.

"Oh my God," I said, breathless. "You beauty you."

The cat stared at me impassively. It was a Maine Coon and one of the finest specimens I had ever seen. I am a cat fan, but my daughter and Margaux are both allergic, so my cat dreams had gone unrealized for all of my married life.

"Oh baby," I said, in awe. The cat blinked at me like, *Open my door, fool.*

So I did. The cat walked out and settled down on my lap. I stroked it, or him, or her, and it made happy little chirping noises, like a bird or a cricket. Such beautiful melodic sounds. And, then, like the screaming episode, I did something I hadn't done in a century. I cried.

3. MARGAUX

"HE'S OVERBOARD," I REPEATED. "We have to send a rescue party. He can swim but a boat might hit him on the head, and he's out of shape. He hasn't exercised in years. There are waves and yachts and boats and ferries. He'll get hit on the head and he'll drown."

"We'll find him," the ferry captain told me. "We'll find him."

It was midnight and we were heading back to our hotel after dinner with Anita, an old friend of mine, a dinner that I knew Lyndon had found tedious and I had felt bad for having made him go. I hadn't seen Anita in years, and yes, admittedly, she was tiring to be with even for the shortest periods of time. But still, when we bumped into her at Circular Quay, she had squealed with delight. How could I have come to Sydney without having gotten in touch? I did know about Facebook, surely? Cowed, I had said yes, dinner would be lovely, and I made Lyndon come with me, and then of course, he had hated the whole evening. My already frazzled nerves were splayed like the frayed edges of an electrical cord as I waited for the flying sparks to erupt into a raging fire. But they didn't, which was only a partial relief. The tension crackled in the air and I felt as if I was trying to spark a flame off an old Bic lighter, while all I was doing was shaving off the top layer of my thumb.

In fact, my whole body had felt as if it had been trying to spark a fire off an old lighter. I was raw and scraped, such was the evening. And I was angry with Lyndon. It was only one night of our whole trip. Just one objectionable night. Why couldn't he have been nicer? At least, nicer to me. Why couldn't he have been a conspiratorial ally about Anita's loud, challenging hospitality? He could have exchanged looks with me, made me feel like we were on the same side, but instead, he ignored me and made snippy comments at her, which wasn't like him either. Although really, he hadn't been himself in ages. Perhaps I'd hoped the dinner would be a catalyst to help him snap out of his malaise, but, like all my other solutions and ideas and remedies, it hadn't done a darn thing except make him act like a sullen schoolboy while I felt like his aging mother, which was hardly sexy or fun.

I had finally slipped a Xanax under my tongue when neither of them was looking, and I kept the wine flowing, and by the time Lyndon and I were waiting on the ferry at Neutral Bay, I was numb to the whole night. All I wanted to do was have a lovely hot bath, add a sleeping pill to the chemistry in my blood, climb between the freshly-laundered crisp hotel sheets, and forget about the dinner, my husband, my life, and this awful trip which had been my ill-advised idea in the first place.

But my hot bath hadn't happened because Lyndon had vanished.

"When last did you see him, Mrs. Blaine?"

"Hmm?" I tried to rally my thoughts. The captain was asking me a question. It was true that fear and adrenalin had stripped me of my cosy Xanax and wine comforter, but it was still hard to think straight.

When had I last seen Lyndon? Good question. I had ignored him on the ferry, taking a seat inside when I knew he liked to be outside, enjoying the waves and fresh air. Although "enjoying" would be a strong term since I hadn't actually seen Lyndon "enjoy" anything in decades. So, I had stared pointedly away from him, pretending to look at the sparkling lights that lined the harbour. But I was really watching the reflection of my face on the window and all I could see was a tired old woman with deep, harsh lines cutting into the sides of her mouth. Her skin had become saggy and dimpled, soft, like cheesecake past its best-before date. While a part of me didn't want to admit it, I knew that woman was me. She was disappointed and hurt and tired, and I wanted to comfort her, but I was angry with her for being disappointed and hurt and tired, and worse, for looking inescapably old, so I turned away. I studied my feet, or the other people on the ferry, and then when I finally looked around for Lyndon, he wasn't there.

Just like him, my first thought shouted. *It's always all about Lyndon. It's only ever about Lyndon.*

A part of me wanted to scream, *So be theatrical then! Vanish and do whatever you want to, you challenging, tiring man. You overgrown child. Just leave me alone. Leave me to have some kind of peace. I'm tired of cosseting and cocooning you from the disappointments and hurts of your life. I have my own problems to deal with. Don't you ever think of that?*

But then a worm of worry crawled through my belly. Seriously, where was he? I stood up, telling myself that he'd be around the corner, leaning against the side of the ferry, waiting for me to come and find him and apologize for making him suffer through such a tedious evening.

But I hadn't found him, so I ran back and forth calling for help, and my Xanax and wine fog only made it harder to look, and I felt my mascara running down my face in salty black trails.

We finally docked at Circular Quay, and it took a lifetime of bumping and nudging the ferry and throwing ropes this way and that—all of which had seemed so romantic to me when we first arrived in Sydney. But at that moment, it was torturous, and took forever.

The captain ushered me through the small crowd waiting to board. They looked at me curiously but without any real compassion or interest. My face was streaked with makeup, my hair was wild, and none of my clothes were sitting as they should. Everything was twisted.

I was led into the main terminal where we waited for an elevator. I wanted us to run to wherever it was we are going. Why weren't we running? Why was everything taking so long? I stared at the captain and the deckhand, but they were pointedly ignoring me and conferring in quiet tones. I wanted to ask why helicopters weren't searching the black waters of the Sydney Harbour—Lyndon would surely have died from hypothermia by now or been hit by a yacht or another ferry.

"Why aren't you out looking for him?" I asked, and the two men exchanged a look.

"It's okay, ma'am," the deckhand said. "We'll find him. Please don't worry. We have protocols in place for these kinds of things."

The captain didn't say anything.

Protocols in place. I wiped my face with a shaking hand. The elevator arrived and we rode up several floors. I was then led by the captain into a room filled with computer monitors, and he sat me down in front of one of them.

"Now," he said, and I hated him, his gingery hair, his weak chin, and his self-righteous manner. "Where exactly did you get on?"

"At Neutral Bay," I told him. "At eleven-thirty. I can't remember exactly when I last saw Lyndon. When we got on, he stayed outside, and I went inside. I don't like the wind, not even in summer. But he wanted to be outside, and I thought he must have walked out of my line of sight, so I didn't worry. Why would I? But then, all of a sudden, I did worry. I knew something was wrong. I searched everywhere and Jerry helped me." Jerry was the deckhand.

"We're going to go through the camera footage that shows people getting off the ferries," the captain said. He told me his name was Brian.

Jerry brought me a cup of hot tea while Brian fiddled with the computer.

"Here's the first stop after Neutral Bay," he said. "Kurraba

Point." I peered at the people getting off. The footage was clear, not like British CCTV cameras in films, where you couldn't recognize anyone.

"No, he's not there," I said, but they made me watch it three times to make sure.

"I am sure," I told them. "Let's try the next one."

The next stop was Kirribilli. That was when I saw Lyndon stroll off the ferry. I couldn't believe it.

"Wait, stop," I said. "Make it go back."

They took it back to the beginning again, and there, unmistakably, was my husband, getting off the ferry.

"That's him," I said. "But why would he get off there? It's on the north shore. He knew we had to come back to Circular Quay. Why would he get off there?"

Brian shrugged. "That I can't tell you, but at least I can tell you that he isn't dead, which is very good news."

I was speechless. Yes, it was very good news, but what on earth was going on? There was nothing for Lyndon to see in North Sydney, no tourist attractions or nightlife. So, if he wanted to go for a walk by himself, why not tell me? Why didn't he tell me? He just left me.

"Can I see it again?" I asked. They showed me how to rewind the recording and I repeatedly watched Lyndon getting off the ferry, while my brain scrambled to find a solution, which was not forthcoming.

At one point, Lyndon turned and glanced back at the boat. I tried desperately to decipher that quick look. Had he been looking for me? Was he trying to tell me something? What was going on at that moment? And why had he turned off his phone? Where was he going? Had he planned this all along?

"Can we file a missing person's report?" I asked.

Brian shook his head. "He's not missing. We can all see him, large as life. Probably wanted to find a pub, have a rum and Coke, some time alone. Blokes need time to themselves. It's not unusual. Look, we'll take you back to your hotel, all right? I am sure he just wandered off for a bit, and he'll be home in a couple of hours. It will be all sorted out."

I understood what he was trying to tell me. This wasn't his problem. Lyndon was alive. Lyndon was behaving strangely, that much was true, but Brian had done his job and it was time for me to take the issue of my problematic husband and my flawed marriage and leave.

I asked Brian if I could watch the recording a few more times and he told me I could. I didn't want to miss anything, in case Lyndon had been trying to send me a message. I watched it for half an hour, and I studied every nuance of Lyndon's movements, but there wasn't anything that gave me a clue as to why he had done what he did.

I decided that Brian was probably right. Lyndon simply needed a bit of time to himself. I decided to go back to our hotel and have my nice hot bath and no doubt Lyndon would stroll in and say he'd needed some air or something or other, and that would be that.

I had to admit to myself that Lyndon hadn't been behaving normally for a while now, and this trip, which I had thought would be a cure for him having lost his job, had only seemed to trigger in him a mid-life crisis and plummeting self-esteem.

"Thank you for all your help and patience," I told Brian who patted me on the shoulder.

"We men can be strange fellas at times," he said, and I tried to smile. He seemed less hateful than before or maybe I had run out of steam.

Jerry drove me back to my hotel, and I thanked him for his help and took my leave. I tried to walk casually through the lobby as if I was simply returning from an evening's dinner after a day of fun-filled sightseeing. Nothing to see here; just a tourist after a long day.

But when I got up to the room, I closed the door, sank down onto the bed and buried my face in my hands. Everything was wrong. Yes, Lyndon was alive, but everything was wrong.

I forced myself to run a bath, but I couldn't luxuriate like I usually do. I scrubbed my body and washed my hair vigorously as if I were in a hurry because I needed to be ready and vigilant. And if I could get clean, my whole life would sort itself out. I just had to get myself moisturized and into my pyjamas and everything would be fine.

But then I was clean, and moisturized, and in my pyjamas, and things were not fine. I sat motionless in the wingback chair that overlooked the harbour, my hands folded in my lap, and watched the blackness of night fade, pushed away by the coming light of day. The sun rose and my phone did not ring and there were no messages from Lyndon, no texts. There was nothing in reply to the messages and calls that I had sent him.

But he is alive, I kept telling myself. *He will come back. Please let him come back.*

He'd never done anything like this before in thirty-five years of marriage—just wander off without telling me. He'd never even taken too long at the store. And his phone was always on and I could always reach him.

I was fifty-eight years old. I was a part-time archivist at Mc-Master University, but mostly I was a wife and a mother, and I thought I was pretty good at both of those things. A niggle of doubt told me that no one was perfect, of course not, but I had tried my best. *Tried my best.* Such a stupid saying. My best obviously wasn't good enough if my husband walked away from me without so much as a goodbye. It wasn't as if he'd ceased to find me attractive. He still jumped my bones two or three times a week and I happily anticipated our encounters. I'd never been beautiful. I was pretty in the girl-next-door kind of way, with a narrow nose that had a little upturned tip—Lyndon called it my "princess nose." He said I was like a Disney princess, but I said Snow White's nose was much more of a button nose than mine. He agreed and commented that perhaps it was the elegant narrow ovals of my nostrils that bewitched him. Only Lyndon could say something that asinine and sound sincere. He also said I had the most perfect philtrum he had ever seen. When I looked blank, he explained that that was the term for the indentation above my lip. A Greek word, he said, meaning "love." A term for the two folds of flesh that, during embryonic development, grew and met in the front of the head. The philtrum was the last bit of the "seam" where the two halves of our face are fused together. All of which kind of grossed me out. I twitched my princess nose and my philtrum in distaste, and we both collapsed with laughter, while he poured me more wine.

I was five-foot-six and slender, except when I bore my children. They had both gone out of their way to double my size, but I soon bounced back to my boyish figure for which I was grateful. I kept my reddish hair short and feathered, coloured in recent years. I never worried about my freckles or the fact that my one eyebrow arched way higher than the other. The ordinary shape of my mouth was counterbalanced by the striking colour of my eyes. I had gotten lucky there. Hazel eyes could be boring, but mine had a starburst of red-brown around the pupils, in the shape of a sunflower, all of which was framed by thick, long eyelashes.

I was a white-capri kinda gal in spring, and in summer, I wore a uniform of white jeans and soft cashmere sweaters. I also favoured colourful blouses with jewellery accents to match. I took care with my appearance, but I was never vain. I didn't have anything to be vain about. I wasn't sexy or curvaceous or sultry. Was that why Lyndon had left me? Did he have a sudden urge for a big-breasted sultry diva?

Meanwhile, Lyndon had always reminded me of Ted Bundy. He had that same patrician look and similar features. I thought that the first night I met him and later, when we hooked up, I joked about it. He told me that I wasn't the first person to make the observation, and he seemed hurt and dejected by the comment, so I dropped the subject and never mentioned it again. But now, I couldn't help but be reminded that Ted

Bundy escaped from prison by jumping out of the law library, and now Lyndon had run off a ferry into the Australian night.

These crazy thoughts and others swirled through my head throughout the night as I sat there watching the blackness become day.

I forced myself to get up and turn on the television. I needed to watch the morning news. I didn't expect to find anything about Lyndon, and I was hoping not to. *Please, don't let there be any stories about tourists knifed in Kings Cross or somewhere unsavoury.* But Lyndon wouldn't walk around unsafe neighbourhoods, would he? But he was a tourist, and he wouldn't know the safe from the unsafe. I clicked on the news and watched a traffic report and a weather report, which said it was going to be another glorious day in Sydney. It was the end of April, and hotter than usual. The day would reach a perfect 27 degrees without a cloud in the sky. Lovely, really but who the hell cared?

I pulled the chair closer to the television and watched the international news roll out, followed by local news. Nothing of note. But then, an announcement. Breaking news: A man had stolen a Jeep from outside a coffee shop in Kirribilli, and what was more, the Jeep had an expensive cat in the back and the distraught owner was about to be interviewed.

Lyndon got off at Kirribilli. It was him, I knew it was. I leaned forward and turned up the sound.

A thirty-something blonde was sobbing into the camera. She had left her car for a moment to go and get a flat white, and the next thing she knew, her car was gone!

What kind of idiot leaves a car running? I asked myself and the interviewer must have thought the same thing because she asked the question of the woman.

"But why did you leave it running?"

"For MooshooBear," the woman wailed. "I was going to drop her off at daycare. I always stop there. Right there. And I go and get my coffee. She hates it when the car is hot. She likes the AC, so I always leave it on when she's in the car. There's never been a problem till now."

"Who is MooshooBear?"

"My cat, of course," the woman wailed. "My Maine Coon. She's only four. She worth thousands of dollars but I don't care about that. She's my baby and someone stole her. I don't care about my car, just give me back my cat."

The blonde turned to the camera and looked imploringly at me. "Please," she said, her makeup as much of a mess as mine had been the night before, "please, just give me my cuddle-wuddle back. Keep the car, I don't care. But please, give me my baby. Wait, here's a picture of her."

She flipped through pictures on her phone and pointed it at the camera. I agreed; the cat was magnificent.

"Please," the blonde wept. "Please, just give her back to me."

The reporter made a signal and someone led the woman away. "If anyone has any information about the Jeep, registration number A, C, 75, W, G, with a cat box in the back, please call the number on your screen. All community help is welcome. Let's help this woman get her cat back!"

The news returned to bombings in Baghdad, so I muted it. I sat there in the wingback chair, all clean and moisturized, in my pyjamas, with my world in ruins. Lyndon had stolen that car. And Lyndon had stolen that cat. I just knew it.

4. LYNDON

I FINALLY GOT MYSELF under control and stopped crying. I examined the cat, prodding her this way and that, and she didn't seem to mind. She was a she and she was huge. She weighted at least fifteen pounds. She let me pet her and roll her over, and her fur was soft and silky. She had a ruff around her neck, like a lion's mane. She appeared to be in good health, and I wondered why she was in the cat box. Was she on her way to the vet? She didn't have any obvious injuries and she seemed happy on my lap. She made little trilling noises, and my eyes welled up again, but I choked down the tears. For God's sake, what was wrong with me? Well, in answer to that question: I had abandoned my wife, stolen a car, and was now sitting crying over a cat. I guess you could categorically say that there was a lot wrong with me.

I stroked the cat's hair, admiring all her colours. She was a tabby with red and gold in her fur, and she was utterly magnificent.

"Wow," I told her. "Wow. Are you okay, baby? Are you sick?" Two minutes into our meeting and I was talking to her like she's a newborn, in a way I never spoke to my own kids, not even when they were tiny. I crooned and chatted to her, and I wondered what my son and daughter would say if they could hearme now.

"Do you actually ever feel anything at all?" my son, Adam, had asked me in one of our last conversations. I had tried to answer him, I did, but I couldn't think of anything to say. There were no words. He had looked at me for a while, waiting, and then he got up and left.

Maybe he had been looking for more of a response to the news that he was gay, but it hadn't really been news to me. I wasn't shocked or surprised, and the worst truth I guess, was that I didn't really care one way or the other.

He had chosen our Around-The-World-For-However-Long-We-Want party to make the announcement. The party—and the trip—had been Margaux's idea, not mine and perhaps it was Adam's fault for choosing that time to tell me. But no, it wasn't that. I would have reacted in the same way, which was, no reaction at all. And it wasn't his fault, that was just me. Besides, at thirty-five, he didn't, or shouldn't, need approval from anyone, certainly not his parents.

I considered myself to be a nice guy, but then, if you have to tell yourself that, you're probably trying to appease the knot of guilt in your gut. Except that there was no knot and there was no guilt. If I were a nice guy, there would be a knot, wouldn't there? Why didn't I feel guilt? Why didn't I feel anything?

I had never been one for introspection. I simply never thought about things much. That was my way—just don't think about it. I had often said to Margaux, "Don't think about it, honey," and she had often snapped back that she couldn't help but think about things. Whereas me, I couldn't think about things if I tried. Obviously, I thought about a lot of things, but they were practical things, like taking out the right garbage on the right day, and putting all the correct things into the recycling and not chucking things in willy-nilly. I was meticulous about that. I thought about recycling a lot and how we were filling the world with garbage, how the level of junk was rising daily, all that packaging and glossy cardboard that couldn't be recycled. I thought about carbon emissions and gas pipelines, about oil and pollution and global warming. So it wasn't like I didn't think about things at all, I just didn't think about emotions or the meaning of life, or why we were here, or where we were going, or where we had come from, or why one's children never seemed to stop needing to be looked after even when they were supposed to be adults.

I was savvy with repartee, and in fact, I was considered to be quite the wit. You could always rely on Lyndon at a party, I'd heard countless people say. I had a dry wit, a cutting wit, and I loved to see people laughing and at a loss with their response. Sometimes people looked a bit alarmed, as if they were worried I would turn my rapier wit on them, but I was never cruel. There was, however, a certain satisfaction that came from being the most clever person in the room, and I had worked hard to achieve and maintain that status. I read the newspapers at breakfast, preparing my commentary for the day, should anyone ask for my opinion, which they invariably did. I had been, until recently, the editor of a business magazine, a post I had held for a very long and yet a very short, thirty-three years of my life.

I was twenty-seven when they made me the editor-in-chief, the youngest hotshot ever. I was already married to Margaux and we had our Adam; he was two years old and our daughter, Helen was on the way. My whole cookie-cutter life had been laid out in front of me, and all I had to do was show up at meetings, say clever, funny things, strategically guide the magazine through its various advertising crises and technological developments, and generally keep the ship afloat.

All of which I did extremely well, primarily by not thinking too much at all. Yes, the physical state of the world distressed me, and I did what I could to save the planet by separating our garbage and taking my own mug to the coffee shop, thereby playing my part in fending off the impending disaster of the death of our planet. I did as much as I could, anyway.

I sat there stroking the cat, and I didn't want to think about my life, but the cat was wonderful on my lap, a heavy, warm comfort, and I didn't want to disturb her—or me. So, I carried on doing that uncharacteristic thing, thinking. Thinking about the unthinking life I had led.

My life had been a blessed one by all accounts. I was born of suburban parents who were acknowledged to be nice people—good people—although my father had been quick with his fists whenever I behaved in a manner, or offered an opinion, that he did not like. He never punched me—that would have been far too crass—but many times he smacked me across the back of the head in a pseudo joking way, a way that brought fireworks of light spinning across my vision and the sting of tears to my eyes. I often wondered if I had suffered from a constant concussion when I was growing up because I didn't feel right a lot of the time. I suffered from headaches, wooziness, and a flulike malaise that my father called my "'Linnie's vapours." "Poor little fragile flower," he would say, "suffering from the vapours like a Victorian heroine." But I never questioned him or his methods of parenting. I had been brought up to believe that my father was a good man, that he merely wanted what was best for me, and I tried to trust that was true. I did try to tell him, as I grew older, that being hit on the back on the head wasn't conducive to facilitating me seeing his point sooner rather than later, that all he had to do was simply say what he wanted to say, and that he could keep his hands to himself. He hadn't appreciated my insight and issued a couple of blows with increased force as if to punctuate for emphasis.

I left home for university and never went back. I phoned my mother regularly, and she and I kept in touch, but she never asked me if she could come and visit, and I never offered.

I did not invite my parents to the wedding.

"Dad will hit me," I told my mother, and she was immediately silent. I was trespassing on forbidden ground, discussing that which should never be mentioned. When Margaux had told me she was pregnant, I spoke to her about my father. It was the only time we ever discussed him, and she was supportive of a clean amputation of the relationship. Certainly, she did not want him around our children.

My mother died of cancer when I was in my mid-thirties. Adam was ten and Helen, eight. They had never met her. We told the children that they died in a car accident, years before they had been born. I attended the funeral alone. I walked up to my father and stared at him in a way that warned him not to touch me, but he was too grief-stricken to even notice I was there.

I skipped the reception and didn't hear from my father until days before my sixtieth birthday when, out of the blue, I got a text message from him. Decades of silence and then a text message for God's sake? "*Got Alzheimer's. Wanted to say goodbye while I still could. Hope you made something of your little life. Don't reply, there's no point.*" I hadn't shown Margaux.

A less-than-happy, rather shrill meow interrupted my musing and I realized I had been kneading the cat as if she was a stress ball, and she looked up at me with an annoyed expression.

I picked her up, nose to nose. "I'm so sorry," I said. "You're quite right. Please accept my apologies. So, what shall I call you? You need a regal name. A queenly name. Queenie. Yes, that's you." I poured some water into the dog's bowl and she lapped up a tiny amount with an adorable tongue, leaving a drop of water on her chin.

"I'll get you some food soon," I said. "I wonder if you need to go to the toilet?" I looked at my watch. A good half an hour had passed, with me just sitting there, talking to myself and Queenie. I needed to get moving, I would be noticed soon, a guy sitting in the back seat of a Jeep, talking to himself. I looked around. Yes, the parking lot was filling up. I couldn't dally. I put Queenie back into her box. "Just for now," I told her. "We'll stop in the next town and get you some food. Okay?"

I got into the driver's seat, turned on the air con and the seat warmer, and we hit the road, heading for Melbourne.

The trouble with thinking was that once you started, you couldn't stop. I was hit by a flash flood of memories and the car was filled with ghosts of old, and they were all talking at the same time. Blowing open this hive of wasps wasn't what I'd had in mind when I abandoned Margaux. In fact, I had been seeking the opposite. My past had been chasing me and I turned and fled unknowingly right into its waiting arms.

I flicked on the radio station, but there wasn't anything I felt like listening to, so I returned to the annoying barrage of memories and unwelcome thoughts.

I had wanted to be an artist when I grew up. I had worked with ink and watercolour but I was also proficient in graphic illustration and I was convinced I would be able to earn a living in an agency, making the time to work on my personal projects at night. But my father had told me in no uncertain terms that my idea was rubbish. However, he said, there was a future in journalism and if I was intent on picking one of the airy-fairy ways to make a living, then at least I'd be assured of a job as a writer.

"Newspapers will always be around," he'd said. "You don't really want to be a starving artist, trust me."

It wasn't that was I was so under his sway that I couldn't fight back, but I heard the logic his argument offered and I had no counter-defense.

I ditched my little sketches and studied the ins and outs of editing and writing, and it all came so easily to me. As did Margaux. I met her when I was twenty-four, we got married when I was twenty-five and she was twenty-three, and we immediately started a family. Back in those days, it wasn't as unusual as it is now, to marry that young and have kids. I had a family. I wanted the warmth and comfort that I had never been afforded and, with Margaux, I set about making that happen as quickly as I could. We had our two kids, we saw the seasons come and go, we put up and took down the appropriate decorations, and I mowed the lawn and shovelled the snow, and I never thought about anything in any greater context than that.

But now, here I was, driving a stolen Jeep, a top-of-the-range stolen Jeep and what was more, there was a cat in the back, a cat that was worth a bunch of money, and I had stolen her and I wasn't sorry, not one little bit.

How had it come to this? I'd like to say it was Margaux's fault, but that was not strictly fair. Things had started to unravel in earnest when I turned sixty and I lost my job, the latter preceding the former, by mere days. You would think they would have had more tact than to fire me a week before such a terrible birthday, but corporations didn't really give a hoot about tact or life-changing birthdays, did they? I wasn't overly surprised, but I was horrified nonetheless. It was like one of those things that you see coming, and you think you are prepared, but you aren't, because you simply can't be.

Like losing your hair. Mine suddenly thinned out—wasn't it supposed to happen sooner or with more fanfare? Mine had waited until I was complacent, certain that I wasn't going to go bald in my later years. But days after my fiftieth birthday, the great recession started. The epicentre was the invisible bull's eye target at the top of my head, which I only knew it was there because of a picture Adam had taken—the first of many pictures in which I simply didn't recognize that man who had once been me. Who was that ordinary-looking middle-aged white guy? He looked so average, so generic, so old. Oh my God, that man was me, and he had a balding crop circle on the back of his head that spread outwards daily like the ripples of a pond. And where had the bags under my eyes come from? I had always pitied people with bags under their eyes. *Get more sleep, look more chipper, do something about it,* I silently urged them. And my chin…. My jawline had softened into a second tier; meanwhile sharp lines cut a parenthesis on either side of my mouth. And I had been a handsome man. Something I hadn't realized I'd needed to be grateful for. I inwardly panicked when I realized that what I had always thought would be there was going, and there wasn't a damn thing I could do about it.

I had told myself I should start working out. I could get a membership at the gym at work. Andy, my associate editor, kept telling me how all the higher-ups went to the gym, that it was a great place for networking. I wanted to tell him that I was way past the need to network, but when he was given my job and I was shown the door, I was glad I'd held my tongue.

Wait until you're sixty, I had wanted to snarl at him, but I consoled myself with the thought that by the time he was sixty, magazines would be long-dead and he'd most likely end up working in a McDonald's or a big-box hardware store. I did wonder if networking at the gym would have saved me, but in all likelihood, not.

I had listened to the woman from human resources explain the unfortunate situation, as she put it, and had nodded agreeably. These were tough times.

"It must be pretty awful, having your job," I told her. She was new. The human resources people I had known had been axed several weeks earlier, and I should have taken that as a sign that my days were numbered. But, with the passage of time, one became arrogant and numb to the idea that all things end for you. I took my severance package—it was a good one—and shook the woman's hand.

I went home to our paid-off, empty nest of a detached Victorian-styled house, and I waited for Margaux to come home from wherever she was, so I could break the news to her. She responded by telling me that we should have a party. A huge, Around-The-World-For-However-Long-We-Want party. It was clear that Margaux, unlike me, had been expecting and preparing for this moment for quite some time.

She had it all mapped out. We had options, we had money, and we were young and healthy. Nothing was tying us down. It was time to live and explore and have fun.

I agreed to everything she said. I couldn't think of a rebuttal, not even to myself, so I went along with all of it.

Adam and Helen thought it was great. We were so bold! Such adventurers! Our friends had also joined the clamour, wistfully saying they wished they too could do such a thing. But they hadn't invested as well as we had; too, they had debt and obligations and responsibilities.

"How long will you be gone for?" was the foremost question and Margaux's answer was always the same. We had no idea; we were travelling lightly and freely, and we would play it by ear.

Margaux threw an enormous going-away bash at Casa Loma, with Adam and Helen's help. Adam had it catered by some famous chef, and he footed the fill. He was such a foodie, my son, I never really understood it. Food was function for the body: eat, nourish, maintain. That was all. But not so for Adam. Even when the kids were young, we'd go on holiday and all he'd see was the food: breakfast, lunch and supper. I was happy with a can of pop and a sandwich or something pedestrian that would do the job, but Adam was into fine dining, from the time he was a toddler. As he grew older, wine began to factor into the occasion. He was a wine master or something; I never really paid much attention. On the odd occasion, when he would insist on taking us out, Adam would list, with unwavering attention to the very last detail, all the things he loved or hated about each dish and the accompanying libation. I tried to pretend to be interested, but I just didn't care. It was hard to pretend otherwise.

When it came to the world's biggest *bon voyage* party, Margaux and Adam and Helen had invited the whole world. I was astounded by all the people who were there. They had been told not to bring presents, since we didn't have a house to put them in anymore; so they were just to bring themselves and their good wishes. I wandered around like a castrated rooster in a crowded barnyard, trying to escape the hordes who wanted to tell me how much they loved this bold, free idea, and how they wished they were me. Perhaps I would write a book, many of them commented. Didn't most editors secretly want to be authors? No, I said, that may be the assumption, but it wasn't true. Not for me, anyway. But I could see them, playing out their own dreams in their heads. They wanted to be authors. None of it was about me. People's conversations were always only about themselves, even when they pretended to be talking about you or world politics or religion or love.

I got mildly drunk, and then Adam found me and took me aside and told me he had fallen in love with a man, and that it was the first time in his life that he'd really been in love, and he hoped he wasn't shocking me or disappointing me, but he wanted to tell me. He needed, he said, to finally come out. Those were his words. He added that he was happier than he had ever been in his life. Happy and free.

"Okay," I said. "Sure, that's fine."

Such a response sounded feeble, even to me, but I hadn't known what else to say. I had been too tired to think of what it was I was supposed to say in this situation. In the past, I had always known what I was supposed to say, but that certain knowledge had vanished. Perhaps it was in the ether, along with my lost hair and firm jawline. My son had realized he was gay, and I had realized I was exhausted.

I had no idea how I was going to survive this marvellous around-the-world adventure. I hadn't even known how depleted I was until I looked at Adam's face, at his earnest, still-handsome face, and I dug inside myself to try to say something, anything, but really, I didn't care one way or the other if he was gay or not.

A part of me knew that this was a great opportunity for Adam and me to bond and hug each other and maybe even cry a bit. But I just stood there, thinking about how my feet were hurting from all the standing and how was I going to manage exploring the whole world when my feet hurt like this?

"Do you want to meet Rick?" Adam asked and I nodded,

thinking he meant in the future, in some distant future, but he told me to stay where I was and that he'd be right back.

But I couldn't stay where I was. I escaped into a small alcove, thankfully furnished with a chair. I sat down and untied the laces of my shoes and leaned back and closed my eyes. I only meant to stay there for a moment or two, but I must have fallen asleep—that's my excuse anyway—because when Helen finally found me, the party was over and my family was clearly unhappy with the manner in which I had conducted myself.

"Sorry," I said to Adam, and I patted his shoulder. "Next time. I'll meet him next time." What next time? What did that even mean?

"Sure, Dad," he said, but he didn't look at me.

"Thank you for the wine and food, Adam," I said, clumsily trying to make amends. "And to you, Helen and Margaux, thank you all, it was a great send-off."

"Well, we had fun," Helen said pointedly, and we drove home in silence—home being a pullout sofa bed in Helen's condo, with our suitcases on guard, ready for the flight the next day.

I had lain on the sofa bed, listening to Margaux sleeping. So what if Adam was gay? It was hardly news these days. Come out, stay in, do whatever you wanted to do; honestly, the whole thing was tedious. Would I have preferred it if Adam weren't gay? Yes, simply because I couldn't be bothered to listen to the saga of self-discovery that saw him summit his Everest. I had steered him through adolescence and into adulthood. I had made sure he got an education and found gainful employment. I had done what I was supposed to do, so I could check successful parenting off the list. Wasn't that the unspoken agreement? That Adam could, should, and would handle things from there? I'd had a tough and nasty old son of a gun for a father, but I had dealt with it, moved on, and taken charge of my life.

I turned over on the sofa bed and studied Margaux's face in the never-quite-dark city glow. She was so lovely. Aged yes, but lovely. Where were the bags under her eyes? Her face had a slightly creased look to it, like a paper bag gripped too tightly then released, but her beauty was still evident. At least I thought so.

I turned and rolled onto my other side. I called up a picture of my son's face and he gazed at me, his expression unchanged. He was earnest, anxious, eager for my approval, and pathetic with need. If there was anything I disliked in this world, it was a whiny adult with Daddy issues. How had he not dealt with that yet? And why was it my problem? And if he hadn't dealt with it, then at least he should man up and shut up because the world was not interested in his diaper dilemmas.

My anger had startled me, and I wanted to turn on the light and make a cup of tea and change the direction of my focus. But I hadn't wanted to wake Margaux, not right before the start of our big adventure. So, I stayed awake all night, shadowboxing with furious arguments that led to nowhere.

5. MARGAUX

"YOUR FATHER HAS STOLEN a car with a cat in it," I told my children. I had gathered them on Skype. It was nine a.m. my time, seven p.m. the previous day their time.

"What?" They were incredulous.

"It's true. He ran off a ferry and left me. He turned off his phone. I haven't heard from him all night. We went and had dinner at Anita's and you know how much he hates her. He was furious with me for that. But he's been behaving weirdly the whole time we've been gone."

"Slow down, Mom," Adam said. "You aren't making any sense. I thought you guys were having a great time."

"I just told you that so you wouldn't worry. Your father has been behaving very strangely, even for him. He wouldn't do anything with me in Vancouver. He said he needed to walk and think, and so I went and shopped and did my own sightseeing, and then he asked me why I was buying things since we didn't have a house anymore, and I told him I was sending the stuff to you, Helen, because one day we would have a new home. And then he got drunk, and the next morning he said we had to leave Vancouver because it was making him feel trapped. So, we went to Hong Kong and that was even worse. He wouldn't leave the tiny room that was about the size of our pantry at home. He said he had flu, but I think he was depressed. I couldn't get him out of bed."

"But you loved Hong Kong," Helen said.

I nodded. "I did. But your father didn't even see it. I brought him back all kinds of food, but he would only eat bread and chocolate, and drink Coke. Then he watched TV he couldn't understand for hours on end. "

"Why didn't you tell us?" Adam asked again.

"Because of course I was hoping that things would get better. So I said let's move on to Sydney and things did improve for a few days. We had a lovely, long walk along the coastline from Coogee to Bondi, which was amazing. I thought your father seemed happy. But then we had dinner with Anita, and it all went wrong from there."

"Anita. She's like a Mac truck hitting you in a dark tunnel a hundred miles an hour," Adam commented.

Anita had come to stay with us a few years back when her marriage was in trouble, and she'd brought a whirlwind of anger and discontent with her. The vortex of her fury had been so intense that Adam and Helen had refused to visit us during her stay, and Lyndon started leaving for work at seven a.m. and coming home at midnight, just to avoid her. After she left, the family made me promise to never let her stay with us again. Her visit hadn't been easy on me either, and I happily agreed that there would be no return stays, but I hadn't thought that one dinner could have such disastrous consequences.

"I thought why not? It was a single dinner, one evening," I told the children. "I thought maybe Anita might snap him out of his funk. But it worked the opposite way, which makes all of this my fault. Everything is my fault."

"No, Mom, it's not," Helen said. "Dad was ready to snap. We were just trying to help, coming up with this idea. What else could we have done? We couldn't let him rot in his study. We had to do something. The trip made sense."

"Wait, back up," Adam said. "You said he ran off a ferry at some random stop and left you?"

"Yes. Exactly. And then he turned off his phone. I've no idea where he is."

"But why do you think he stole a cat and a car?"

"Because that was where he got off. In Kirribilli. How co-incidental is that? He goes missing and next thing someone takes off with a car that has a cat in it?"

"He probably had no idea the cat was there," Adam said. "If it even was him. I mean, who knows? Maybe it wasn't him? You're making a big assumption here. Did he hot-wire the car? I can't see Dad knowing how to hot-wire a car."

"I think Dad has many skills we don't know about," Helen commented.

"The car was running when he took it," I explained impatiently. "The cat was on its way to daycare and it likes the air conditioning on full. The woman stopped to get a coffee. She was hysterical."

"Hysterically ridiculous, if you ask me, to bow to a cat's demands like that," Helen said. "Well, good luck to Dad if he stole such a high maintenance pet. It will be hilarious when he realizes what he's done."

"MooshooBear," I sighed. "That's the cat's name. It's a very beautiful cat. Worth thousands, the woman said."

"Does she have a chip in the cat?" Helen asked. "A cat like that, you'd think she would have a chip in it. Or the car, can't it be tracked?"

"Obviously not, or she would have said," I replied, tired of the conversation. "They put the number of the license plate on the news."

"Did you fill out a missing persons' report?" Adam asked.

"I can't because he's not missing. He got off the boat. You can see it on the video. I watched it about a hundred times. And he wasn't deranged or in any distress. He was fine, absolutely fine. He looked normal."

"Did you tell the police you think he took the car and the cat?" Adam asked.

"Of course not. I don't want to incriminate him. And anyway, there's no proof except that it makes sense to me. Oh God, what if he gets arrested for stealing a car with a cat in it?"

"Let's not get ahead of ourselves," Adam said, in an effort to calm me down. "We don't even know for sure that he took the car and the cat."

"What are you going to do?" Helen, always practical, asked.

"I have no idea. Wait, I suppose. Wait for him to contact me."

"Do you like Sydney at least?" Helen asked.

"I suppose I do but I can't very well go sightseeing. I can hardly concentrate."

There was silence for a while.

"Yes," Adam agreed. "It's not easy to know what to do. He makes me so angry. Once again, here we are, talking about Dad and how to make our lives work around him. I am so tired of his passive-aggressive drama."

"He lost his job after thirty-three years," Helen argued. "It meant everything to him. It was his whole identity."

"He was going to write a memoir. He knew he would have to retire soon," Adam argued back. "What did he think? That he could stay there forever, captain of his empire, until the end of time? The writing had been on the wall for years, he was lucky to have stayed for as long as he did, and he knew it. I kept telling him, Dad, you need a Plan B but no, he just thought he would carry on forever, the life and soul of the dinner party, the guy everybody wanted to be."

"Kids," I said, "please, let's not argue now." And I must have sounded tired and sad because they didn't admonish me for calling them "kids" like they usually do.

"Sorry, Mom," they both chorused.

Then Helen said, "I just worry."

And, at the same time, Adam said, "he makes me so mad."

And then we sat for a while with none of us saying anything.

"I wish you weren't so far away." Helen was close to tears.

"Don't worry honey," I told her. "I'm okay. You guys go and get on with your night. I'll let you know if I hear anything."

"But what are you going to do?" Helen asked.

"I'm going to keep my phone on me and wait to hear from him." I was suddenly confident. "Your father will contact me soon. I'm going to go on that walk again, along the coast. It was lovely. And I'm sure he will be in touch. Okay? Let's not worry."

They agreed to let me go, but I could sense they didn't share my assurances that Lyndon would be in touch soon, or that the famous world trip would get back on the rails and continue on its way.

We said our goodbyes and as soon as I closed the laptop, all my doubts returned. My brief rush of cheer had been based solely on the fact that husbands don't just abandon their wives in the middle of a trip, in the middle of nowhere, although Sydney wasn't exactly the middle of nowhere. But it was the middle of nowhere for me, and Lyndon knew that.

I didn't go for a walk. I didn't go anywhere. I sat in the room in my pyjamas and waited for my phone to buzz or chirp or ring but it did none of those things. Soon it was nightfall and I was still alone, watching the Sydney Harbour blaze into beauty, while normal people went about their normal lives.

6. LYNDON

QUEENIE NEEDED SOME FOOD. I had been driving for four hours, depleting the dollar store stash of junk food. It was mid-afternoon when I decided to pull into Batemans Bay and get a motel for the night. But the cheapest motel was well over a hundred and fifty Canadian dollars, so I told Queenie we couldn't do it. I felt bad for her. She must have needed to pee by now so I drove until I found a small park. I put the tiny dog's leash on her, which fit perfectly, and turned my head away to give her some privacy.

It was peaceful, and I would have liked to stay longer, but I needed to buy Queenie her dinner. We got back into the car and I drove until I found another ubiquitous big-box strip mall with a Petbarn where I bought her a variety of Purina Fancy Feast cans with handy pull-tabs. I got a Double Big Mac and fries, and together, Queenie and I munched on our respective feasts. She even helped me finish off the burger. She loved melted cheese and lettuce on a bun. I was sleepy and wished I could take a nap. I had spent the previous night on a park bench and I'd hardly managed any shut-eye at all. My back certainly hadn't appreciated roughing it.

I returned to McDonald's for an extra-large black coffee. I hoped the caffeine would kick in and help me continue with my journey because I was compelled to keep driving. I would have welcomed a night in a motel but, since I had to watch the cash, I had no choice but to carry on and reach my destination.

Which was where? Melbourne? It was a vague idea at best, and I had no plan as to what I would do when I got there. I was sure that my time was running out with the car. Sooner, rather than later, we'd be spotted.

"The only way out is through," I remarked over my shoulder to Queenie who was back in her box. "I can't remember where I heard that but it's true."

She didn't answer me.

I drove for another four hours until we got to Bairnsdale. By that time, I was blinded with exhaustion. The radio was on, with Justin Bieber and Drake, Canada's homeboys, screaming at me. The seat warmer was off and the air con was blasting full force, helping me stay awake. I stopped to fill up on gas and visit the washroom but other than that, we powered through.

Sleeping in the car overnight was not an option. We'd arrived in Australia less than a week prior, but it was long enough for me to realize that these descendants of prison wardens—and prisoners—took the rules seriously, and one did not want to get caught breaking them. This was a bit rich coming from a car thief and catnapper, but, dollars to doughnuts, they'd catch me for unlawfully spending a night in a car before my more serious trangressions.

It was only eight p.m., but it felt like midnight to me. I'd changed my tune and was willing to pay anything for a room. I needed to crash.

I drove around Bairnsdale for a bit and found a motel on the edge of town. It was eighty dollars and I didn't tell the guy I had a cat. I paid cash and prayed he wouldn't ask me for my license or registration number and he didn't. He didn't seem to focus on much of anything and he handed me a proper, old-fashioned, real key, and I hustled out of the office as quickly as I could.

I parked the car in the shadows of a laneway that ran along-side the motel, and I scurried Queenie into the room. The neighbourhood looked pretty dubious, and I hoped the Jeep would make it through the night. The Jeep was the only thing I had, apart from Queenie and while I knew that neither of them were mine, they had quickly become my world.

I locked the motel door and sat down on the bed which sagged like a half-filled air mattress. The bed tried to swallow me, like a tongue taking a pill. There was a foul smell to the place, as if the unwashed bed linen and sweat-soaked towels and pillows had absorbed too much lost, greasy hair. I reflected upon the place's shortcomings, and then I acknowledged, with some horror, that the fog of body odour was coming from me. I sniffed my armpits. Yep. It was bad. This was the second night that I would have to sleep in these clothes. I knew I would have to do something about this predicament, but not right now.

I fed Queenie and gave her some water and then I found it hard to make myself do anything. I lay on the bed and turned on the TV. To my surprise, there was nothing on the news about Queenie or me or the stolen Jeep.

"I guess I am overestimating both of our importance," I said to Queenie. She had jumped up onto the bed with me and was trilling like a little budgie. I stroked her head. "What will become of us?" I asked her and she butted my hand with her tiny pug nose and my heart broke.

I fell into a doze, woken by the nightmare that someone was shining a flashlight directly into my eyes. I struggled to sit up on that marshmallow swamp of a bed. I couldn't get upright, so I rolled and landed on the floor with a thud. The carpet was crunchy under my cheek and when I sat up, my face was crusty. The light wasn't a dream. It was shining through the window, swinging back and forth.

"Oy!" I shouted. "What are you doing?" The light swung in the direction of my voice and then disappeared.

I jumped up, making sure that Queenie was nowhere near the door, and I went outside. I held the door closed behind me, so it didn't lock, and I stared this way and that, but the flashlight and whoever was holding it was nowhere to be seen.

Great. I went back and got the car keys and I moved the Jeep so I could see it from my window.

Goodnight to any further semblance of sleep. I pulled up a chair and kept a vigilant eye on the car that I had stolen, fully aware of the irony. I told myself to get as much rest as I could in the chair since there was no point in leaving while it was still dark. It was hard enough to find my way around during the day.

In the morning, I finally took a shower, telling the devil I'd sell my soul for a pair of flip-flops to protect my feet from the poor-man's-motel foot fungus. I could practically see it growing like grey moss on the tiles. The devil ignored me, and I scrubbed my body with a small cake of soap that smelled faintly like dish detergent and which refused to lather. Then I sandpapered my body with a towel that had never brushed shoulders with fabric softener in its life. But I was cleaner than before, and that was a step in the right direction. I fed Queenie and waited while she ate. I had laid down some newspaper in the night, which she had obligingly used for her toilet.

"Such a good girl," I crooned, scratching her behind her ears. "You're Daddy's good, good girl. Who's Daddy's favourite little princess?"

Where had the real me gone? Where was Lyndon Blaine? *Good girl, good cat, bad me.* When had I, Lyndon, ever talked like that? Lyndon. And who called their kid Lyndon? What was wrong with a simple name like Henry or David? But no, I was Lyndon and here I was with Queenie, both of us running away from home. Not that Queenie had any choice in the matter.

I loaded her into the Jeep and we continued our journey southwest to Melbourne. I gradually weaned Queenie off the air conditioner, decreasing it in slow doses, and soon, all the windows were open and there was nary a howl from her. I told myself that this was a sign that she was happy to be with me.

We hit Melbourne after lunch, but I wasn't ready to stop. I felt compelled to carry on driving. My gut would tell me when to stop. "Who knows?" I said to Queenie. "Maybe we'll drive all the way to Perth or around the perimeter of Australia!" I wondered how long that would take. But I didn't have enough money, so I pushed that thought out of my mind along with my thoughts of Margaux or Helen or Adam.

We turned into the town of Apollo Bay, population 1,598. I pulled up at a small park on the edge of Cape Otway. I gleaned this information from a plaque that said that the Henty brothers had founded the whaling station in the area around 1840, and that the bay had gotten its moniker from a Captain Loutit, who grounded his boat there, the Apollo, during a terrible storm in 1845. Much like me. Seeking shelter from the storm of my life. I attached the lead to Queenie and let her do her business. Then I picked her up and sat at a table, looking out at the sunset. The clouds were on fire.

"Tasmania's over there," a voice said. Startled, I jumped and clutched Queenie to me.

I hadn't noticed the man sitting under the tree, next to the picnic table.

"You can't see it," the man said, folding his arms behind his head and leaning back in his chair. It was a vintage lawn chair, with blue-and-white criss-crossed interlocking plastic strips on the seat and back. The rickety aluminum frame creaked, and I wondered how the thing didn't collapse under his weight. He was a big fellow, I could tell that, even with him sitting down.

I nodded but didn't say anything. I didn't want my Canadian accent to sound any alarm bells. The man was British, with a thick cockney accent. He was about my age but in much better shape than me. He had the quiet energy of a bare-knuckle cage fighter and he was adorned with tattoos.

I drew Queenie closer to me for comfort. Even the man's scalp was a cap of tattoos. I sat up straighter, trying to ignore the flabby belly spilling over my belt. I was easy prey for this guy. I knew the best course of action was to leave, so I was about to stand up when his words sat me right back down.

"That's the stolen cat from Sydney," he said casually. I made a strange noise, an admission of guilt, and immediately wished I could suck the sound back into my throat.

"And," the man said, turning around in his chair, "that's the stolen Jeep. Nice model. Fancy. It's got all the shiny bits and pieces."

He nodded, turned back to the sunset, and rocked in his chair. I was frozen in place, clutching Queenie and I didn't know what to do.

"What are you going to do?" the man asked, and I felt like I was talking to Michael Caine in *Get Carter*. A film that did not end well for anyone.

"I don't know," I managed to sputter. "What are you going to do?"

The man laughed. "You mean, am I going to report you?"

"Yes. Exactly. Report me."

"Not me, sunshine. But if you like, I can help you."

"Help me how?"

"Help you off-load that expensive and very flashy motor vehicle you've got there."

"Why would you do that?"

The man looked surprised. "Because you, sonny, are very clearly in need of help. Your clothes are a bit ripe, to put it mildly. You're hugging a stolen cat, and you're in the unenviable position of being far too close to a hot car. The egg timer's about to blow."

"But why help me?"

"Why not?" the man replied, and he got up and folded his chair neatly. "Don't be so suspicious. Come on, sunshine, let's get you sorted. We've still got time."

"Do we?" I had no idea what he meant.

"Yeah. Footy's on in an hour. In an hour, you've lost me. But until then, I can help you. Throw us the keys."

"What?"

"Throw us the car keys," the man repeated slowly as if he was talking to an idiot which, from his perspective, he probably was.

I looked at him, my expression guarded.

"Okay," he said. "Fine. Get into the car. You drive, and I'll show you where to go."

I loaded Queenie gently into her box, taking care not to turn my back on the man, but he wasn't even looking at me. He was gazing out into the setting sun.

"Never gets old," he said, and he gave a sigh of pleasure. "Thirty years of living here and I never get tired of the sunsets."

Surely the lover of sunsets can't be too evil? I reassured myself with the thought.

My hands were shaking as I drove, and I followed his instructions to a garage on the outskirts of town.

"Pull around the back," he said, and I drove the car down a narrow lane to the rear of the garage. A bunch of men were standing around a Harley Davidson, talking and smoking, and my armpits flooded with hot shameful sweat. The Hells Angels. I had unwittingly delivered myself and an innocent cat to the Hells Angels.

"Relax, sunshine," the man said. "Everything's copacetic. I'm Jason, by the way."

"Lyndon," I managed to say, and I parked where he told me to.

"Wait in the car for me," he said, and I got in the rear with Queenie, leaving the back door open as if flabby old me could outrun these fit gangsters with an unwieldy cat box in my arms. I realized that I had never previously even vaguely understood the concept of terror. I hoped my heart wouldn't give out. It could. It was doing a weird thing, as if a rat was having a panic attack in my chest.

Jason returned with one of the men, and I hung onto Queenie's box like a life raft. I wondered if my scrotum would ever recover from this ordeal. I faced the facts. This was the end of my life. I had nothing with which to defend myself, nothing. My wit and repartee were of no use to me now. Nothing and no one could save me.

"Five k.," the man said to me. I stared at him, speechless.

"Colin is kindly offering you five thousand dollars cash for your stolen car," Jason helpfully translated, and I nodded as quickly as I could.

"O-o-okay." I stuttered. "I mean, great. Yes, thank you."

The man shrugged, and he and Jason strolled off.

"I don't know about you," I whispered to Queenie, "but that just about killed me."

Jason and the man returned and, this time, the man handed me a bulging manila envelope. "It's there," he said, and I knew better than to insult him by counting.

"Thanks," I said, hauling Queenie's box out of the vehicle.

"I'll take the cat too," Colin said, eyeing her. "My kid wants a pet."

I clutched the box to my chest and hoped he couldn't see how badly my legs were shaking.

"No, she's mine," I said, and a tremor ran through my voice. When Colin smiled, I thought, *hockey-player teeth*. He took a step closer to me and I wondered if my bladder would hold.

"We've no problem with that, do we, Colin?" Jason said, and he put his hand on my shoulder. "The cat's yours, sunshine. Colin, can you give us a ride back into town?"

"Yeah," Colin replied, grumpy at not having scored Queenie. He gestured to a rusty old panel van, and I climbed wordlessly into the windowless back with Queenie. We sat on the floor among the tires and greasy mechanical junk and listened to them shoot the breeze.

I didn't breathe until Colin dropped us off at the park and drove away.

I sank down onto the bench and gasped. "I can honestly say I've never done anything like that in my life. I thought I was going to have a heart attack."

"Yeah, man, you do look unsteady. Listen, come on in and have a cuppa with me."

I nodded and followed Jason to a row of stores across from the park. He led us into The Anarchist's Tattoo Parlour and Barber Shop and my balls, which had started to unclench a fraction, shot back up into themselves. At least I still had my cat.

7. MARGAUX

I COULDN'T SLEEP. I couldn't eat. I couldn't do anything. I scoured my computer for updates of stolen cars and cats, but there was nothing. There was no word from Lyndon. I walked around the Rocks, watching people come and go from the large cruise ship docked in the harbour. I sat on the grass outside the Museum of Contemporary Art while acid sloshed around my belly. I couldn't sit still for long. The didgeridoo player's music felt like an assault on my splintered nerves and I had to leave. I paced the streets, wandering into stores, picking things up and putting them down. I could see shop assistants talking to me, but I couldn't hear a word they were saying.

How could he do this to me after thirty-five years of marriage and two kids? How could he just up and leave?

Granted, a part of Lyndon had always been inaccessible to me, but he was a good husband: funny, good looking, and a good provider. We'd met when we were both so young. But I had never regretted our youthful marriage or the decision to have children early on. A family was the only thing in life I had ever wanted. And I knew Lyndon wanted that too.

I had always known that his job meant a great deal to him and that he was terrified by the chasm of change into which he'd been flung. And I also knew, which the children did not, that aging felt increasingly like a road race run on spavined feet and the words "weight-bearing exercise," simply meant making the effort to stand up. This was why I had suggested the trip. And yet it hadn't only been for Lyndon's sake but for mine as well. Did Lyndon think getting old was easy for me? Wait, Lyndon's motto was, *Don't think about it,* remember? *Just don't think about it.* Like that would fix everything. But I was a thinker. I thought about everything and I'd thought that this trip would be good for Lyndon and me. It would shake us out of our little Oakville lives and kick-start us into a new future together.

All I had wanted was to feel the optimism of having something to look forward to. To know that there were new adventures in the world that would push bone density scans, middle-age hearing loss, and weakening vision to the back of my mind. I had wanted to feel alive, not decrepit. And now Lyndon had thrown me into a terrible limbo where time and place lost all meaning.

I picked up a paperweight at an outdoor market stall in Paddington. A blue peony lay unfurled in the round, solid clear glass. Somehow the weight of thing in my hand reassured me. It was a ridiculous purchase, this irrelevant heavy glass ball, but I needed it. The weight made me feel grounded. As long as I held onto it, the fragments of my mind wouldn't scatter into the wind like so many dandelions gone to seed.

I clutched the ball in both hands and held it against my belly as I walked. A semblance of calm replaced the floaty restless fever of my confused railings at Lyndon and cleared the way for a quiet, white-hot, seething fury.

8. LYNDON

WE WALKED THROUGH The Anarchist's Tattoo Parlour and Barber Shop, and I was amazed. This had to be the coolest place in the world. The front half of the store was a barber shop and the place was filled with men being foamed and shaved and trimmed. The barbers looked like fashion models, all buff, lithe and beautiful. Of course, they were all covered in tattoos. And no one was over thirty. The décor was black, white, and silver; the floor was checkered and huge mirrors lined the walls, along with black-and-white photography of impossible male musculature. Next up was the reception area of the tattoo parlour, filled with hanging boards displaying hundreds of designs, against a backdrop of red, bordello-style wallpaper. Jason led me past three tattoo artists who were all concentrating hard. One man was having a sports club logo tattooed onto his thigh; a woman was face-down while angel wings were etched onto the span of her back; and, a woman who looked to be in her early seventies grimaced as the finishing touches to *eternity* were tattooed on her shoulder.

We took the stairs to an apartment above the store where Jason showed me to the kitchen, and I stared past my reflection in the window. "Pretty black out there," I commented.

"The bay," Jason said. "You'll be amazed in the morning. If you look closely now, you'll see ship lights, but that's it. Sometimes, we get storms. I love them."

He waved me to a chair at the round, white table. "How long have you been in Australia?" I asked.

"Twenty-four years," he said, getting out a rose-covered china teapot with fluted edges and gold trim, which I found a bit unexpected. "Came when I was thirty-five. I had an early mid-life crisis and decided I needed to find out who I was and what I wanted to do with the rest of my existence."

I was uncomfortable. Adam was thirty-five and he'd just had his self-realization or whatever it was, and I had let him down badly. True, his wasn't a mid-life crisis so much as a turning point, an acceptance and acknowledgement of who he really was, but regardless, I'd let him down.

"What are you thinking about?" Jason asked me, putting the kettle on and handing me a box of custard creams.

"That I let my son down. Not that that's anything new. But never mind that, you came to Australia when you were thirty-five?"

"Yeah. Went to Sydney first. Bunch of stupid wankers. I went to Melbourne next and liked it better. I found this place by luck. Back then, it was just a barber shop and nothing like it is now. The old geezer who owned it was dying, and he took a liking to me. So, he sold it to me for a quick thousand, which paid for a fancy coffin for him. Dark cherry wood with a red velvet interior and a comfy mattress. He said he wanted his tired old bones to have a good thick mattress upon which to rest. He had his gravestone all done up, and he'd bought his little piece of land in the cemetery. And he asked me to make sure he got to his resting place in good style."

"You took care of his burial? Didn't he have any family?"

Jason gave me a look. "There are lots of us wandering the earth who don't have family," he said. "We take care of each other. I made sure he was all taken care of and that he got buried right and I got this place which I take care of."

"How sad," I said. "That he didn't have anybody."

"He had me when he needed me," Jason said, and he filled

the teapot with boiling water and covered it with a cheerful yellow crocheted cozy.

"Here we go then," he said, and he reached for two teacups in a cupboard. The cups matched the teapot. They were delicate, elaborate china, with scarlet, pink, and apricot-coloured roses with the same gold leafing on the scalloped edges.

He arranged the custard creams on a matching plate and sat down. "I'll be mother," he said, and I wanted to smile because the whole thing was so odd and yet so right.

"Can I take Queenie out of her box?" I asked,

He looked startled. "Of course, pardon me, I should have said. We'll get her a box and some kitty litter later. In the meantime, I'll put down some newspaper."

After he laid down a few sheets of newspaper, I took Queenie out her box. She chirped and trilled and batted her head against my hand. I fed her and scratched her head as she ate.

"Jason," I asked, getting up slowly, aware of my aging knees, "from what you said, do you think I'm going to stay here? I mean if you are making kitty litter plans and things."

"Well, it's not like you've got any other place to go, do you, sunshine?" he asked, and he poured the tea, adding half a cup of milk and four teaspoons of sugar to his. "I'm used to helping strays from time to time, and you definitely have the look of a pup who ran away from home. We'd need to get you some new clothes though to start."

"Where would I stay?"

He gestured to a stairway to my right. "There's a guest bedroom there," he said, gulping his tea and sighing with obvious satisfaction. "You can think of me as your guardian angel for the time being. I've got no idea how you made it this far with that flashy stolen car, not to mention the cat."

"How did you know about the car and cat?" I asked, and took a cautious sip of my tea. It was the colour of caramel and was tart and strong and abrasive, but I liked it.

"Police scanner. Better than a TV set for entertainment. They tied the car theft to you, by the way. Canadian tourist causes a stir, then a car is stolen in the neighbourhood where he vanished, and some ninety-year-old lady said she saw you jump into the car and speed away like Steve McQueen."

I laughed. "Yep, Steve McQueen. That's so me. And how is my wife?" I asked though it was hard to get the question out.

Jason laughed. "I am many things, but I am not psychic. How would I know?"

"I thought maybe it was on the police scanner?"

"Nope. Only that she thought you had fallen into the Sydney Harbour, and that she wanted them to search the water. Kicked up a big fuss. That's when they saw you on the camera, getting off at Kirribilli and disappearing into a park. The New South Wales Government's transport authority has to report any suspicious activity to the coppers. Terrorism and all that. So, you just left your wife?"

I put my head into my hands. "I can't talk about it now," I said. "I can't think about it."

"That's quite all right," Jason replied, and he leaned over and patted my shoulder. "Drink your tea. Couple of hours time, I'll heat up a fantastic tofu curry I made yesterday, and we'll play a game of Scrabble. But first, my friend, it's hot shower for you and a bar of lye. You've had a long couple of days."

To my astonishment, I burst out laughing. Maybe some of it was hysteria, but I really laughed, a deep belly laugh that reached right up into my lungs.

"There you go, you see," Jason said with satisfaction and a slightly bemused expression, "life can have its better moments."

9. MARGAUX

I NEEDED TO FIND a cheaper place to stay. Helen and I had planned the hotel budget carefully, and if this episode of Lyndon's mid-life crisis was going to necessitate a longer stay in Sydney than we had planned, I had to get organized, so as not to go bankrupt in the process.

Sydney was viciously expensive. I weighed my options and threw hostels into the mix. I could get a single room for less than forty dollars a night. I'd secretly always wanted to have a backpacking adventure, but I then met Lyndon and it never happened. I felt a tiny glow of excitement at being able to do it now, but to my chagrin, most of the hostels had an age limit of thirty-five. On a very good day, I could pass for fifty but that was it. The tiny glow of happiness was extinguished by a bucket of ice-cold water. I had to face the facts. Who wanted an old fogey in the midst of young folk in the prime of their lives?

I picked up my peony paperweight and lay down on the bed. *Lyndon. Look at the mess you've dragged me into. And I have to clean it up. Me, me, me.* I wanted to throw my glass flower at the mirror and do as much damage as I could, but I couldn't afford to lose my temper—literally—like that.

I'd had a temper second to none when I was a kid. As a teenager, I had routinely destroyed the contents of my bedroom and scored my arms with a razor blade, trying to release my inner scream of rage. But having to pay for the damage, and my parents' policy of zero tolerance for such behaviour, taught me restraint. That, and the fact that my mother had sent me to a therapist for half a dozen years. I hadn't felt that terrible anger in decades. Lyndon's calm demeanour, his unruffled reliability, his way of making a joke out of things, had helped me. And I loved the kids. While Adam drove Lyndon nuts, the kids brought me joy, pure and simple.

But now the anger had returned, full force. I wanted to smash my computer, slash my arms with the ballpoint pen, shatter the mirror, and trash the room.

I had to get myself under control. I forced myself to continue looking for a place to stay and found one that had potential, only it was in Kings Cross, the red-light district in Sydney. I decided to check it out in person and assess how dubious the area was. It was also a hostel so, they might not even take me.

It took me an hour to walk to the hostel and, on the way, I picked up a slice of sourdough toast with jam and a large coffee. I hadn't eaten in days, and wolfed the food down, hardly chewing.

I stood outside the hostel and tried to summon the courage to go inside. It was still early in the morning and really, all things considered, Kings Cross didn't look too bad. A bit grimy, but nothing I couldn't handle.

A bunch of excited young folk piled out of the hostel and clambered into a minivan. They were so carefree, and I wished I was one of them.

I pushed myself forward by sheer will and opened the door to the hostel. A bell sounded, like wind chimes and I jumped, on edge. I was a mom from Oakville, Ontario. What on earth was I doing here?

Inside, the dark blue hallway was shadowy, lit by a single lamp on a small red table. Tiny twinkling lights lined the banister railing. I recognized a poster of the seven-headed, ten-horned wild beast of Revelation, only it was pink and yellow and crazy, with meowing lion heads. I couldn't help myself; I had to see who the artist was. Bob Motown. It was titled, "Beast of the Sea" and the kind of pop art I loved and Lyndon hated. I studied the poster for a while, lost, not sure what to do next.

"Can I help you?" A deep voice materialized out of the darkness at the end of the tiny hall and I pressed back against the wall. If I closed my eyes and wished hard enough, maybe I'd find myself back in my high-rise luxury hotel room. This was too grassroots, too close to the ground.

I opened my eyes. I took a step forward and another and then I stopped. A man moved into the light. He didn't look the way his voice sounded. I had expected, I don't know, a middle-aged balding man who was tall, lean, close-shaven, tidy, slightly biker-like perhaps. And this man was nothing like that. He was huge, like an older Marlon Brando, obese, with a wild lion's mane of shaggy white hair. His skin was the colour of white flour and his eyes were black raisins set deep into his face. His mouth was a slash of black and his nose was tiny and elegant. This man was a study in black and white.

I couldn't speak. I just looked at him. I was frozen.

"Chickadee," he said, and he sounded kind, "I can't help you unless you talk to me. Come on over. I don't bite." His voice was deep and beautiful, and I started crying.

"I am sorry," I said, digging in my purse for a Kleenex. "I'm here on holiday with my husband and things have gone a bit wrong."

"Canadian, eh?" he asked, and he came out from behind the reception counter at the end of the hallway. "I'm from Saint John, New Brunswick. Not to be confused with St. John's, Newfoundland."

"I know the difference," I told him. I blew my nose and didn't care when I honked like a goose. I couldn't pretend things were fine anymore.

"Come and have a cup of coffee with me," the man said, and he moved his bulk gracefully into the kitchen where a group of kids studied maps and planned their days. Unlike the hallway, the kitchen was bright and breezy, and there was a bookcase filled with leftover reads from long-gone travellers: paperbacks, maps, brochures, and magazines.

"Sit down," the man gestured at one of the two armchairs that faced out into the garden. The garden was filled with more hostellers, eating breakfast while studying brochures or scrolling through their laptops.

"Latte?" The man asked.

I was startled. "What?"

"Would you like a latte?"

"I would love a latte," I said, and relaxed for a second. Then I remembered I shouldn't be relaxing while Lyndon was out there, absent without leave. I took out my phone and studied it. Still nothing. I put it away.

"Sugar?"

"Yes, please. Two."

He handed me the latte and when I took a sip, an insane happiness flooded my body.

"Maybe I could just sit here and drink lattes and be happy for the rest of my life," I told the man.

He laughed. "I do make good coffee," he said. "But your life must be pretty bad if a latte is make or break. What's going on with you? I am Tim."

Tiny Tim, not, I immediately thought, and he laughed again.

"As in not so tiny," he said, and I flushed. How could he have known what I was thinking?

"Everyone thinks it," he said as he wiped foam from his black lips. Why were his lips so dark? He must have weird pigmentation issues. I tried to stop thinking about it in case he tuned into that thought too.

"Tiny Tim. But you can just call me Tim."

"How long have you lived in Australia?" I asked.

"Twenty years. I was on the police force and got shot when I was fifty-five. Was pensioned off, which was fine by me. Had enough of the winters by then. I came here for a holiday and decided to stay. I had enough money so the Aussies didn't kick me out, and I've been here ever since. I bought this place right off the bat."

I did the math. "You don't look seventy-five," I told him, and it was true.

"Seventy-six this year. And thank you."

"And what about your wife? Did she come too?" I blurted out the questions without thinking, and he laughed.

"Chickadee, I'm gay. Although I do make a beautiful woman. You should come and see me."

"I'd love to," I said, and then I remembered my plight. I'd been enjoying myself, and I'd forgotten about Lyndon for three seconds and the mess he had created.

Tim saw my expression change and leaned forward.

"And now, what can I do for you?" he asked.

"I need a room. A single room. Just me. And me and my husband's suitcases. He's run off. I don't know where he's gone. I haven't heard from him and need to stick around for a bit. He stole a Jeep in Kirribilli with a cat in it. Please tell me you have a room."

"I have a room," he said, as he patted my knee.

My eyes filled with tears. "I must stop crying," I said.

Tim shook his head. "Cry as much as you like," he said. "What happened?"

I told him the whole story. He listened and didn't say anything.

When I finished, he looked at me. "Let's go and get your stuff," he said. "I'll put a boy on the front desk. Come on, where's your hotel? I'll drive you there."

"But I have to pack everything," I told him. "I'll go back, settle up the bill, and come back by cab. It's no problem."

I needed to do this alone; I wanted to be able to take my time. I appreciated his kindness, but I didn't want to think about him downstairs, waiting for me while I gathered my things. I needed a moment to myself. The world was spinning too quickly.

"No worries," he said. "I'll be here when you get back." He

took our mugs to the sink and washed them. When he turned back, he said, "Take your time. Like I said, I'll be here." He smiled and it was disconcerting—his black eyes, his dark mouth, all that white hair, and his vast pale skin.

"Thank you, Tim." I was grateful.

I slipped out in the hubbub of Kings Cross and walked back to the hotel. I checked my phone repeatedly, but there was nothing. Rage bubbled up inside me again like corrosive lava and I choked it down. The coffee I'd had rose in my throat and I threw it up into a flowerpot. I was worried that someone would take me to task for this, but no one noticed or cared.

I was invisible to the world. I wiped my mouth and stood up tall. And I thought about how much I hated Lyndon for what he had done.

10. LYNDON

"IT'S BETTER IF YOU DON'T SPEAK," Jason said to me in the car. We were on our way to Vinnie's, the St. Vincent de Paul Society to get me some new clothes. Jason had washed and dried my clothes, but he said my energy field needed addressing. Besides, I needed more than one outfit.

The previous night, Jason had inflated an air mattress and given me a stack of clean bed linen, a leopard-print fleece blanket, and a pillow. The guest room had been empty when he pulled the air mattress out of the cupboard, and apart from navy-blue curtains, the room was without décor. The floors were pale varnished wood and the walls were white. The washroom was similarly utilitarian, with thick, fluffy beach-sized towels. I had noticed that while Jason had few possessions, the ones he did have, were fine quality.

We were on our way back to Melbourne in a metallic-blue, twenty-year-old Chevy Cavalier that Jason had borrowed from a friend. The windows were cranked.

"Your accent is a dead giveaway," Jason continued. "If you do speak, tell people you're from America. They won't know the difference."

I nodded, my lips clamped shut.

Jason grinned. "I didn't mean don't speak to me, you tosser,"

I pulled down the mirror on the passenger visor. "When did I turn into Santa?" I grumbled. To my horror, when I took the shower, my mirrored reflection's three-day growth was white.

This was a development I was unprepared for. "I am so old," I said, miserably. "I look about eighty, never mind sixty."

"We'll designer you up when we get back to the shop," Jason said. "You do look like an old hobo, but we'll make you into the Tom Ford of granddads."

"Can't wait," I said, slumped into gloom. "It's the end of the world as we know it."

"*And I feel finnnneeee!*" Jason sang loudly, finishing off the song and smiling.

Once we got to Vinnie's, I started sifting listlessly through the plaid shirts and tan trousers. Jason arrived with his arms full. "Come on," he said. "Try these on."

I followed him to the changing room, still depressed about my freshly-minted Father Christmas face. I took the stack of clothes from Jason and started trying things on without thinking about what I was doing. I pulled on a pair of black jeans, a black linen shirt with silver decals on the lapels, and a black leather waistcoat. I looked at myself in the mirror. I had never worn black. The fellow staring back at me looked as disconcerted as I felt and neither of us moved. "What the heck," I told the old guy in the glass. "Maybe it is time to ditch the plaid and tan." Next thing I knew, my shoulders straightened up and I saw a semblance of the man I used to be.

I left the change room and Jason was waiting. He gave a wolf whistle and stupidly, I blushed, losing whatever semblance of cool I had gained in the previous moments.

"Now you need some boots," he said. "And my friend, we are going to buy you some good boots. A man needs a pair of good boots that will be his mates for life. This whole walking in other people's shoes is for the birds."

We paid for my clothes and I folded my old trousers and jacket and put them neatly into a bag, and Jason told me I should throw away.

"Look. There's a rubbish bin, right there," he pointed.

"But they're Tilley's," I objected. "They were expensive."

"They were that," Jason agreed. "They nearly cost you your life. They depressed you that much. Throw them out and give them the finger while you're at it."

I couldn't do it. I gave them to Vinnie's instead. A memory of Margaux shopping to buy those clothes flashed through my mind. She'd been so excited. And now, here I was, giving them away. But at least I hadn't thrown them in the garbage.

Jason took me to a store where the boots were so expensive I wanted to throw up and leave. Five hundred dollars for a pair of boots!

"You've got the dosh, sunshine," Jason said. "There are times for budgeting in life and there are times for appropriate spending. This is the latter. Now, let's find your solemates, or footmates, whichever." He grinned, deep dimples cutting into his cheeks. "Gotta luv a pun," he joked.

It took hours. I was quickly exhausted. Jason made me walk up and down relentlessly. He watched me from the front and back, and asked me a hundred questions about how the boots fit.

"Dear God," I said querulously, "is it always this much work to buy a pair of boots?"

The assistant nodded. "It's worth it," he said. "You only have to do it once."

"Ah, he's not that old," Jason protested. "He may have another pair left in him yet." He winked at me, and I tried on a new set, and it was like all the pieces slid into place and locked neatly.

"These ones," I said dreamily, strolling around the store. "These are the ones."

The boots felt like butter or marshmallow, soft and kind, but when I looked down, there was nothing kind about the way they looked. They were tough and mean and kick-ass and I loved them.

We paid for them and headed out of town but not before I convinced Jason to let me get a latte from Starbucks. I offered to get him one too, but he looked like I was trying to poison him. I let that go and ordered my venti, no foam, no fat latte, along with a slice of lemon loaf cake. And for a moment, it was as if I had stepped out of my office and the world was exactly the way it should be, the way it used to be, when I was a person I understood and my place in life was guaranteed.

"Come on, princess," Jason said, shattering the glass illusion of my back-in-time moment and I immediately felt depressed. Until I looked at my boots.

Back at the barber shop, Jason sat me down and lathered me up. "I'm going to set you on a path here," he said. "I'll show you how to trim it daily and keep it nice and tidy."

"Sounds like a lot of work," I replied, sounding whiny.

"All art is work," Jason said, and he started shaping my facial hair.

He was done half an hour later, and I was utterly relaxed from the feeling of his sure hands working so carefully on my face. I was sleepy and peaceful when he whisked the plastic cape off of me and told me to look in the mirror. I stared at my reflection. Geometric stripes intersected my chin, and a designer goatee looked flattering on my face. There wasn't as much white as I had thought. I looked incredibly stylish.

"Wow," I said. "Okay, I can live with this."

"Put your glasses on," Jason said. "You need to wear them all the time. You are a wanted felon, after all."

He had made me buy a pair of squarish black glasses with clear lenses, and I must admit, they made me look good. I looked like Robert Downey, Jr., if you added ten years, ten pounds, and minus the hair. Jason had shaved my scalp clean, so the clown ring of hair was gone. I looked sharp and mean and I loved it. My expression improved too; gone was the saggy, woe-is-me, my-ass-got-fired, hangdog look.

"Thank you, Jason," I said awkwardly. "I wouldn't recognize me, in a good way."

"No problemo, sunshine. A friend in need and all that. And now, I've to go and attend to an appointment. Keep yourself out of mischief. Hang around the shop and see if the boys need any help."

He vanished, and I was filled with anxiety. Was that an instruction? If so, what was I supposed to do? What could I possibly do to help? The barber chairs were full, the tattoo chairs were full, the place was buzzing. I had no idea what I could do to help.

"You can sweep up," one of the young barbers called out to me, having heard what Jason said.

"I'm Sean by the way," he said, and shook my hand. Sean was super-cool, with a handsome narrow face and a trendy ginger mullet. Who knew that was even possible, a trendy mullet? He was outfitted in skinny grey jeans, a tailored white shirt, and a narrow maroon tie. He was wearing winklepicker boots no less and a Rolex watch. He must be an awfully good barber, I thought, to have a watch like that.

He gestured at the hair-covered floor. The old me would have told this young 'un where to get off, but the new me was so grateful to have a task that I immediately grabbed the broom and attended to the mess. I spent the remainder of the afternoon sweeping, collecting towels, and tidying up. Sean showed me how to work the cash register, answer the phone, and make appointments, and the rest of the afternoon passed in a remarkably pleasant manner. I had a brief thought about Margaux and Helen and Adam, and I knew I should be doing something about them, letting them know I was okay, but I couldn't do more with that thought than let it drift away.

"You want to see how a tattoo is done, up close?" Sean asked. Apparently, he was the foremost tattoo artist, after Jason.

I nodded eagerly. I followed him and watched him prepare his equipment.

He explained the difference between coil and rotary machines, and he told me that you call it a "tattoo machine" not a "gun." "And we are called tattooists, or tattoo artists, not artists. We always wear gloves. We have different kinds of needles for lines and for shading. Generally, we use five needles on the line needles; seven on the shading. They all penetrate the dermis with ink. A word to the wise: do not tattoo yourself."

I watched him clean and prep a guy's skin, apply a stencil, and get to work. The machine sounded like a drill, and it was a bit off-putting, but soon, I didn't even realize it was there.

Sean told me get in really close, and I asked the guy being tattooed if he minded.

"Nah man. Help yourself to the view," he replied.

"Does it hurt?" I asked him, and he nodded. "A good kind of hurt," he said, his eyes screwed tight. "But I'm addicted. Once you start, you can't stop."

I was fascinated, and by the time Jason returned, I had found my new calling in life.

I followed him upstairs and tried to find the words to tell him about my epiphany.

"I want to become a tattoo artist," I announced, watching him carefully for his reaction. We were in the kitchen and he was putting groceries away.

"Excellent career choice," he remarked. He left the room and came back with a pile of books. "Here's some light reading for you while I make supper."

He handed me the stack—all books about tattooing. I called Queenie to come with me, and I sat on the sofa, book in hand and cat on my lap. For a moment, I marvelled at the place I was at, and how my life had so astoundingly and quickly evolved, but then I was equally flooded with paralyzing guilt at all the damage I had caused. So I turned my attention to the book and to Queenie's sweet chirps as I rubbed her head.

11. MARGAUX

MY ROOM AT THE HOSTEL was a far cry from the up-scale, luxurious hotel I had left. My new view was a large red-and-blue neon dildo that waved back and forth. The room was tiny, but at least I had my own washroom with a toilet and a shower.

Tim kindly stored Lyndon's suitcase in the basement so it didn't take up room, but more importantly, I didn't have to look at it. Lyndon had hardly unpacked, so at least I hadn't had to handle his things. I might have been tempted to rip them to shreds. I threw his expensive electric toothbrush into the trash, a small act of childish petulance that somehow made me feel better for a moment.

My hostel bed was a small double, not the bountiful king-size I was used to. The mattress was overly soft, and I could feel the dents where other bodies had lain before me. I rolled into the corpse-sized impressions and tried to fall asleep.

But I was wide awake.

I hooked up to Skype and updated Helen and Adam as to my whereabouts and neither of them was too happy about it. We had a long online argument in which they insisted I stay in a better part of town, but I told them I was already ensconced at the hostel and that I liked the owner. I sensed he'd look out for me and that I was as safe there as as I would be anywhere.

"He's an ex-policeman from Saint John, New Brunswick," I repeated for the umpteenth time. "How can you not trust a man from Saint John? The people are nice there. Think about David Adams Richards."

"First, he is an author, which isn't the same as a normal person, and second, he is from Fredericton," Adam said.

"No, he's not. He's from the Miramichi, but he lives in Toronto now," Helen said.

"Kids, I don't care about David Adams Richards. I don't even know why I brought him up. We're getting off topic here. I'm fine, okay? Just fine."

"You haven't heard from Dad?" Helen asked me.

"Not in the five minutes that passed since you last asked me, no. Oh honey, I don't mean to sound snappy. This whole thing is so weird."

"I wish one of us could come out there and be with you," Adam said, and I rushed to tell him in no uncertain terms to please not think that way.

"What would be the point? Both us waiting? I may have to give up and come home after a while. I don't know when. We'll just have to see what happens."

"But what about the rest of your trip?" Adam asked.

"It wouldn't be the same without your father," I said.

"You're right" Adam agreed. "But it might even be better."

I sighed. "No dear, it wouldn't. I do love your father although I'm very angry with him right now."

"They didn't find the Jeep or the cat?"

"They did not. Not a trace. He has vanished into thin air. And he hasn't used his bank cards. I have no idea how he's managing. But how are both of you?" I asked. "This affects you too."

"Well, less us than you," Helen said. "I know Dad will be fine. I don't think it's fair what he's done, but I also don't think he could help it."

"Why do you always stick up for him?" Adam asked. "He really hurt Rick's feelings. Dad is always only about himself."

"And you are only about *yourself*," Helen retorted. "Listen to you. Mom's stuck on the other side of the world with this huge problem and all you can think about is Dad not meeting your boyfriend."

"That's not fair. I was just using it as an example of his self-ishness. He's the most selfish man in the world."

"Not the most," I interjected. "But I'm not happy with him either, at the moment. Helen, I understand what you are say-ing, but he could find a way to get in touch. This really is a bit much. I have to agree with Adam. But anyway, there's nothing we can do, so let's not argue among ourselves and make it even worse. I'm going to let you two go. I'll email you if anything comes up, of course."

We said our goodbyes and I tried to sleep, but I was too restless.

I spent half of the first night tossing and turning and then gave up. I got up and got dressed. I went outside and walked around. Kings Cross at night was a far different cry to Kings Cross by day. I shrank into the shadows when I realized I was intruding on some drug deal or other clandestine activity between three young people who fell silent and glared at me as I backed away. I looked around. I didn't understand this world.

I saw a sign for a bar—*Dames*—and I remembered Tim telling me he hung out there. Tim was a drag queen, and he'd said he made a mean old hag, so I decided to check the place out.

I climbed the narrow stairs that led to the club's entrance, gripping the railing. The narrow stairwell was dark, and it was hard to see. Every nerve in my body screamed for me to turn back but I kept going. When I reached the top of the stairs, I found an empty bar apart from the bartender who was studying his phone.

"Show starts in fifteen minutes," he said looking at me with an expression that told me he was as surprised to see me as I was to be there.

"Do I have to pay?"

He looked confused. "No. For what?"

"The show," I said, and he shook his head.

"They pass around a hat at the end." He looked at me. "They might get you up there too."

I shuddered. "No. That's not going to happen. Is there a washroom I can use?"

He pointed down a hall. I felt like Alice in Wonderland, lost.

And then I got even more lost, looking for the washroom. I passed a large empty room with a single sofa. An enormous flat-screen TV on the wall showed a porn flick from the seventies—all soft focus and flickering lights. A man with a large handlebar moustache was going down on a blonde woman while she raked long red nails through his thinning hair. There was no sound, but her mouth was rounded into an O, and her head was thrown back. The room was black; the linoleum floor was in need of a clean. There was a man on the sofa, jacking off, his eyes closed. His jacket, shirt, and tie were in place, but his trousers were down around his ankles as if he was sitting on the toilet.

I backed out and turned into another room that had a bare green air mattress and on it three young, muscled men were making out. I saw a camera stand at the end of the bed. They were filming themselves, and I was mesmerized. I stood there, watching their muscles ripple. I told myself that I was being a terrible voyeur, a disgusting old woman but still, I couldn't make myself leave. One of the boys met my eyes and he grinned while I shuddered. Jolted into action, I rushed down the red corridor and stumbled into a dressing room filled with laughter and cigar smoke.

And Tim. "Chickadee," he said, and he seemed delighted to see me. He took a puff of his cigar and a cloud of smoke filled the room. Tim was dressed in a glittering gold muumuu and high heels. His black-and-white face was the same as always only he'd added large patches of red blush to his cheeks. A white feather boa with gold tips was flung around his neck.

"Are you okay?" he asked, and I shook my head.

"Here," another voice said. "Help her sit down."

I felt very odd. The room was melting. The walls weren't solid, and my vision became a distorted fish-eye lens. I sank down onto the sofa and closed my eyes. I could feel myself crushing a pile of ballet tutus and I heard myself mumble an apology. I tried to stand up, but the kind new voice told me there was nothing to worry about. "Lie back, darling," the voice said. "I'll get you some water."

I lay back as a hand stroked my head, which helped. The panic started to ebb from my body. I gathered myself slowly and opened my eyes. A tall young man with eyelashes two feet long was hunkered down next to me, gently running his fingers through my hair, looking at me with concern.

"Meet Dammit Janet," Tim said.

"Put out that disgusting cigar," the young man told him. "It's probably making her feel more crook."

Tim nodded and stubbed it out.

"I'm Janet," the young man said. I wished he would stroke my forehead forever.

"Nice to meet you. I'm Margaux."

"Oh, you're Tim's new boarder."

"I guess I am. Are you guys on soon?"

"We are. We sing. We do karaoke and look beautiful." Janet grinned. "At least I do, anyway. You'll stay for the show?"

"I wouldn't miss it for the world." Then I remembered something. "The bartender said you might call me on stage. Please don't call me onstage."

"We won't, darling. Here, drink some water."

I took the water he offered.

"I can't take you back to the front," Tim said. "The audience can't see us. Can you find your way back? Just go straight, unlike the rest of us here."

Janet gave a high-pitched cackle. He was snapping at his fishnet stockings and adjusting a large blonde beehive wig.

I stood up slowly. "I'm fine," I said, and I was. "I'll see you out there. Break a leg or whatever one says." I left them and walked back the way I came. The rooms were empty now, and I wondered if I had imagined everything. Perhaps the stress was getting to me even though I thought I was coping.

The bar room was jam-packed and it was hard to find a place to stand.

Tina Marie and Dammit Janet came out and the crowd leapt up, chanting and applauding. Tim was an amazing singer. He sounded so much like Cher that it was freaky while Janet sounded like Sonny. They were hilarious and fantastic, and their rendition of "I've Got You Babe" nearly set the room on fire. I watched, feeling outside of myself, not really there, not really a part of it.

How I wished I could stop thinking about my life just for just one moment. And I wished my goddamned stupid husband would tell me where he was and what on earth he was thinking, running away like that. I almost wished he was dead because then I could take his body home, bury it, and get on with the rest of my life. No, I didn't mean that. Not really. I just hated this limbo he'd stuck me in.

But then again, I asked myself, was this limbo anything new? Hadn't Lyndon stuck me in limbo the moment I married him? I'd simply been too foolish and naïve to know it at the time, but, looking back, it was exactly what he had done, right from the very start. And this, our retirement holiday around the world, this was supposed to be my reward, my big gold star for being a good, solid, supportive wife. Even now, he had taken it away from me, had left me hanging like a balloon that floated away from a parade and got stuck in a tree. No one ever rescued those balloons. They were just left to wither and die. And even if the tree released me, where would I go?

12. LYNDON

MY APPRENTICESHIP AS A TATTOO artist started the next day. I read late into the night, and Jason wanted me to observe the other guys for a couple of days before picking up a machine. I was filled with exhilaration and joy pumped through my veins. Having a purpose and being powered by passion was nothing short of a miracle.

The days flew by and, if I were a religious man, I'd be on my knees thanking God.

Jason, to my surprise, was an intensely spiritual man, and he invited me to join his early morning yoga sessions on the rooftop of the building.

"It's just not right to get up at this hour," I grumbled, the first morning he woke me up. "I haven't been up this early in my entire life." It was five a.m. "And I've never done yoga," I told him for the fiftieth time. "I'll probably break into several hundred parts. I've calcified. It's best to leave these things undisturbed."

"No, it is not best," Jason said, and his smile looked quite evil. "We're going to introduce your body to movement. It may feel a bit shocking at first, but your body will get used to it, and soon it will even like it and long for it. Our bodies are meant to move, not sit all day in office chairs."

"I shovel snow at home," I protested, following him up the stairs and feeling ridiculous as I lay down my yoga mat. "I mow the lawn in summer. I take out the garbage. I am very active."

"You take out the garbage for exercise?" Jason thought this was hilarious. "Well, we're going to make you do a bit more than that today, sunshine. I'll talk you through it. Follow my lead and don't overdo it. Only do whatever your body can do."

Which was not a lot. My body was indeed like a bunch of desiccated twigs and stiff parts, and nothing was willing to bend. I was horrified at how out of shape I was. I'd always assumed my body would naturally retain its mobility, but my joke had backfired on me—I had indeed calcified.

"I am going to fix this," I said to Jason while we lay in savasana, the only pose I thought I would be able to do, but inexplicably, even that hurt. "My whole body hurts. Even just lying down like this. Do you have any books on yoga?"

"Many," he replied, his arms splayed out slightly from his sides, his eyes peacefully closed. "But don't worry about books. Just stick with me, and I'll show you what's what."

"How long have you been doing it?" I sat up and rubbed my shins. I rubbed my feet and my thighs and my head and my neck.

"Since I came to Australia. It was the only good thing about godforsaken Sydney. It got me started on yoga. By the way, we're supposed to be silent during savasana to fully reap the benefits of the practice."

"Oh, sorry," I replied, about to chat to Queenie when I remembered Jason's comment about silence, so I stroked her quietly. The sunrise was glorious, and the air was quiet and fragrant. Were it not for the incredibly noisy Australian birds that sounded like they were simultaneously barking and throwing up, the moment would be a peaceful one.

I wondered if Jason had fallen asleep. I was about to leave him on the roof when he rolled himself up in a single smooth fluid motion and hopped to his feet. For a large man, he was very graceful.

"Time for breakfast," he said, and I picked up Queenie and my yoga mat and followed him into the kitchen where I put the kettle on. According to Jason, I now made a decent cup of tea, which meant I had learned how to brew his caramel-coloured beverage exactly how he liked it.

We sat down and Jason spooned steel-cut oatmeal onto my plate and I added a dollop of Greek yoghurt and a teaspoon of raw honey. I wondered if I was losing any weight. Margaux would like that. She hadn't been happy with, as she put it, "the layer of pudge" that I had allowed to encroach over the years. I hadn't been too happy about it either, but I also hadn't been unhappy enough to do anything about it.

"I've never asked," Jason said. "What did you do with your life before you came here?"

"You haven't asked," I replied, "and I love that about you. Why do we have to take a perfect relationship and ruin it?"

"We're not ruining it. Are you afraid I won't like who you were before? We all have snakeskins we need to shed. I don't care about your past. I am just interested in how it will affect your present. Maybe there are areas in need of healing."

Areas in need of healing? Who was this guy? A six-foot-five, tattoo-headed bundle of lean muscle and coiled-up energy. A gangster in his past, I was sure of it. And yet, he was also an an organic-food eating, yoga-practicing spiritual guru. Who was Jason?

"You yourself are an interesting contradiction of moving parts," I said, and he shook his head.

"Deflection won't work."

"I am a married man," I told him with reluctance. "I married young. I was twenty-five. I don't regret that. I have two kids, Adam and Helen. I don't regret them either."

"Have you contacted any of them since you disappeared?"

"How would I have?" My tone was sharp. "I had to turn my phone off or the police would find me. Anyway, I wouldn't know what to say."

"You could tell them not to worry," Jason said, getting up.

I collected the bowls and washed them. I set them on the

drying rack and straightened the table. I poured another cup of the bitter brew and I felt miserable. He was right. I should have done something, and yet again, I had done absolutely nothing. How quintessentially me. You could dress me in designer black and have me step out in the world's coolest boots, but you couldn't change my fundamentally useless nature. I picked up one of the tattoo books and opened it.

Jason returned with his computer and set it down on the kitchen table. "We're going to send one of them a message," he said.

I sat up and snapped the book shut. "Who? What message? What do you mean?" But I knew who and what he meant. "Then they'll know where I am," I objected. "I don't want them to know."

"They won't know. They'll get an email from dadisokay@aussiemail.au, and they won't be able to trace it. Trust me, if there is one thing I know better than the inside of my mouth, it's computers. I am a computer whiz. There's nothing I can't find my way into either. A handy skill if I say so myself. What do you want to say? Let's send it to all three of them."

"Oh yes, let's," I retorted sarcastically. "And say whatever you want. I'm not part of this."

"You know you want to do this," Jason said, and he was right. My heart was beating erratically, my mouth was dry, and my armpits were lakes of sour sweat. But yes, I did want to do this. I needed to tell them not to worry. I needed to tell that that I loved them.

"Tell them…" I said, my voice cracking. "Tell them not to worry. Tell them I love them."

"A good start, sunshine," Jason said, and I wanted to hit him. He typed it in. "And then? Dictate. I'm a fast typist, so off you go. What next?"

"And then nothing. Nada, zip, zero." I folded my arms across my chest. "Okay, okay. Just tell them that I am fine and that I'll be in touch with them when I can. I don't want them to ask me any questions, and I don't want them to know where I am or what I am doing. I need some time to myself. Tell Margaux I'm sorry I ruined the trip. And tell Adam I'm sorry I didn't meet his boyfriend at the party. I'm sure I have to apologize to Helen for something, but I don't know what it is right now. Just tell them I'm sorry I wasn't a good dad. Tell them also that I didn't plan this—it just happened. And tell them I love them. And that's it, okay? Please, enough."

"That will do," Jason said. "Now, email addresses?"

I told him.

"Sent," he said, pushing enter with a flourish. He looked at me as I wiped the tears off my cheeks.

"Let's go for a walk and get some ice cream," he said kindly.

I got up and blew my nose loudly. "What am I? Five? Ice cream? We just had breakfast." But I was smiling, and I did feel as if several boulders had been extracted from the centre of my chest.

13. MARGAUX

I WOKE UP TO AN EMAIL from Lyndon:

> I am fine. I need some time. I will be in touch when I can. Please don't ask me anything about what I am doing or where I am. I won't answer if you do ask. Margaux, I am sorry I ruined your trip. Adam, I am sorry I didn't meet your boyfriend at the party. Helen, I am sure I have to apologize to you for something, but I can't think what it is. Just know I am sorry I wasn't the best dad. I didn't plan this. It just happened. I do love you all.

This bombshell from dadisokay@aussiemail.au.

Of the three of us, I was the first to open it. It was sent at eight-thirty a.m., Sydney time, ten p.m., Toronto time. Adam checked his email moments after me and he tried to get me on Skype. But I needed time to think, so I didn't respond, which I knew would drive him nuts.

I messaged him to let him know that I was fine and needed time to think.

But the poor boy simply had to talk. After he sent me a barrage of text messages and emails, I finally told him to call me, which he immediately did.

"I can't talk louder than this. Rick's asleep. He's got an early meeting," he whispered and for some reason, this annoyed the hell out of me. If he couldn't talk, why did he have to phone me? I reminded myself that he loves me, and that he was worried about me, and of course, that he wanted to talk about it. I knew I was annoyed with his whispering simply because I was so angry with Lyndon.

"Adam, if you can't talk properly, then perhaps phone me back when you can," I snapped at him. "Okay? I'm fine. Let's talk when you can really talk. Phone me whenever. I'm sure I'll be awake. Your father has killed my ability to sleep, along with so much else."

"No, Mom," Adam was clearly upset, and I was angry with myself now, too. "I don't want talk later. What do you think Dad meant?"

"About what?," I said. "His note wasn't exactly confusing. Oh, Adam, look, listen to how horrible I'm being to you. I told you I don't want to talk now and I don't. I can't. Please, don't be hurt or angry but I need to think, okay? I can't add any illuminating knowledge as to the insights of the note. I know as much as you do."

"No, Mom, don't hang up. Please don't. Did you reply?"

"Of course, I did not reply. He doesn't deserve a reply. Did you reply?"

There was silence.

"When did you reply?" I asked him. "We only got the note about half an hour ago."

"I sent him a reply immediately," Adam admitted. "A few actually. Well, a dozen. Asking him where he is, telling him how unfair this is, telling him what this has done to you. Telling him how selfish he is. I must admit, Mom, I didn't hold back. But why should I have? He did this. He started all this. I sent them immediately because I thought he'd still be online and that he'd see them."

"And now we might never hear from him again," I said, tremulously. "He was clear. He said don't ask him. And you did. That's the thing with you, Adam. You always push his buttons. Why do you do that? You always have, and then you're hurt by your own actions, and we're all taken along with you."

"I'm sorry Mom," Adam said. This wasn't a new conversation.

I caught my breath. "Look, don't worry about it. Your father's going to do or not do whatever it is he wants. That much is clear. So please, don't worry about it. I shouldn't have said that you shouldn't have replied. You have every right to reply as much as you want to and tell him how you feel. But please, let me go, okay? I really can't talk right now. You're thirty-five years old. Please don't make me feel like you're a toddler who can't manage without me. I just can't deal with your neediness right now."

Adam sucked in his breath. I could tell by the hurt puppy sound that he made that I had devastated him. The whole conversation was a disaster, which was exactly why I didn't want to speak to him in the first place.

"Adam," I said, rubbing my forehead and digging my fingers into the pressure points of my eye sockets, "I didn't mean to hurt you. But sometimes you need to hear what I'm saying to you. You put your needs above mine by calling when I asked you to give me some time. And maybe yes, as my son, your needs are supposed to come first and trump mine. And I know you have been deeply affected and hurt by your father for your entire life and you know I've always done what I could to help you. This situation isn't something any of us know how to cope with. We're all struggling."

"Fine," he said, but his voice was strangled. I knew he was fighting not to cry. Like all the other times he had argued with Lyndon and I tried to comfort him, I had failed.

There was silence. Then I said, "I'm going to go now, okay? Book an appointment with Brenda today." Brenda was his therapist. Great, I thought. Some mother I was, telling my son to go and see his therapist. But I couldn't help him. I couldn't even help myself.

"Okay." Adam sounded sulky, frustrated. "Okay, Mom. Call me when you want or text me or whatever."

"I will honey, I will."

I hung up. I needed to get out of the hostel. I needed to walk, run, scream, and shout. I knew exactly where I needed to go.

I put the phone in my purse and rushed out to wait for the bus. After Lyndon had vanished, I'd bought a weekly bus, rail, and ferry pass, figuring I might as well ride around and see some of Sydney while I waited for him to grace me with some kind of message or contact. We were into our third week and I was on my third pass, and I had pretty much explored Sydney from top to toe.

After I moved into the hostel, I established a routine of sorts: I woke when my body told me to, which was usually late since I stayed out with Tim and Janet until the early morning hours. I had found it increasingly easy to lose myself in the noisy glamour of their vibrant show, unlike that first night.

After I woke, I showered and grabbed some toast in the kitchen. Then, I caught a bus or a ferry or a train to somewhere where I'd walk around or people-watch. Or I'd spend the day on a beach somewhere, trying to read. Then I'd head back to the hostel to get ready to go to Dames and hang out with Tim and Janet. This routine had become my life, and it was amazing how the days passed in this way. And although I had established a certain rhythm, I was still waiting to hear from Lyndon, constantly checking my phone. And now, finally, limbo had given way to the next step although what that step actually entailed was remarkably vague.

I took the bus to Coogee Beach and by mid-morning, I was sitting on the hilltop at the Coogee Virgin Mary's shrine. Worshippers swear the Virgin had been seen in the very spot I was sitting, so a shrine had been built in her honour. Gold-and-silver Christmas balls, tinsel, and glittering pink-and-purple carnival beads were draped across the aging laminated newspaper clippings of the sighting. Rosaries and burnt-out candles were mementoes of prayers, all of them desperate, no doubt.

This was not my first visit to the shrine. And that was why I was so extremely blunt with Adam. I did have my own issues to deal with. Because, the previous day, yes, not even twenty-four hours earlier, I had asked the Virgin for help.

I had prayed for the first time in my life since I was a school-girl. And even back then, I hadn't really prayed. I had gone to church with my mother, but as soon as I could wrangle myself out of it, I stopped going.

So, I had prayed for the first time in decades, begging for help. *Please let me hear from Lyndon, please. I can't go on like this. I need your help. I need to know what's going on.*

And then, first thing the next morning, my husband sent me an email. There was no way around it. My prayer had been answered. And I didn't know how I felt about that.

Life was easier to manage without religion muddying up the waters. I felt guilty for having asked for anything. Who was I to ask for favours from God? And who was the God who'd answered me? And this led me to wonder, had they done other things along the way, in my life, that I hadn't acknowledged? Would I be punished for not having acknowledged them? But I hadn't known any God was there. Maybe He or She had never been there. Maybe I just felt guilty for having snapped at Adam, my poor sweet boy, whose needs would most likely remain unmet for the rest of his life. He was was an open wound, always had been. He was a delicate, finer prettier cast of Lyndon, slim and dainty. When he came out, it had been no surprise to me. I had only wondered what had taken him so long. And I had tried, over the years, to encourage him to be whatever he needed to be, without pushing him this way or that way. But he had done things in his own time, in his own way.

He seemed happy with Rick, a nice enough, well-dressed lawyer built like a stocky rugby player with broad shoulders and a solid chest. And then there was my Helen. I wondered what she would make of Lyndon's email. She would no doubt find a way to excuse and forgive him. She had always understood him whereas I judged him, and Adam feared him. Why were we all so intrinsically, inescapably ourselves?

I was sick of all of it. I was sick of being needed in the wrong ways. I was sick of standing on the pinnacle of the mountain of my life and looking down at such a mess. My life was a littered Everest and I hated that. It had always been an inside joke between Lyndon and me, that life was like mountain climbing, and somehow, we'd felt so superior to everyone else. Why was that? The arrogance and naivety of youth?

I stared at the Virgin's shrine. All I had were unanswered questions and a crushing guilt. I couldn't sit still. I was angry with the Virgin, which confused me. Perhaps it was because while she had answered my prayer, it hadn't changed anything. Perhaps I hadn't asked for the right thing. I should have asked for Lyndon to come back and fix this mess. But instead, I said I wanted to hear from him, and I had, but not in the way I wanted.

"So pretty much thanks for nothing," I told the Virgin with no small amount of sarcasm. I wondered if I only imagined the sun ducking behind a cloud because the world darkened for an instant, while my body felt lit up like a human biofield image. My anger was radioactive, nuclear. I shut my eyes and tugged hard at my hair, needing the pain. I had asked for help and what had I received? A cryptic message—not that that should be any surprise, coming from Lyndon.

I wanted to smash the shrine, rip the newspaper clippings, and scatter the stupid old shiny Christmas ornaments. Why were there Christmas ornaments in April anyway? I wanted to throw the rosaries and candle stubs across the lawn, but I knew I couldn't do that, so I kept my hands buried in my hair. I needed to bring this terrible mood under control, and as the wave of anger slowly ebbed, I felt exhausted, eviscerated by life.

I had no idea what I was going to do.

I needed to leave, that much was for sure. But I decided to take a photograph of the shrine of the Virgin of Coogee to mark the moment, as a reminder for me to thank her later. Great, I was getting like Lyndon: *Don't think about it now.*

I snapped the shot on my phone of the Virgin with her outstretched hands, her beatific smile, and her flowing robes. I checked to see if the image was in focus. But something very strange happened, and I wondered if my phone was broken. Because, where Mary should have been, there was no image, only a black outline, a cardboard cut-out, like the outline of a body on a crime show.

I took a picture of the bathing station archway, just beyond, to test my phone. Nope, it was all good. And I snapped a few pics of a frolicking dog and they were all fine. I took a few more pictures of the Virgin Mary and it was the same in all of them: she was a black cardboard cut-out. The tinsel, the gold balls, the rosaries, and the candles were all there, but the Virgin was solid black.

I shot backwards, terrified. I scrabbled up the slope, grazing my hands on the grass, such was the force of my panic. My heart had grown the wings of a vulture, and my ribs were clawed with sharp talons.

I couldn't breathe. My chest was blocked. I engaged a breathing method a friend had taught me years back. I held my breath and then breathed out, just a tiny bit, and gradually each in and out increased until I was nearly back to normal.

I approached the Virgin again, and I took several more pictures from various angles, all with the same result. She was a black cardboard cut-out. I zoomed in and out and it was the same, every time.

I tucked the phone in my purse with shaking fingers, zipped it closed, and walked away. I walked to Bondi, along the coastal path I loved so much. The day was scorching hot, but I was shivering, covered in goosebumps. I couldn't even appreciate the beauty of the waves crashing below me, or the aqua sea to my right, or the perfect clouds above me. I took comfort when I reached the gravestones in the Waverley Cemetery that overlooked the ocean. Death and despair, the unknown, the occult, the various religious persuasions, all spun around in my mind. I had unleashed something, that much, I knew. Something dark. I felt as if I was walking in the shadows although I could see the sun on my skin. I should have brought a hat. Even if I couldn't feel it, I'd get sunstroke at this rate. I had run out of the hostel without thinking, and I didn't have any sunscreen or water with me. It was lunchtime, and the heat was peaking. I was thirsty and I knew I should stop for water, but I powered on, trying to figure out what happened.

I got to Bondi and stopped for a moment to admire the view and catch my breath. Despite everything that happened, I still loved the curve of the beach and its soft, pale sand in the crescent-moon bay. I'd be safe, here.

But I felt dizzy. I needed food, water, and rest. I needed to find an outdoor café where I could have a glass of wine, take a Xanax, and try to calm down.

I knew I should be thinking about Lyndon and his message, but I was too frazzled by the Virgin and the call with Adam. It was all too much for me.

I walked into the first restaurant I could find. I ordered a cocktail with rum and pineapple and coconut, and I told the waiter I needed to visit the washroom, that I'd be right back.

I studied myself in the mirror. I wished my twenty-year-old self could see the face I was looking at now. Because I had no idea what I was looking at. Was I really old? How old was old? Old people always said they didn't feel old, but I felt old. I looked at my withered cheeks and the puckered lines along my upper lip, even though I'd never been a smoker. Why did I have those lines when I had never smoked? I reached into my purse and smeared on some makeup, but it made things worse, as if I was trying to fill in the cracks, which now only stood out even more. Lipstick turned me into a demented clown, the Joker. I was the Joker, but nothing was funny.

"If there is a God, then you're a cruel one for having invented aging," I told the mirror. "How come we never see pictures of the Virgin older? She's stuck at what, an eternal twenty? The math doesn't add up. If Jesus died when he was thirty-three, Mary would have been at least forty-seven. Where are her wrinkles? Where are her sunspots? Her hands are unlined. All of her is unlined. Talk about creating unrealistic body expectations. I realize that my observations are not endearing me to you, and I should be more careful after your recent display of anger...." Then the washroom door opened, and a woman walked in. A woman who stared at the crazy lady who looked like the Joker and who was shouting at the mirror or rather, at the Virgin Mary and at God.

"Margaux? Oh my God, it's *you!*"

Oh *my* God. Just what I didn't need. Anita.

I let her hug me. She twisted me into an awkward embrace, and I felt like I was being crushed by an iron maiden. She finally let me go.

"I'm here having a girl's lunch," she said. "Are you here with Lyndon? I didn't see him out there. I would have spotted him, the gorgeous man."

Gorgeous man? "No, he's back at the hotel," I lied. "He isn't feeling too good, but I love Bondi, so I thought I would come and have lunch by myself."

"How *brave* of you, dining alone! Well, I'm here to save you. My word, I would have thought you'd have been off to your next big world stop weeks ago! We had dinner what, three, four weeks ago? What have you been doing in Sydney all this time, without getting in touch again? Well, never mind, come and join me and my friends! But wait, I have to tinkle."

Who even uses the word "tinkle"?

She carried on chatting to me while she "tinkled" loudly. I wondered if I should make a run for it, but I'd have to pay for my cocktail on the way out. She'd find me and the whole thing would be strange and rude, so I stood there until she came out, adjusting her panties. I looked away. She was six-ty-five if she was a day, and I didn't need to see her adjusting her leopard-print thong.

I wished I had taken my Xanax, but I hadn't had the chance. Now life was roaring at me in full colour, teeth bared. I was caught in the gale force wind of Anita's chatter, staring at the uvula of a tiger's throat, which hung there like a deformed, bloody teardrop. And Anita's teeth looked like giant yellow Brazil nuts, half skinned. There was a rushing noise in my head and suddenly there was silence.

Anita was staring at me. "Darling," she said carefully, "are you all right?"

I couldn't tell her she was the open mouth of a tiger with Brazil nuts for teeth. I couldn't tell her my husband had left me. I couldn't tell her anything real. So, I said, "Coogee's Virgin Mary turned black," and then I felt myself fainting. I fell fast. I hit the floor and it was nice and cool down there. And then, there was nothing at all.

14. LYNDON

A COUPLE OF NIGHTS LATER, I was sitting at the kitchen table, working on some sketches. I felt like a kid at Christmas—Jason had said I could try my first tattoo on him as soon as I was ready.

"Never forget the first time, do you?" he said, winking at me. He was digging in the fridge for the makings of supper. He hadn't mentioned the email to my family, and I hadn't asked if there were any replies.

"Any ideas on what I'm getting? Good luck finding a place on my body."

"I've got a few ideas," I said, and I showed him. I'd done a couple of versions of the Tree of Life, and I was nervous that he wouldn't like any of them. He put down the vegetables he had taken from the crisper and a lifetime passed before a great smile spread across his face. "Beauty!"

I wanted to run around the kitchen table like Adam did when he was a kid—run from the sheer exhilaration of being alive and having done the right thing. It occurred to me that perhaps I was substituting Jason for my father, but I didn't know what to do with that thought, and I wouldn't let anything diminish my happiness. Besides, Jason was hardly old enough to be my father.

"I like this one," he said, pushing the more intricate sketch at me, and I inwardly winced. I'd hoped he choose the easier one.

"Sean will help you learn," he said, noticing my concern.

Then he folded his arms across his chest when my face closed at his suggestion. "Lyndon, if you can't take help from those who know more than you do, then you're a stupid git and you'll never get to be any good. You've got the chance to learn from the best and you should take it. Sean went to art school after he decided to get into this line of work. Plus, he's been doing this for years. You couldn't find a better teacher if you tried."

"You're right, I'm sorry," I said. "I used to be the one who ran the show, so I'm not used to being the rookie."

"What did you do when you ran the show? What kind of show was it?"

"Well, I've always been an asset at dinner parties," I offered, trying to change the subject. "I'm famous for being the epitome of wit and bonhomie."

"Basically, you're a dickhead at other people's expense."

"I don't know why, Jason, but coming from you, that's not the insult it would be from anyone else."

"And I will take that as a compliment. What else did you offer this world besides your amazing sense of humour? How did you make filthy lucre to support you and your family?"

"I was the editor of a business, marketing, and investment magazine for thirty-three years." I proudly announced, and Jason sprang up as if I'd tasered him.

"Bollocks you were! No way? You, my friend, are the *enemy*! You are *Satan*!"

I shrank back in my chair. I had expected him to be impressed. But he was trembling, his long lean wiry body was shaking and rippling, like a blow-up air doll at a car wash. It was clear he was outraged, but by what, I had no idea. I'd never had anyone react this strongly to my job description. I sat there, my mouth open, my world in flames around me.

"Jason? Please explain. I am not Satan or your enemy. I don't understand."

Jason finally sat down, to my relief. "If I had known that about you," he said, "I never would have opened my door to you. I thought you were one of us. You stole a car, and a cat, for God's sake. You showed up here with nothing but the horrible old clothes on your back. I thought you were a brother."

I was confused. "Jason, I don't follow. And they weren't horrible old clothes, they were brand new Tilley Around-The-World-For-However-Long-We-Want travel clothes that Margaux picked out for me. They were expensive. I like my new clothes a lot more, don't get me wrong, but I wasn't some kind of homeless thief." I stopped and rubbed my head. "Okay, so I was homeless and I was a thief, but it was the first time for either of those things. I took Queenie by accident."

"Capitalism," Jason said, and he spoke slowly as if I was the village idiot, "is the occult bruise on the body of the earth. That's the truth, Lyndon, and you need to understand it. Please, open your heart to what I have to say." He stopped and got up and paced around the kitchen. "No, first I have to think about how to approach this. I can't go the obvious route. I can't come barging in through the front door. I have to think about this."

He sat down as Queenie jumped onto my lap and started chirping. I hung onto her for dear life.

Jason muttered and pinched the bridge of his nose and closed his eyes. I tried to think of something to say, but I came up short. I quietly picked up my book and started paging through it while Queenie kneaded my thighs.

"I know what to do," Jason finally said. His eyes had calmed down and were focused. He wiped away a small piece of spittle that had landed on his chin, something I'd thought best not to point out. "Come with me," he said.

I got up and followed him into his bedroom and saw six cardboard boxes lining a wall. The room, much like Jason's entire apartment, was sparsely decorated. It had a king-size mattress on the floor, a ridiculously neatly organized bookcase, and a spectacular view of the ocean. Apart from a framed print of earth as seen from space, the walls were bare. Jason's blanket was bright yellow and his pillow was red, and his bed, unlike mine, was neatly made. My clothes were strewn all over the floor. His were not. I made a note to tidy my room as soon as this conversation was over.

I was still trying to figure out how I had metamorphosed from being a brother to being Satan, simply by being the magazine editor of a financial publication. And how capitalism was the occult bruise on the body of the earth? That Jason didn't approve of my former, lifelong job, was obvious. I had thought my job was laudable, impressive, worthy of respect even.

I stood there, struggling with my thoughts while Jason opened one of the boxes. It was filled with copies of the same book and he handed one to me. It was a slim volume titled, *The Occult Persuasion and The Anarchist's Solution*. The author was Jason Deed, who I presumed to be the same man standing in front of me.

I looked up. "You wrote this? What is it?" I was perturbed by the look in Jason's eyes. I'd seen that gleam in the eye of many an author, hell-bent on selling me their book. Authors of all shapes and sizes had made appointments with my assistant to meet with me, under the guise of having a proposal for a magazine story, but then they'd try to persuade me to do a book review. Most of their offerings had been amateurish and filled with implausible speculations about the financial industry.

Jason forced me out of my trip down memory lane and back into the moment.

"Yeah, I wrote it," he said, and he rushed over to the bookcase. "But wait. Before you read that, you need some background information. You can't just go in, blind."

He pulled a book off the shelf and handed it to me.

"*The Dispossessed*, by Ursula K. Le Guin," I said out loud and then studied the blurb on the back. "'Shevek, a brilliant physicist, decides to take action. He will seek answers, question the unquestionable, and attempt to tear down the walls of hatred that have isolated his planet of anarchists from the rest of the civilized universe. To do this dangerous task will mean giving up his family and possibly his life. Shevek must make the unprecedented journey to the mother planet, Anarres, to challenge the complex structure of life and living, and ignite the fires of change.'"

I looked at Jason. "Seriously? You want me to read science fiction about anarchy?"

"I do," he replied, and he took his own book back from me. "You can have this one after you've read that one. You'll be ready then. I can't throw you in the deep end without giving you a few swimming lessons first."

"I hate science fiction," I told him. "In fact, I hate fiction in general. It's a waste of time."

"You poor fellow. How your soul has not shrivelled up and died is beyond me. Listen, sunshine, you need to read that book. More than you need to read books about tattooing. Please trust me. Have I let you down yet?"

No, but it always happens in the end, I thought. "Sure," I said with obvious reluctance. "I'll start right now. This must-read trade paperback that was published in 1974. It looks like a book you could pick up on one of those revolving metal stands at the checkout counter of a drugstore."

"And your point would be?"

I returned to the living room and Queenie jumped onto my lap. I held the book over her head so as not to disturb her and began to read. Jason interrupted me, handing me a pen, a highlighter, and a notepad. "Make notes about questions you might have. And feel free to write in the book. It's your copy now. Mark things that resonate with you or things you don't understand but want to talk about. I'm going to make us more tea."

I consoled myself with the thought that I was a speedy reader. I turned the book over in my hands. I'd be done in a couple of hours easily.

But once again, I was wrong, and once again, Jason was correct. Page six stopped me in my tracks: *"He had always feared this would happen, more than he had ever feared death. To die is to lose the self and rejoin the rest. He had kept himself, and lost the rest."*

That was me. That was who I was and what I had done. I stared out into space. I needed to read this book properly. I settled back and concentrated.

I couldn't stop reading. I devoured the book with the hunger of a rabid animal and when I finished it, I stroked Queenie and thought about many things. Yes, I actually thought.

I fell asleep on the sofa. Jason woke me with breakfast on a tray. I could tell it was much later than our usual sparrow's fart sunrise hour, as Jason liked to call it.

"I let you sleep in," he said. "I came in and turned the light off around three a.m."

"Why were you awake at three?" I asked, sitting up and yawning and rubbing my face.

He shrugged. "So you liked it, did you?"

"Liked it? Understatement. Wow, it blew me away. Shevek and his observations? I felt like he was talking about *my* life. But Jason, that was science fiction. I loved things like names having no gender and being generated by a computer, so they are all unique, and I loved the idea of sharing and doing away with excess. But things like countries not having their own flags and there being no vertical hierarchy in organizations—no captains, bosses, chiefs-of-state—well, that's just not practical. And the whole ethos of people's natural incentive to work coming from spontaneous energy, well, that wouldn't work at all either. People work for money; people want their own things. People like to own stuff."

"People think they want to own things," Jason said, handing me a bowl of oatmeal off the tray. "Look at you. You owned a house, I presume, a car, maybe two. Now you don't own anything."

"And I'm living off the proceeds of a stolen car. It was fortunate that I ran into you."

"Were it not for me, the universe would have provided. *You* would have provided. You are more resourceful than you might think."

"Without you, I would have been arrested. And the book says this…" I flipped to a passage I had marked: "'*We have nothing but our freedom. We have nothing to give you but your own freedom. We have no law but the single principle of mutual aid between individuals. We have no government but the single principle of free association. We have no states, no nations, no presidents, no premiers, no chiefs, no generals, no bosses, no bankers, no landlords, no wages, no charity, no police, no soldiers, no wars.*' That simply won't work!"

"You're overthinking the specifics," Jason told me. "Finish your breakfast. And have some more tea. Then go and watch Sean and chat to him about your sketch. And go for a walk. Get some air. Let your brain process what you've read and for once I'm going to tell you not to think about things. Your mind will sort things out if you keep your hands busy. Sweep the floor, help out where you can, and the rest will take care of itself."

He left and I ate my oatmeal, still thinking about Shevek and the book. Jason returned and handed me a copy of *The Occult Persuasion and the Anarchist's Solution.* "Whenever you feel ready. No pressure and I mean that. I've got some errands to run. I'll see you later, in the shop. Enjoy the day, Lyndon. It's a good day to be alive!"

15. MARGAUX

WHEN I CAME TO, Anita's face was inches away from mine. Her breath was minty and not unpleasant. I realized I was still lying on the floor of the washroom. "How long was I out for?"

"Not long. Twenty seconds or so."

"I need some water," I said thickly, and I got to my feet, shrugging off Anita's outstretched hand.

"Yes, darling, we'll get you some. And something stronger," she said, as she turned back to the mirror and checked her makeup. "Now, what were you saying about the Virgin Mary being black?"

"I'll explain later. Give me a minute, Anita, for God's sake."

"You're out of sorts, darling. I think you may have had too much sun. Happens to lots of tourists. They underestimate the sheer force of the Australian summer."

By now, I had washed my face and adjusted my clothing. I wanted to leave that horrible little washroom where I was trapped with the predatory Anita.

I turned to leave but Anita was right behind me, her hand on my waist, guiding me to a table of women who were all chattering like starlings. Even from a distance, the noise made me want to turn and run, but Anita had a firm grip on me.

"Darlings," she said, "this is Margaux from Toronto. The one who saved my life when Eddie was being a bastard. Let's get Margaux a drink. She fainted in the loo."

The waiter spotted me and brought my drink over, and I took a large gulp before I even sat down. It was delicious although the ice had melted a bit.

"Are you all right?" the woman nearest me looked close to normal with short cropped grey hair and a no-nonsense expression. "Here, sit down."

She pulled out a chair next to her. "You should drink some water too." She poured me a glass, and I drank it in one go. She was right. Rehydrating with a rum cocktail was hardly sensible. "I'm Graham. I know," she said to me, "boy's name. Still, that's me."

I looked at the menu Graham was holding.

"I'm going to have prime rib on the bone," I said to her. "Rare. I think I need some protein to pep me up."

"So, darlings," Anita shouted from across the table, "let's order our food pronto and then Margaux can tell us her story about the Virgin Mary at Coogee. Apparently, she had an encounter."

A loud series of *ooohs* and *ahhhs* rose at this, and they all turned to me with wide-eyed expectation.

"Well," I began, but the waiter came and took orders around the table. It seemed there was a lot of indecision and he was stalled with one woman for quite some time.

"How do you know Anita?" I asked Graham while we waited for the server to reach us.

"Writer's group," she said. "We've been together for nearly ten years. We all write different things and are at different stages in the writing process. I've had a work of non-fiction published, while some of the women have had short stories in a few anthologies. There are a couple of novelists here too."

"I can't see Anita as a writer," I said. "I never knew that about her."

"She's a poet. Won a few awards, actually. And another woman, Nora," Graham gestured across the table, "also writes poetry, but Anita's been published a few times."

"She has?" I was surprised. "She's never said."

"She's really very good. Mostly rants about love and men and how it all goes horribly wrong, but she's very funny."

"And what's your book about?"

"*The Idiot History of Australia*. I know, the title sounds the opposite of any kind of politically correctness, doesn't it? But that's what people with mental health issues were called back then. 'Idiots.' It's about insane asylums and how badly women were treated in them, back when being called an 'idiot' was actually considered a medical term."

"Sounds fascinating," I said and I meant it.

"It's more of an academic publication than anything. I'm a psychologist at the University of Sydney, and they like their professors to be published. I thought the field sounded interesting and I enjoyed researching the asylums. But now, I'm trying to write fiction, which is much harder. For me, anyway."

The waiter has reached us and after we had placed our orders, Anita raised her hands as if she was about to start a mass. The table fell silent.

"So, darling, the Coogee Virgin Mary. Tell all."

I froze. I didn't have my story ready. I couldn't exactly say that I had been sitting at the shrine praying to hear from my husband who had left me weeks ago, and that I needed a miracle, which had then unexpectedly fallen into my lap.

The whole table was looking at me, in silence, waiting.

"I thought it was a quaint tourist attraction," I finally said. "And so I took a picture, and where Virgin was supposed to be, there was just a black cardboard cut-out. Now, bear in mind I fainted in the washroom, so maybe I imagined the whole thing."

I dug into my purse for my phone.

"Nice purse," one of the women commented. "Coach?"

I nodded.

"I've always wanted one," the woman continued, "but I've never been able to spend that kind of money on something like that. That's a five-hundred-dollar purse," she told the table, and I flushed beet red.

"It was an anniversary present," I said, wishing I hadn't just tossed my phone into my bag where it had clearly sunk to the bottom of the disarray inside.

"Margaux's husband is such a lovely man," Anita commented. "So handsome, so successful. I'm not surprised he's generous too. You ladies should meet him. He's such a dish."

I wanted to tell Anita that, in fact, I had bought the purse for myself as an anniversary present for Lyndon's and my thirtieth because he had told me that Coach purses were obscene examples of successful marketing campaigns that tapped into the ever-growing trends of consumer-driven greed, and that he would rather take us out for dinner. What, so he could lecture me the entire night about something that had caught his eye in the newspaper that day? I preferred the purse.

"If we must spend, let's buy experiences, not things," he had said, sounding so pompous that I went ahead and bought the gift for myself on the credit card we shared. Lyndon and Adam had been going through a particularly tough patch, and I had been frustrated with Lyndon for no reason I could clearly define. And though it was fine to say that about experiences, when it came down it, what experiences had he been referring to? There had been no further suggestions about our anniversary dinner, which morphed into the Chinese takeout that he liked. My anger at his hypocrisy—or, at the very least, his self-blindness—had contributed in a big way to the booking of this trip. He had said he wanted experiences? Well, here was an experience. And hadn't that just worked out well for me? He should have been more specific. He should have said, "I want experiences without my family and without you, Margaux."

I found my phone. "I bet I was just imagining it," I said as I flipped to my photos. But no, I hadn't imagined it. There was the Virgin, a black cardboard cut-out, in all the pictures.

"Pass the phone around," Anita barked, and I couldn't exactly refuse. I hoped she wouldn't start scrolling through my emails and text messages when it got to her, but she behaved herself, limiting her curiosity to the various images of Mary that I had taken.

"My God," she marvelled. "Well, group, here's a writing prompt if ever there was one. What do you make of it? Trish, you're our local psychic, what do you think?"

We all turned to Trish, a tiny, seventy-year-old woman with purple hair and large dangling silver earrings. "It's definitely a message," she mused. "I believe there is a soul in trouble, and she's asking for your help."

Could she be talking about Lyndon? Was he in trouble? I leaned forward. "Are you sure it's a woman, not a man?" I asked.

She nodded. "Definitely. Otherwise, the effigy would have found another way to manifest itself to you."

"What am I supposed to do with it?" I asked. "Even if it is a message, it's highly improbable that it's meant for me in particular, and it's even more improbable that I am supposed to do something about it."

"The thin line between the improbable and the probable is known in magic as 'the sphere of availability,'" Trish told me. "You need to widen your sphere of availability, so there is more of the probable within your grasp. And then you will find your answers."

"I've got no idea what you are talking about," I replied bluntly, finishing my cocktail and waving for another.

"White magic, religion, it's all the same thing," Trish said, and the others around the table nodded. Even Graham nodded and I was surprised. I would have thought her feet would be more firmly on the ground than that.

"Oh, come on!" I objected. "You're not being serious?"

"Absolutely serious. Magic goes way back in history."

I wondered if, instead of a writers group, I had fallen into a coven of witches. It wouldn't surprise me if Anita was a witch. I looked across at her. She was listening to Trish with the kind of rapt attention I didn't think was possible of her.

"As I was saying, I do think there is a soul in trouble, and I do think you should be careful. You will need to keep yourself earthed and grounded during your search. For example, all acts of white and positive magic must be conducted facing east."

"Acts of magic? What exactly am I supposed to be doing while I face the east?" This woman was infuriating. She was talking in riddles. "I think my picture is just a trick of the light. Some odd coincidence or something for which there is a scientific, logical explanation."

"Magicians know there are no coincidences in the physical or spiritual worlds and that so-called fortuitous happenings are simply predesigns of the cosmic forces that can see everything. Even Jung thought that what he called synchronicity, in other words, coincidence, is the result of our unconscious blending of the past, the present, and the future."

"My unconscious made my iPhone see a blacked-out Mary?"

"Believe it or not, yes. And now you have a choice. You can try to find and help this soul in distress or you can turn away. But remember the rules of magic: to see, to know, to will, to dare, and most importantly, keep silent. Some people cannot keep silent and that is their downfall."

"Should I have kept quiet about the Virgin and my pictures?" I was suddenly terrified that I had unloosed the demons of chaos and destruction and that my children would be harmed. I told myself that I was overreacting and that perhaps I shouldn't have finished my cocktail so quickly on an empty stomach, which didn't stop me from reaching for the replacement that had appeared in front of me.

"Not at all. That's not what I mean. I mean that on your path to find this soul, you will encounter magical forces, and you will need to be grounded and respectful in your handling of that."

I didn't know what to say to that. Fortunately our food arrived and I hoped that it would be the end of the discussion but Trish, her fork poised over her lobster with garlic butter sauce, had one more thing to say. "Just remember, there are no limits to the powers of the human mind. All angels, demons, and gods of nature slumber deep within the human unconscious." She nodded sagely at me and attacked her food with delight.

I was exhausted. I wondered how I was going to get away from the group without letting Anita know about Lyndon. I was trapped at a lunch I didn't want to be at, and I didn't care about some lost soul. I was lost, Lyndon was lost, we were all lost. I just wanted my normal life back. I wasn't interested in the spiritual or mystical side of things.

I looked up to see Graham watching me, a frown of concern on her face. She put her hand over mine. "I can help you if you like," she said, sounding kind. I wanted to ask her how she knew about Lyndon, but then I realized she was talking about the lost soul in the photograph.

"I would like to see you again," I told her, out of the blue. "But don't tell Anita. She'll barge in. She and I have been friends since we were little kids, and I love her, but she can be a bit overbearing."

"A bit?" Graham smiled, which transformed her stern face. "Give me your phone. I'll give you my number and email address. I'll pretend to just be studying the Virgin again. Otherwise Anita will get territorial!"

I handed my phone to her and felt like maybe things weren't quite so awful after all. I had Tim, and now, I had Graham. I also had the ghost of a blacked-out Virgin Mary, but I took a leaf out of Lyndon's book and decided not to think about that.

16. LYNDON

JASON'S BOOK SEEMED EASY to read but it was quite hard to pin down the specifics of what he was trying to say. Never mind that the content wasn't my cup of tea—many of the rambles were elaborate and unwieldy, and I wasn't exactly sure what his point was.

"I thought anarchy meant embracing violence and chaos," I said to Jason over lunch. "Your book doesn't have that at all."

"You're right. We don't believe in violence. Many anarchists are violent, but that's not what the purists subscribe to. You'll always have splinter groups who use violence as an excuse to vent their own rage, and they hide behind a convenient philosophy that allows them to behave in the destructive manner they desire. We believe in the individual, in complete freedom. We want a society where individuals can co-operate freely and equally. We're opposed to all forms of hierarchical control, and most of all, we oppose capitalism. Capitalism is killing the world, and man. And by man, I mean men, women, all of us. Capitalism is founded on acts of genocide and greed and it's responsible for the current global ecological crisis. Most people put their head in the sand and don't want to admit how evil capitalism is. They don't want anything to get in the way of their next big car, or computer, or whatever else it is they want to buy. And all they want to do is buy, buy, buy. And, in doing so, they become complicit and contribute daily to the pollution and destruction of our world."

"But I can't ever see capitalism being tossed out the window," I said, insistent. "It's the only system that works. Socialism, communism, imperialism, and monarchism have all failed or are failing. So, what's the solution?"

"Ah Lyndon. So solution-driven. Next thing you'll tell me that anarchy is a beautiful ideal but impractical. Emma Goldman spotted that problem in the early nineteenth century. But should we abandon an ideal simply because it is hard to attain?'

"There was a nice thing in *The Dispossessed* about ideas," I said, and collected the book from the living room and paged through it: "'*It is the nature of the idea to be communicated, written, spoken, done. The idea is like grass, it craves light, likes crowds, thrives on crossbreeding, grows stronger from being stepped on.*' All of which is lovely, but what does it mean in terms of action and changing the hold that capitalism has over us?"

"Our role, as anarchists, is to bring the idea to the oppressed people and get them thinking about a collective emancipation. Capitalism's demand for ever-continuous growth is draining our finite planet and putting the whole human species in jeopardy. We want to save the individual, save the pure human being, save the planet."

Very noble, I thought, but once again, how? And to what end? I turned to the first line of Jason's book. "Why is 'capitalism an occult bruise on the body of the earth'? I get that it's a bruise, but why occult? Doesn't that mean supernatural?"

"It does and it doesn't. It's also a scientific term. According to the internet, and I quote, it refers to a 'disease or process that is not accompanied by readily discernible signs or symptoms.' So, when we talk about capitalism causing global warming and killing the planet, people respond by saying, oh well, there's no proof really. They say that what we take to be signs and symptoms of our planet's demise are nothing more than the usual weather patterns that have always had their ups and downs. Some people say that Noah's Ark was built when the world's weather patterns changed, and look, there wasn't global warming then."

"Noah's Ark is fiction," I protested. "But yes, you are right. There are people who refuse to accept that global warming is real. And I see what you mean about the occult bruise. There is no doubt that the world is bruised from our constant pollution."

"Which is directly caused by capitalism. Capitalist expansion is forever seeking increased profits. That's the fundamental core tenet of the system. But we already have an over-abundance of stuff, so what do capitalists do? They invent and manufacture new needs and new wants among consumers who continue to buy their products, and thus subscribe to their ethos of greed."

"Yes!" I sat up, accidentally dislodging Queenie. I immediately apologized to her and tried to pick her up, but she was offended and she stalked out of the kitchen. "It drives me nuts," I said. "We buy things willy-nilly, but the products are not biodegradable, and they have limited lifespans, which means you are forced to throw them away, constantly adding to the garbage that we are littering on the earth. And space! Space is filled with garbage! And the oceans! Plastic bags are killing our seas, pollution from ships is deadly, our skies are clogged with the exhaust fumes of thousands of planes, there are regular oil spills, and no one says or does anything. There isn't a single part of this world that, to put it in your words, isn't bruised by our greed. It all comes down to greed. You're so right. Want, buy, have, repeat *ad nauseam*. And the packaging." I waved my hands around, relieved to finally have the opportunity to tell someone about something that had been making me anxious and frustrated and furious for so many years. "Cosmetics, kids' toys, gardening equipment, you name it. They all come bound and clad in layers of packaging, none of it recyclable. I tried to do my bit. I recycled so carefully. I took all the family's garbage and sorted it and rinsed cans and bottles and put things in the right place. But my contributions meant nothing, and did nothing!" I sat back and rubbed my head hard. "I even used my own cup at the coffee shop to try to help and do you know what they did? They used one of their cups to fill mine and then they threw theirs away! So why bother? Why bother at all?"

I was furious, all fired up. Jason looked at me calmly. "The solution is to bring it back to the individual," he said. "What you were doing was right. You felt frustrated because no one was on the same page as you. But I want you to think about this too—how many people actually like their jobs? 'Anarchism aims to strip labour of its deadening, dulling aspect, of its gloom and compulsion. It aims to make work an instrument of joy, of strength, of colour, of real harmony, so that the poorest sort of man should find in work both recreation and hope.' I am quoting Emma Goldman there, by the way."

I blinked. "But I loved my job," I said. "I was gutted when I lost it. I think the loss sparked off my entire breakdown or whatever this episode is or was."

"You weren't having a breakdown, you were having an epiphany. You were suffocating as the seas of capitalistic enterprise threatened to overwhelm you. Your world trip forced you to confront the reality out there, and your psyche couldn't handle seeing the destruction of the planet on the global level."

At first, I wasn't sure I agreed with his diagnosis of my motives. I couldn't imagine my psyche being that altruistic. I flipped through *The Dispossessed* again. "'*Reality is terrible. It can kill you. Given time, it certainly will kill you. The reality is pain—you said that! But it's the lies, the evasions of reality, that drive you crazy. It's the lies that make you want to kill yourself.*' Maybe you're right, Jason. The world trip forced me to see the lies for what they are."

"Your soul realized you needed to break away, do something, and find meaning. Do you think it's an accident that you are here? Nothing in life is random, not to those who seek meaning, anyway. You found me, us, because you want to make a difference."

That made sense. "I knew I was tired, but I didn't realize I was angry or anxious," I said.

He laughed. "No one ever does. But there are those of us who will not remain silent. You were deadened, numbed by your comfortable job. But you liked it because it was an opiate, it made you feel lulled, reassured, sleepy, and calm. And then when it was pulled out from under you, you had nothing to kill the pain, the pain of realization that this world is on its last legs, and we're the buggers to blame."

"I will carry on reading," I said as Jason started to clear away our lunch plates. "And we will converse more."

Jason looked delighted. "And watch Sean work," he said. "We want to get you into the game soon."

17. MARGAUX

WHEN I RETURNED to the hostel, having successfully evaded Anita, I decided not to tell Tim about Lyndon's email, though I had to tell him about the blacked-out ghost of the Virgin Mary. But Tim was over at Dames getting ready for his show.

In the meantime, I realized I hadn't checked in with Helen to see how she felt about Lyndon's message. I texted her to Skype if she was awake. It was her three a.m., but she immediately dialled in.

"Are you okay?" we both said at the same time, and we laughed. I was relieved. I could always rely on Helen. I was afraid of her at times, afraid of her brusque no-nonsense self, but I could always rely on her. I felt like she got the best of Lyndon while poor Adam had got the worst of me. Helen looked like me, but she wore her hair platinum blonde and spiky. She had a nose and brow piercing, along with half a dozen earrings in each ear. Helen was broader than me and taller, and she had generous breasts. They were so large that a doctor had told she could qualify for surgery, should she wish to have them reduced. But she'd laughed him off. "I like them," she'd said, shrugging. And that was that.

"Adam is upset," I told her. "And I really hurt his feelings this time." I relayed our conversation.

"Don't worry Mom," she said. "Adam's old enough to deal with his own shit. I love him but he needs to see that the world doesn't revolve around him and his daddy issues. And the same with Dad. He needs to do whatever he needs to. It's not our problem to solve and at least we heard from him. But Mom, I've got some news."

She paused. From the expression on her face, my gut clenched, and I gripped the laptop with both hands. "What is it Helen? Are you ill?"

"Um, nope. I'm pregnant," she said, and I let out such a squeal of joy that she looked startled, then relieved, then delighted.

"Oh Helen! That's fantastic! I didn't even know you were seeing anyone."

"He's married," she admitted. "He works with me. I've been seeing him for three years actually."

And then it all made sense. Her sense of private happiness while seeming so alone; her constant texting at the dinner table at family events; her long working hours; her odd disappearances; and her mood swings, which went from euphoric to dark.

"I've told him. I don't know what he's going to do. I didn't get pregnant on purpose to make him leave his wife, but I did stop taking the pill. I wanted to get pregnant with or without him in the picture, and I figured, after three years of promises and lies, that at least I deserved to get a baby out of it. And I really want a baby. And I do love him, so I wanted his baby. He's angry with me right now and I get that. But I'm not sorry for what I did."

"I'm not sorry either," I told her. "I'm going to be a granny! That's wonderful! Well, you can count on me, Helen. I'll change nappies, babysit, make formula, whatever you need. How far along are you? Do you know if it's a boy or a girl?"

"Twelve weeks and they think she may be a girl, which is also hilarious since Alex has four boys and they wanted a girl for the last two."

"How old are his kids?"

"Twelve, eight, six, and two."

"Two? He had a child while he was having an affair with you?"

"Yes. That didn't make me happy, I can tell you that, Mom. That was when I started thinking that I wanted a baby too, and why couldn't I have one? It wasn't a rash decision. I thought about it for ages."

I was certain it wasn't a whim or an impulse based on a ticking biological clock. Helen, my neat little accountant daughter, would never do anything rash. I knew she would have done all the math to make sure she could afford a child.

"Helen," I said, "I'm so proud of you. I really am!"

She looked thrilled, and I wondered if she ever thought I harboured any other kind of thoughts or feelings towards her, other than love and pride. I hoped that wasn't the case.

"So, what are you going to do about Dad?" she asked.

"I'm not sure yet. Adam sent him a bunch of emails. Do you know if Dad replied?"

"Nothing more from Dad to Adam," Helen said, laughing. "Adam told me he's petrified he scared Dad off, but I said I really didn't think it would have made any difference if he replied to him or not."

"I agree. I don't know what to do. But I might tell him that I will stick around for a bit while he thinks about his life and see what he says to that."

I realized, as I said that, that I wasn't ready to leave Australia yet. I had unfinished business, and not just with Lyndon but with Tim, the ghost of the Virgin Mary, with my new friend Graham, and even with myself.

"Are you okay if I stay here for a bit?" I asked.

Helen nodded. "Of course, that's fine. I figured you'd be gone for at least six months. And while she's growing inside me, there's not a lot any of us can do, but once she's born, I will need you. Mom, don't tell Dad. He doesn't have the right to know. And I don't want him to emerge from wherever he is out of some misplaced sense of patriarchal guilt. If you ask me, his mid-life crisis began when his hair started falling out. He needs to come to terms with his balding old-guyness by himself, and then we'll take it from there."

"I agree. Do you remember all the shampoos and potions he bought?" We both laughed. "I told him it didn't matter to me if he lost his hair, but he said it mattered to *him*. And I told him it happens to all of us, but he snapped at me and said, 'What, you're going bald too?' And I said no, but I am aging. But you know your Dad. He's like Adam in that way. Their drama is more worthy than anyone else's."

"Yes. He told me he went to get blood tests done to see if there was anything he could do to stop the hair loss. He had found some doctor, a scam obviously, who said he could tell by Dad's blood if there was anything he could do to stop or slow down the hair loss."

"I had no idea he did that!"

"I know. Anyway, so he told me he was sitting in the waiting room of the blood lab, and he looked up and saw a friend of mine sitting across from him. Ava. You remember her? She was on her phone. So, he thought he'd check Facebook to see if she was who he thought she was before he made a fool out of himself by saying hi to her. And then he read her status, and it said something like, '*Sitting here in a lab full of sick old people doesn't exactly increase my will to live.*' and it made him so depressed. And you know how cool Ava always thought Dad was, and then she didn't even recognize him. In her mind, he was just one of the sick old people. He left and went back later when he was sure she wasn't there. But it really depressed him. And then he wasted a bunch of money on that doctor who said the blood work revealed that there was nothing he could do, but the consultation cost Dad five hundred dollars."

The price of my Coach purse. Consumerism wasn't acceptable, not even for a thirtieth wedding anniversary, but vanity justified spending. I told myself I was being ungracious. No one wants to lose their looks.

I looked at my watch. "It's nearly four a.m., honey. You need to go to sleep. Have you thought of any names yet for the baby?"

"Not yet, but I'm having fun doing research. Oh, and Mom, don't tell Adam about the baby either. Not yet. And don't worry about Dad or Adam, okay?"

"I won't. I can't. I'm too happy about your news! Keep me updated. And you know you can talk to me about Alex anytime if you want to, but I don't want to invade your privacy."

"Thanks, Mom. I will let you know what he does. It affects all of us now, not just him and me. Sleep tight."

I switched off the computer and lay down on the bed. A granny! A beautiful surprise just when I needed it most.

18. LYNDON

"THIS IS FAKE SKIN," Sean told me. "You'll practice on this first a few times."

I nodded and followed his instructions for putting the transfer of my Tree of Life on the stuff that, weirdly, did feel like real skin.

The first time I held the tattoo machine, I was giddy with joy, the likes of which I hadn't experienced since my first beer or the first time I cupped a girl's heavy breast in the palm of my hand. "I need a moment," I said to Sean, and he grinned.

"Cool, I know," he said.

The buzzing left my eyeballs and I could concentrate again. "Good to go," I told him. Tattooing wasn't as hard as I thought it would be. My hand was steady, and my lines were clean. Seemed like I hadn't lost my artistic talents, even though they had lain dormant all these years.

"Good one," Sean said when I was done. "I say you can do the boss tomorrow."

"Where is he?" I looked around, but Jason was nowhere to be seen.

"Had an appointment in Melbourne," Sean replied, and a large stone dropped to the bottom of my stomach, cold and hard.

"What? Why didn't he tell me?" I asked.

Sean laughed. "Don't worry, mate. I'm sure it just slipped his mind. He's been distracted lately with all of us, not just you."

But I was living with him. He was my friend. I told myself

I was reading too much into it and behaving like a lovelorn schoolgirl, so I shook myself.

"Feel like coming for a run?" Sean asked.

I barked with laughter. "Sean, I haven't run for about the last forty-five years, give or take. I'd break something."

"Okay then, how about a nice power walk?"

"Sure, but not too fast."

He eyed my boots. "Better change out of those, yeah. And get into your tracky dacks too." Sean had a very thick Australian accent and he tended to mumble out of the corner of his mouth. And he spoke in a hurried rush. There were times I couldn't understand him, but I got the gist of what he was saying.

I nodded. "I'll be right back." I returned wearing my sneakers and sweatpants. I was ready.

We started on a small path that ran along the ocean, and I inhaled large quantities of the salty fresh sea air. I was about to explain to Sean that we didn't have oceans in Ontario, only very cold, very deep, very still lakes, but then I figured that conversing with him would be too hard, particularly as he had us going at a quick pace. I was already in a sweat and finding it hard to keep up.

"You read Jason's book, yeah?" Sean asked. He had no problem walking and talking.

"Yes," I huffed. "Well, about three quarters of it. Are you an anarchist too?"

"We all are, mate. All the guys at the shop."

"How come there are no women in the shop?" This was something I had been meaning to ask Jason, but I kept forgetting.

Sean shrugged. "No reason. We had a receptionist for a long time but then she got preggers and we never replaced her. We just answer the phone ourselves."

"I like the sound of anarchism," I said, "but I don't think it's practical. Even if we get the individual all fired up to do his part, how will we make it work?"

"Computers and biogenetics," Sean said.

"What do you mean?"

"It's called transhumanism. First you upgrade and enhance the human mind, or brain, if you prefer, by computer, nano-technology and biotechnology. The upgraded individual will realize that anarchy makes the most sense, given that all the other systems have failed us. But we will need to restart our brains."

"I have never heard of that," I said diplomatically. I thought it made little sense.

"It's called techno-optimism. It's a political-positive outlook that's becoming more popular. And then there will be uncon-scious robots to replace human labour, and they'll be run by unconscious computer algorithms."

"Why will the robots help? I get why they need to be uncon-scious, but why do we need them?" I was struggling with the fact that I was even having this somewhat bizarre conversation while trying to power-walk along the shores of Cape Otway on a southern tip of the Australian continent.

"People won't have any power," Sean explained. "There won't be any top-down power. We'll vote, yeah, and the computers will make sure there's no corruption."

"But what about hackers and the like?"

Sean sighed. "Yeah. They're a problem. Did you know that Jason is a legend in the hacking world? He can get into gov-ernment websites, banks, the army, you name it."

I came to a complete stop, my hands on my thighs. I used this jolting bit of news to get Sean to stop for a moment, but I was genuinely astounded. "He said he was savvy, but he's that level of good? There is only one small laptop in his apartment."

"Crikey, mate. A genius like him? He doesn't need more than that."

I recalled Jason's telling me something about his skills when we emailed my family, but I hadn't realized he could hack in at government level.

"Sean," I said, "I need to take a breather."

"Sure, yeah, no problem, mate. Here's a bench. Let's sit for a while." He handed me a bottle of water, and I chugged it down gratefully.

"Does he do that a lot?" I asked. "Hack into the government?"

"No way! He runs a website called *The Occult Persuasion*. He's got millions of followers worldwide."

"Millions? Seriously?"

"Yeah. At last count, he had eight million subscribers."

"Wow." I couldn't think of anything to say.

"And he loves Sid Vicious," Sean added. "He's got a tattoo of him on his leg. He says he even saw Sid live one time. He was a real punk rocker, Jason was. Have you seen all the scars on his chest? Thought he was Sid, burning himself with cigarettes and cutting himself. Sid would have been sixty this year, can you believe it?"

"Yes, I do know. I loved Sid too. We're the same age." I felt nostalgic for dead Sid. I had been twenty-one and heartbroken when he died. Like many of Sid Vicious's fans, I had cursed Nancy Spungen and the horse she rode in on.

"You got any tattoos?" Sean asked.

I shook my head. "I never thought about them."

"And now you're going to be a tattooist?"

"I hope so," I said fervently. "We can carry on walking, but maybe a bit slower?"

Sean nodded and we got up. Sean, I had already noticed, was covered in tattoos.

"Which was your first one?" I asked.

He shook his head. "Can't remember. This is my most recent. Emma G." He shows me a monocled, stern woman on his calf muscle.

"Nice," I said. It was very well done.

"Ta mate. Jason did it. I love Emma. I mean I'm into transhumanism and all that, but you have to go back to the basics too. I can lend you a copy of her essays if you like."

"I would like that, thank you."

We carried on walking, and for a while neither of us said anything for which I was grateful. I managed to keep up, and Sean, kindly, kept it slow.

"It's all about nature, for me," Sean burst out.

I turned to look at him. "What is?"

"Anarchy," he said. "I love the earth."

"Yes, I know what you mean," I said, waving my hand around. "Look at this. So unspoilt, so beautiful. Meanwhile, we are killing the planet with garbage and pollution." I was about to go on my garbage rant, but Sean interrupted me. He took my arm and we stood face-to-face. I felt a bit uneasy all of a sudden.

"No mate. You're not getting my point. I really *love* her," he said, and he dropped to his knees and started caressing the beach sand. "I make love to her. She's my sexual partner. I don't need or want anybody except for the earth. And it's not some mother issue, before you start analyzing me. It's a nature thing."

"I see," I said. But I didn't, and I was concerned he was going to take off his trousers and demonstrate exactly what he meant. But to my relief, he stood up.

"Even decaying earth is sensual," he said. "Flowers, the bees, all of it. It's eco-eroticism. There are lots of us, right? People think it's weird, but what's weird about making love to a flower? It's the most natural thing in the world."

I nodded, trying to imagine it and trying not to imagine it. "And that's why you're an anarchist?" I asked, confused.

He shook his head. "I was into anarchy first and then I realized earth was my sexual partner for life. Anarchy frees my spirit, so I can engage with my true love. Anarchists are freethinkers, not judgmental like the rest of the world. We're into freedom of self-expression at every level. We don't discriminate. You read *The Dispossessed*?"

"Yes. An enlightening book. Wasn't there a piece in it about loving the earth?"

"'*There are souls ... whose umbilicus has never been cut. They never got weaned from the universe. They do not understand death as an enemy; they look forward to rotting and turning into humus.*' That passage, yeah? Well, it got me thinking. I've always loved nature so much, so I started meditating on my feelings for the earth and flowers and grass and mud and everything. And then, one thing led to another, and now she's all I need. She's my eternal sexual partner, and will be, even after I die."

"I think I have gone as far as I can today," I said faintly. I didn't mean the walk, but Sean took it that way and patted me kindly.

"You did very well, mate," he said.

19. MARGAUX

IT WAS TIME TO WRITE to my husband:

> Lyndon, to just leave me like that, even while I can
> understand that things were derailing for you, wasn't
> fair. Fairness. You love to tell me that fairness is a
> childish concept, that only the very foolish and very
> naïve subscribe to the notion that they are entitled
> to fairness, but am I not, as your wife of thirty-five
> years, entitled to at least a modicum of fairness? We
> have been through so much together, and the key word
> there is *together*.
>
> Perhaps you didn't want to have your mid-life
> crisis in front of me. Perhaps you preferred, even at an
> unconscious level, to do it in the privacy of your own
> new world, and I can understand that.
>
> And perhaps you simply don't love me anymore
> and would like to start a whole new life without me.
> If that is the case, then even if you consider fairness to
> be a foolish concept, it would be only fair to tell me.
>
> Less than a year ago, you lost your job, you
> turned sixty, Adam came out, we had our thirty-fifth
> anniversary, and then we threw our lives up in the air
> and decided to explore the world. It was a lot to take
> in. And what you don't seem to understand or pay
> credence to, is that all of this has affected me too. You

lost your job and it affected me. How could it not? You are/were your job. It defined you, the you I am married to. I wasn't exactly sure how to cope with a moping sullen you, the you who sat in your study eating smart popcorn and scattering the crumbs everywhere while I sold the house and did all the preparation for the trip. You couldn't deal with the unfairness of the hand that had been dealt to you, but you wouldn't acknowledge it either.

I am not really sure what you want me to say. You probably don't want me to say anything. You probably just want me to leave you alone.

Fair enough. There it is again, that word, *fair*. Don't you think it's time we all tried to bring some fairness back into this world where such a beautiful concept is considered improbable? We need to widen our spheres of availability so there is more of the probable within our grasp and that includes the concept of fairness.

I can't hang around Sydney indefinitely, waiting for you to tell me what's going on. I will give you another two weeks and then I am leaving. I may continue the tour by myself, I will see. There are the parts of the world I have always wanted to visit. Angkor Wat, for one. I am not going to miss out on that because of you.

I am not going to recite a list of the sacrifices I made for you because really, there weren't any. I loved you. I love you still. I love our family. In such instances, acts of love are not sacrifices. I do feel like I spent most of my life waiting. I was waiting for you to retire, so we could do more together and see the world, and I was waiting for you to do it with me. And now, if you don't want to do it with me, then I will do it alone.

You know, I don't even miss you right now. Maybe it's because I know you are fine, just acting selfishly. You haven't been easy to be with lately, either. But I don't want to get into a mud-slinging match although I'd like to say that you should contact Adam. Actually, don't. Let him deal with this. He also needs to realize that not every one of his needs can be met, not that that will be news to him, but he needs to learn to deal with it. You and he are more similar than either of you would care to admit.

I am going to go now. Please let me know what is going on.

I sent the message and didn't expect a reply. I was getting ready to go and meet Graham for breakfast. She lived in Balmain, and she said she had something to show me, something that was relevant to my encounter with the Virgin. I'd come to think of the eyeless statue in the images as my ghost, an apparition from another world, and I was eager to hear what Graham had to say. She also said that the Balmain Market was open and she thought I'd enjoy walking around there.

I was about to close my laptop when I saw a reply email from dadisokay@aussiemail.au.

Why did you say, "We need to widen our spheres of availability so there is more of the probable within our grasp and that includes the concept of fairness?"

I typed back, "This isn't Lyndon, is it?" and pressed send.

There was a brief pause and then, "No. It's the man he's staying with. Why did you say that? Do you believe in magic?"

"I don't," I replied. "But apparently there's a lost soul who needs my help. A white witch said that to me and I liked it. I thought it was relevant to Lyndon and me. You sent the email, didn't you? Not Lyndon. The first email, I mean."

And he responded, "Yes. I did. Lyndon didn't mean to hurt you. He can't help himself right now."

I replied, "I'm not going to comment on that. And you obviously read my very private email to him. Isn't that horribly voyeuristic of you? Frankly, I feel violated."

And he said, "Understandable, but not my intention at all. I apologize. I was only trying to help facilitate communication. I knew Lyndon wouldn't be in touch, and I felt you had the right to know that he's okay."

Furious, I lashed out. "You're God, are you? How nice that must be, dispensing wisdom and justice at your discretion."

And he said, "Actually, I'm a sixty-five-year-old ex-punk rocker from England. Not any kind of god I know."

Oh. I didn't have any idea how to respond to that, so I typed, "I have to go."

"You're going to find your lost soul?"

"Not today. Today, I'm just going to a weekend market in Balmain with a woman I met. It would be nice to spend some time with someone normal."

"No such thing, darling," the man replied, and I knew I should object to a perfect stranger calling me "darling," but actually it made me smile like a teenager passing notes in the classroom.

"Have fun," he said. "Roger, over and out."

And that was that.

Interesting. Lyndon had found himself a punk rocker to shack up with. I smiled. Both Lyndon and I had been into punk when we met—tartan trousers in the university beer hall, anarchy signs scribbled on our wrists, and all that. Both of us had been into street art and self-expression. How times had changed.

I locked my door and rushed to catch the bus to Circular Quay where I took a ferry to meet Graham at Balmain. I joined crowds of people going places, and I suddenly felt a bit glamorous,which was silly. But it was delightful to have a purpose. I had missed that, having a purpose, even one as small as a walk around a weekend market.

The ferry dropped me at Balmain, and I walked up the hill where I had arranged to meet Graham. I felt nervous, as if I were on a date or something. I was about to reach for a Xanax when I stopped myself. I wanted to see if I could do this without the aid of my calming little peach-coloured friends. I blamed Lyndon for my attachment to Xanax—it had been because of our dinner parties, with him being so clever and everybody being so afraid they'd be the next one he'd line up in the sights of his rapier wit. He had thought he was hilarious, and he was. He had been careful to never take it too far, but he certainly scraped up against the edge and dragged us all with him.

People had loved and hated our parties for that very reason; it had been like a gladiator sport. Who was Lyndon going to rip into that night? If you were the poor sap who got called upon, then it was hell for you, but hugely entertaining for the others. The others but not me. I'd had to resort to tranquillizers.

"Do you have to be quite so cutting?" I had asked him dozens of times afterwards while I cleaned up, and he'd laughed and come up behind me and I could feel his erection.

"My debate-winning techniques used to work for you," he said. "Used to be quite the aphrodisiac."

It was true. That was how we had met. Lyndon had been the captain of the debating club at university, and I'd thought he was brilliant. The best sex we ever had was when he'd verbally dissected and destroyed his opponents. He had needed to triumph over his teammates. And I got off on it too, watching him go in for the kill. I had applauded, my panties wet with the knowledge of fantastic sex to come.

But then, somehow, along the years, it had turned nasty, and I couldn't take it anymore.

"You've got soft and old on me," he'd said one night as he lay on the bed and watched me undress.

I had turned to him, still in my bra and panties, still as lean as I'd been when we met, unlike him. "You think so?" I asked.

"Intellectually," he jousted in a way I hadn't found funny.

"Perhaps you've become a sadist in your old age," I had countered. "Which isn't very attractive."

"No? This isn't attractive?" He had stroked his engorged dick, and I couldn't help myself. I had laid down and taken him in my mouth.

So there had been advantages to his cruel wit, but soon after that, I started taking a Xanax here and there, just to help see me through, which extended to times of being alone with him, or when we were out in company.

But I was not going to take one now.

Graham was leaning against a wall, waiting for me. She was smoking and she looked so together that I didn't think I could do this, with or without chemical help. I have never been "together," not like that, not even when things were at their best.

I always felt scattered, as if there was something I had forgotten to do or forgotten to tell someone. Or maybe I had said the wrong thing. In all likelihood, I had said the wrong thing. It used to drive Lyndon crazy when I'd come home from social events and I'd say to him, "I think I said something really stupid," or "I feel like I made a real *faux pas*," or "I'm sure that person will think I'm such an idiot," or "Why do I say such strange things to people?" And then I'd tell him word for word what I'd said, and generally, he'd say something like, "Most people aren't listening to you anyway," which wasn't helpful. Why weren't they listening when I was talking to them? Was I that insignificant? Or he'd say, "Most people have very short memories. They'll forget about it soon," meaning that I had indeed said something bizarre. So the odds were, I was going to say something awkward to Graham, and she'd think me a foolish woman, but I was going to take that chance.

I waved at her and she smiled at me, and that radiant smile transformed her face. My chest released—for the moment anyway.

"I'm so glad to see you," she said, and she gave me a hug. I wasn't a good hugger, and I worried that I had responded a fraction too late. Had I already ruined our friendship by not being as engaged in the hug as I should have been?

But Graham just looped her arm in mine, and we walked to the market that was set around a church. I've always loved markets and she and I shared the same tastes, stopping to look at pieces of antique jewellery we both liked, and both of us laughing quietly at some of the artwork on display.

We walked around for nearly two hours. I hadn't noticed it had been that long until Graham asked me if I was hungry, and I realized I was ravenous.

"Let's buy a picnic and go and sit in the grounds of the old Callan Park Hospital for the Insane," she said, and I was startled.

"Don't worry," she told me. "It's the Sydney College of the Arts now, and the grounds are lovely. I often go for walks there."

We bought muffins, lemon tarts, and coffees to go and set off for Callan Park. The acres of mowed green lawns featured several large buildings, and it was surprisingly peaceful and lovely.

"We'll just walk down that hill a bit," Graham said. "There's another writers' group here, a famous one in Sydney, the New South Wales Writers' Centre, but they are so full of themselves. I've been to a few meetings, but all they do is compete to see who's read so-and-so's book before anyone else has, and how many literary journals they've all been published in."

"Do they do any actual writing?"

"Oh yes. A lot of them are very well-known. They're the real literati of Sydney. It's a vicious little circus."

She led me down the hill and pointed at the building. "The Garry Owen House. That's where they meet. The Guild of Craft of Bookbinders are also in there, with all their fascinating tools of the trade."

"When was the Garry Owen House built?" I asked as we settled down on the grass under a large tree. It was a hot day, and I was glad to find shelter in the cool shade. We ate our muffins and tarts, and washed them down with lukewarm coffee.

"Around 1839. It started out as a luxury mansion and later became part of the Callan Park Hospital for the Insane, then later still a school for nurses. Hard to imagine the horror that those folk in the asylum suffered."

"I don't suppose they had air conditioning," I commented absently, which was typical of my stupid *faux pas* comments that I would later use as a self-flagellation tool for hours.

Graham laughed. "They did not. And there were twice, even three times as many people inside the asylum as there were supposed to be. Those poor people. Many women sought refuge from abusive husbands, but you could end up in the loony bin for domestic trouble, or so-called religious 'excitement,' or even love affairs and sexual seduction, or sunstroke, or overwork, or sexual intemperance, or even nostalgia."

"Nostalgia?"

"It is listed as a cause. And then, once you were in, that was it. Complaints were seen by doctors as further evidence that you were nuts, and it was nearly impossible to get out. There were scads of normal people in these places, but by the ends of their lives, they were crazy from the horror of it all."

"That wasn't so long ago," I said, "One imagines things like that happening to women in the dark ages, not a couple of hundred years back."

"True. The state government bought the Callan Estates in the 1870s in order to build what they thought would be a state-of-the-art psychiatric institution. And the Garry Owen House started being used as part of the asylum in 1875.

"My mother tells a story of having to bring her boss here," Graham continued. "My mother was a typist in an ad agency, and she arrived at work one morning to find her boss in terrible distress. He'd been drinking all night, and everyone knew he was an alcoholic, but all of a sudden, he demanded that my mother bring him to Callan Park Hospital to dry out. She did what he wanted. She brought him here and helped him get admitted, but then shortly afterwards he left. He drank himself to death. That was around 1960. So, this place has a long history of housing tormented people.

"I'm thinking of writing a new book about it, looking at madness as a subversive form of resistance to gender oppression. Madness was considered primarily a woman's condition, under the powerful hand of patriarchy."

"I remember reading that nurses could be terrible to the patients," I said. "I read that in a book, but it was about an institution in Canada that also no longer exists, so maybe it wasn't the same here."

"Oh, they were terrible all right, even here. These places were sometimes home to sadists who enjoyed wielding their power over those who had no way of fighting back. And yes, nurses could be cruel to their patients. So sad, the awful human tendency to kick those who are down, to take advantage of a situation to express our most base desires to torment others."

And it was then that I began to feel odd. The black cardboard cut-out of the Virgin Mary flashed before my eyes and I felt cold, as if I'd been out in the snow wearing only summer clothes. I rubbed my arms, which were covered in goosebumps, and Graham noticed.

"Are you okay?" she asked.

"Freezing all of a sudden," I said. "And I feel sick too, as if the flu has just hit me with full force. How odd."

"Let's move into the sun," Graham said, and she gathered up our picnic. "It was most likely my horrible stories of all the locked up and tortured women here."

"I don't know what it was," I told her as we shifted into the sun and as we did, I looked up and screamed, then grabbed Graham's arm.

"There," I said, and pointed. I was shaking, and cold sweat ran down my body. The muffin I'd just eaten rose in my throat, making me gag. "Look up there, at that window. A woman is looking at us."

Graham looked up, but I could tell she couldn't see anything. I was transfixed and shaking, and my fingers were digging into Graham's arm.

"Tell me what you see." Graham was calm, and she put her arm around me. "What do you see?"

"A woman. Her eyes are black holes. Her mouth is wide open, and she's screaming. She's wearing an old-fashioned nurse's hat and uniform, and her hands are up against the glass. Now, she's trying to tell me something. Oh dear God, her black eyes are bleeding and the blood is running down her face."

"What is she trying to say to you?" Graham talked to me as one would a child, in a soothing, quiet way.

"I don't know, I don't know. Oh wait, she says she's sorry. She says, 'Tell them I'm sorry.'"

"Tell who?"

"I don't know. I don't know." I screamed again, and Graham hugged me closer to her.

"White light's coming out of her eyes," I gasped. "Like lasers. I can't look anymore. It's like looking into a camera flash only much stronger. I want to look away but if I do, she might go away, and I have to hear what she wants to tell me."

But as I watched, the woman started to fade. She dissolved into a shadow, and then finally, there was nothing left but the shadow of a tree branch.

Warmth slowly returned to my body as if my frozen bones were being lowered into a hot bath. And all the shards of ice that had felt lodged, deep within my muscles, disintegrated.

I leaned into Graham. "I'm sorry," I said, "I don't know what that was."

"I do," Graham said. "That was your cardboard Virgin Mary. She wants your help." She looked at me and rubbed my back. "Margaux, please don't be angry with me, but that's why I brought you here. I just had a feeling this place might be helpful in some way. Don't ask me why, it was just an idea. Because I've had that feeling too, walking through here, that here's a soul in need of my help. And then, when you and I met, and you told us your story, I thought coming here might be helpful. I thought that perhaps it might jog your lost spirit into action which it did. Because I can't tell you the number of times I have walked through these grounds trying to speak to this distressed soul and ask how I can be of help. But I thought she was a patient, not a nurse. That's very interesting. Let's go up into the building and see if we can access that room."

"I don't know if I want to," I said. "That was terrifying. Those holes for eyes. And the blood pouring out of them. And that terrible light. I don't think I ever want to see that again. And why me?"

"She knows you can help her," Graham said with confidence.

"But why me? I mean really? I'm just a suburban wife and mother from Oakville, Ontario. I'm nothing special. I thought I had some psychic abilities when I was a teenager but I haven't even thought about that in years."

"Maybe you're in the crux of some crisis you don't even know about," Graham suggested. "Have you had any life-changing events happen to you recently? At times like that, if one is the kind of person who is receptive, then these things can become stronger."

Life-changing events. My husband had left me stranded in a strange country. My daughter was pregnant. "Yes, there've been a few things," I said vaguely. "But I don't know if this ghost wants my help. She frightens me. She looks so evil."

"But she said she was sorry. She wants to atone."

"Maybe she wants to draw us into her trap, possess our souls," I argued because what Graham was saying didn't feel right.

"Why would she want to do that?"

"Evil is evil," I shivered. "Maybe she's apologizing in advance for luring us into the trap of her darkness."

Graham laughed, and I could hear how foolish that sounded.

"Come on," she said, "let's go inside. I'll protect you."

I staggered a bit and Graham caught me. "You could have warned me this might happen," I said to her. "You knew it might."

"It was just an idea. And I didn't want to colour your behaviours with any kind of suggestions. It had to come from you."

"Well, it did do that," I replied.

We had reached the front door of the Garry Owen House and we slipped inside. We heard voices, a lively debate, and Graham pointed down the hall. "Writers' group in progress," she whispered.

"Are we allowed to be in here?" I asked.

Graham shrugged. "Why not?" She started to climb the winding, curved staircase, and I grabbed the wooden banister to steady myself. A colourful stained-glass domed skylight was set high in the ceiling and it cast rainbows and reflections on the walls. Our tread was silent on the thick floral-patterned carpet, and, despite the light and the colours, I didn't like the place one bit.

But my body temperature regulated, as did my mind, and I began to convince myself that nothing had happened. But then I pictured those black holes for eyes and that terrifying, open-mouthed scream, and I knew it had been real. I told myself to think about something else, to focus on being here, now, so I followed Graham. I was safe with her. We had reached the top landing. Graham was opening doors and trying to find the room that we would have seen from our position on the lawn.

"Here," she said, and my gut told me she was right. There was something evil in the room, and the air was thick. I shrank against the wall while Graham went and studied the window.

I closed my eyes. I was afraid to open them in case the woman appeared again, but then I felt something brush against my skin and my eyes flew open. It wasn't Graham who had touched me. She was still at the window and I was pressed up against the wall, against the wallpaper. I smelled starch and bleach and old-fashioned hairspray, and there it was again—the brush of fabric against my arm.

"Who are you?" I whispered. Graham turned to me, and I

hoped she wouldn't say anything. She didn't. She froze and watched me. I repeated my question.

The shape of a figure formed, a white-light cardboard cut-out this time, instead of black. But the light, although the opposite of darkness, was not soothing or warming but icy and terrifying. There was movement to the whiteness, like the static on an old television set, and I could hear crackling, snapping sounds, like the needle on a record being scratched back and forth.

Nancy. I knew her name was Nancy. "What do you want from me, Nancy?" I whispered.

Sorry. Tell them I am sorry.

"Tell who? And how can I tell them?"

I felt Nancy's anger slap me. She was furious at my unintentionally obtuse stupidity.

"Okay," I said quickly. "I'll find a way. I'll find a way to tell them you're sorry."

And the white light of her anger dimmed. But the force of her former fury frightened me, and I thought that if she was a nurse and she tortured people, then what she was expressing wasn't contrition but simply more anger.

I decided to risk more of her wrath. "Excuse me, but you don't seem very sorry to me," I said and the white light glared again, pulsating and malevolent. Then I realized something. "It's because you're stuck," I said. "That's why you're angry. You can't move on."

The light dimmed to a less ferocious shade, and I took that as a yes.

"But I don't know how to help you with that," I said, and the light flared so brightly I flinched and had to close my eyes.

"Quite the temper you've got there, Nancy," I said. I was beginning to feel less fearful and chatting to this angry ghost was starting to almost feel normal.

"I'll have to do some research," I told her. "And I will. When were you a nurse?"

Nineteen sixty-four popped suddenly to mind. That was it.

"Great, good to know. Okay, Nancy, we'll help you."

And then, just like that, she was gone.

I slowly peeled my body off the wall, and Graham walked over to me.

"We?" she said.

"We," I said, and I sank down to the floor and wrapped my arms around my knees. "That was intense." I exhaled. "Yep, that was intense."

20. LYNDON

LATER THAT NIGHT, Queenie, Jason, and I were in the kitchen. Jason was making his tofu curry of which I could easily eat vats. "So," I said, and I affected a casual tone, or at least, I tried to. "Where were you today?"

He gave me a look as he added freshly chopped lemongrass to the bubbling curry.

"Why," he asked. "Did you miss me?"

"Actually yes," I said. "You weren't doing anything illegal, were you?"

He laughed. "Like what?"

"Well, Sean told me you have eight million followers on an anarchy site, so I thought maybe you were at a meeting or something, planning to blow up Parliament."

"I'm not into violence," he reminded me mildly.

"How long have you had your website? That's quite the following."

"You love the facts and figures, don't you?" he said. "How long this or that, what are the numbers, let's be practical."

"Numbers are everything in the magazine world. Circulation figures, deadlines, print runs, paper costs, advertising sales. And then it became iPad visits, iPhone clicks, how many likes, how popular your web links are. And then there was my family, bringing up two kids, balancing a mortgage, Margaux's income. So, you're right, my whole life was numbers and facts and figures. What's wrong with that?"

"What did Margaux do to make money?" Jason asked.

I shook my head. "I can't talk about her yet," and I knew I should ask whether any of my family had replied to my email, but I didn't want to know.

"Fair enough," Jason replied, and he spooned the curry onto two plates and brought them over to the table. "You want to know where I was today? I wasn't doing anything illegal, unless you call dying an illegal act."

I dropped my fork into my food. "What do you mean, Jason?"

"I'm dying. Pretty quickly too. I've had renal cancer for a while, and it has metastasized. They say I've got only months left at most."

I buried my head in my hands. "Oh my God. But I've just found you."

He laughed. "I wish you could hear how that sounds. 'My darling, I've just found you!' No, it's fine, Lyndon. I've had two years since I was first diagnosed. My emotions have run their course. I'm ready."

I was crying like a baby. This man and his kindness had saved my life. He had rescued me. He'd given me a new life. I pushed my plate away, folded my arms on the table and buried my head in the darkness of my body. Jason came and put his hand on my shoulder. He let me cry myself out, which took a while, and I eventually blew my nose on a piece of paper towel and looked up at him.

"Well," I said. "Do the others in the shop know?"

He nodded and sat down and picked up his fork. "Don't worry," he said. "I cried a lot when I first heard. Then I got angry. Then I wept again. And so it went on and eventually I reached acceptance although there will probably be more tears and anger."

"I am here for you," I said and I had never meant anything more in my life.

"Ta," he said, and his eyes were wet. He wiped his nose and attacked his food. "You had a good chat with Sean today I take it?" We were both glad to change the subject.

"He's certainly got some interesting viewpoints," I said, and we managed weak smiles. "Transhumanism, eco-eroticism."

We both laughed. "I've never wanted to know too much about that last one," Jason said. "Sweet kid. He was a lawyer when he came here. He was passing through, on his way to see the Twelve Apostles, which I still have to take you to see, and then he stopped in at the shop, just curious. He'd been a tattooist since he was about fourteen, but his family forced him into law which he hated. I had an opening and he never left. He went back to art school in Melbourne for a while, about eight years ago. He's really come out of his shell. He was very prim and proper, Sean was. He went to all the best private schools, and now, he's got a flower for a girlfriend. His family disowned him, which didn't seem to worry him too much. He worked hard to lose his posh accent, and sometimes I can't understand what he's saying. I still rely on him for legalese when I need something done or when the government threatens to shut down my website."

"Does that happen often?"

"Fairly regularly. I'm under constant surveillance they tell me. In cyberland, not here. Not to worry."

"Sean said you met Sid Vicious?"

"I saw Sid," he corrected me. "My God, he was so beautiful. Bloody Nancy. He stabbed her, you know? And his mother? I heard she gave him the lethal dose; did you know that? The theory was that she knew he'd never be able to cope in the nick. Who'd kill their own kid? But it was Nancy who put him on the path to ruin. She introduced him to heroin, and she got him hooked."

"I know," I interrupted his rant. And I did know, and I felt the same.

"Just think. All the life we have lived while Sid's been dead. Stupid bugger. He was only twenty-one. I was a pretty boy back then too, young and unscarred. Now look at me."

I had looked. And I had seen. Jason was a craggy cliff of scars and dents and tattoos.

"When is your birthday?" I asked, and what I meant was, would he even see another one in?

"In four months," he replied. "I'd love to go out with a bang. Not an explosive bang, mind you, but a bang nevertheless. And let's not forget, "'Dead anarchists make martyrs, you know, and keep living for centuries. But absent ones can be forgotten.' Is anarchy making a bit more sense to you? Have you read more of my book?"

"I have read more, and yes, it's making more sense, but I wish I could get a practical handle on it. Find the crank to make it turn in this world, instead of it just being some abstract ideal. Abstract ideals are no good for stocking the pantry. You know, I used to be a punk too."

Jason burst out laughing. "No," he shook his head. "You never were."

"I was," I insisted. "I just remembered. Actually, so was Margaux. All kinds of memories are returning to me. Living with you is like being in a flotation tank or under hypnosis or something."

"You just remembered?"

"Yes. I had red-and-black tartan trousers with zips all over them and safety pins, and I used to dye my hair black. I used to spray-paint anarchy signs everywhere even though I didn't know what it meant. I used to play bass guitar too," I added. "And I used to draw. I wanted to go art school. I wanted to be a graphic novelist at night while I worked in an ad agency during the day."

"What happened to you?"

"My father," I said. "He pretty much hit the rebel out of me. I truly had forgotten most of that until now. I didn't forget that he used to hit me, but I forgot about my punk stage."

"You've given me an idea," Jason said thoughtfully as I looked at him. "I have decided I must go out with a bang.

You're right, I must make a statement, a practical, tangible touchable thing to make a stand. My website isn't enough. I need to do something big, something the world will see and take note of and remember. You see, all your practical talk and your punk rocker reminiscing has led me to great things!"

I was filled with misgiving. "What great things?" I asked reluctantly.

"Well now, sunshine, don't rain on my parade. I don't know that yet! But the first step has been taken. The idea has been had, and once it's been had, it cannot be unhad! I'm going to celebrate my birthday punk-style! Even if it's not on my exact birthday. Who knows, I probably won't be around for that." He paused and his face lit up. "Sid's birthday! Let's do it then! Moves the timeline up but nothing we can't handle. 10th May! Genius! But the first thing I'm going to do is order myself a pair of those trousers. Would you like a pair too?"

"Hell, yes," I said.

"I wonder what we can do," he mused. "It can't be graffiti. It must be beautiful, a work of art. We need to do Sid proud."

"Sid is dead," I pointed out. "He won't know."

"I'll be dead soon too. And Sid will know. The dead do know. Don't be such a cynic. We'll have to go into Sydney though, meet some people. I'll take you to the Black Rose, show you around. I'll set up a meeting, and we'll take a trip."

"You can't take me to Sydney!" I was horrified. "Margaux's there. Everybody's looking for me."

"You don't look anything like you used to," Jason said. "You've gotten skinny. Anyway, I meant to say, I've got a gift for you."

He vanished into his bedroom and came out holding a passport. "Here you go. Meet the new you. I officially anoint you Mr. Liam Lemon."

"Oh seriously?" I asked. "Liam Lemon?" I opened the passport. The guy did look like me. Or I looked like him, whichever.

"Where did you get this?"

"Off the back of a truck, where do you think? Stop asking me questions and say thank you. You can do a lot with a passport. Get a whole new life."

"A whole new life," I echoed. "As Liam Lemon. I'm not sure I'm ready for that. From Lyndon to Liam. You stuck with the L at least."

"Take it or leave it," Jason said. And he looked out into the distance. "I never wanted to be one of those tossers who said to himself, 'Where did all the years go?' But Lyndon, where did all the years go?"

"It's Liam," I replied. "And the hell if I know."

21. MARGAUX

THE MORE I THOUGHT about what Lyndon had done, the more I wanted to rip his balls out. I hadn't realized how angry I was. It was true that I had sent him a measured, calm reply, but now I wished I had been more honest and spewed some of my vitriol. But who knows, Mr. Ex-Punk Rocker might have intercepted the reply. I wondered if my email had even reached Lyndon. Perhaps it hadn't. No, Mr. Ex-Punk Rocker would have passed it along.

"Anger is unseemly," I used to tell Helen. She's always had a temper, and I wondered if she had inherited it from me. I reasoned that was why she hadn't had a long-term boyfriend in years. And whenever I made my "anger is unseemly" comment, she'd look at me calmly, and reply, "Letting things eat you up inside is worse. You've got a lot of anger in you, Mom, you just don't let it out."

Of course, I denied it. I was happy with my life. "Nonsense," I'd reply. "My world is very serene."

That made Helen laugh. "Fine. Serene. But one day, you'll let it all out, and then, beware world."

I hadn't remembered our discussions until now, and the reason I was thinking about them was because I was staring at my laptop, back in my room at Tim's hostel, and I was furious over Lyndon's silence. He didn't even have the courtesy to dignify my gracious email with a response. I thought I had sounded so rational, so balanced, even kind. I thought that would guarantee a reply from him, but there was nothing.

I wanted to pound my keyboard with my fist, but it was a move I knew I'd regret. "You're cutting off your nose to spite your face," I had told Helen along with other clichés. "You rush through your life burning your bridges. A man in passion rides a mad horse. You're like a bull in a china shop when you're angry."

"Mom, I'm assertive, not angry. There's a big difference. I stand up for myself."

"And all your hard work will go out the window, and for what? Life's about playing the game, Helen, that's all. We don't like some of the rules on the playing field, but if you don't do what you need to, you'll lose."

"So, I should let Professor Danner accidentally touch my breast when he gives me back my essay? I should let him brush his crotch along my arse when there's more than enough room for him to pass around me in a room? Is that what you are saying?"

"I'm saying, don't poke a stick at a sleeping wolf."

"Mom, you're full of ridiculously old-fashioned sayings. And he's not a sleeping wolf, he's a very awake, on-the-prowl wolf."

"Just don't rock any boats, Helen," I said, and she laughed.

"That's what you always say, Mom. Acquiesce, be gracious, be ladylike. For God's sake, you'd think we were in the fifties Your mother really did a job on you. I bet your home was full of woman's magazines telling you how to be kind to your man when he's had a rough day at work, how to never bother him with your silly little problems, and how your opinions were actually irrelevant and useless."

She wasn't wrong. My mother was the epitome of ladylike support when it came to my father and his rages. He was a man, therefore, it was quite all right for him to express his anger at his job, his boss, taxes, the broken car, the endless money that needed to be poured into the house, school fees, unreasonable people he had to deal with, bad drivers who shouldn't be allowed on the road, and the stupidity of politicians. But I had never once heard her express anger about anything. I had learned my lesson well—anger was unseemly.

My father shouted when his team lost at a football game and in summer when his baseball team lost and in winter when his hockey team lost. There was a seasonal sports game for his every anger while I sat upstairs in my bedroom, listening to him shout at the television season after season, and dreaming about my future home where peace would reign. Where my husband and I would have civilized, adult conversations. My life wouldn't be determined by a sense of righteous injustice at the vicissitudes doled out by an invisible hand, seemingly by random whim.

I watched my mother's jaw clench as she nodded in agreement to some outrage, and while she nodded, I noticed that her eyes were far away. Even our family holidays were exercises in anger: anger at bad breakfast toast, inferior coffee, knives that were not sharp enough, overpriced restaurants, and shabby motels. There was, it seemed, a reason to be angry about everything. And yet, I was the one who had to go for therapy! That in itself was reason enough to make me spitting mad. No wonder I scored my arms and wanted to break things. I had been conditioned.

By the time I left home, my mother was riddled with a cancer she'd not told any of us about, and my father didn't seem to notice I was gone. He didn't notice that my brother had also left—my brother who had refused to engage in the testosterone-driven anger games, which rendered himself irrelevant in my father's eyes.

And when my daughter shouted at her first doll and ripped its head off for being stupid, pincers of terror gripped my bowels, and I bent down and gave her a first lesson in the dangers of unseemly anger. And I hadn't done too badly. I helped Helen harness her temper, get through school, keep friends, have a boyfriend, get through university, and find a job.

It hadn't been easy. Take the Professor Danner incident, for example. I had told her that in my day, you shut up and managed the situation. You accepted that he was a man in a position of power and so what if he touched you a bit. It wasn't like he was actually raping you, and final exams were just around the corner. "Suck it up," I'd said. "Keep your eye on the bigger picture."

But Helen told him if he ever touched her again, if he so much as patted her on the shoulder, she'd report him to the dean. And she told him that if her final grades dipped at all, she would take the conversation she was recording, to the dean. Recording a threatening conversation! Why put yourself in such a potentially damaging situation when she was so close to the home plate? It was incomprehensible to me.

"That's just Helen." Adam shrugged when I tried to discuss it with him. Adam was never an angry boy. He was simply born wounded by the world.

And Lyndon laughed. "She should be studying law," he said, "not accounting."

"I just think she lets her anger compromise her," I said. "How will a man stay married to her? How will she ever find a man?"

"I don't think Helen cares about that too much," Lyndon replied. "Besides, you seem to see her as a fire-breathing dragon. She is very level-headed and calm. She just doesn't let anyone get away with any crap."

I had thrown my hands up in fury. Why couldn't I get support from anyone? I was trying to look out for Helen. Helen's anger had, ironically, made me storm off to spend time on my own more than once, and Helen teased me, saying I was a passive-aggressive angry shopper—that whenever she or Lyndon or anyone annoyed me, I retaliated by shopping. Of course, her comment made me even more angry.

"I'm trying to create a lovely home environment for all of you," I retaliated. "Don't you want me to cook something delicious, or buy you two nice clothes or keep a nice house?"

Sometimes, I wanted to rip down the curtains I had sewn, or smash the lovely, fluffy, perfectly browned-in-all-the-right-places dinner soufflé I had made, just pound it with a ladle so the egg and cheese and flour spattered against the windows, floor, and walls as if thrown by a demon. But what was the point of doing that? Dinner would be lost, money would be wasted, and then I would have to clean up my own mess. It would be cutting off my nose to spite my face. What I didn't understand, was why I was so angry. Why did I want to grab a fistful of soufflé and throw it at the wall? Why did I want to smash a glass in the sink and then cut my thumb, already imagining myself sucking on my wound, tears welling up in my eyes? Where did all that anger come from and why couldn't I make it go away? I was happy; I had everything I wanted.

Lyndon had done so well in life, and my children, despite Adam's hurts and Helen's over-feisty nature, did just fine too. My house was lovely, and our dinner parties were impeccable social successes, even if they were given a helping hand by my friend Xanax. I was fit and trim, sculpted by cardio at the gym, and life was good.

And then I had the idea for this trip. I had thought it would be the answer. My guilty secret was that I was tired of trying to keep a good house and I loved the idea of getting rid of it all. I'd leave at the top of my game and never have that pressure again. No more parties, no more soufflés! The relief was enormous. We would get rid of everything, be young at heart, free, unencumbered by baggage. Lyndon had never appreciated everything I had done, he hadn't acknowledged all my work, so I thought, fine, let's just sell it then, and see how you feel Lyndon, when you don't have this home. Then you'll see just how much work I did. Then you'll appreciate it, but by then it will be too late.

It occurred to me now, as I sat on the saggy old hostel bed in Sydney, that I was the one who had cut off my own nose to spite my very own face.

I had lost my home, the one I'd built, the one that no one noticed but me. I'd lost out. But, I asked myself now, had I really? Maybe I wasn't angry because no one noticed my beautiful new curtains but because I was furious with myself that the sum total of my contribution to the world was curtains, soufflés, champagne-coloured taps, and a marble countertop for the kitchen island.

I was glad it was gone. The monument of my life's work was an insult to me. Yes, I had wanted Lyndon to feel regret when he realized it was gone forever, but deep down I had also known that he wouldn't really notice or care.

I dug the bristles of my hairbrush into the palm of my hand and stared at my computer on which there was no message from my husband. I looked over at my cellphone, charging on the little desk Tim had brought in for me to use as a makeup table.

"It was me," I said to the phone. "My anger caused the Virgin Mary to turn black. I was so angry when I saw the message and what it said that I caused this to happen. My anger opened the portal so Nancy could find me because I am just as angry as she is. I have been so angry all my life, angry with everything, just like my father, but I suppressed it. Although I didn't really suppress it. Helen knew it was there. Lyndon knew and probably so did Adam. The only person who never knew I was still angry all that time was me. And now that I do know, so what? You see, there is no point to anger. Even if you admit to it, so what? It doesn't change things a bit. It just makes things worse." I was talking to myself out loud. And I suddenly felt deflated.

It didn't help that a long, empty day lay ahead. Graham was going to do some research on Nancy, and I was going to meet her later that evening. But in the meantime, there was nothing I needed or wanted to do.

Tim and Janet would still be asleep. There was nothing left in goddamned Sydney that I felt like doing. I was sick of the city. It was nothing more than a glittering, sunlit prison. I didn't feel like writing to Helen or Adam. There wasn't anything I could add about Lyndon, and Helen had never been one for small talk, and Adam would just make it all about him and find something to complain about.

I looked at my laptop. I might as well do some research on insane asylums although Graham pretty much knew all there was to know. While the colourful spinning ball of death tried to find Google, I picked at the cuticle of my thumb until a tiny bead of blood welled up and I sucked on it, finding release in the pinprick of pain.

When Google finally came to life, I looked up Callan Park Hospital for the Insane. The listings confirmed what Graham had told me, but I wanted to see if I could find anything about Nancy and I kept clicking until I came across a link in *The Daily Telegraph*. "Sydney's shameful asylums: The silent houses of pain where inmates were chained and sadists reigned." The article was utterly horrifying, particularly the bit about the Chelmsford sleep therapy.

I admit that my first thought was that sleep therapy sounded like a lovely way to relax, but the full story read like something out of a horror movie. I had to find out more. I had a strong feeling that Nancy had something to do with the sleep therapy treatments, although there was no obvious or immediate connection. I told myself to keep looking.

The article said that a Dr. Harry Bailey had administered "deep sleep" therapy at the Chelmsford Private Hospital in Sydney in the sixties and seventies. He would put his patients into coma for up a number of days, supposedly to cure a variety of ailments. He combined this with electro-convulsive therapy, which he performed without patient consent, and without anaesthetics. As a result, many otherwise healthy people would either die or be left with serious kidney damage or various other potentially fatal ailments. It seems many of his patients died and countless others had their health and lives ruined, before he was finally stopped.

But what did this have to do with Nancy? Nothing apart from an increasing conviction that there was a connection between her and the Chelmsford Private Hospital. But what was it? And why had she found me? Was the Virgin shrine at Coogee her portal? I told myself to stop thinking absurd thoughts and using words like "portal," but the fact was that I'd had the crazy experience and I had to follow the clues, insubstantial as they were. I felt as if Nancy was leading me by the hand and I could almost sense her telling me I was on the right path. This made me wonder about the state of my own sanity. I decided to take a break and grab one of Tim's coffees and a few white chocolate and almond cookies that Tim left out on the counter.

Thus fortified, I returned to my computer and found Wikipedia had this to offer:

> "Deep Sleep Therapy, DST, was Bailey's invention, a cocktail of barbiturates that put patients into a coma lasting up to thirty-nine days, while also administering electro-convulsive therapy (ECT). Bailey likened the treatment to switching off a television; his self-developed theory was that the brain, by shutting down for an extended period, would 'unlearn' habits that led to depression, addiction and other psychiatric conditions. Bailey claimed to have learnt DST from psychiatrists in Britain and Europe, though it was later found that only a mild variant was used there, sedating traumatised ex-soldiers for a few hours at a time, not the median fourteen days under which Bailey and his colleague Dr. John Herron subjected their 1,127 DST patients at Chelmsford between 1963 and 1979."

Dear God. I read further, wondering how such brutality had been allowed. I kept clicking, desperately trying to find something about Nancy, but there was nothing. Nothing except the feeling that I had hit a home run. I felt certain that Dr. Harry Bailey was the key to this. Another link reported that Bailey had committed suicide in September 1985, "in response to the ongoing media exposure of his practices and disquiet from among the ranks of other health professionals." In his suicide note, he wrote: 'The forces of madness have won.'"

I wondered what he was like, this Dr. Bailey. "Who are you, Dr. Harry Bailey?" I asked out loud.

I found a pic of him. He was handsome. He looked to be a tall man by the way he held himself and by the breadth of his shoulders. He seemed self-assured, and he had a movie-star smile, and a forelock that twisted and curved over his forehead.

Back off, he's mine! The thought thundered through my body, hitting me like a punch that pummelled my spine to my ribs and back, and I gasped.

"Okay, I get it," I said, when I could breathe again and I felt the pressure slowly release. "He's yours. But why me? Why did you pick me? And why did you appear at Callan Park? It doesn't have any connections to the sleep therapy."

Nancy shimmered in front of me, a hologram of distorted rainbow pixels, fractured by flashes of white light. She trilled with girlish laughter that echoed like a child's music box, tinny and terrifying. "Well now, aren't you a keen little sleuth! Firstly, you opened the door, not me. There you were, all wide open at the Virgin and I was lonely. I've been wandering around in what I can only describe as a grey space, a fog if you will, and then there you were, a lantern in the mist! I walked towards you, so very delighted to have found a friend!"

"But why did you appear to me at Callan Park?" I asked and I felt her mood change. I was being too demanding, asking questions she didn't like. I could feel her mounting irritation with me.

"You're becoming tedious," she announced. "Because places like that are home to me. I feed off the ravaged pain of the suffering. Besides, don't be so pedestrian. I could have found you anywhere, because you wanted to be found. You almost summoned me at Callan Park, you and your annoying friend. You both wanted evidence of me and so I obliged, but of course only you could see me. Because we're soulmates, don't you know?" There was that laughter again. "But you're boring me now."

I felt her fade and I shouted at the ether of nothingness that she left behind. "But wait, what do you want with me? What do you want?" But there was no reply and I hoped that the hostel was empty and that no one had heard my anguished cries.

I took a deep breath and closed my laptop. I rubbed my temples. I felt exhausted and drained. I had gotten myself into this mess. Perhaps if I took a nap, I would wake up and discover it was all a bad dream. But I knew that wasn't the case. I needed to think this through, and figure out a solution.

I wondered if Nancy had administered the sleep treatments. If she had, no wonder she was stuck in a limbo of hell and well-deserved punishment.

I clicked on a few more links and found that women left their abusive husbands to seek sanctuary in institutions, only to find the situation there far worse. And they could never leave of their own volition. Graham had been right about that. And, all of this hadn't even happened that far back in the past. It wasn't like we were talking about the 1700s, this had happened in the mid-1900s. Dogs and women were considered to be much on the same level then, and I was grateful to not have been born in an age of such ignorance and powerful misogyny.

I couldn't find anything else to hold my interest and was about to turn off the laptop and go for a walk when a ping let me know that an email had arrived. Lyndon! He had answered me. My breath left my belly like a released balloon and I clicked on my email, eager to see what he had to say.

But the message wasn't from him, it was from the Mr. Ex-Punk Rocker, who he'd shacked up with.

"Find your lost soul yet?"

I looked at it for a while. I couldn't think of anything to say. I wanted to write back that I was the lost soul, and that I didn't know if there was even a me to find. If I had spent my whole life angry like my father, discontented with the world and hiding from my true self, how could I be sure there was even a real me to be found?

I bit my cuticle until it bled again, and I sucked the tiny wound while I stared out into space.

22. LYNDON

JASON INSISTED I PRACTISE one tattoo a day on him. "Consider me your canvas," he said generously. "And in return, you can scatter my ashes when I'm gone. Go down to the sea, stand in view of the shop, say 'Jason says thanks, that was one helluva ride,' and then let me be dust in the wind."

"Like Buddhist sand art," Sean offered,

Jason nodded. "Exactly. A mandala. Jason Deed was irrevocably and invisibly here."

"I don't want to think about you not being here," I said, and my eyes welled up with tears. Jason handed me a Kleenex.

"Rule of thumb," he said. "Don't cry when you're tattooing people. First, you can't see what you're doing, and second, it doesn't give a good impression."

"I was the same as you," Sean told me while I dried my eyes and blew my nose. "I cried like a baby for two weeks solid."

"He did," Jason said. "You lot all cried much more than me, and for that, I thank you. Listen Sean, I want to make an anarchist statement that the world won't forget. Any ideas? We need to be ready for Sid's birthday."

Sean screwed up his eyes and shook his head. "Not off the top of my head, mate. But I'll think about it. I'll ask the other boys to think on it too. Lyndon, the shading will work better if you hold the machine at more of an angle. Here, let me show you."

"His name's Liam Lemon," Jason said, and Sean snorted.

"You see?" I said. "Couldn't you have found me a more normal name?"

"Where's the fun in that? As a matter of fact, I chose it for you. I wanted to make you think, shake you up. My last name isn't really Deed. I chose it because actions speak louder than words and I am the sum of my deeds on this planet."

"You wanted to shake me up how?" I asked, not impressed.

He laughed at me. "Your world view is so narrow. I thought the whole lemon analogy would be good for you."

"What is your real name?" Sean asked.

Jason shrugged. "Can't remember. But we're getting off topic here."

"I've got an idea," I said. "For the protest. But let me finish this."

"Right, keep us in suspense," Jason grumbled. "Hurry up then, I'm dying to hear it, *har har*."

I finished the tattoo and whipped off the gloves.

"Installation art," I said to them. "Like Jeanne-Claude and Christo. You remember them? They wrapped buildings and monuments and trees with fabric. But we won't use fabric. We'll use biodegradable toilet paper! There are towns in the USA, and I kid you not, that lay down asphalt, or tar as you call it here, and then, to help it dry and also to help it stop it from sticking to bike tires or shoes or car tires, they put toilet paper on top of it. The toilet paper is biodegradable, so it breaks down and disappears in a few days."

"And you are thinking we do what, specifically?" Jason asked.

"I am thinking that we create a very large piece of installation art. We cover the Sydney Harbour Bridge with toilet paper and the message "Stop Shitting On Our World" as our mantra."

"I love it," Jason said, and Sean grinned like Alice's Cheshire cat.

"It has to be single ply," I added.

"But how will we do it, mate?" Sean asked. "Lyndon …

oops, sorry … Liam, you're our practical guy. That's an ambitious idea."

"We'll figure it out," I said, breezy and confident. "There has to be a way. Jason, we may need a bunch of your followers to come out and help us, and I think we may need to take that trip to Sydney after all, as much as the thought horrifies me."

"Come to think of it, I know a guy who takes people up the bridge," Sean said thoughtfully. "He's gives tours to the top. I'll invite him to come to the meeting. He'll have all the intel about the bridge and I bet he can get us access too."

"I'll set up a meeting now," Jason said. "Lemonhead, you did well."

A rush of pride hit my belly in a warm flood.

"Lemonhead," Sean chortled. "Crikey mate, I love it."

I didn't want to admit that I quite loved it too.

Two days later, we left for Sydney. The plan was to take Sean's black BMW which I didn't even know he had. It was all gangstered up, with black-tinted windows, a red stripe, and a rear-wing on the trunk. It was low-slung, sleek, and boxy.

"Cool car," I said and Jason nodded. We were standing outside, waiting for Sean who had gone to fetch something.

"A rare one," Jason said. "Only six hundred of them were made. One of these babies went for over $150,000 in Hong Kong recently. Last model was produced in 1990. They're collector's classics."

My mouth fell open. "How can Sean afford such a car? I thought his parents had disowned him."

"His granny gave him a truckload of money when she died."

Just then Sean arrived, not with something but someone. A woman. She was about six-foot-three, and she gazed over my head when we were introduced. The iron in her handshake rattled my spine. She must have been seventy-plus, and she wore her steel-grey hair long down her back, like a defiant old Barbie doll.

"This is Martha May," Jason introduced us. The woman

looked me in the eye like she was reaching into the back of my head, and I felt reprimanded for something, only I didn't know what.

"I'll sit in the back with you," she said to me. I made an unmanly squeaking noise and Jason grinned.

"I'm sure you two will have lots to talk about," he said. "Let's go."

But when we got into the car, Martha made a point of staring out the window, ignoring me.

And, two hours down the road, Martha May still hadn't said a word. But then again, neither had Sean or Jason. I fell asleep, a thing I am prone to do when I am a passenger, and I woke with my neck bent at a weird angle and my glasses askew.

I checked my watch. Three hours. We had been in the car for only three hours, which meant we had nine more to kill. I yawned. "Anyone want to play I Spy?" I asked.

Martha whipped around to face me. "I spy with my little eye, something beginning with a C," she said.

"Car?"

She shook her head.

I went through all the things I could see that started with a C, but none of them were right.

"Capitalist," Jason finally said, and he sounded amused but also tired, in the way parents told their kids to stop fighting.

I looked at Martha and her eyes were lit up with hatred.

I recoiled. "Hey," I said, my hands raised in peace offering, "you don't know anything about me. Maybe hold off judging me for a while."

"I Googled you," she said.

I was startled. "Really? And what did you find?" I was curious. I had gone through a spate of Googling myself after I won my last award. I had been gratified to see that I had a whole three pages, primarily dedicated to the accolades my magazine had won but also featuring my keynote speeches at industry functions.

"Report on Industry and Investments," she said. "RII. You were the ringleader of that circus for what, thirty years?"

"Thirty-three," I said, correcting her. "And despite what you and Jason think, I am not Satan. I was just your average Joe, making a living to support my family."

"I'm sure that's what the Nazi guards said too," Martha replied. "Just doing my job, boss. Putting food on the table for my wife and kids. Giving in to the man because I had to. No one held a gun to your head."

"And what would you rather I had done?" I was angry. "Run an anarchist newspaper that earned me diddly squat and lost me everything? Would that have met your approval, Martha?"

I spat out her name, and Jason turned around.

"Imagine," he said, "if everybody didn't do what they had to, to put food on their families' tables? Imagine if we all lived noble lives, if we took care of the planet and tried to fight for a way of life that wasn't fuelled by the American Dream of having so much stuff you needed storage lockers to keep it all. Imagine that."

"Yes, you all keep saying things like that," I told him. "But none of you actually says *how* we should do it. What job would I get? You tell me. Don't attack me because I was part of the system. Yes, I was an unthinking part, but you guys, all of you, none of you have even got *one* suggestion about how we can realistically live in a different way. Jason, some old guy gave you the shop. Sean, your granny gave you freedom, and Martha, I don't know, maybe you are living a true and noble life, and if that's the case, good for you. But back off attacking me. Until you actually come up with a plan to live differently, don't use me as your whipping boy."

There was silence in the car for a while, which made me feel victorious.

"Google said you stole a car and a cat and abandoned your wife after thirty-five years of marriage," Martha said, breaking the silence.

I ignored her.

"Internationally-acclaimed editor, husband, and father of two steals a Jeep with a prize-bred Maine Coon in the back and subsequently disappears."

"I hope Queenie will be okay," I said anxiously to Jason.

"She'll be fine," he said for the hundredth time. We'd had to leave Queenie behind. Jason had said it wouldn't be a great idea to breeze back into Sydney flaunting a spectacularly memorable cat who was on a most-wanted list. Queenie had the apartment to herself and would be visited twice a day by one of the barbers who had promised me with his life that he would take good care of her.

"You're not very good at addressing the issues," Martha said.

I folded my arms. "I don't owe you anything," I said. "You're a stranger to me, and you don't know my life story."

"And your life story would justify all your actions?"

I turned away from her. Abandoned my wife. It sounded so terrible. But I hadn't abandoned her. I had just stepped out for a bit. I was just taking a moment to think about my life. Didn't I have that right? And Jason had emailed her. If anything, I had given her freedom to think about her own life. It was true that I had done it in a brutal sort of way but sometimes things just happened, opportunities presented themselves, and you had to run with them.

I didn't want to think about Margaux. I turned back to Martha. "Okay stranger," I said. "Tell me about you."

"I was the high-school principal of an all-girls' academy just north of Sydney. We took the troubled offspring of rich parents and stopped them from getting into more trouble than they otherwise would have. I did that for forty years. I've written two feminist plays, one of which, *Call Me Bitch*, had one of the longest runs in the history of Sydney theatre, although it was a very small operation. But still. I'm the author of three non-fiction works about capitalism, greed, and climate change, all of which have sold to a small but passionate audience."

"You ever married? Have kids? Toast marshmallows over a fire and do normal things?"

Martha brought out the sarcasm in me, but she ignored my tone.

"I have three children, two sons and one daughter. A doctor, a lawyer, and a baker."

"Will we be seeing Robert?" Sean piped up enthusiastically from the front. "Oh crikey, Lyndon—I mean Liam—you have to taste his cinnamon buns. They are to die for, mate."

I had assumed the baker was the daughter, and chastised myself.

"My husband was a poet," Martha said. "He was considered a national treasure."

"Of course, he was," I retorted, worn out. "Serves me right for asking. Look at you, Martha. I bet Google is all over you and your many successes."

"It certainly is," she replied. "I'm Australia's leading anarchist feminist."

"Great," I said and sighed. "I am honoured." My sarcasm filled the car like smell of a wet dog.

"I'm just trying to jolt some life into you, Lyndon," Martha said, and she patted my hand.

Suddenly, I wanted to cry. I blinked my eyes shut and held fast until my tears went back into my nose and ran down my throat.

"We will be seeing Robert," Martha told Sean. "He's coming to the meeting. He's bringing an assortment of baked goods."

Cookies and anarchism. Burn down the establishment and annihilate the authorities with cupcakes in hand. Great. Ah, who cared? I was so tired. I didn't want to go the meeting anymore. My flash of energy had burnt out. I was fine when it was just Jason and Queenie and me and sometimes Sean. But this, the prospect of returning to the real world, drained me. I didn't want to do anything except lie down on my bed with Queenie and find refuge in sleep, or take a walk on the beach and watch the sunset, or go home and eat curry with Jason, or read a book about tattooing. I honestly didn't give a fig's ass about anything else.

23. MARGAUX

I DIDN'T REPLY TO the Mr. Ex-Punk Rocker's email. Instead, I went to find Tim. I made his coffee the way he liked it, and I knocked on his bedroom door and let myself in.

He was asleep, but I woke him up.

"Lyndon emailed me a couple of days ago," I said, and he shuffled himself into a sitting position, the covers pulled up to his third chin. I was constantly disconcerted by Tim's massiveness, the mountainous expanse of his pale body.

Janet was in the bed too although I hadn't noticed him until he crawled to the surface. "Where's my green tea?" he asked, blinking, last night's mascara running raccoon rings around his eyes. Janet refused to pollute his body with coffee. I went back to the kitchen and returned with a mug of green tea.

"Reveal all, darling," Janet said, cuddling up to Tim and sipping with relish. I told them everything. I started with the email from Lyndon, only it wasn't Lyndon. I told them about the black cut-out Virgin Mary, lunch with Anita and her gaggle, and about Graham and Nancy.

Janet was delighted by my story. He skipped out of bed. "Darling," he said, "let me read your tarot. It will help us get to the root of this. I always carry my cards with me, so please, indulge me. Let me help you in the best way I know how."

Tim smiled at me. "Even if you don't believe in it, Janet will amaze you." He raised an eyebrow at me. "Corresponding with a punk rocker?"

"Ex. I get the feeling he's our age."

"He would be by now. God knows the children of today wouldn't know a bona fide punk rocker if they got their dicks sucked by one. Margaux, do you want me to find Lyndon for you?"

I gaped at him. "Can you? But how? The police can't find him."

"Because they haven't been looking," he said. He got out of bed and added, "I can find him. But only if you want me to."

"Yes, I want you to! Of course I want you to!"

"Wait," Janet cautioned. "Maybe you don't want to. Maybe you only think you want to. And if Tim does find him, then what? Do you want a divorce?"

"Of course not! I want him to stop this nonsense and let us get on with our lives."

"I don't think he wants that or he wouldn't have left," Janet said, shuffling the cards and sitting cross-legged on the floor. "Timmy can you make me some toast with Vegemite? I can't do this while I'm starving like a rabid dingo. You never feed me, darling."

"I'll make you toast," I offered. "I want to get a latte too. If we're going to read my cards, let's get settled and organized."

"God forbid we should be disorganized," Tim shouted after me, laughing. But more than toast and coffee, I needed a moment to think about this. What if Janet saw something terrible in my cards and told me something I didn't want to know? I was a hundred percent certain that nothing good lay ahead, at least not in the short term. I was about to tell Janet that I didn't want to do it, but then I thought, *What the heck?* My husband had already left me, and the Virgin Mary hated me, so how much worse could things get?

"Now, this isn't like fortune-telling," Janet warned me, and he took a big bite of his toast. "Ooh, goody, the ratio of marge to Vegemite to bread is perfect. You can make my toast any time, darling. If all else fails, you can become a short-order cook. So remember that. It's not like I'm reading your fortune here. This is just an indicator of what may or may not be going on, and what may or may not be relevant."

"If it's so vague, then what's the point?" I asked.

"It's helpful," Janet said. "You'll see. First, we need to choose a significator card that represents you. Pick one, whichever you feel like. Don't worry. There is no right or wrong."

I picked one. The High Priestess.

"If you look inward, all the answers you're looking for will be revealed," Janet said.

I immediately shook my head. "You're wrong. I don't have any answers," I replied sharply. "This isn't going to work."

"Oh, stop it," Janet said, swatting at me. "We haven't even started. Now pick seven cards and put them down as I tell you."

I did what he said. Death. The Devil. The Tower. The Four of Pentacles. The Ace of Swords. The Two of Swords. The Three of Swords.

"Death," I said, horrified, and a cold shudder ran through my body. I hugged my arms to my chest. I immediately thought of Helen's baby. "This is metaphorical, right? No one's going to really die, are they?"

"Of course not. And despite your instinctive reaction, this card is actually a good one. It means you need to find your way out of a dead-end road. Something has brought you to a halt, something is sucking the life out of you and you can't move forward."

"Yes, his name is Lyndon. No news there."

"This card doesn't mean the end of a relationship. It means rebirth. But it won't be easy. It does mean change."

"Oh, fabulous. Let's move on. Excellent, the Devil."

"This, like Death, can actually be a good card. Yes, it is the card of rage, violence, force, and fatality, but it can also be seen as a sign that you need to face the constraints that hold you back. The Devil appears when you need to liberate yourself from your thoughts, your actions, and from people and patterns that are creating negativity in your life. You can free yourself from the oppression of other people's thoughts or actions."

I thought about my anger. The anger I thought I no longer had, or that I thought I had handled with ladylike grace. I liked the power the card seemed to represent. I liked that it sanctioned rage. I had been powerless for so long and had nobody to blame for that except myself. But now, I wanted others to feel the force of my power. I wanted others to feel the wrath of my righteous fury at having lost my youth and wasted my life on a man who hadn't deserved me. Nancy shimmered into the room in my peripheral vision, and I looked right at her and her white-light anger burned through her cut-out. I knew she understood what I was feeling. I had asked her what she had wanted from me, but the truth was, I had summoned her. She was the manifestation of my anger. She wanted people to suffer too, to feel hurt and pain. I wanted to hurt people, to crush them, to crush Lyndon and make him pay. I wanted him to be sorry for what he had done, for letting me down, for not understanding me all these years, for not appreciating me and my efforts. I dug my fingernails into the palm of my hand and closed my eyes, willing myself back into the moment.

"What do you want to break away from?" Janet was talking. "Where are you holding back? Do you hesitate to express yourself? What does the Devil mean to you?"

I shrugged and forced my thoughts away from Lyndon and my desire for revenge. "Nothing."

I felt Nancy smile. We had a secret—our anger was our secret. "What's next?" I asked. "The Tower. That's surely good?"

"Well." Janet hesitated. "It is our destiny to constantly evolve. Some growth comes as upheaval. The Tower card calls for acceptance of whatever comes our way and some of the lessons in life can be distressful. This is the card of adversity, but let's face it, it's accurate. You are in distress; you're miserable. The Tower card signifies the breakdown of old structures and old ways of being. That's true for you, wouldn't you say?"

I nodded.

"Maybe the relationships in your past have stunted your personal growth," Janet continued. "Maybe Lyndon was like a security blanket, but one that stopped you from moving forward with your life."

I shook my head. "I've always done what I wanted to," I argued. I couldn't let him know that what he said was true because it would make me feel like I had failed. "And this trip was my idea. I tore down our old tower. I sold our house. I made a lot of changes."

"But did you change your heart? Did you open your heart to the unknown? Maybe you did those things, but perhaps you are still resistant to real change?"

"Moving on," I said. I wasn't enjoying this in the least, and I pointed to the next card. "What is that, anyway?"

"The Four of Pentacles. This card is about blocked energy. You think you are protecting yourself but what you are doing is counterproductive and nothing new can enter your life. You are still too attached to the materialistic, to the specifics that you think are important. You're trying to control things, to get them to be what they were. You're afraid of change, but ask yourself, what's the worst thing could happen if you loosened your grip, even just a bit? You feel like things are out of your control, and you're responding by trying to control them even harder. You can ask yourself what would happen if you let go, just a little?"

"He's already left me," I said, and I sounded bitter. "And it looks like he won't be coming back. The card is wrong. It's already out of my control."

"Too much or too little restraint can create blockages. There is a balance between taking control and letting go."

I noticed that Tim had gone back to sleep and was snoring slightly. I was getting tired and depressed, and Janet saw this. "Margaux," he said gently, "this will help. It will open up your mind even if you think it won't. It will help you see. Just bear with me. Next is the Ace of Swords. This is a card of great force, in love and hatred."

"Hatred, anger, death, the devil. Very helpful. Okay, carry on."

"This card will help you to communicate. It helps you stay open. Part of the message of the Ace of Swords is that you're not supposed to know something that you may be aching to know. You might need more information or there still might be a lesson for you to experience or a realization that needs to take place. But you will get there. Clarity will come."

"Sure it will," I said. "Maybe with the next card. Although from the look of it, I'm not hopeful."

"Two of Swords. You are stuck at an impasse. But the saving grace of this card is that the block causing the impasse begins and ends with you, so this card can bring up a lot of issues around avoidance and denial. We face choices every day, and some are easier for us than others. When the Two of Swords appears, it can indicate that you are letting a decision keep you where you are because you are refusing to do anything about it."

"I am not doing anything about it because I don't know where it is," I said tartly.

"Which is why I'm going to look for it and I'm going to find it," Tim said. He had woken up, and we hadn't noticed. He started getting dressed. "When you are done here, email me a few pictures of him to show people. But carry on. And Janet's right, this is helpful for you. See the reading through. You've only got one card left."

I clenched my jaw. "More swords I see. And right through my heart. That one's not hard even for me to understand. Three swords have been driven through my heart. Faith, loyalty, and love have been stabbed to death."

"Traditionally, the card stands for removal, absence, and delay but I believe this card stands for release. You'll be released from your pain and heartbreak. Whether you're holding onto something from the past or if your pain is fresh, trust that it will be lifted. And in this case, I sense that the pain is from the past and the present. But healing is on its way. I'm delighted that this card has come up in this particular position because it is indicative of outcome and you'll be able let go of pain that you have held onto for too long. You're grieving now but you'll move on. You will be released."

I was unconvinced. "The card has a massive heart pierced by three enormous swords. I really don't see how you are reading healing into that."

"I know my stuff," Janet insisted. "Trust me. This is one of the more emotional cards in the suit, as indicated by the heart. Swords also indicate our thoughts, and thoughts have a lot of influence on how we feel. We can't always separate our thoughts from our hearts."

"That's true," I said. "I don't even know what I'm feeling now except for anger. I look at the Devil card and feel so much anger. I have caused so much damage. Lyndon must have hated me all those years and never told me. How else could he have left me without so much as a backward glance? He hates me. And that makes me doubt myself and hate myself. I am anger-filled and unlovable. I'm as dangerous and sharp as all of these swords we're looking at, and I did so much damage."

"Realization of feelings is the first step towards healing. I bet you didn't even realize how angry you were at Lyndon for doing this. You certainly never expressed it to us. You were so calm, so in control, but it was suppressed pain."

"I should have suppressed more when it came to Adam. I really hurt him. But selfishly, I just couldn't deal with his issues anymore. He's a man, for God's sake. I'll always be his mother, but he needs to take responsibility for his life."

"He does. And maybe that is also what is in these cards—you're tired of carrying him and his burdens. You're aching to be free from the responsibility of his feelings all the time."

As he said this, a ton of steel melted off my shoulders. I sat up straighter. I felt lighter and free and my whole spine felt aligned. "I do want to be free of that. I love my son. I love him dearly, but I don't want to do that anymore. I'm here to love him, and support him, but not enable his constant need for drama and attention.

"And what about my angry ghost, or whatever we should call her?" I asked. "That's why we're doing this." I saw Nancy hovering in the room, her uniform starched and pristine, her gaze vengeful and dark, despite the whiteness that glowed from her. She was so white that she was the darkness, and I tried to look away.

"Pick a card," Janet said. "With the intention of symbolizing her."

I closed my eyes and drew a card. "The Moon. Surely that's good? It symbolizes the light? The ghost is full of white light too, only so much so that it is like darkness."

"The card indicates hidden enemies and danger. There is darkness, terror, deception, error."

"So, I can't trust her when she says she is sorry?" I asked.

"Perhaps you can. But the card can also mean that things come to light in the darkness that can easily be ignored during the day. And it's time to face them in order to find a path to healing. Your ghost may be deceiving herself about something. She's in denial about something. Something is unresolved."

"You're certainly making her very angry," I told Janet as I watched Nancy pulse and glow. Blood flowed from her black eyes, and her mouth opened in a wide scream. "She doesn't look like she's on any kind of path to healing, as we speak."

"You can see her? I wonder why I can't feel anything. Where is she?"

"She's moving around. Right now, she's at the window." I pointed and Tim and Janet both looked.

"I don't feel anything either," Tim said. "But she obviously has a very strong connection to you."

"It's because of my anger. I was so angry when Lyndon's message came through that my rage opened up a portal for her to emerge. Oh my God, listen to me. My whole life to this point has been about drapes, marble countertops, paint swatches, and dinner parties. Where am I getting all this mystical stuff? Portals and tarot cards. This isn't me."

"I think it is," Tim said. "And in my opinion, Lyndon did you a huge favour. You would have run around the world in the same unthinking materialistic fashion that you conducted your life. Now you're actually starting to really live."

"Wow, don't hold back Tim," I said. "Why don't you tell me what you really think?"

"I think you should come up on stage with us and sing," Tim told me. "I think you should let it rip, starting with the trapped song in your chest. Stop holding onto the tent pegs of your life and let yourself fly. Now, send me some pictures of Lyndon."

"No, wait," Janet said. "We haven't finished here. I want to plant a few seeds in Margaux's brain, from this reading. Margaux, please select one card from the ones you have chosen so far. This will indicate what will help you move forward. It will incorporate all the messages from the ones we read earlier."

I picked the High Priestess.

"There are secrets as yet unrevealed. You have reached a point where you are ready to align yourself with your soul's purpose. This path requires you to be able to know and trust your intuition, and The High Priestess will help guide you on this path. Your mantra is this; say to yourself: 'I allow for quiet reflection, I allow my inner voice to be heard. And the more I listen to that voice, the louder it becomes and the more my intuition grows.'"

I repeated what he said, and I did feel happier and more peaceful. The horrible, restless fury that has been gnawing at the marrow of my bones left, and I felt the lovely buzz of harmony instead. "Thank you. Janet. You're very good at this. Not that I've had a reading before, but still."

"He's famous," Tim said. "How do you think he makes money? Not by being Sonny Bono, that's for sure. Janet earns up to two grand a week, cash. Travels all over Sydney giving readings. North Sydney, Cremorne Point, Double Bay. The ladies love him."

"I had no idea."

"You thought I was a kept man." Janet preened. "Loved for my beauty and my long, long legs."

"Actually," I said with smile, "yes, I did. I'm sorry."

"I'm flattered you think my beauty is worth such a fortune," he said, and he gathered up his cards. "Now, what are you going to do with the rest of your day?"

"I'm going to send Tim some pics and write an email to Adam to tell him I love him and that I'm sorry I hurt him. Because I am sorry. But I'm going to say that it's up to him whether he lets this thing with Lyndon run or ruin his life because it won't run or ruin mine."

"Don't tell him I am looking for Lyndon," Tim said. "In case I can't find him."

"You'll find him," Janet said breezily. "He can find anyone," he told me. "That's what he's famous for."

"And here I thought you two beauties did nothing but emerge at night to sing," I said. "I'll grab my phone, Tim. Back in a flash."

24. LYNDON

WE STAYED OVERNIGHT in a little town called Tarcutta. It was the midway point between Melbourne and Sydney. Actually, we stayed there for most of the afternoon and the night. Sean wouldn't let anyone else drive his baby, and he was too tired to be on the road anymore. We three guys were sharing a room at the Tarcutta Halfway Motor Inn, a double-storied pale yellow building that reminded me of a couple of stacked custard cream biscuits. The spacious room had a view of the ocean with palm trees waving in the breeze. It was all very idyllic, but I was sulking after Martha's cruel treatment of me. I told Jason and Sean I was going out and rushed out like a child, before they could say anything. Not that they would have, in all likelihood.

I took the time to wander around and think, and I argued viciously in my head with an invisible Martha and Jason.

I would have liked to have seen either of them cut it in the corporate world of magazine publishing. It was a harsh gig. You needed the stamina and the endurance of a long-distance runner or a triathlete. Plus you needed magicians' skills and a Harvard business grad's knack for numbers. I had done well to keep my head above water. It took a certain personality to stay afloat, and I had managed to be that person, unremarkable but indestructible, and on the right side of whoever was in power. And you never knew who would take the reins next, in an ever-changing world, so you constantly had to pay it forward, just in case. Yes, life was an old boys' club and I had always known that. And yes, I had been mildly obsequious to my brothers in power, and there were days when the stench of shit stuck to my nostrils from having my nose so firmly attached to their asses.

Keeping one's job was a life-or-death chess game. One had to be strategic at all times, and I wanted to see either Martha or Jason manage that. I had been kind but firm to the reports on my org chart, and I had tried not to let anyone go who had children, understanding their situation too well. I had been a positive and helpful mentor to my underlings, and I had a fine hand when it came to editing copy and polishing a magazine for print. I had kept my sense of humour under pressure and made sure my flock were acknowledged for their efforts. I had also been known for my incisive interviewing skills, not to mention my savvy insights into the stock market, which admittedly also helped Margaux and me feather our nest with the finest down.

There had never been a hint of insider trading, but I was given solid clues as to where the treasure lay, and I had made sure to mine every nugget of gold I could. Yes, I told myself now, as I stood outside a craft store advertising locally made mementoes to remind one that you had been to Tarcutta, New South Wales, I had done well. And yes, by way of thanks, they axed me in the end, the mere reminder of which forced me to acknowledge the ball of toxic sludge that lay at the bottom of my belly like an acrid old battery, oozing out poisons and leaking humiliating images of my being escorted out of the building without even being allowed to clear my own desk.

Yes, that memory leached my joy and corroded the perfect storyboard of my life. The powers that be had ruined the overall picture. They made a mess of the seamless slide show of who I had been and what I had achieved. They tripped me up, just before the finish line. Successes did not end their careers by being walked out of the building by human resources; no, they did not. They were given fabulous parties and a Breitling watch or some token of appreciation and everybody got far too drunk. And when you woke up the following morning, hungover and yet released, the rite of passage had been performed and you were on track to move on to the next elegant passage of your life. In my case, I had planned to write a memoir tracking the history and trends of financial gains and losses as measured against the timeline of my life. I had been certain I had a story worthy of telling, and I even had a publisher who had expressed interest. I had penned notes, preparing with complacent satisfaction for the final five years of my career. I daydreamed about the speech I would make at my farewell to announce my memoir—the cherry on the top of a stellar career.

But instead, my box of awards and framed certificates, lauding me with employee recognition, had been delivered to my house, along with a few books that had lined my office, although I had wanted none of them. There, stacked in the box, were my five-year, ten, fifteen, twenty, twenty-five and thirty-year certificates, all thanking me for my valuable efforts. I wanted to take a hammer to them and shatter the glass and crack the frames, but I couldn't.

I couldn't because I needed to keep them for when management realized the error of their ways and welcomed me back to my desk, back to my magazine, and back to my job, but of course that never happened. They had moved on and my underling moved into my office, and he even messaged me about how much he loved the view but envied me my "freedom." Bigger cuts were coming soon, he said, and he was sure they were going to shut down the magazine and he would be out of a job. I could only hope so. But in all fairness, it wasn't his fault he was sitting in my chair, looking out at my view. It wasn't his fault I was left with the ugly stain of failure—yes, I had clearly failed or I wouldn't have lost my job. I had lost it. No one else had lost it but me.

My shameful exit no longer afforded me the luxury of a shiny memoir. I had been forced out and who wanted to hear the bitter ruminations of a loser? And, in addition to losing my job, I had lost all notion of how to begin the book. I couldn't even remember what it was I had planned to say. I had studied my notes, but it was as if they had been written by an alien. I hadn't been able understand what any of it meant. This, in turn, filled me with panic—was I losing my mind? Was I getting dementia? I had sped off to my doctor on the quiet and he told me I was "simply" filled with anxiety. He recommended anti-depressants, which made me snort with sarcasm.

"Pills," I said. "I've lost all the things in life that meant something to me. Drugging to forget would be an easy way out. As long as you don't think I have dementia, there isn't anything I want from you. And really, you should stop being such a pawn to the drug companies. That's all you are. You listen to me with half an ear and then you prescribe. I tell you the story of the sad ending of my life, and you find a way to fund the drug companies at my expense. If I am not suffering from dementia, then I am suffering from grief and loss and I need to find my way through that, God knows how. Can't you see how unethical you are? How you abuse your power?"

The doctor had looked at me mildly, as if my rant added more fodder to his suggestion that I needed the pills and, in my anger, I marched out, much as I had marched away from Margaux and from Jason and Sean in the motel.

I had wanted to write an article about how doctors played into the hands of large pharmaceutical companies and the consequential effect that had on stocks and shares, but then I remembered I no longer had a forum—my soapbox had been whisked out from under me.

Shortly after I saw the doctor, Margaux and Helen announced that the plans for the Around-The-World-For-However-Long-We-Want trip were finalized. We were ready to go. The change of topic had been a welcome excuse to flee from the pebble in my shoe that was the book, and I took that stone and cemented it to the wall of my life's failures. The trip had been a way to keep fleeing the person I couldn't bear to be, but I hadn't been able to escape him. And even now, even as Liam Lemon in black clothes and killer cool boots, I still hated myself as much as I ever had.

25. MARGAUX

I WROTE TO ADAM. I told him how much I loved him and that I was sorry I had been cruel to him. I told him that I just wanted him to be happy and free. I said I was sorry about the conflict between him and Lyndon, but I couldn't fix it for him, only he could. If that meant seeing a new therapist, then he needed to do that. I hoped I said all the right things to my son, the boy that I loved so much.

I also wrote back to Mr. Ex-Punk Rocker:

> I think the lost soul is me. I think my anger manifested the angry apparition. Don't get me wrong. I'm not usually the kind of person who uses words like "manifest." I'm too much of a practical realist. Or, so I thought, anyway. You know when people say "Everything happens for a reason," or "It happened for the best"? I always thought that was just a loser's way of making a stupid excuse when things went wrong, but I do think that Lyndon's crazy action was for the good. For me, anyway. I have no idea how he's doing and that's not why I'm messaging you. Please let's not talk about Lyndon. I don't really know why I'm messaging you. It's like some pen pal thing back in the day when you decided to write to someone in Iceland, or somewhere you knew you would never go in life before the internet. And you could ask them about their country and

their life. So, Mr. Nameless Ex-Punk Rocker, tell me about your exotic life and in exchange, you can ask me anything you like.

Margaux, over and out, for now.

And then I went to meet Graham.

"I got my cards read today," I said. "By Dammit Janet. Have you heard of him? Apparently, he's famous in Sydney."

"He is," she nodded. "Wow, that's impressive. He's got a waiting list as long as my arm and you just 'got your cards read'—you're hilarious. I see him once a year because that's all I can afford. I love him to bits. And you got a free reading? Lucky you. Listen, are you up for a drive?"

"Sure. Where?"

"To find Nancy's nearest and dearest. She lives out near Parramatta, not the best area, but I thought it might be helpful to you to meet her and talk about her."

"You found out a lot then?" I asked.

"I found out some things. Our nurse is Nancy Simms. Or she was. She would be ninety-six now, but she died when she was only sixty-two. Ha, you know you're getting old when you say things like 'only sixty-two.' When I was in my twenties and thirties, I thought people would be happy to die then, that they must be awfully tired of life. The article I found didn't say what she died of. She worked as a nurse at the Chelmsford Private Hospital."

So my feelings had been correct when I had made the connection between the sleep therapy, Dr. Bailey and Nancy. "I read about Chelmsford. It's where the doctors performed terrible sleep treatments on their patients. I'm pretty sure she had a relationship with Dr. Bailey who was responsible for the therapy."

"The math adds up. She was born in 1925, and started nursing in 1945. She died in 1987, two years after the not-so-good doctor committed suicide. Bailey practised his deep sleep therapy from 1963 to 1979, and she was on record as working there during that time."

We were driving in Graham's little Opel, and it was clear we were leaving the more affluent part of Sydney and heading for the western suburbs where graffiti covered the walls that ran along the train tracks. Small houses with a derelict air lined the roads, and the muffler parlours were a dime a dozen.

"From what I've seen," I told Graham, "people around here go through mufflers like Kleenex."

She laughed. "We're nearly there. Brace yourself for a whole new Australia, my dear."

She wasn't wrong. We pulled up at a tiny house with a chain-link fence and sturdy gate. A Doberman was running around the yard, sniffing at car parts that lay scattered around like innocuous lawn ornaments.

The dog started barking as we approached the gate and both Graham and I paused, neither of us keen to go any further. We waited for a while, hoping someone would come out and see what the dog was barking at, but nothing happened.

We inched forward, and the dog only increased his volume. A neighbour emerged, clad in filthy white boxers, his hairy belly a massive straining water balloon.

"What's your problem?" he shouted, and Graham pointed to the house.

"We want to talk to whoever lives in there," she yelled back, and he looked at her for a moment and didn't say anything. None of us moved.

I studied a child's bicycle that was leaning up against the fence. It was fuchsia with shiny pink and purple cheerleader ribbons on the handlebars. It was missing the seat and the front wheel.

The man lumbered down the path and hitched up his shorts. He brushed in-between Graham and myself, and opened the gate. We stepped back, expecting the dog to rush out, but it cowered and crawled away, skittering to the house.

"More like a kitten than a killer, that one," the man grumbled, and he ushered us into the garden and closed the gate.

"You've got visitors," the man shouted. "Open the door."

"What? Who?" We heard the letterbox open slightly. "Who are they?"

"Don't be so paranoid, Nancy, open the door. They're some yobbos from Sydney, rich folk."

"I'm not rich," Graham said indignantly, but we both knew that compared to these lives, we were millionaires.

"We just want to talk to you about Nancy Simms," Graham shouted, and there was silence. Even the dog stopped barking.

"Auntie Nan? Why?"

"We just want to talk, that's all."

"Offer to buy her dog food," the man whispered helpfully.

"We'll buy you dog food," Graham shouted.

"Two bags?"

"Two bags."

There was a pause before a series of locks started clicking and the door opened. A tiny woman, no more than four-foot-two, skinny like a child and wizened like an ancient elf, stood there in a yellow floral print dress with a wine-coloured apron on top.

"Come inside, Mite," she said, and the dog slinked past her. "Vegemite's her name," she told us. "On account of how she loves it on toast. You want some tea?"

We turned to thank the man, but he had already left and was closing the gate behind him. He didn't look our way.

"I'm Nancy too," she said. "Named for my Aunt. Not that I was happy about that when I realized what an evil woman she was. Let's go and sit in the kitchen."

We followed her through a hallway that was maybe two feet wide. It was as dark as a cave, with a low ceiling. We emerged into the kitchen—at least, we realized it was the kitchen when Nancy flipped the light switch on. If there were windows, they were covered with yellow-and-maroon striped wallpaper that was adorned with enormous tiger lilies. Nancy closed the door behind us, and I saw that wallpaper even covered the door. It was like being trapped in a surreal cage of giant flowers, and I couldn't breathe.

I sat down at a child-sized table in the centre of the room. My butt spilled over the chair, and I worried I might break the thing.

Nancy put the kettle on and popped two slices of bread into the toaster. She poured some water for Mite who guzzled it. "Strange you wanting to talk about Auntie Nan," she said conversationally, pulling down a Brown Betty teapot. "I've been having visits from her lately."

"I thought she was dead," Graham said, struggling with her chair. She gave me a look and I nodded. Whatever we had been expecting, it wasn't this.

"She is, yup. But she comes and moves the pictures around when she's in a mood. And the furniture too. This used to be her house. Although I did all the redecorating. She didn't like my flowers, I'll tell you that. When she lived here, everything was white. There was hardly colour at all. Except for the curtains. They were navy blue. And the carpet was grey. Those were her colours. Nurses' colours, she said. Her bedspread was navy and so were her towels. The sofa was grey, the carpet was grey, the throw rug was navy. And she never would have let an animal in here. She was not happy when I got Mite, or the ones that came before Mite. But she died and left the house to me, and if she thought I was going to live in a navy-and-gray house, she had another thing coming."

She sat the teapot down, filled a milk jug, and arranged some cookies on a plate. She pointed at a large bag of dog kibble in the corner. "Ninety dollars a bag," she said pointedly.

I opened my purse. "I've got $120," I told her.

Graham opened her purse. "And I've got $40," she says. "$160. Not bad for a chat."

"Except that I didn't have to talk to you at all," Nancy said agreeably. She took the money and tucked it into her bra. Then she poured us each a mug of tea and put the sugar bowl next to the milk. "Help yourself," she said.

I took a cautious sip of my tea and then a generous gulp. "This is good tea," I said, sounding surprised. Nancy beamed.

"Tea leaves. That's the trick. Never use tea bags. Try a biscuit too. Homemade."

Graham and I each bit into a biscuit, and they were excellent.

"Shortbread is my favourite," Graham said dreamily. I wondered if we were both being hypnotized by the giant flowers and the crazy colours inside the tiny room or if maybe there was something in the tea. The room began to melt, and the flowers curled and slid down the walls. I, too, slid off my chair, managing to put my mug on the table in the nick of time. I was lying on the wine-coloured floor, grateful that it was cool. I heard Graham and Nancy's voices and then felt a wet cloth on my forehead.

Mite licked my hand, which made me feel better. I started to come to. I struggled into a sitting position with Mite helping me along by licking my face.

"I forgot your toast," Nancy apologized to the dog, and she slathered the slices with Vegemite and gave them to the dog who turned away from me and gnawed at a slice.

"Let's try that again," I said, and I returned to the tiny chair. I concentrated on my mug. I could feel Graham's concern so I flashed her a quick look to tell her I was fine although I wasn't. Not at all.

"That would be Auntie Nan having a go at you," Nancy told me, and she handed me the cool wet dishcloth. "Keep that pressed to your face. Bugger off Auntie Nan, or, if you're going to stay, behave yourself."

The weird feeling behind my eyes began to drain away, and I could breathe again.

"Thank you," I said with relief. "Your aunt wants me to help her, but I don't know how."

"She needs to apologize to all the souls she tortured," Nancy said in a matter-of-fact tone, and the white figure of the enraged nurse flashed as she spun into the room, filling it like a whirlwind. I skittered off my chair and pressed myself up against the sink. Even Mite stopped chewing on his toast and looked quizzically in the direction of the light.

"Doesn't like it when I say that, does she?" Nancy commented. "I can't see her, but I can feel her anger. Auntie Nan, I don't know exactly where you're stuck, but I know you don't like it. If you want to move on, then you've got to say sorry, even if you don't mean it." The figure continued to spin, a crazy tornado of light in the tiny kitchen, and I turned away from her and peered into the sink instead.

"She used to be the one to give shock treatments to the unconscious patients," Nancy explained. "She was so in love with the doctor, Harry Bailey, and although his treatments were never approved, she thought they made sense. You went to sleep and got all the benefits of a good eight hours. Only, they added barbiturates in large quantities and when the patients woke—if they woke—suffered devastating consequences, like kidney damage, deep-vein thrombosis, bowel hemorrhages, and sometimes pneumonia. Many died."

"How did they get away with it?" I was horrified.

"No one questioned doctors in those days," Nancy said. "They were like God. I was a nurse too, but for kiddies. And I would never have done what Auntie Nan did. And she didn't just do it because she was in love with Harry. She did it because she was cruel. She used to hit patients when they were tied up or when they were stuck in ice baths with sheets over them and they couldn't move. She broke their fingers for fun when they were all drugged up, and she thought it was funny that they didn't know what was happening. And those sleep patients didn't even give their consent. It was just done to them."

"How do you know all this?" Graham asked, and Nancy went silent for a moment. I still had my head in the sink to avoid the spinning vortex that was Nancy Senior.

"She told me," she finally said. "She told me from when I was a very little kid. I told my mom and dad, but they said Nancy just liked to tell tall tales, that none of it was true. My dad said she was a bully to him, but that she'd never hurt the patients. So, no one did anything. I started nursing in 1957, and I went to live in Queensland. I didn't want anything to do with Auntie Nan. I wanted to be a good nurse. My parents knew why I left. And then when she died, Auntie Nan left me this house. By then my second husband had taken all my money and run off with a waitress. So, I came back just like she wanted to me to."

"Do you have any pictures of her?" Graham asked.

"Yup, I'll get them. Maybe you want to take your friend out into the garden."

Graham took me by the arm and led me outside, I sank down onto the sunburnt crackly grass. Mite came out with us and he licked my face with his Vegemite breath. I put my arms around his doggy warmth and felt the life seeping back into my bones.

"Auntie Nan was a real piece of work," Graham mused, and she lit a cigarette. "This whole thing leaves a terrible taste in your mouth."

Nancy returned with a shoebox. "The medical authorities tried Harry Bailey. He was charged with manslaughter, but nothing came of it, and he got off. But he was disgraced, so he killed himself. I think Auntie Nan offed herself too. She hated being without him." She sat down next to me and rifled through the box.

"Here you go," she said, and handed me a photo. Nancy Senior was stunning. She was in her nurse's uniform, with her hair tied back. The clarity and symmetry of her features were spectacular: high cheekbones, large eyes, dark eyebrows, curved mouth.

"She was gorgeous," Nancy said. "And she was pure evil. You know you hear about kids who kill kittens and puppies? That was Auntie Nan. Even my father, her brother, was scared of her. He said she would hit him for no reason, just punch him or slap him, and then she would laugh like it was the funniest thing. He was older than her and much bigger, but still she bossed him like there was no tomorrow. He tried to tell his parents but they wouldn't hear a word of it. And then, he didn't believe me about her either! The irony of it."

"Maybe they all knew the truth," Graham said. "But they were too afraid to do anything. I can imagine she was pretty scary."

"Such beauty," I marvelled as Nancy handed me more photographs. There was my ghost, a vision in a swimsuit, one leg bent at the knee, model-style, a smile on her perfect mouth.

"And she was obsessed about being clean. She loved the bleach, did Auntie Nan. There was never a speck of dust in her house. But when the women in the asylums had their periods, she would give them one pad for the whole time and told them they stank and were disgusting. She wouldn't let them wash and then she held her nose when she walked past. Sometimes, she tied them up until they couldn't hold their bowels anymore. She made them sit in it for a day or two before she got an orderly to clean them up. She told them they were filth, and that they didn't deserve anything else."

"She told you all of this?" I was horrified.

"Yes. She thought it was funny and in a way, I think she liked to brag. What kind of sick person tells things like that to a kid? Like I said, I told mum and dad but they swept it all under the carpet. 'Don't hang your dirty laundry out in public,' mum would say. And my dad would add that, 'Family is family, never forget that.' None of us did anything. But then again, what could we do?"

"I can't help this woman," I said, and I was desperate with fear for my own life.

"A part of you must identify with her," Nancy said, and she started to put the photographs back in the box but then hesitated. "Do you want one?"

I recoiled. "No. But thank you. So, you think if I fix myself, the part that relates to her, then I'll be able to get rid of her?"

Nancy shook her head. "I don't know what you can do. But don't be afraid of her. I'm not."

"I think we should go now," Graham said. "Margaux, you look shattered. We've been here for an hour. Thank you for your time, Nancy."

An hour. We had only been there for an hour. It felt like an eternity. I struggled to stand, and Graham helped me.

"Good luck," Nancy said, and she watched us leave, with Mite sitting obediently next to her.

Graham helped me into the car. She buckled my seat belt into place like I was a child. As we drove away, I craned my head and saw that Nancy was still watching us. I hoped we had left Auntie Nan behind, with her, but I knew better than that.

We were halfway back to Graham's house when I realized something. I should have taken Nancy Junior up on her offer of a picture of Auntie Nan. It would help me with the exorcism or whatever it was that I was going to have to do to get rid of her in my life. "Graham," I said reluctantly, "I'm sorry, but we need to go back. I need a picture of Nancy. I should have taken one. I wouldn't ask, but I think we should."

"No problem," Graham said, and she swung the car around in a neat U-turn. "It was my fault. I rushed us out of there. There was probably more that Young Nancy could have told us, but I was worried about you."

"And you weren't wrong. I felt like the world was made of wax and that an evil witch was holding it too close to a flame."

We drove back in silence and parked outside the house. This time there was no Mite running around barking, and the place looked locked up and quiet.

"I wonder if she went out," Graham said, as we let ourselves in the garden gate.

We walked up the cement path, dodging those inexplicable car parts that I never asked Nancy about. I couldn't see Nancy Senior allowing such debris on her front lawn and Young Nancy, as Graham had dubbed her, didn't strike me as a nat-ural-born mechanic.

We knocked at the door and there was a mewling noise sound.

"Mite?" Graham guessed. "What a weird noise though. He barked last time. That's odd." She leaned down and pushed the letterbox open. "Oh no," she shouted, and she turned the door handle, but it was locked.

"We have to get in," she yelled. "Nancy's on the floor. Here, use my phone. Call 0-0-0 and tell them to track the location from my phone."

I called while she grabbed one of the heavy car parts and started smashing at the door.

"Oy! What are you doing?" The man in the filthy boxers came out of his house and shouted at Graham.

"She's on the floor," Graham yelled back. "I'm trying to get in."

The man ran to the fence and vaulted over it like a hurdler, enormous belly and all. "I'm coming!" he yelled.

I was open-mouthed, but I was trying to give the operator the details as I had them. Graham stepped aside as the man hit the door with a series of blows with his shoulder and it crashed open, swinging wide.

Graham rushed inside and felt Nancy's pulse. "She's still breathing. Ask them if I should give her mouth-to-mouth or chest pumps. "

I relayed her questions. "Is she breathing regularly?" I asked.

Graham knelt down close to Nancy's mouth and nodded.

"Then don't do anything. Just wait for the paramedics."

The neighbour was pacing the small living room, his eyes wide. Mite was still sitting at Nancy's head. There was nothing we could do except wait.

The sirens took forever to sound, and even after we heard them, the ambulance took an age to arrive. But once they were inside the house, things moved with great speed.

"We're taking her to Westmead," one of the paramedics said. "What's her name?"

"Nancy Simms," I offered. "We just met her. We don't know much else."

"She has a bad heart," the neighbour added. "But she hasn't had an attack in ages. You lot probably brought it on," he told us accusingly, and I agreed with him. I was willing to bet anything that Nancy Senior made an appearance after we left, and her visit had not been a friendly one.

"We'll stay and get the door fixed," Graham said to the paramedics as they left with Nancy bundled up on the stretcher. "And we'll come and check on Nancy in the hospital."

"I'll fix the door," the neighbour said brusquely. "Youse both should leave now. I'll take care of the dog too. You've done enough harm."

"But I need to find a picture," I was insistent. "Nancy said I could." I stared at him, not brokering an argument, and he backed down.

"Get what you need and go. I'll be back now to fix the door. Don't hang around."

I rushed into the flower-wallpapered kitchen cave and flipped on the light. Sure enough, the shoebox was on the table. I whipped it open and screamed, jumping back, hands to my mouth. The pictures of Nancy were damaged, as if lighter fluid had been spilled on them and they'd been set on fire. But, just like the Virgin Mary, only Nancy's face and body were blacked out, each image a perfect silhouette while the rest of the photograph remained unblemished.

I grabbed the box and hurried out to find Graham. She was talking quietly to Mite and rubbing his pointy little Batman ears.

"You get them?" she asked, and I nodded, thinking I'd explain later. Just then the neighbour returned with a toolbox and a nasty expression on his face.

"Get on with youse then," he said. We didn't need to be told twice.

As soon as we were in the car, I showed Graham the photographs. She winced. "We're going to need the help of a white witch I know. Wait, you met her. Trish. She was at lunch that day."

"I remember her. She told me I needed to widen my sphere of availability so there was more of the probable within my grasp. She said I'd find the answers that way. Yes, let's talk to her."

"But let's go and check in on Nancy at the hospital first, yeah?"

"Absolutely," I said and we drove off, with the ruined photographs in my lap, taunting me.

26. LYNDON

I WALKED AIMLESSLY and wandered into a park with neat flowerbeds filled with yellow and violet pansies. The curving asphalt path had a broken white line in the centre, like a mini-highway. The path took me to a yellow brick memorial wall with a black marble plaque bearing hundreds of names. It was the Australian Truck Drivers' Memorial Wall.

This Memorial is dedicated to the memory of truck drivers who have been accidentally killed on Australian roads while performing their duties in the transport industry.

Henderickus W. Davis, "Ricky the Rat," twenty-eight. Timothy "Porky," thirty. William J. Blake, "Bill," thirty-six. Gordon R. Blades, thirty-three. He'd lived the same number of years my career had lasted. Then I too had been swerved off the road of my life, reduced to being researched by an aggressive feminist grey-haired Amazon ... who suddenly appeared at my side.

"I want to be alone," I snapped at her.

She didn't say anything for a moment. Then she sighed. She pointed at William J. Blake's name. "He was my mother's brother. He died when I was eleven. I remember him very clearly. And I remember his death."

There wasn't anything I could say. I studied the plastic flowers stuck into the wall, flowers that had outlived the people they were commemorating. I thought about my glass-etched trophies and my certificates and how they would outlive me, and how they meant nothing.

"A man is following us," Martha told me. I looked around quickly, but I couldn't see anyone. "He comes and goes," she said. "I saw him hanging around Jason's shop too, just before we left." I was convinced that the man was just a figment of her angry imagination—all men were the enemy.

"How come I haven't seen you around the shop?" I asked. "If you're such a great friend of Jason's, then how come?"

"Jason and I were lovers, not friends. And we have political affiliations. After my husband died, Jason and I enjoyed one another's bodies for a time." She looked around. "He's gone. The man I told you about."

I wanted to tell her that there was no man, that she was imagining things, but I couldn't be bothered.

"You don't need to belittle me to empower yourself," I told her.

She shook her head. "I'm not belittling you. I merely commenting on your life as I see it. You're as free to comment on mine. And as for empowering myself, I don't need you, or anyone, to do that. You need to find a way to be comfortable with yourself, Lyndon."

"I am very comfortable," I instantly asserted. "My whole life I have been extremely comfortable." Something about this woman made me feel like I'd been caught stealing marbles?

Depression hit me like a wave. I was not, nor had I ever been, comfortable with myself. And I had worn this secret shame like the lining of my suit—out of sight, but there, rubbing against my shirt, my skin. But shame about what? I wanted to ask Martha what it was I felt so ashamed about, but that in itself stunned me. Why would I want to ask Martha anything? I hated this trip to Sydney. I hated Martha. She ruined my happiness with Jason. Things would have been wonderful if she hadn't come along. We would have had fun. Instead, I was more depressed than ever. I wanted to walk away from her as quickly as I could, but I was so mired in gloom that all I could do was stand there and look at the names of dead truck drivers.

27. MARGAUX

LATER THAT NIGHT, Graham and I were still at the hospital. We wanted to be there when Nancy woke up, but we had no idea when that might be.

I went to grab coffees from the cafeteria. I was standing at the vending machine when I sensed crazy Nancy Senior next to me. I looked at the reflection in the vending machine and yep, there she was, with all her terrible beauty.

"I don't want any part of your damaged life," I told her. "I was angry, yes. But I'm moving on, and I'm moving on without you."

Her face stretched wide like an elastic doll in a House of Horror carnival ride and her black mouth was dark as a cave. She screamed her silent scream, and thousands of tiny green worms poured out of her mouth and swirled around me, cloaking me with their sticky wet skin. My worst fear. Worms. I froze. I couldn't scream or move. The worms like a cold, living, writhing, porridge, crawled all over me.

"You're not going anywhere without me." Nancy's voice was clear and loud inside my head. "You think you've dispelled your anger? You've dispelled nothing. Actions, sugar, actions. Actions speak louder than words."

"I emailed Adam. I made things right," I muttered, addressing her less with my voice than my thoughts. "What else do you want me to do?" The worms were inside my clothes now, wriggling and squirming.

"Sacrifice." The word echoed. "I want you to sacrifice something dear to your heart."

"No. I won't. It will feed you. I'm going to fight you. I'm not you. Yes, I was weak for a moment, and I gave in to hatred, but I'm not you."

I heard her mocking laugh. Then the worms became moths, tiny as dandelion seeds and as suffocating as a woollen blanket. So, I drew into myself as much as I could. I told myself they weren't real, but they felt real. The moths fluttered around me, a malevolent cloud of evil intention, but I stood my ground, although my heart was pounding. My mouth was so dry, I feared I would choke. The moths became a black swarm of midges, closing in on me, filling my ears, my mouth, and my nose. I was going to choke to death. I could not breathe.

And then, they were gone. There was nothing there. I took a cautious breath and tried to steady myself.

"You gonna use that thing or not?" a man behind me said.

I turned around, startled. "Sorry. You go first, I'll wait."

He didn't need to be told twice. He nearly pushed me aside. I waited until he was finished, and then I made two coffees and took them back to Graham. She glanced at me and immediately knew that I'd met up with Nancy again.

"She hates me now. Whatever that lie was, about her wanting me to help her apologize, it was just a ruse. She wants a patsy to help vent her anger and I was there." I told Graham about the moths and the worms and the midges, and she shuddered.

"I am sorry. That's so gross. But don't worry, Trish will help us. You sit with Nancy, and I'll give Trish a call and bring her up to speed. We need to see her as soon as we can."

I sat down, and shortly after she left, my phone rang. Part of me hoped it was Adam but another part of me feared that crazy Nancy had found a way to get inside my phone. But it was Tim.

He sent me a text message with a single line: *Found him.*

28. LYNDON

MARTHA HAD LEFT ME at the wall. "Things can improve for you," she'd said. And with that parting shot, off she went, that tall, grey-haired Amazon.

I sat down on the grass and stared at the wall. How could things improve? Jason was dying. I kept trying to push the thought away, but it kept coming back. He had rescued me, and now he was dying. I'd be all alone. I had Queenie, that much was true. But little else. What would I do with the rest of my life? Was my work on this earth done? Was it time for me to die? Perhaps I should kill myself. I wasn't suicidal, but what was the point of being alive? No one needed me, and I couldn't stand being me. Everything was so uncomfortable. Queenie would go back to her original home, the world would carry on turning, and I would simply be dead.

I lay back in the grass and put my hands behind my head. The sky was cloudless and alarmingly uniform. I searched for a small discolouration, anything to break up that monotonous blue, which echoed the bleakness inside my chest. My rib cage was supporting nothing more than a hollow man. I was nothing. Yes, I thought. I should kill myself. I would support Jason through this venture and his illness, and then kill myself in the least problematic way so as not to make things difficult for my family.

But then, out of the blue, and I later amused myself with this pun, a contrail shot diagonally across the sky, marking it with a thick chalk line. And then another contrail came, and it intersected with the first one and stopped abruptly. The result was a cross. A cross? What did that mean? It had to mean something. I sat up. Only seconds before, I had been convinced that my life lacked any kind of meaning, and that the entire universe lacked meaning, and that the only solution was death. But now there was a sign. A sign that was telling me what? That I had meaning?

I needed to see Jason. I leapt to my feet and scurried back to the motel and burst into the room. Jason and Sean were sitting on the verandah, watching a fiery sunset settle over the ocean.

"Heya. Are you going to come to dinner with us, mate?" Sean asked. I was about to say that if Martha was going, then it was over my dead body. But before I could open my mouth, I remembered that Jason was dying. What kind of friend was I being?

"Of course," I replied, rallying cheer into my voice. "Where are we going?"

"Amazing vegan place," Jason said. "Who knew Tarcutta had such a variety of vegan places? We are going for Thai. Did you have fun on your walk?"

"I saw a really depressing memorial wall for dead truckers," I told them, pulling up a chair. "Then Martha came over and depressed me even more. She said there was a man following us. After she left, I lay down on the grass and thought about killing myself when two contrails made a cross in the sky. And that was when I realized I am being a poor friend to you." I looked at Jason. "I am henceforth going to be a better friend."

"You're fine as you are," he said. "Don't kill yourself until I am gone. I'll send you a sign to tell you if the other side's any good or if you should hang in here for as long as possible. Which might be the case, you know. You had a busy afternoon. What man? Who was following Martha?"

I shook my head. "I didn't ask her." I didn't tell him my theory that Martha hated all men except Jason.

"I'm going to find her and ask her," Sean said, and he left.

"He gives credence to what she said?"

"There are constant nutters out there, trying to shut down the anarchist movement," Jason said. "Mostly retired policemen who never managed to catch us at any real crime during their careers and can't give it up. It's always worth checking out."

I felt terrible. When it came to Martha, I kept getting it all wrong.

Sean came back with Martha in tow, and we moved the chairs until we were all sitting in a row with our feet on the railing, watching the sun.

"Magnificent," Martha said, and she was right. The sun in Australia was enormous compared to the one in Canada, or so it seemed to me. Of course, I knew it was the same sun, but this one was an angry ball of fire. I could practically see the flames coming off the surface and lashing out.

"Who's following us?" Jason asked once Martha was settled.

"A very large man. A man who looks like he could be the incarnation of evil but most probably is not."

"Okay. But we need more that. Describe him with more of the usual kind of details like height and age."

"He was about sixty or older. He was shorter than me but not by much. He was as broad as he was tall, and he looked like he was a boxer or a bouncer who had melted around the edges. He had a lion's mane of white hair and his skin was white, albino white, with a pinky-yellow tinge. He was a flat, even white, not like us with some darker areas than others, or patches of colour. He was so creepy. And his eyes were like black olives, and even his mouth was black, a Halloween-lipsticked black. I think he might have tried to smile at me and it was ghastly. He was ghastly. His face was like a floury moon and there were those two black olives for his eyes and two smaller ones for his nostrils,and then a black slash for a mouth."

"Anything else?" Jason asked, although I thought that was quite a lot.

"He was wearing black."

"And he tried to smile at you. What do you mean he tried? Did he smile or not?"

"It looked like he was making an effort because he wanted to, but it didn't work and so he stopped."

"Where did you see him?"

"First at the shop, after Sean came to fetch me from his place, and later just near the memorial where I was talking to Lyndon."

I had wondered why she stayed at Sean's and not at Jason's, and then I realized it was because of me. I also wondered why Jason hadn't told me about her, but then again, it wasn't like he spilled his guts on a daily basis or was a contender for the chatterbox-of-the-year award.

"Why do you think he looks like the incarnation of evil but most likely isn't?" Sean asked.

"I don't know. Maybe he's just afflicted by his strange appearance. He looks like an enormous fleshy ghost. And he had extremely long eyelashes."

"You saw his eyelashes?" Naturally, I was the one to voice the objection.

"You'd be amazed by what we humans see in a fraction of a second," Martha said. "Yes, they were very long, girly eyelashes. And they were real, I could tell that."

"Was he wearing makeup?" Sean asked.

Martha thought about that. "Maybe eyeliner. But I can't be sure."

"We will keep a watchful eye out," Jason said. "Let the sun lay its body to rest upon the water and we will go out and get dinner."

We sat in silence for the rest of the sunset, and I was sorry when the last tip of the great circle dipped below the horizon.

I traipsed out after the others, the last in line, not looking forward to dinner during which I was sure that Martha would further attack me for my long list of failings. But I was wrong.

She regaled us with tales of celebrity parents of her troubled schoolchildren and the evening passed in a chatter of good humour and excellent food. We went back to the motel and Jason left to share Martha's room while Sean and I bunked together.

"Martha does like you," Sean told me through a mouthful of toothpaste foam. "She's just putting you through your paces."

I wasn't sure if that was the correct expression, but I knew what he meant.

"I don't care what Martha thinks," I said, and Sean grinned at me, like yeah, right, and spat in the basin.

"So this thing with sex with flowers," I said. "Do you ever get it on with a bouquet?"

"No way, mate. I'm not into orgies," Sean replied, and he changed into a pair of plaid boxers. "And before you mock me, you should try it."

"Not likely," I told him, but then I thought that at one point in my life, I wouldn't have thought my current situation would be likely either. But sex with flowers? The odds were extremely slim.

29. MARGAUX

TIM SAID THAT LYNDON was on his way to Sydney. I didn't know what to do. I couldn't believe that Tim had found him so quickly. I had a sneaking suspicion that Tim had started looking for him shortly after we met, but that he'd been waiting for me to give him the heads-up to track him down for sure.

But I couldn't waste time thinking about Lyndon because Nancy woke up. We told her that Mite was safe with the neighbour and then Graham and I got going, to meet with Trish.

It was early, not even nine a.m., and the day was going to be a scorcher. I would have loved to have a shower and a change of clothes, but we needed to see Trish as soon as possible. I could still feel the fluttering moths flaking their dandruff onto my skin, and those awful clammy, bug-eyed worms rubbing up against me. And how could I forget those suffocating midges flying up my nose and my mouth?

As Trish welcomed us into her home, I thought, *Just your average white witch*. Her purple hair was Einstein-wild, and she was wearing blue-framed glasses, a tie-dyed skirt, and silver platform boots.

I was apprehensive. The moth-cloak episode had scared the bejesus out of me, and I knew that Nancy's power was growing.

Trish took us to her back garden, and we walked through a spiral of stones to a table in the centre. There was a pitcher of water with slices of fruit in it: oranges, lemons, cherries.

I hadn't realized how thirsty I was, and I gratefully polished off the first glass that Trish poured for me and sipped at the second.

"Water is holy," she said. "Merely by virtue of being water. Every time you take a drink of water, imagine the skies and the earth and all of nature that brings this magical elixir into being. And when you take a bath, thank the molecules that make up the droplets that cleanse and heal you."

I could see Graham looking at me questioningly, as if she was worried I would dismiss Trish as a flake and run out of the spiral without looking back. But I was so terrified of Nancy that I did as Trish said. I imagined the water blessing me and cleansing me of those awful moths.

"Graham has told me all about your plight," she said. "The demon has grown in power since we had lunch."

"Demon?"

"Yes, a supernatural being that possesses a person, alive or dead and torments them. We will need to find the right spell to ground her power."

"What does she want? To possess me?"

Trish shook her head. "She wants to do as much damage as she can, however she can. You will most probably end up dead if we don't try to stop her. She'll burn you out. She needs to go to hell and take up permanent residence there. That is her rightful place. A part of her wants to be there with her companions, so we will help her with that."

"Do you have a spell like that?" I asked.

"Spells have the same basis," Trish said. "Most magic can be worked with the same formula: 'That which is above is the same as that which is below.... Macrocosmos is the same as microcosmos. The universe is the same as God, God is the same as man, man is the same as the cell, the cell is the same as the atom, and so on, ad infinitum.'"

I was curious as to what was smaller than an atom, so I asked the question.

"Oh, lots of things. Quarks, electrons, neutrinos. And then there is, of course, the Higgs boson particle which was fairly recently discovered."

"Of course," I echoed, clueless.

"Also known as the God particle. That's its nickname. The God particle gives mass to matter. Some particles are responsible for giving matter different properties. The God particle fails to explain gravity, and there are gaps, but nevertheless, its discovery is remarkable. Not surprising if you recall what Christ said: 'For by Him all things were created: things in heaven and on earth, visible and invisible ... all things were created by Him and for Him.' That's from Colossians chapter one, verse sixteen."

"You believe in God and Christ?" I was surprised by this, and she was equally surprised by my astonishment.

"Of course I do. God, Jesus, the Universe, Buddha, Allah. They are all one and the same. They are all water. They are all us and we are them."

"And Nancy is a demon," I added, wanting to realign her with the urgent matter at hand. "And I want to get rid of her."

"Not that easy to do," Trish said. "If you recall the power of your anger when you opened the door to her, you will know the sheer force of energy that you felt at that moment. That kind of energy is hard to reawaken by whim or will."

She was right, and I felt dismayed. I'd been consumed by a fury the likes of which I had never felt before. I had no idea how I could match that.

"I see." I was exhausted and couldn't do anymore. "Trish, Graham, I think I need to go home, to my hostel, to rest. Is that okay? I don't think waiting one more day will hurt anyone, do you? I can't tackle this any further today. I'm spent."

"No worries," Trish said, and it was funny, hearing the pukka Aussie saying coming from an actual Australian. "It will give me time to do more research. I'd like to suggest that we go to the Garry Owen House tomorrow night and conduct a spell there. We will need to be there for midnight. It's a new moon, which augurs well."

"Okay," I said. "Whatever you guys think is best. I'm beyond tired."

"We'll chat about the specifics later," Graham said to Trish as she helped me up. Even my legs were weak, and I felt rude rushing our meeting to a close, but I was shattered. All I wanted was have a shower, take a Xanax, and go to sleep. I didn't want to have to think about any of this. Of course, a part of me just hoped it would all go away.

Trish saw us out. I could hardly keep my eyes open on the way home. I remembered that Lyndon was on his way to Sydney, but I didn't care. It had been a long two days, starting with the tarot card reading with Janet the previous morning, then meeting Nancy Junior, and staying overnight with her in the hospital.

"You've been amazing," I said, thanking Graham. She looked sheepish and uncomfortable, and I stared at her.

"What's going on?"

"It fascinating," she admitted. "I'd like to work it into a book, if you don't mind? But if you do mind, I won't."

"That's all?" I laughed. "I really don't mind. Knock yourself out. Let's just try to get a happy ending for me, okay? No *Exorcist* or *Poltergeist* sequels!"

She smiled and nodded before driving away. I walked into the hostel and remembered that Tim wasn't there, and I missed him. He had texted me to say he was on his way home, and that he was following Lyndon and his crew. Lyndon was travelling in a rare and expensive BMW, along with the ex-punk rocker. The BMW was owned by a kid named Sean with too much money for his own good and a tall woman with steel-grey hair was travelling with them. Apparently, she and Lyndon were at loggerheads with one another, a conclusion reached by Tim via binoculars, and apparently by the manner in which the two backseat passengers put as much distance between them as they could, and hardly spoke. This made me smile. Good—someone who could challenge him. God knows, I had tried.

I was about to walk up the stairs when I saw someone familiar out of the corner of my eye. And, sitting there, in the red lounge, was my son, Adam.

30. LYNDON

WE DROVE INTO SYDNEY, and I felt strange, returning to the scene of my crime. The rest of the journey was uneventful—there were no floury, black-olive eyed white man sightings and no sparring with Martha. She looked happy and peaceful, and I had the somewhat bitchy thought that it was amazing what a good shag will do.

I thought about the last time I had sex with Margaux. The funny thing was, it had felt like the end of something to me, although I had no idea I was going to leave her the following day. She hadn't had a clue how I felt, and was impressed with my passion and my imagination—I did things to her I hadn't done in years.

"I guess this trip is starting to work out for you," she had said. "I wasn't sure you'd get into it and you worried me in Vancouver and Hong Kong, but you're happier now?" I hadn't replied.

I had never been less happy in my life. I had wanted to go home, and to go back to my job and my house, neither of which existed anymore.

I had hated Vancouver. I felt hemmed in by the mountains and the ethos of West Coast cool. It didn't rain the entire time we were there, and I felt denied. I was tired and wired at the same time, and I spent a lot of time walking around while Margaux shopped.

"Where are you going to put all the stuff you are buying?"

I asked. "We don't have a house, in case you had forgotten."

"I haven't forgotten," she said. "I am going to post it to Helen, and she's going to put things into her storage locker, and once we see where we're going to live, we'll take it from there."

I hated it when people said, "We'll take it from there." I didn't reply. I poured another glass of wine and then another and I ended up drunk until I fell into bed, knowing I would snore like a bulldog with a sinus problem. When I woke at three a.m., Margaux was asleep on the sofa in the living room of our hotel suite. I leaned against the window and watched Vancouver wake up while my wife slept. I told myself there were thousands of reasons I should be happy. I had two grown, healthy kids who were forging successful careers. Both of them seemed fairly problem-free, although there was this new development of Adam being gay.

I wondered about Helen. I hadn't actually talked to her about her love life in years. Helen was an investment banker although Margaux always referred to her as an accountant, which drove Helen nuts. I loved Helen. Of all the members of my family, she was the one I understood the best and she understood me.

I wondered, as I watched the West Coast sun rise, if there had been something about Margaux's and my relationship that had warned Helen off long-term commitment. I had tried to talk to Margaux about this in the past, but she always shook me off.

"Helen's just finding her feet," she had said. "She's having fun. She's young."

"She doesn't seem to be having fun," I'd said. "But it's her life. We can't change that."

I wanted Helen to be happy. I wanted her to have fun. I worried that she was too much like me but I wasn't exactly sure what I meant by that.

I knew I had let Helen down at the party by not meeting Adam's boyfriend, and I resented that more than I regretted upsetting Adam. Adam would forgive me, just like he always had—that was the way our relationship worked.

I wondered what Helen had made of my getaway, and if she had replied to the email that Jason had sent. I wanted to talk to Helen, but I didn't know what to say. How would I explain myself? Would she see this as a run-of-the-mill mid-life crisis? I hated that expression, mid-life crisis, and I had always been so proud of myself for never having had one.

In the car, on the way to Sydney, I had wanted to ask Jason if he thought that today's world was populated by a genera-tion of self-centred selfie people whose whole lives revolved around their mood charts and careful monitoring of what was going on with them at the expense of the bigger picture. Sure, no one wanted to feel irrelevant and now, with social media providing a reality TV platform for the intimacies of our daily lives, we were all celebrity stars in our docudramas. Everyone screamed at everyone else: "Look at me on Face-book! Look at me on Instagram! Look at me on Pinterest! Look at my career successes on LinkedIn! Me, me, me! Aren't I so bloody marvellous?"

But I hadn't wanted to disturb the peace in the car just when we were all getting along. So, I thought about my son and daughter and how I had asked Margaux if we would leave Vancouver as soon as she woke up.

She agreed we could. "Hong Kong?" she asked, and I nodded.

But Hong Kong was a mistake. As we rode up to the sixteenth floor in a tiny elevator that crammed both of us in along with our two suitcases, I felt claustrophobic and panic-stricken. I was going to faint. When I later read *The Dispossessed*, there was a passage that perfectly described how I had felt. I kept rereading it: "*He saw space shrink in upon him like the walls of a collapsing sphere driving in and in towards a central void, closing, closing, and he woke with a scream for help locked in his throat, struggling in silence to escape from the knowledge of his own eternal emptiness.*"

Margaux was delighted with the room into which we barely fit. A tiny washroom with a shower was crammed into the corner and suitcases that defied being opened at the same time—there simply wasn't enough room.

Margaux leaned out the tiny window and marvelled at the vast city below. We had landed at night and it was a surreal nightmare trying to get a cab. The drive from the airport disoriented me further—I felt like we were moving backwards while the world was spinning in a counter-clockwise direction at an increasing speed.

I blamed the flight from Vancouver to Hong Kong for frying my synapses. Thirteen hours in the air, with self-flagellating thoughts whirling around my mind. I took some of Margaux's sleeping pills, but they didn't work. They towed me into a no-man's land of madness. While Margaux napped next to me, my brain was on speed dial with every crazy thought and then some. I pulled a pen and paper from my carry-on and started scribbling wildly. I thought that if I could get my thoughts out of my brain and onto paper, that I would be able to find some peace, but I was wrong.

I am flying around the world in the wrong direction like a deranged bird. It's no wonder I am losing my mind. It's no fun, losing your mind. It's not like going to the Bahamas and drinking tequila. Not that I even like tequila, mind you. I hate that godforsaken syrup's hallucinogenic stomach-turning, strobe light, finger-jabbing drumbeat. I am upset.

I have failed by growing old. I never meant to. I swear I didn't. I thought I was better than all the rest. Do I have a sensory processing disorder? Disorders everywhere we turn.

Over seven million people live in Hong Kong. Fruit flies sleep too, you know. Who are the people who run backwards? There are sacrifices. Yes. A ghostwriter is for hire: "I don't promise the world, just a well-written book." Coconut is the new kale, don't you know? Time to tip the hat and call it a night.

I wrote and wrote until it was time to land and once we did, my condition, if one could call it that, worsened, and then, in that tiny room on the sixteenth floor, I fell onto the bed, huddling my body around my belly and groaning.

Margaux spotted a night market below and wanted to go out. I wanted to wail, rub my balding head, and die.

"You don't look too good," she told me. She pulled out her purse. "Here, take a Xanax. I'm going to go out. Don't worry. Try to rest."

I dry-swallowed the pill, and she left me coiled in my fetal position, shoes and clothes still on. Thankfully, I fell asleep but the following day, I was unable to leave the room.

"I just need to rest," I told Margaux. "I must have caught a bug. I am sorry. Please, go and explore. Please don't worry about me."

She brought me buns and water and Cokes and chocolate bars. She went to find the Jade Market and various art galleries. She took a ferry to main Hong Kong—we were in Kowloon— and she came back to that tiny room with ropes of pearls and precious gems and tales of a wonderful city that she loved.

And she went out at night while I slept. When I woke, I flipped through the channels of the tiny TV. We spent a week like that—Margaux exploring the city and me lying in bed.

"Let's move on to Australia," Margaux suggested. "I don't think Hong Kong's right for you. Let's leave and find some wide-open spaces and beaches. You can rest there. You're exhausted. We need to find you a place to rest."

Which found us on the third stop of our famous Around-The-World-For-As Long-As-We-Want-Tour, a tour on which I seemed to be hurtling towards a nervous breakdown.

So, thinking back, I guess it was not all that surprising that I left Margaux in the awkward and amputated way that I had.

And, as the BMW pulled into Sydney, I felt my new sense of self start to disintegrate. Jason must sensed it because he turned to me. "How are you?" he asked.

I shook my head. "Not great."

To my surprise, Martha took my hand. "Things can improve," she said, just like she'd said at the wall.

My eyes filled with tears and I nodded. *Sure they can.*

And then it was time to meet the anarchists.

31. MARGAUX

"ADAM!" I WAS OVERJOYED to see him. I buried myself in his bear hug. Adam wasn't small like Lyndon or myself—he was a good six-foot-three and just as broad. He would have made a superb quarterback, were it not for the complete absence of any kind of sporting skills.

"You're not angry I came?" He pulled back and looked at me, unsure.

"Of course not!" My eyes filled with tears. "I thought I was doing fine by myself, but now that you're here, it makes all the difference in the world to me."

"Howdy Mizz Margaux," a deep male voice said. Rick had come with Adam and I gave him a big hug.

"How did you boys get time off work?" I asked.

"Family emergency, which is true." Adam said. "I just got your email, Mom. Listen, I'm fine. I go on rants that I know aren't fair to you. I'm going to try to stop that, and I'm going to try to stop being so dramatic all the time."

"Don't change a thing," I said, and I realized I meant it with all my heart. "I love you completely, just the way you are, Adam. That email and my reaction, that was all me, coming from my pain and confusion. Where are you boys staying?"

"Here. I got us a room. Not a dorm, a single room. Quite the place. We've been here since early this morning. I didn't want to message you. We wanted this to be a surprise. We had a sleep because of the jet lag and now we we've been sitting here and waiting for you. Where have you been?"

"I've been to hell and back," I said, "and I'm not joking. I'll bring you up to speed. I've been in these clothes for two days, so I really need a shower."

Just then, Tim arrived. Both Adam and Rick were startled by his gothic largeness, but they recovered their manners, shook his hand, and made their introductions.

"The package is in Sydney," Tim said to me. "At the Black Rose Café in Newtown. It's a regular anarchist hangout."

"Anarchist. It must have something to do with Mr. Ex-Punk Rocker. But Tim," I said, "and Rick and Adam, there's something I need to tell you."

"I must get something to eat," Tim said. "I'm starving. Then you can tell us what's been going on, which judging from the expression on your face, is serious."

We settled around the kitchen table, which was conveniently free of other hostel residents. Tim made a fresh pot of coffee and a tray of sandwiches, and I inhaled a ham and swiss cheese on toasted sourdough bread before I realized how hungry I was. I ate the second sandwich more slowly while I told the story of Nancy. I started from the very beginning, with the Virgin of Coogee's statue and I didn't stop until the very end, with my walking into the hostel, craving sleep.

"But seeing you," I said, and squeezed Adam's hand, "revived me."

"Dear Lord have mercy," Rick drawled, and he launched into a story. Rick was from Kentucky, and he had the smoothest Southern voice. When he talked, I got lost in the melody of his words and forgot to listen to the lyrics.

"We had a demon take over our house," he said.

"What?" Rick's nonchalance at the statement caught me off guard. "What kind of demon?"

"Perhaps demon is too strong a word," he amended. "More of a spirit that didn't want to leave. Kentucky is quite famous for its paranormal activity. We've got the Hillbilly Beast in the foothills of Kentucky just to mention one. He was around at the time of Daniel Boone and there are all kinds of other ghosts. People come to visit just for the ghosts!"

Rick looked set to launch into a history lesson of the supernatural in southern America and I quickly interrupted him. "But what about your demon? Spirit, I mean."

"Shortly after my Nana died, we started having disturbances in the house. Pictures fell to the floor, cold winds swept through the house, knocking over vases and one time, a bath started running all by itself! I figured Nana was annoyed at having passed. She loved life, that woman! Horses! The race track in particular! Couldn't keep her away. If you ask me, she was genuinely peeved that the rest of us were still able to enjoy the delights of the Derby and whatnot, while she was off, wherever she was, missing out on all the fun."

Rick took a gulp of his coffee and grinned at our expectant faces. "So I called in our local Reverend and I told him that Nana needed a good ole talking to and he obliged. We had more of an intervention than an exorcism. We had a big party for Nana, even though she'd had the biggest send-off reception the South had seen in a long time! We got caterers in, mint juleps, the works! Everybody had to wear their finest, with a fancy new hat just for the occasion and they all had to tell a story of how they missed Nana. I was direct when it came to my turn. I told her, 'Look Nana, I love you and miss you but you've got to stop this nonsense. You broke a Wedgewood vase and that running bath could well have ruined the parquet flooring on the second floor.' I told her she had to find peace with her lot and that we'd all join her as soon as we could but then again, not too soon. I told her to be patient. Not Nana's strongest point."

"Did it work?" Adam asked.

"Kind of. She stopped being as vehement. She still wanted us to know she was there, so she'd rearrange things and have some fun but she held off with hurting the antiquities and such."

"She listened to reason," I mused. "I'm not so sure Nancy will."

I reached for the box of pictures and laid them out on the table like a deck of cards. Rick leaned in close to look at them, and he recoiled. I knew what he meant. A sense of evil ricocheted from them.

"Do you think Trish knows what she is doing?" Adam asked.

"I hope so. I have faith in her, but I have no idea what her plan is. We have to meet them at midnight."

"Here's what we should all do…" Tim said, but just then my phone pinged and I picked it up, wondering if it was Helen, who I had been neglecting.

But it was an email from the ex-punk rocker.

"You want to meet me at three p.m. at Circular Quay?"

"Yes," I wrote back.

"Good. I'll be outside the Museum of Contemporary Art."

I looked at my watch. "I'm going to have a lie down after all," I said. The others looked puzzled, but I couldn't explain. "And a shower first. I have to be somewhere at three. But I'll be back around seven at the latest, and we'll regroup and go to Garry Owen House."

"I'll drive you all there in the van," Tim offered. "I'm coming with you. The more powerful energies we have to counteract this thing, the better."

I messaged Graham and Trish to ask them if ten p.m. was a good time for us to meet. and Trish immediately replied that it was perfect.

Main gate at ten p.m., she said. *No wandering around the grounds on your own.*

I confirmed this and then I went and had a long shower before lying down on the bed. There was so much going on in my brain that I was certain I wouldn't be able to sleep but before I knew it, my alarm was going off and I had half an hour to get to Circular Quay.

32. LYNDON

WE WERE AT THE Black Rose Café in Newtown, Sydney. Home of the anarchists. I paused outside the place while the others filed in. There was a bookcase outside, a rickety bamboo thing, and it held a strange selection of reading matter: *The Drifters* by James A. Michener, *East of Eden* by John Steinbeck, *I Never Promised You a Rose Garden* by Joanne Greenberg, and others. The books were all calcified with dust, and when I picked one up and tried to open it, it was a solid brittle brick. All the pages were stuck together.

I put the book back and wiped my hands on my trousers, wishing I had some of that hand sanitizer Margaux was never without.

The storefront window was smashed and broken, and there was a torpedo-sized hole in the centre with thick spider-web cracks radiating outwards. I peered through the hole and noticed that whatever had made it had penetrated a good three inches of glass. A face came up to mine and glared at me. Startled, I took a few steps back.

There were anarchy signs and posters stuck to the broken window, with only the spider-web cracks and the hole visible.

I forced my feet to move with great reluctance, and as I entered the store, which was no more than a cramped, hot, airless, low-ceilinged room, it was hard to breathe. The place was encrusted with filth laid down by a century of sticky fingers. I wanted to run out and buy paper towels and cleaning products, but I knew this would not endear me to my new friends. To be honest, my new friends frightened me. I wasn't sure if any of them knew how to smile. They were dressed in faded ill-fitting black clothes, the garments too loose or too tight. The clothes were speckled with rips and holes, not designer-style but worn to the bone, exhausted holes. The anarchists looked to be about anywhere from fifteen to forty, and the place was packed. There were only three chairs. I had no idea how this meeting of the minds was going to work.

And the noise. Everybody was shouting at the same time. It was like a hundred auctioneers were all selling their wares at full lung capacity. This continued for half an hour. I flattened myself against the wall and felt a meltdown approaching, similar to my Hong Kong episode. If things didn't change soon, I'd have to turn and run and who gave a fig about paper towels and cleaning products? I just needed to get the hell out of there.

I had noticed a lovely pub as we walked down the main street. I could escape there, have a cold beer, enjoy some peace, and meet the others back at the hotel later. At a quick glance, the pub had polished checkerboard floors and a ceiling fan that whirled quietly. The red booths were both welcoming and kind, with large open windows that faced out onto the street.

Meanwhile, I was stuck in this lockbox of hell and sweat was running down my face and my spine. I couldn't see Jason or Martha or Sean, so I turned to leave. But just then, Jason climbed onto a table, raised his fingers to lips, gave a piercing whistle, and the room fell into a blessed silence.

"We're going upstairs," he shouted. "Shut it, all of you. I mean it. This meeting's now called to order. We're going upstairs where you'll load up your plates, sit on your bums, stuff your faces, and let the meeting commence. You know the rules."

There were rules? I thought "anarchy" meant no rules? Sean appeared next to me. He must have known what I was thinking because he whispered, "Jason had to make some rules or this lot would never come to order. Follow me, I'll take you up."

The stairs at the back of the room thankfully brought us into a vast empty loft, three times the size of the area below. I calculated that the loft must span three of the buildings below us. The place was light and airy with all the windows open, and my heart finally stopped doing the fandango. However, hundreds more anarchists streamed in. I had no idea where they could have come from. There was no way they could have all been hanging out in the store below. But at least they had listened to Jason. There was a resolute silence and they were orderly.

Sean lead me to a long table, and I joined the tail end of the lineup. The anarchists piled baked goods onto their paper plates like there was no tomorrow. A man I assumed to be Martha's son was clad in chef's whites, and he was busy replenishing the pastries from boxes he brought out from under the table. It was a good thing he had more because the anarchists were ravenous beasts.

The aroma of butter, flour, sugar, cinnamon, vanilla, chocolate, and raisins baked to perfection filled the air. My mouth watered. I took a thick slice of banana bread, a vanilla cupcake, and a slice of lemon loaf with thick frosting.

I sat down on the floor next to Sean, and we faced Jason and Martha who were standing at the front.

"So," Jason started, "Sid's birthday. A big day for us all. The idea came from Liam Lemon over there. Stand up, Liam, and take a round of applause."

Of course it took Sean to nudge me in the ribs before I remembered that I was Liam since I was focused on my astoundingly delicious slice of lemon loaf. There was an awkward pause as I clambered ungracefully to my feet, carefully clutching my plate. Besides, I hadn't sat on the floor since I was six years old, and my hips and knees were aghast.

I folded back down after the anarchists had given me a dribbling round of applause. Granted, most of them, like me, had their hands and mouths full of cupcakes and date squares.

"I have sent out the message and it has been widely accepted and well-received." Jason continued, "and apparently several thousand—eight thousand at last count—people will be flying in to Sydney to celebrate with us. They know to stagger their arrival times over a few days, and they are keeping an eye on the website for details of the event. They are all coming, ostensibly, on holiday or to visit relatives or check out universities." He looked around. "To reiterate and clarify in case you missed seeing the newsletter or the details have slipped your mind, we will start gathering at the bridge at five a.m. Sunrise is at six-thirty-seven a.m., and, by that time, we will be in place. We have from five a.m. until six-ten a.m., to get sorted. An hour and ten minutes should be enough time to climb the arch and put ourselves all over the bridge. Ideally, we want to be like ants, swarming the place. Those on foot will enter at the south end via The Rocks and those from the North Shore will come in at Kirribilli. For those of you with vehicles, the plan is to create gridlock on the bridge from both sides. All bikes, trucks, and cars are welcome. If you can borrow a car, then you should. Our goal is to turn the Sydney Harbour Bridge into a wall-to-wall parking lot."

I looked around. The anarchists were still chewing with concentrated focus and didn't seem to be paying much attention. Some were going back for seconds and thirds, and Martha's son was unpacking more food. I cleaned my plate and felt slightly nauseous from all the sugar. I wished I had a bottle of water.

"The plan is also to have as many bodies on the bridge as possible. And everyone needs to bring as many bog rolls as they can. It's light, so load up. Single ply, people, single ply. Our friend Mark … please stand up Mark…. He is our key man, literally. He's got the keys to the bridge climb, and he'll open it up for us."

Mark leapt to his feet. He was addict skinny, and when he grinned, he revealed the stubby brown remains of his teeth.

At first impression, I wasn't sure Mark was the most reliable of fellows, but that was Jason's call.

Jason continued. "Note, we will only be utilizing the east side of the bridge. The action is directed away from Paramatta, Planetarium, and Luna Park side. You will be facing the Opera House and Kirribilli. We want to get as many people up into the arch as possible. I will be sending out diagrams of the bridge again, and if you can, take a walk and do a recce in person. But do *not* draw any attention to yourselves by hanging around and looking suspicious. You know we're under constant scrutiny.

"And if you are going to climb up to the arch, be safe, because if anyone dies, it will work against us and our message. So, please, no deaths. You are responsible for your own safety. Mark has said that if you're planning to climb the bridge, then it's strongly suggested that you get a helmet with a flashlight, even though we will be doing this during the day. Order them online. Do not visit camping stores en masse.

"At the hour of sunrise, a siren will sound, and we will unfurl our banner 'Stop Shitting On Our World.' This will run the length of the bridge and will be fifteen feet in height. We're going to order it tomorrow, so if there are any mathematical geniuses here today, please stay back to chat with me after this meeting. I need help double-checking that our scaling is correct in terms of font size. The last thing we want to do is look like wankers by having a sign that no one can see or read.

"The sign will hang for half an hour to make sure that the news helicopters can get good coverage. And then, I will sound the siren again. You can see why we will need to do this in silence. If you're all yammering, no one will hear the siren. So, keep schtum and focus. The second siren is when we will unfurl our toilet paper to create the white wall of ignorance and shame.

"Now, here comes the most crucial part of the whole thing.

The bog roll drop. It has to be perfect. Once again, we don't want to look like wankers. Google Jeanne-Claude and Christo, and you'll get an idea of what we want. We want artistic perfection. No less. You have half an hour while the banner is being photographed to prep for the bog roll drop. That's way more time than you even need.

"Huddle as close to one another as you can, really squeeze in, side by side at the railing. We will each drop a minimum of three rolls, more if you can. We have to create a solid white curtain, preferably from the arch as well as the from the sidewalk area. Make sense?" He looked around. "The white curtain of shame and ignorance. We will hold the white curtain of shame and ignorance for half an hour, which is a bloody long time actually, so be prepared for your arms to get tired. Maybe try it at home. Sounds daft, but we can't be too prepared. And then, again at my signal call, we will all drop the toilet paper at the same time. And then one final siren call lets you know that the protest is done and you all leave. Any questions so far?"

We all looked around at one another, and a few people shook their heads.

"Good," Jason said. "Mark is staying back after the meeting in case you've got any questions about climbing the arch. This room is booked for the night.

"Now, onto wardrobe. I don't know about you lot, but I'm getting dressed up for the occasion: tartan pants, safety pins, the works. If you don't have tartan or red, then wear black trousers. Also, I want everybody to wear a black T-shirt with an anarchy sign on the back and front. Do not buy these online. Make them using white spray paint. Wear a colourful T-shirt under your anarchy T-shirt and as soon as the final signal sounds for the end of the protest, take off your anarchy T-shirt, drop it on the ground and walk away.

"No one sticks around to chat, that's crucial. If you do, you will get arrested and it will not be fun. And for God's sake, don't meet up after to have a few drinks and talk about what heroes you all were. Get as far away from the bridge as you can and look normal about it.

"And here's the most important thing of all: we do *all* of this in silence." He held up his hand and the room, which had a swell of murmured chatter to it, fell deathly silent. "You guys were supposed to be quiet this whole meeting and listen to you already—a bunch of bloody sparrows! I know, the temptation to just whisper something is huge. I get it. But the power of silence is incredible. If we're all running all over the bridge, making an ungodly racket, it makes us look disorganized, like a bunch of schoolkids let loose. We are not a bunch of schoolkids. We are adults with a serious message. Silence is ominous, meaningful, and dangerous. All good?" The room nodded in unison, and I was impressed by Jason's cohesion.

"And to that point, no running. You walk. Even when you leave, you do not run. Running indicates a riot or panic. We are not rioting. We are staging a world protest. Big difference."

I was flooded with a rush of pride that I was involved in this and that it had all started because of my suggestion. Jason still maintained the whole thing was my idea, and maybe I'd had the kernel seed for the thing, but his thorough attention to detail was deft and military in its precision.

"In case you forget any of these details, you will receive them all again, sent in the usual way. All newsletter subscribers will receive two messages just like you did about this meeting; one with the details encrypted and a separate message with a script to convert that document into a readable file. This is nothing new. You guys know how it works. And while we want spectacular amounts of media coverage on the day, we do not want to tip off the police, so watch yourselves. No bragging beforehand, via verbal, or text or email. Don't talk to anybody about this, Consult the website and only visit the bridge if you'll be normal about it. No chat sites will be used in getting this set-up and not a hint on social media. The less noise out there, the better."

A single hand shot up into the air.

"Yes, Nerissa," Jason asked. Nerissa was a tall black girl, with long dreadlocks.

"Why the bridge? Why not the Opera House?"

"Because the bridge is easier to make happen. We thought about the Opera House, but it isn't feasible."

"But Jeanne-Claude and Christo did more buildings than bridges," Nerissa objected.

"And they had permits and everything was legal and it took them months. We are illegal, we've got no time whatsoever, and we have to do it however we can. The bridge is the most viable option."

I hadn't realized that Jason had looked at other options, and I felt slightly hurt at being excluded from that discussion.

Another hand shot up.

"Yes, Scott?" Jason asked.

"Why don't we cover images of colonialism like statues or QVB? Why the bridge when it's really an Australian thing? We should be using this to protest against colonialism too."

"A very good point," Jason replied politely. I thought that the boy was an irritating moron who should be swatted into silence.

"What's QVB?" I whispered to Sean breaking the rules of no talking.

"The Queen Victoria Building. That big old shopping centre in the downtown core."

Right. It had been the first stop on Margaux's map.

"We wanted one pivotal icon to be the focus," Jason explained to the boy. "And while QVB would have been that for sure, it also would be too hard to do, from a security point of view. And covering a bunch of statues would be too scattered and wouldn't have the same impact visually. Besides, the bridge has easy access and although there are cameras, we're all allowed to walk across it, and we'll be able to take it relatively easily. And I do say relatively because you know the fuzz. They'll be like an army of red ants as soon as the alarm is raised. This is why the rules of silence and no running are crucial."

Another hand was raised. I sighed. Why couldn't these people just take direction and accept that Jason had considered things from all sides, as was clearly the case?

"What will happen to the toilet paper?" A skinny little girl, who looked about twelve years old, asked.

"It drops it into the harbour," Jason replied.

"But isn't that bad for the water?" the girl asked.

"It's biodegradable and it's a symbol. We have to use something. If we were going to be absolutely environmentally friendly, it would be a protest without a symbol. But we need a symbol, and it ties in perfectly to the message."

"But what about all the damage done to the environment with all that toilet paper that we're essentially just going to waste?" A boy stood up, angrily. His acned face was burning, and he folded his arms aggressively and jutted his chin.

"Sit down, please, Paul. The toilet paper would have been generated anyway, so we are just using it for a different purpose. We are using it as art to send a message. If anything, the environment will suffer for an even better cause than us wiping our bums."

A smattering of laughter rippled through the room, and Paul turned an even deeper red but he sat down.

"And what about the pollution generated with all those extra people coming?" another man asked. He was older than most of the kids there, and he had the look of a fat, geeky creep. I pegged him as the sort who lived in his mother's basement and played violent video games while scoffing greasy pizza. "Increased flights lead to increased carbon footprints. And tourists generate more garbage. They hire cars, which increases pollution. It all adds up, you know."

Jason sighed. "I do know. But all the people who are coming

will be contributing to a protest that will be seen on a global scale. If we try to avoid any kind of expense, be it pollution or otherwise, we would do what we have done until now, which is nothing. We want to do something, for God's sake, and this seems to cover all the bases. Any other questions?"

I hoped not, but another woman waved her hand around as if she was trying to hail a cab. She had frizzy, unkempt hair, and her front teeth were splayed yellow bricks. I wondered if she could actually close her mouth. She ran her tongue across her chapped, pouty lips and put her arms on her hips.

"I don't have enough money to buy toilet paper to throw into the harbour," she said. "I barely have enough money to buy it for me."

There was a murmur in favour of what she said. A large contingent of hands shot up, and people started shouting in agreement.

"Let's hijack a truck of toilet paper," one voice shouted out, and there were cheers.

"We are not hijacking a truck," Jason said loudly. "Don't you recall what I said moments ago? Do nothing to draw attention to yourself. Nothing. Hijacking a truck full of toilet paper is calling attention to yourself! Think, people, think!"

"Well, I can't pay," the frizzy-haired woman said, and shouts of support greeted her statement.

"I'll pay!" I yelled, and I jumped to my feet. Sean tugged me down.

I sat down and waved my hand. "I'll buy the toilet paper. For those who really can't." I was willing to spend however much was needed of my ill-gotten gains to support Jason.

"Thank you, Liam," Jason said. "All those in need of assistance with toilet paper, please raise your hand."

Three quarters of the room was a flurry of raised hands. And then, the rest followed.

"Oh, come now," Jason said, disgusted. "Most of you can't spring for a few bog rolls? Let's try that again. Put down your hands. Think about this for a moment. Think about the contribution you are going to make to try to change the world. This is an honour, to be part of this. Don't be wankers. Those of you in need of real assistance, raise your hand."

There was a small show of hands, including the frizzy-haired woman.

"If you go to Costco, it will be cheaper," a helpful individual piped up.

"Kmart are pretty good too," another offered, and Jason, clearly getting weary, signalled with a throat-cutting gesture. The room fell silent.

"I think we can all figure out where to buy bog rolls," he said. "But can anyone do the maths on the banner? I don't want to get that wrong."

"I can," a fellow in his mid-thirties with porn-star sideburns offered. "I'm a mechanical engineer and an architect. We can chat after, and I'll call you from a burner phone to confirm the specs."

"Great. Thanks. Okay then, so that's that? Any other questions? I'm getting tired here. Come on, people, it's not rocket science. It's a protest. Plus, all info will all be on the website."

"What if I want to bring a friend?" A skinny young man asked nervously. His railway-track braces made it hard for him to speak.

"Friends are fine as long as they follow the rules: silence, black T-shirt with an anarchy sign, listen to the signals, bog rolls, don't run, don't talk about it, before or afterwards. Friends who follow the rules are welcome, but we're serious, and they need to be too. Anything else?"

There was silence. Then one hand was raised, stretching upwards in the slowest of slow motion gestures. I clenched my teeth.

"What if we get arrested?" the voice whispered tremulously. The man looked like Muhammad Ali in his prime, but he was shaking and quivering like a bowl of jello.

Jason let out a belly laugh. "Don't be such ninnies. Where's your sense of adventure? You're anarchists for God's sake, not conservative democrats or republicans. Grow a pair, will you? All of you, women included, grow a pair, and do it fast or don't show up. If any of you in this room don't have the balls to do this, then unsubscribe when you get home. That way I'll have a true count of the numbers. If you stay subscribed, then you're in. Are we clear? No shame in backing out. Well, I will consider you all to be a bunch of tossers, but hey, if you don't have the balls, you don't, it's as simple as that. All right, we're done here. Meeting adjourned. Thanks Robby, for the snacks, they were great as always."

At this, the anarchists broke into the most enthusiastic applause I'd heard all day.

"Lots left," Robby shouted out. "Come and get it on your way out." There was a stampede to the table. I saw Jason talking to the mechanical engineer who was also an architect, while a large group had gathered around Mark, the bridge man.

I was behind the now-empty table, with Robby, Martha, and Sean. Robby reached under the table and brought out a thermos. "Coffee," he said, producing cups as if by magic, and we each took one, gratefully.

Sean opened up a closet I hadn't noticed and wheeled out a stack of folding chairs. He set them in a circle at the far end of the room. We all, mostly me, sank down into the civilized comfort with relief.

"That went well," Jason said, joining us. "What do you think?"

We nodded various forms of approval, and Robby handed Jason a plate of goods he'd kept aside.

Jason bit deeply into a vanilla cupcake with pink and white icing, and he shook his head. "Who knows if we'll pull it off," he said, and he sounded tired. He looked tired too. I was annoyed that the nervous nellies had tired him out with their questions.

"We will," Martha told him. She leaned forward and squeezed his hand. "Don't give it another thought. We're going to rock the world."

After the meeting ended, we all went our separate ways. I hadn't known that was going to happen, and I was a little disconcerted to see everyone scatter. Jason was vague about his plans, and I assumed they had something to do with a doctor. Sean just waved and said he'd see us later back at the hotel. I hoped he wouldn't be arrested in the Royal Botanic Gardens for sexual misconduct with a plant. Martha left with Robby, and I wasn't sure if she was coming back to Apollo Bay with us or not. I stood alone on King Street, watching the traffic and the people coming and going. I decided I might as well drop into the pub I saw, the Newtown Hotel.

I found a booth, just as I had imagined myself doing, and I admired the artwork on the walls while I waited for my beer. The interior was upscale, old-world colonial spiced with New York graffiti. One of the walls would have, at one point, been considered hard porn: it had pictures of sexy girls with their legs spread and large women holding their breasts. I supposed that anything could be called "art" these days, and if it was art, it was allowed, even right in the open and in your face while you drank a beer. I sat there, musing, thinking that in all likelihood, I was an old-fashioned prude. But I liked looking at the images, and my cock stirred, startling me. And there was me, thinking the thing was quite dead.

My beer arrived, and I drank it in two swallows and ordered another one. The afternoon was hot and drowsy, and I was worn out, but I felt fired up too, and I wished the march was happening sooner. I finished my second beer and ordered a third. I wondered what the others were doing. I felt lonely and alone, left out. I wondered what Margaux was up to and if she would recognize me if she walked into the bar. I doubted it—my entire demeanour was different, not just my appearance.

"You were at the meeting," a voice said to me, and I turned and tried to focus on the speaker. It was the tiny girl, the one who looked about twelve, the one who asked what would happen to the toilet paper.

"Should we be talking about it?" I replied, trying to keep my words crisp.

She smiled. "That was all I was going to say about it," she said, and she slid into the booth next to me. Right next to me. My cock sprang to full attention.

"You're like what, twelve?" I asked. She laughed a deep and sultry laugh, and my cock strained even further. I shifted in my seat, trying to ease the pressure of my trousers. She was doe-eyed and it felt like I was hitting on a Disney princess. I wanted to put a stop to my seemingly perverted inclinations, but I couldn't put the brakes on.

"I'm twenty-four," she said, pouting her perfect little heart-shaped mouth. That upper lip. Oh my God. Those teeth. "I'm studying physics at the University of Sydney. I've nearly got my Masters. What do you do?"

"I am retired," I said. "In other words, I am very old. Ancient. Old enough to be your granddad or even your great-granddad."

"You're making my pussy very wet," she replied, her face pure innocence, and she reached out and rubbed my rock-hard cock. "You don't feel like my granddad."

I squirmed. This was torture. "How would you know? You feel him up too?"

"You should come back to my apartment and explore my garden of carnal delights."

"As a matter of fact, I really, really shouldn't," I told her. "But, you know what? I will."

She tongue-kissed me, and I was transported back to another time, a time of my youth, when girls' tongues were a source of infinite and astounding pleasure.

"Let's go then," she said when she came up for air. I threw enough money on the table to cover my bill and a generous tip. I managed to follow her outside into the brilliant sunlight where I was sure she'd see how horribly old I was and run screaming. But she took my hand and we walked a block south. Then, we were at her apartment and I was lying on her bed. She was going down on me and I couldn't help myself, I came much too soon. She wiped it all over her face and grinned at me. Such perfect tiny white teeth.

"Sorry," I said, chagrined and deflated, my cock shrivelled and damp. There I was, in a Moroccan-styled boudoir with a sex angel, and I was done.

"Don't worry, Daddio," she said. "We'll get you going in no time. Ever tried Viagra?"

"Of course not! I've never needed to."

"And you most likely don't need to now, but let's err on the side of hours of erotic pleasure."

She dug in her bedside table and put a blue tablet on her tongue. She fed it to me and I swallowed gratefully, anything for that tongue, that tongue that tasted like strawberries and sunshine.

I was concerned I'd fall asleep before the Viagra kicked in. I wasn't used to that many beers, particularly not in the mid-afternoon of a hot summer's day.

"What's your name?" I asked.

She smiled. "Polly." We both laughed. "You haven't seen me naked," she said, standing up. "I'll put some music on."

She dropped the needle onto a vinyl copy of "Sea of Love" by The Honeydrippers, and removed her clothing, swaying, her eyes dreamy, watching me. Soon, I was solid and powerful, and so I pulled her down, rolled over, and took her, missionary style, pounding with fury until we came together. We lay there, replete. I rolled off her and closed my eyes. I was buzzing from the beer, the Viagra, and the whole day.

"You can go now," she said sharply.

I raised myself up on one elbow. "What?"

"You can go now. Thanks and all that, but off you go." She

swatted at me with my underpants and widened those enormous blue eyes and I realized, with great sadness, that I was never going to taste that strawberry and sunshine-flavoured tongue again.

I gathered my clothes, uncomfortable and taken aback. Had I failed her? Did she regret what we'd done? I was shaking—the exertion of it all had caught up with me. I didn't want her to see me old and tired, so I tried to dress with cavalier nonchalance.

"Eight," she said.

"What?"

"You're an eight out of ten."

"What's the average?"

She thought about that for a moment. "Six point five."

That made me feel better.

When I left, she was still naked, and she was still on the bed, only she was painting her toenails sky blue. She didn't look up when I opened the door and I closed it quietly behind me and walked down the flight of stairs. Outside, the day had spun into dusk.

I had no idea what to do with myself and decided to go back to the hotel. I was about to hail a cab when I spotted a woman who looked familiar. Margaux! It was her. I was sure of it. I shrank into the doorway of a storefront and watched her walk decisively to the subway. It was definitely her. And behind her, I saw a man watching her leave, and he looked like he could be the incarnation of evil, only he most likely wasn't. Margaux disappeared into the subway and the pale, floury man, and yes, he was incredibly pale, walked quickly away. I tried to follow him, but he had already vanished.

33. MARGAUX

I CHECKED MY FACE In the mirror. Pillow creases lined my cheeks and my eyes were swollen with sleep that had not wished to be disturbed. I put on some makeup and was once again painfully aware of the crevices in my face where once, not so long ago, it had been smooth. I told myself to put my vanity aside but still, I wanted to look good. I wanted to be desired. I did not want to be put out to pasture to graze the green grass and have the days of flirting and fun far behind in the rear-view mirror.

Did I want to flirt with Jason the ex-punk rocker? Yes. I did, I knew that from our email exchanges. And, with school-girl pride, my feelings would be hurt if he simply saw me as someone's granny. Not that I was someone's granny, just yet, I reminded myself.

I was nervous in the cab ride and unattractively sweaty. My hands were shaking when I paid the driver.

Along the path, in the shadow of the enormous cruise ship in the harbour, I walked to the edge of the museum, worried that I wouldn't find Jason in the milling crowd of ice-cream eaters.

But he was a hard man to miss. He was leaning against the wall, tall and lean, like a piece of solid steel. His head was covered in a cap of tattoos and he had full sleeves of Celtic and Maori designs.

I had no such distinguishing features. I walked towards him hesitantly, preparing my introduction but he bounced off the wall and beamed at me. "Margaux, I presume?"

He had a bad boy gangster accent, deliciously cockney, and I found it incredibly sexy. I found him incredibly sexy.

"Hello," I said, nervously, stupidly, and he laughed.

"Yes, hello. Look, there's a nice little pub we can go to, to talk, away from all these shopaholic cruise nuts. Come with me."

He took my hand and my belly melted with warmth. I was sixteen, in love with this boy I'd just met. I'd be happy to never reach a destination; we could just walk around holding hands forever.

But we arrived at a pub that adjoined a hotel, and I ordered a glass of red wine and Jason got a pint. We sat in a curved booth and it was with the greatest of difficulty that I refrained from sitting on his lap.

"Your detective found us," he said. "He's not exactly the most unobtrusive figure in the world, wouldn't you agree?" He smiled and the granite harshness of his features softened.

I laughed. "Yep, Tim isn't unobtrusive."

"And now that you know where Lyndon is, what do you plan to do about it?"

"Nothing. I've got a few things on my plate that I need to sort out first."

"With regard to your lost soul?"

"Yes. That." And for second time that day, I recounted the entire story and I dug out a few pictures of Nancy that I had brought to show him.

"The facts I found about Chelmsford and the use of deep sleep therapy are unbelievable," I told Jason. "There were apparently at least two dozen known deaths. False death certificates were signed by the Chelmsford doctors to cover things up. Consent forms were forged; the patients had never seen them. And other patients committed suicide a year after leaving the hospital.

"One fellow, an actor, went in because he was suffering from anxiety because his plastic surgery had gone wrong—his facelift had made his eyes look weird and he was freaked out by it. They gave him a pill telling him it was a mild sedative to help him calm down. Next thing, he was unconscious and given the sleep therapy treatment, which was, in fact, a potentially fatal dosage of barbiturates combined with other drugs. And on top of that, he was given electric shock treatment for two weeks and fed through a stomach tube."

"Your nurse was involved in all of this?"

"Yes. Graham, this other friend of mine, found evidence that she worked there. We think she was in love with Dr. Bailey. But she was born cruel, the sort who tortured puppies."

I was finding it hard to concentrate. I was talking about the worst cases of abuse and cruelty by man to man, but all I could think about was how much I wanted Jason to kiss me. Me, practically in my sixties, wanting to be kissed like never before!

Jason's arm ran the length of the booth, and somehow I ended up closer to him than I was before. I didn't know if I could manage to conduct myself with any kind of decorum for the rest of the afternoon. And my feelings must have been obvious, because the next thing I knew, I turned to him and Jason leaned down to kiss me. I put my hand on his neck, his rough neck, and we French kissed like high-school kids.

"I am thinking maybe we should get a room?" he said and I agreed.

We went to the front desk of the hotel and Jason got us a room. The whole thing took much too long, and I waited for him to change his mind. I wanted to apologize for the fact that my body wasn't young and tell him that I hoped he knew what he is in for, but from the way he kissed me when we got into the elevator, I knew that everything would be fine.

It was far from fine. It was every kind of superlative in the book, and afterwards I lay curled up next to him, with my face buried in his shoulder. "So, we finally meet," Jason said, smiling. "Does this feel odd to you?"

"Not in the least. Do you mean because you're Lyndon's buddy?"

"Exactly." He grinned. "His buddy. Look." He showed me a recent tattoo of a tree on his leg. "Lyndon's work."

"He's a tattoo artist now? That's really good."

"Yes. Well, he's learning to be. He has to keep practicing. We go back tomorrow, you know, to Apollo Bay."

The thought of him leaving me ripped me in two and I sat up. "Oh," I said, stupidly, clutching the sheets to me.

"Margaux, there's something I need to tell you. A few things, actually. I don't want any secrets or lies between us."

I had a sense of foreboding. By the time he finished his story, I knew that he was dying and that a huge toilet paper protest was being planned for the near future.

"I want to help," I told him, and I couldn't stop crying. This man built of muscle and steel, this man who I was in love with after five minutes, was dying. What was wrong with life? I felt my anger rise, so I got up and pulled on my clothes, yanking and tugging with fury, still crying.

"Ah Margaux. I'm sorry, this was a mistake, coming here today," he said.

I stopped buttoning my shirt and shouted at him. "This wasn't a mistake. Not for me, anyway. This was one of the best days of my life. I'm just sad, that's all. We haven't even gotten to know each other and now it's over."

"It's not over yet. And, at least we met each other. I'm very glad we did," he offered. "I really wanted to meet you. You are right. This was no mistake. I'm sorry I said that."

I managed to stop crying. "Are you going to tell Lyndon you saw me?"

He shook his head. "No. That's between the two of you."

"If we ever even talk to each other again."

"You will." Jason was confident.

"Oh God." I looked at the time. It was nearly seven p.m. "I have to go."

"Yeah, me too." Jason got out of bed and I watched him dress, admiring the grace of his movements and the beautiful lines of his body. I couldn't believe I wouldn't see him again or that we wouldn't have this moment again.

"Listen," he said, and he took me in his arms. "We will be planning the protest for the next two weeks. But I'll find a way to come to Sydney and be with you for a day, if you'd like that?"

"I would love that," I said, and that made leaving him bearable.

He put me on a ferry to Balmain and I watched him turn and walk away. I wanted to dive off the boat, swim to the shore, and cling to him until the moment he died. But that wasn't possible and I soon lost sight of him. I wondered why life was such a complicated and contradictory thing. I tried to tell myself that was what made it interesting, but all I felt was heartbroken.

34. LYNDON

"YOU ARE SURE it was him? And her?" I was back at the hotel with Jason and Sean, neither of whom offered any information about their post-meeting activities, and I didn't feel that I could ask.

"Yes," I said. "It was both of them. It was."

Neither Sean nor Jason wanted to talk about what I had seen, and I was baffled.

"Maybe he's a private investigator?" I said.

Jason shrugged. "Could be," he said. "Or maybe it wasn't him or Margaux you saw."

"It was," I insisted.

"You were sober?" Jason asked, and I realized that I looked dishevelled.

"Sort of," I replied. "I can recognize my own wife, you know."

"And would she say the same of you? Maybe she's had a makeover too and looks nothing like her former self."

I was stunned by this thought but before I could pursue it, Jason asked me where I had been for the rest of the afternoon.

I turned bright red. "I was at the pub, the Newtown Hotel, and this girl, she was at the meeting, Polly…"

I didn't get any further. They both burst out laughing.

"Cleaned your pipes, didn't she?" Jason said. "Took you back to hers, fed you Viagra from her sweet little tongue, and then she practiced the Kama Sutra with the "Sea of Love" in the background?"

"I see," I said, and I was as deflated as my cock had been after the first time I came.

"Don't feel embarrassed," Sean said. "It makes you truly one of us. It's an honourary rite of passage being with Polly."

"Even you?"

He nodded. "Even me. And then, seconds after the greatest orgasm of your life, she kicks you out."

"Does it ever happen again with her?" I asked hopefully, but they both shook their heads. I sank down into a chair. "Well, it was Margaux that I saw," I insisted.

"Go and have a shower," Jason advised me. "And if you have a change of clothing, I'd opt for that too. You have the distinct odour of a dog having had his day."

"Nice," I replied, but I felt happier. I hadn't realized how lost I felt without him and Sean, and it was no wonder I had fallen for Polly's charms. Although, admittedly, I would fallen for her even if my pals had been right by my side.

"Here's the plan," Jason said, when I emerged from the shower. "We're getting room service and then we've got work to do. Sean's driving to Frenchs Forest and Lyndon, you and I are going to Wollongong. I've rented a car for the night. We're going to time how long it takes for us to get onto the bridge at exactly five a.m. from both those places. It may take a few tries, so we've got a lot of work ahead of us."

35. MARGAUX

IT WAS TEN P.M. Rick, Adam, Graham, Tim, and I were gathered at the gates of the Callan Park. A few dog walkers were still entering the park. I wondered what kind of spell Trish was going to cast and whether we would go unnoticed. I didn't want to get picked up by the police for vandalizing the place.

Nancy Senior had been remarkably quiet, which led me to harbour the hope that she had left, satisfied with having nearly killed her niece. Graham told me that Nancy Junior was doing well in hospital and would be released later that day.

"Maybe crazy Nancy is done with me," I said hopefully to Graham.

"Perhaps. But I doubt it."

"Where's Trish?" Adam was anxious. I hugged him close.

"She'll be here soon. I know this feels a bit weird."

"A bit?" Adam laughed, a shaky sound, and I wondered what I was getting him into.

Trish arrived, pulling a little shopping cart with her. I introduced her to the others. She was dressed entirely in white—even her glasses had white frames.

"Is this dangerous?" Adam asked her.

"Very. Of course, but we'll take every step to make sure we are safe," she said, and we set off down the hill.

Adam looked at me doubtfully. "Very," he mouthed, and I shrugged.

"We have to do it," I whispered to him and he nodded.

Rick offered to pull Trish's cart, and she thanked him but declined.

"So where to now?" Graham asked the question we had all been wondering.

"The Garry Owen House. We need to be in the same room where she first appeared to you." Trish was matter-of-fact. "One of my friends is part of the writers' group here, and so I have a key to get in.

This made sense and so we didn't say anything more. We reached the front doors of the Garry Owen House, grateful that the small parking lot in the front was empty. There were no lights on inside and when Trish unlocked the door, the interior was dark and shadowed. "There's no security," Trish said. "They're awfully trusting, which is good for us."

We filed up the stairs, using the flashlights on our phones.

We got to the room and the first thing Trish did was take out a folded-up sheet of black paper and a roll of duct tape. "Here," she said to Adam and Rick. "Put this on the window. Make sure it's thoroughly sealed. We will be lighting candles and can't have anyone spotting us."

Rick and Adam did as she asked while she unpacked the rest of her bag. There was a solid object wrapped in purple satin, as well as an abalone shell, a smudging wand, incense, an incense burner, charcoal, and a wand that looked like something out of a Harry Potter movie. It all felt a bit ridiculous, and I wanted to smile and make a joke, but I realized the seriousness of the situation.

Trish also placed a number of candles on the floor, along with six water glasses and a carton of eggs. She added a jug of water to the gathered pile and unwrapped a black-handled knife from the purple cloth.

The room was empty apart from a small desk and chair. Trish moved these against the wall and stacked the chair on top of the desk. She took out a large piece of chalk and a length of string. She asked me to stand in the centre of the room and hold the string. Then, using me as her central compass point, she drew a circle around the perimeter of the room with the chalk, her knife in hand. She did this in a clockwise direction and she completed the circle three times. She explained what she was doing as she worked.

She placed candles at the north, south, east, and west ends of the circle and lit them. She then lit the sage, and blessed and cleansed the room.

I was convinced this would have the smoke alarm going off pronto, but she didn't do it for long. Then she poured water into four of the glasses and gently dropped an unbroken egg into each one. She placed these next to the candles. She further blessed the circle with her wand as she scattered a small rain of salt round the perimeter of the circle. She lit a cone of incense and placed it in the centre of the circle, along with the abalone shell. She put an opaque crystal at the north candle, explaining that it signified the earth. Then she put a feather near the west candle to represent air; an additional lit candle at the south, for fire; and a glass of water at the east to represent the strength of the rising sun.

In final preparation, she took the photographs of Nancy that I had taken from Nancy Junior and she put them in the abalone shell. "When the time comes," she said, "you'll need to light these." She placed a box of matches near the shell.

"But how will I know when that is?" I was panic-stricken.

"You just will."

Trish then sprinkled holy water around the circle. She invited us to join her in the circle and she asked me to bring my phone with the pictures of the Virgin Mary as well as the photographs of Nancy.

We stood in the circle, facing east. "Breathe," Trish said. "We will be protected. Relax your bodies. Stay present. Stay calm. We will be safe."

I could not help but recall the last time I was in this room when I was anything but safe. But I closed my eyes and tried to believe in the power of the white magic that Trish was evoking.

"Spirits of Air, I call on you," she said. "Air, beautiful friend, caress us. Spirits of Fire, I call on you, the pure flame of spiritual energy. Spirits of the Earth, I call on you. Spirits of Water, I call on you. Mother Earth, come, protect us. Father Sky, come protect us. Bring your strength and wisdom into this circle. Now, let us be seated."

We sat down, but my knees were not what they used to be. Sitting cross-legged on the floor was too painful. I tucked my legs to one side and hoped that my body would co-operate with the evening's activities. I looked over at Tim, wondering how he was doing, but he seemed serene and relaxed. Clearly, his knees weren't troubling him. I told myself that I needed to get back to doing yoga as soon as the trip was over. My mind was wandering, thinking about what my life would be like after all of this was said and done. Was there a way to resume a normal life? And did I even want that?

"Please let us hold hands," Trish said, and my reverie was interrupted. I grabbed her hand to my left and Graham's to my right.

"True," Trish began to recite, "without falsehood, and most true, that which is above is the same as that which is below, and that which is below is the same as that which is above, for the performance of the miracles of the One Thing. And as all things are from One, by the mediation of One, so all things have their birth from this One Thing by adaptation. The Sun is its Father, the Moon is its Mother, the Wind carries it in its belly, its nurse is the Earth. This is the Father of all perfection or consummation of the whole world. So thou hast the glory of the whole world—therefore, let all obscurity flee before thee. This is the strong force of all forces, overcoming and penetrating every solid thing. So the world was created." She fell silent and let go of my hand.

"Nancy Simms," Trish called out.

I jumped at the sound of her name.

"It is time to set you free. It is time to end your unholy alliance with Margaux. You need to go where you belong. We are here to set you free."

She turned to me. "Delete the pictures off your phone," she said, and I scrambled to do as she said. My hands were shaking as I scrolled and found the images. I selected them and deleted them and the very second I did that, my phone died. It instantly turned black, and at the same time, all the candles in the room were snuffed out. The temperature dropped by twenty degrees. I shivered.

"Welcome, Nancy," Trish said, which I couldn't really support. *Welcome?* My heart had swelled to three times its size and it was blocking the back of my throat.

Trish got up and relit the candles. But as soon as she sat down, they were extinguished, as if with one breath.

I wanted to run away as fast as I could, but I was frozen with terror. I was a block of ice, unable to move or blink.

Trish calmly lit the candles again. She took my phone and placed it next to the abalone shell in the centre of the circle. "Nancy," she said calmly, "I can light those candles as many times as you blow them out. Stop being childish. We simply want to help you."

To my surprise, the candles remained lit, and the room resounded with peals of laughter. It was the pretty, happy, summer-day laugher of a carefree girl except that it was unmistakably chilling and evil. A cold wind blew around the circle, dropping the temperature even further. Our breath was visible as we exhaled, clouds around our faces, and I saw that the others were as cold as I was.

The wind gathered shape and a vortex of fury spiralled and darted around the circle, pausing in front of each of us, as if considering us carefully, and then moving on. It did this twice before stopping in front of Adam. My belly clenched and I gritted my teeth.

The vortex formed the shape of a hand. The long, slender fingers flexed and stretched. It was clearly a woman's hand, elegant and fine, with oval, tapered nails. The hand clenched into a fist and to my horror, the fist pulled back, took careful aim, and drove into Adam's solar plexus, knocking the wind out of him. He fell out of the circle and lay there, curled up, groaning. But the hand didn't let him lie there—it grabbed him by his hair and hauled him back up into a seated position. And then it slapped him across the face, left, right, left, right, leaving ugly red welts. My boy. She was attacking my boy. Attacking me was one thing, but no one was allowed to touch my baby.

The hand grabbed him by the throat and squeezed. I had to save him. Adam's eyes were bulging, and he was turning purple. I grabbed the matches and set the photographs of Nancy alight in the abalone shell. I launched myself across the circle to Adam. The hand was choking him. Rick was also trying to reach him, but he was being held off by a force field as if he were leaning into a wind tunnel, straining to move forward but unable to do anything.

But I was Adam's mother. "Leave him alone," I shouted, and I grabbed the hand. It felt like any woman's hand would, with soft skin. It was silky, cool, and definitely alive.

"You *bitch*," I shouted. "You barren bitch, let *go* of my son! Let go of my child!" I leaned down and bit the hand until it let go of Adam and he fell backwards. Rick was released and he rushed to Adam.

The hand slapped me hard across the face, and I got to my feet.

"Let me see all of you, you coward," I shouted. "Stop playing your stupid tricks and show yourself to me."

And she did. Beautiful Nancy, cool in her starched uniform, her hat jaunty, her eyes wide and innocent. She put her hands on her hips, as if to say, *Now what?*

"And now," I said, shaking with rage, "I condemn you to hell. I condemn you to the live in the excrement you forced upon others. You will not be allowed to wash, and you will be tied up. You will be given drugs and made to think that you have gone insane. You will suffer from paranoia, delusions, and frantic frenzy. You will claw at your own skin to try to escape, but you will be trapped forever. And, you will watch yourself become a deranged filthy beast. You will stand outside of yourself and bear witness to the piece of human garbage that you truly are. Your teeth will fall out, leaving bleeding holes in your mouth. Your skin will wither, and you will lose your hair. And you will watch *all* of it happen. And you will be powerless. You will be like a newborn baby, without the strength of a kitten. I summoned you by the power of my rage, and, by the power of my rage, I banish you. BE GONE!"

And with that, I grabbed Trish's sacred knife, the knife I knew I wasn't supposed to touch, and I buried it deep in that bitch's cold heart. The knife glowed a fiery red and turned black. Nancy opened her mouth to scream, and instead of moths or worms, she spewed maggots, so many that she choked on them. She began to fade, but still, she fumbled for the knife, trying to tug it out of her chest. The knife turned a violent aquamarine blue, seemingly lit from within, and then, the thing that was Nancy shattered like an exploding glass vase, and the fragments and remnants flashed radioactive green before fizzling and disappearing.

The knife fell to the floor with a dull thud.

I whipped back to Adam who was still holding his throat. Rick was hugging him, and I put my arms around both of them.

"My baby," I said, my voice was hoarse. "How dare she. Are you okay? Please tell me you are okay."

"Mom," he managed to say, "you were awesome. Wow!"

This made all of us laugh and the release was beautiful.

"I'm sorry I used your knife," I told Trish. "I'll get you another one."

Wide-eyed, Trish shook her head. "Please, don't give it another thought. I am relieved it worked. You never really know what will work and what won't."

Tim held out his arms. "Group hug," he said. "For me, if no one else. I'm shaking like a leaf. I swear I thought I was going to have a heart attack. I've seen some things in my life but nothing like that."

We all gathered in a hug, and no one said anything for a moment. With our heads bowed and our arms around each other, I knew we were all counting our blessings that we were alive.

I pulled back, exhausted. "I can't wait to have a hot bath," I said. "I feel like I've run a marathon." I, like Tim, was shivering and covered in goosebumps.

"It's shock," Graham said, and she yanked off her cardigan and wrapped it around me. I hugged it close, thanking her.

"Let's get the heck outta here," Rick said, and even his drawl sounded speeded up.

"I know we want to get out of here as soon as possible," Trish said, "but we need to close the circle and cleanse the room. We have to finish this properly."

Tired as we were, we assured her that we understood, although our reluctance to remain in the room was palpable. Trish walked us through the closing circle ceremony, and we packed up the candles, the incense, the abalone shell with the ashes, and the rest of the tools. We all kept glancing around nervously. I think we were all worried that Nancy would find some way to come back and put us through another round of hell.

But everything went smoothly. Rick took down the window covering, and by the time we were ready to leave, there was no evidence of us ever having been there, except for a very faint chalk circle on the carpet and the smell of smoke and incense in the air.

"I'll cleanse everything when I get home," Trish said, "but we still need to break the eggs outside and pour the water on top of them at the four points around Garry Owen House."

We followed her lead, stopping to do as she said. The air

outside was cool and fresh and when we poured the final drop of water on the last egg, I knew the others felt as I did. It was over. We were free. We were finally ready to leave. It was close to three a.m.

"Tell me something," Rick said, and we turned to him. "Do they have all-night diners in Sydney? Because I'm starving!"

"Yeah man!" Adam said, high-fiving Rick.

"I'm starving too," I said, grinning. The hot bath could wait. It was time to celebrate.

"Yep," Graham said, and Tim nodded. "We've got all-night diners all right. And I'm going to take you to the best one I know."

36. LYNDON

WE LEFT SYDNEY and Martha stayed behind with Robby, for which I was grateful. And I was right—the dynamic without her was entirely different. We were close to giddy, like schoolboys planning the biggest party in the world. I hadn't realized how depressing getting old had been, that there had been nothing ground-breaking or new to look forward to, that there was nothing that hadn't been tried. Everything was the same old same old, literally. But this—a world protest against capitalist greed—this was something different! We were going to take the bridge and make a statement, and the whole world would wake up and watch. We felt, in equal parts, as if we were going to war against the establishment as well as putting on the greatest protest show the world had seen in a very long time.

I couldn't say I didn't have my doubts. The anarchists in Newtown had seemed more focused on cinnamon buns than the strategies, and I voiced my concerns to Jason and Sean.

"They were the tip of the iceberg," Jason said with confidence. "There were what, three hundred of them? We're aiming for eight or nine thousand. There will be people coming from all over the world as well as the rest of Australia. The Newtown meeting," he explained, "was a dry run of what I'll post on the site. I wanted to see what kind of questions they'd raise so I could address them in the follow-up post. And the response was great—they asked ecologically sound questions and voiced valid concerns."

"Aren't you worried the website postings will be intercepted?" I asked. "Sean told me you are constantly under surveillance."

Jason nodded. "I am. But I bounce the posts off different IP server addresses and change the script code every time I log in. I've done it for years. I mix my own code with the message interface. This decouples the software from its external interfaces and creates a smoother role by maintaining backward compatibility. It works brilliantly."

I gave him a blank look and he shrugged impatiently. "We don't have time for me to explain the logistics of it all. Just trust me, sunshine."

"The protest's going to be filmed by two guys with drones," Sean cut in. "That's where I was yesterday while Lyndon was experiencing the delights of young Polly. There'll be a livestream on YouTube and Facebook, with Instagram stories and, wait for this," he paused dramatically, "we'll be live on national news and radio. A guy I went to school with is a vice president at ABC, and he guaranteed it."

"Great work," Jason said, and I felt annoyed. If he had asked me to do something important, I would have, but instead they all just left me and attended to their own heroics. I felt like a child who had been left to play in the sandbox while the adults talked. I leaned back in my seat and sulked.

"I got the call from our engineering genius and our banner is a good size. We'll need a core team tending to that because it's going to be as heavy as a small car. I'll post for volunteers with a specific skillset. They'll need to do a few practice runs in a field. The banner's going to be bloody huge! That lot will need to be the first on the bridge."

"They had a Breakfast on the Bridge in 2009," Sean said, "and six thousand people pretty much filled the space, but they were sitting down in the middle of the lanes."

"Good point," Jason replied. "Not everybody's going to be able to fit at the railing. The more climbers, the better. I'll let people know and I'll tell them to bring harnesses to attach to the bridge. Mark gave me some tips to post. The safer, the better. And you, Lyndon, have got one of the most important jobs of all."

He turned around to face me in the back seat. I looked at him with some surprise. I'd given up having a role to play. So far, I had been as useless as a wet noodle while Sean and the engineering genius had been sparkling heroes. I had convinced myself there was hardly any point to my even being there.

"What do you mean?" I sounded truculent, like a kid who knew he was being duped into thinking he had a role when his real chore was sweep the stage before the show started.

"We need you to write a speech. The most kick-arse speech the world has ever heard. About capitalism, greed, anarchy, global warming—all of it. It needs to be like Martin Luther King, Jr.'s "I Have a Dream" speech, only don't copy him— come up with something original. While our banner is the perfect and eloquent "Stop Shitting On Our World," we want a more elegant and memorable manifesto. Something beautiful and historic."

"Sure," I said trying to sound casual, my heart pounding. "But you do remember that I'm an editor, not a copywriter?"

"I do. But you've had an intimate, up-the-arse experience of living that life. You have the knowledge of how big business is screwing us over, and you know what it's like to no longer be welcome in that club—the club of the chosen brotherhood of big swinging dicks. I want your anger to shine through. I want to feel your pain and loss—how the system failed not only the world, but the individual. There's no job security or sense of identity or community. We are rudderless, blown by the winds of greed, with capitalistic, corporate hands grabbing at the ship's wheel and hanging on for dear life. Lifeboats are things of the past. People are just chucked overboard into the shark-infested waters without a hope in hell of maintaining their integrity. Good men are compromised because they'll do whatever it takes to put food into the yawning squawking beaks of the starving chicks in their nest."

"You should write it," I objected. "What you just said is great."

"Then write it down and work it into your speech," Jason grinned. He handed me a pad of hotel stationery and a pen, and I scribbled furiously.

"It can't be longer than five minutes," Jason added. "Powerful and to the point. Use short sentences too ... packs more of punch.

"I really don't know why don't write it yourself," I muttered. "You wrote a whole book, remember? I've got no idea why you need me."

"I just do, so please oblige me and stop arguing," Jason said, and his voice brokered no room for objection.

I wondered if I could just paraphrase a few things from Jason's book, like the title for instance. *The Occult Persuasion and the Anarchist's Solution.* But most people associated the occult with ghosts and the paranormal, not with capitalism and global warming. I frowned and chewed on the pen, oblivious to the rest of the conversation in the front seat. Maybe I could pick up something from Shevek's protest speech in *The Dispossessed,* but all the anarchists would know it, and I'd be shamed for the rest of my life. But the rest of the world wouldn't, and wasn't that more important?

"And you must carry on practicing your tattooing," Jason said, breaking into my thoughts. "A tattoo a day, on me. I want you to be a real tattooist by the time I'm six feet under or dust carried away on a sea breeze. Do two a day even. I want you to work off a complex variety of stencils that I'll pick. I'm serious about this."

"That would be great." I beamed from ear to ear as my bad mood evaporated.

I had thought that the tatooing would be pushed aside, given the magnitude of what was coming up, and I had been disappointed, but one hardly wanted to whine about something so trivial in the face of a world-changing event. And by this point, I really believed that our protest could change the world. We just had to pull it off perfectly.

37. MARGAUX

JASON WAS COMING to town and my heart was filled with joy! He was flying in to save himself the drive. I booked us a room at the Marriott with a view of the harbour, the Opera House, and the bridge. I was in the room, waiting for him to arrive. I wanted to jump up and down with excitement but that would make me feel ridiculous. Besides, I might tear a ligament or something. Imagine the embarrassment, not to mention the inconvenience, as I was looking forward to more rigorous sex with the gorgeous man.

I tried to sit still but I couldn't, so I paced around the room. I had even brought new underwear.

When he finally knocked at the door, I was exhausted from overthinking and worrying, but we fell onto each other with glorious passion, discarding clothes willy-nilly onto the floor.

"Do you like the view?" I asked, sweeping my hand towards the window, and he laughed and raised himself up on one elbow.

"In case you didn't notice," he replied, "I've been a bit preoccupied since I arrived." He got up and looked out the window. "This is fantastic. I'm going to take a bunch of pictures and they'll help with the final calculations."

"That's what I thought," I said, over the moon to have the done the right thing. "Can I help in any way?"

"You can come up with a catchphrase. I asked Lyndon to write a speech and not to say he's botching it up, but he's not exactly setting the world on fire."

"That's because I used to write his speeches," I said. "I'll write one for you too. Shall we order room service? I'm starving."

"Look at her! Not just stunningly beautiful, but brilliant to boot! Yes, I'm famished. But back to the slogan. I want something that encapsulates how capitalism is killing the world. I also want something to make people to *think*, goddammit, *think*."

"Okay. And to eat? Or do you simply require a speech for sustenance?" I loved joking with him, and he grabbed me and lightly spanked my bottom. I told myself not to think about the fact that he was dying.

"What did you tell Adam you were up to, tonight?" Jason asked.

"I said I was staying over at Graham's. She'll cover for me. She thinks it's very funny that I can't tell my son that I'm engaging in a sexual rendezvous with the man who rescued my husband who ran away from me. I see her point. I still haven't told Adam that I know where Lyndon is. I just can't go into it because it would open up a huge can of worms. He's still a bit fragile after the Nancy attack even though he's trying to pretend he's fine."

"Having a demon sucker-punch you in the gut, bitch-slap you left right and centre, and try to strangle you to death, would affect any man," Jason mused.

"I told him about Helen's pregnancy though she asked me not to. I was trying to distract him and cheer him up. He and Rick are looking to do all kinds of worrisome adventures like skydiving, deep-sea diving, and motorcross. It's Rick's bucket list, and if he's not careful, it will end up being Adam's death list. Adam's not what you'd call a natural at sports. Helen was much more talented. She's a brilliant tennis player and a great golfer while poor Adam is a muddle of limbs on any playing field." I paused. "Have you told Lyndon that Helen's pregnant?"

"No. He doesn't ask me about the family, and I don't volunteer."

A flash of hurt whipped through my heart and Jason saw

it. "I'm sorry," he said. "That was bollocks of me. If you ask me, he still loves you all very much. He's just traumatized by his life, by getting older, and by losing his job. He's not seeing straight. He found a cave of refuge with us and crawled inside. But once the protest's over, he'll have to move on with his life."

"Why? Can't he just stay with you and the tattoo people?"

"I'm on my way out and I'm not sure he'd want to stay after I'm gone," Jason replied. "But hey, come here you. My nether regions are stirring, brought about by the vision of your entirely magnificent breasts. We've got urgent matters to attend to."

For a dying man, Jason had a lot of stamina.

"A catchphrase," I muttered out loud as we lay back, staring at the ceiling.

"Oy, no thinking about the job now," Jason said, and took me in his arms.

"It's tricky," I told him, my face against his chest, which had exactly the right amount of hair. "I mean, you want something short and punchy. But fine. I won't work on it now. You're right, now's not the time."

"What're you going to do with your life once this is all over?" Jason asked idly.

"I'm going to run for government," I said, and he sat up in horror.

"Think about it," I said. "What's the point of flailing and protesting if you can't actually make a difference? I'm not saying protesting doesn't make a difference, it does. But if I were in power, even in local politics, I could do some good. Some real good. It's actually something I've wanted to do for some time. I did a lot of envelope-licking and cold-calling for our MP, and I think I would stand a good chance. I'd start very small, with our riding, and see how it goes."

He lay back. "Dear God. Here I am, in bed with the government."

"The future government," I reminded him. "It may not work out."

"If you want it to, then it will. You're a woman of sheer determination and titanium will. You are the banisher of demons to the hellfire caverns of eternal excrement. You can do anything."

"When you put it like that, yes, I can." I traced the hair on his belly down to his balls. "I can't bear to think that I won't be with you again. I'm sorry, I know I'm not supposed to get maudlin, but this, being with you, is so fantastically wonderful. It's like I've met my true love and soon you will be gone and all I'll have are memories. Nothing tangible."

Jason stroked my hair and kissed my head. "If you like," he said, "we can go and visit a mate of mine who has a tat shop. He'll lend me a machine. I could do a tattoo on you. That's tangible."

I jumped up in delight and started pulling my clothes on. "Yes! Let's go now."

He grinned at me. "Do you know what you want have done?"

"Not a clue. I'll think about it while we go." And, sitting in the cab, heading to Newtown, I knew what I wanted. "I want you to choose," I said. "You decide. It will be your message to me. I won't even look while you are doing it. I would like it on the top of my left foot. So, when I lie in the bath, I can look at it and think of you."

"That's a lot of responsibility. Okay then. But can't I tell you first? They're permanent things, you know. Well, you can get them removed, but at great cost and a lot of pain."

"I'm sure. I don't want to know. I just thought of something else. What if the catchphrase is "Be Your Revolution!" taken from *The Dispossessed*?" I too had read the book, as soon as Jason recommended it. When I snapped the book shut, I had fleetingly wondered what Lyndon had made of it all. At one point in our lives, it would have made for a great discussion, along with a few bottles of wine, and a grand finale of explosive sex.

I had always been a huge fan of science fiction and I couldn't believe I hadn't read this classic. In a way, Shevek's relationship with his partner, Takver, reminded me of Lyndon's and mine. We had wanted to be each other's support system in our journey through life. I wondered if Lyndon's vanishing, was, in a sense, like the years of separation that Shevek and Takver had suffered. They eventually reunited, and I wondered if the same thing was in store for us. But since Lyndon was the very last thing I wanted to be thinking about at this precious moment, I pushed the thought away.

"I know the book said 'be the revolution.' So, how about 'Be Your Revolution!' With an exclamation point, to get people excited!"

"'Be Your Revolution!' I love it!" Jason said. "Will you write about how the revolution needs to start with each of us individually? That's anarchy in a nutshell. Start with yourself, develop a sense of community and responsibility, and go local. It doesn't need to be bigger than that and it certainly doesn't have to be violent. We need to make sure that people understand that anarchy doesn't mean violence. Anarchy isn't one person saying, 'I don't give a dog's bollocks about the rest of you and I'll do whatever I want, no matter what it takes.' That's bullying and domination and oppression, which is the antithesis of anarchy. We want to tell people to focus on community, think about social justice. Anarchy can start with an action as small as having a community garden. Many people out there are unconscious anarchists, working for the good of man and woman."

I scrabbled in my purse for a scrap of paper and tried to remember what he'd said.

"It's like Gandhi's saying, 'Be the change you want to see in the world.'"

"He never actually said that you know," Jason continued. "He said, 'We but mirror the world. All the tendencies present in the outer world are to be found in the world of our body. If we could change ourselves, the tendencies in the world would also change. As a man changes his own nature, so does the attitude of the world change towards him. This is the divine mystery supreme.' I forget the rest of it, but it's something about what a wonderful thing this is, and it's the source of our happiness."

We arrived at the tattoo shop, and I scribbled as much as I could while Jason paid the driver.

The owner of the tat shop welcomed Jason like a long-lost brother, and said he'll get him sorted with a machine, no problem.

"I wish you'd give me a clue as to what you want." Jason's face was puckered like a Shar-Pei's.

I gave him a kiss. "I just want something of you to carry with me for the rest of my days until I can meet you on the other side. It will be your hand on me, touching me."

I could see he was anxious, but I didn't care. I just needed visible proof that he was here with me now, that this was real.

I sat back in the chair and Jason began to prep my foot.

"I'm worried I will be a coward," I said, and Jason grinned at me.

"Demon slayer," he reminded me, and I nodded, unconvinced.

And it did hurt. A lot. And it took a lot longer than I thought it would. And, true to my word, I did not look. And when he was finished, he straightened up and looked at me.

"There you go then," he said. I raised my leg up and brought my foot up onto the chair.

True Love. Written in a beautifully expansive, swirly script. I sobbed. "I love it and I love you," I cried. I was a mess. I threw myself into Jason's arms. The shop was full and people looked at me briefly, then shrugged and went back to their own lives.

Jason's demeanour had shifted from Shar-Pei to Cheshire Cat. "Glad you like it. Now, let's go back and enjoy more of our luxury accommodation while we can. "*Let's spend the night together.... Now I need you more than ever...,*" he sang loudly and tunelessly, and it was utterly marvellous.

38. LYNDON

N O ONE COULD SAY we didn't prep the event to death. Every single detail was taken care of. We knew how many drivers would be coming from the north and south ends of the bridge. A guy who owned a porta-potty business said he'd provide twenty units to be placed at intervals on the bridge. We arranged for his truck to be the first to enter, followed by a van with bottled water and the banner guys. We had an ambulance on loan from a high-end retirement village, offered by a physician who wanted to contribute. Another van was stacked with energy bars and snacks. The protestors were instructed to take their garbage with them and not drop empty wrappers and bottles on the bridge. Jason was adamant. Not one piece of rubbish was to be left on the bridge—zero littering.

We went to Costco and filled four U-Hauls with toilet paper. No one asked why we needed that much, so we didn't offer an explanation. We spent hours ripping them out of their plastic wrappings and restacking them.

Jason had sent out detailed instructions of how the T-shirts should look. He was insistent that we needed to look united. We were an army, not a ragged bunch of losers. That was how he put it.

And he kept sending reminders about the silence. There had to be silence. Apart from the siren calls, there would be no noise from us. He warned people that the helicopters would be deafening and that, most likely, there would be police. The police and traffic officers would be screaming at us to disband and all of that needed to be taken in stride. There would be barking dogs and, if crowds gathered, which he hoped they would, they'd be making a lot of noise too. And he kept re-iterating that no matter what happened, there was to be no running and no screaming. He said, bluntly, that if people thought they might be runners and screamers, that they should please stay at home rather than ruin the whole thing. He said it was vitally important that people walk calmly. They could walk quickly, but there was to be no running. He wanted us to look calm, in control, assured.

"Silence is more powerful than chatter," he wrote. "The world is littered with chatter, on social media, in the workplace, on television. Let us go about our protest with the strongest message of pure silence. No matter what happens. If they tear-gas us, we will stand in silence. If they fire rubber bullets upon us, let us be silent. If they arrest us, let us be silent. From the moment you get up in the morning, shut it, zip it, and don't open it until you are back home and the day is done. We will move through the day with precision and purpose."

His approach was clear: he wanted us to be zen warriors.

"We are not panic-ridden nutcases," he wrote in his newsletter. "If we want to change the future and be a part of the future, we need people to see that we are trustworthy, not chaotic. Do NOT break anything, do not steal anything, and for God's sake, do NOT mark or tag the bridge. The bridge remains untouched. NO CANS OF SPRAY PAINT ARE ALLOWED. This is vital. We do not harm, mark, or tag the bridge. Respect the code."

He was worried that the pack mentality would spark off anarchy in the most expected form of the word, and he tried his best, in the two weeks preceding the event, to re-educate his followers and keep their focus on the message.

"There is beauty in symmetry," he wrote. "Think about murmurations, about how groups of starlings swoop and swirl at exactly the same time. If they were all whirling about in different directions, would that send the same message? No, it would not. Think about the *corps de ballet*, how they are often more breathtakingly powerful than the soloists because they are so precisely united. We must move together as one.

"Our protest is artwork and each of us is a piece of that art. It won't be easy. We don't have the time or opportunity to practice. There can be no rehearsal—only the real thing."

I told him, as I was working on my second tattoo that day, that perhaps he was overestimating the intelligence of his audience. He sat up quickly, nearly causing my machine to slip and ruin the butterfly I was working on. Jason said butterflies were one of the most popular tattoos requested, so he wanted me to have them down pat. By the time he died, his body would be a butterfly arboretum. I had already done more than a dozen on him: on the top of his hand, on his neck, a few on his arms and legs, torso and back.

Jason had explained that there was a big difference between tattooing older skin as opposed to younger skin and what he said was fascinating as well as depressing. "As we age, we lose fat, our skin gets thinner and we heal less easily. The ink doesn't work as well because the skin has lost elasticity." Jason had also told me to accept and learn about these limitations, to find my way around them, instead of avoiding them or pretending they didn't exist.

"There's a huge market in old people wanting tats," he'd said. "Get it right and you'll be set for life."

"Until they all die," I had joked, which was pretty rude of me considering his condition.

"I think you can rely on there being an endless supply of aging people," he replied. "We spend much more time being old than we do being young."

I hadn't given much thought to the actual people I'd be tattooing. I had only focused on the art. And when he started telling me about aged skin, I was turned off, revolted. I had silently vowed that I would only tattoo beautiful young flesh. Jason had understood this and was trying to change my perceptions. I, in turn, tried to learn, so I paid attention to his skin texture and the interaction between it, the needle, the ink, and my art.

"You can tat me too, try some different skin," Sean had kindly offered. "But not a butterfly, okay? Do a rose. People love roses."

Becoming a tattooist had made me face the fact that there was no going back from aging. As stupid as it sounded, I'd kept waiting for my lines and wrinkles, as well as the other various symptoms of aging, to reverse or at the very least, politely stop. I had felt like my body had betrayed me by getting old and I was angry. I had felt a sense of alienation from my younger self, who'd abandoned me, like a fickle friend. Working with Jason and his dying body was bringing me, I hoped, some kind of self-acceptance. Although, honestly, I was still waiting for that self-acceptance to take effect.

When I said that, about him overestimating the intelligence of his followers, he shot up in the chair. I dabbed the butterfly and assessed the damage, which was minimal.

"I need my laptop now," he said. Sean handed it to him and he started pounding away. I had to stop working since he was jiggling all over the place.

"Do not underestimate your own intelligence," he read aloud to us when he finished typing. "The politicians and the corporations want you to feel stupid. When you feel stupid, you look to them for guidance and don't question them. You are not stupid! You never were stupid. But you have been made to feel that way. You have been made to fear your own thoughts, your own instincts, and your desires. You need to get in touch with the power of your own decision-making. Perhaps some of you have never been in touch with your own decision-making, as it has come to you from your schools, from your parents, your religions, your leaders, and the culture of your country. I want you to say two things to yourself every day. The first is this: *I am an intelligent human who can and will think for himself.* The second is this: *I am making this decision.* No one but me. And do that at least once a day. Even with the smallest thing. Why am I eating this sandwich on this bread? Think about the bread, the ham, the butter. Think about the chain of events that brought the sandwich to you. And then, if there are things about it that you do not agree with, think about how you can change them. Boycott companies whose ethics you do not agree with. Spread awareness. Think for yourself."

"People will be upset you wrote, 'himself,'" I pointed out. "It should be himself or herself or themself."

Jason looked at me and nodded. "You're right, good point."

"I think people will be alarmed by having to think for themselves," I added. "Most of them have never done it because it is too much work. It's far easier being told what to do and the general population wants what is easier. Added to which, the capitalistic regime instills in them the fear that any thoughts they have of their own, will be wrong, and they'll be forced to face the worst consequence, that of alienation and poverty. They will be social pariahs. Fear fuels the success of capitalism, and fear is one of the hardest things to eradicate."

"My God, you're depressing me today," Jason said. "Try seeing the happy side, why don't you?"

"I am being realistic," I replied. "People view thinking in the same way they view exercising or eating correctly. It's much more fun to binge-watch TV, eat crap, go out and spend money, and not think about what you're buying or why. Accumulating stuff makes people feel good. Stuff is who and what we are. It's like the core matter, the fibre of our being. Our sense of self is tied up in our stuff. I have stuff, therefore I am. I think you expect too much of humankind."

"You're making me glad I'm dying," Jason told me, and he sent the message to his followers and slammed his laptop shut.

"There have always been those kinds of people," Sean piped up. "The ones who don't want to do anything. But not everyone's like that. And we aren't trying to change the whole world in one day with one action. We're trying to encourage intelligent thinking, and that is possible. We're trying to nudge the beast, tell him, or her or it or whatever, that we're still here. We're trying to tell each other that a wink can lead a nudge to a shag and then, things can be different. We don't need to focus on the bigger picture. We've got no way of knowing what the end result of our actions will be and, actually, the outcome is irrelevant. *'Society was conceived as a permanent revolution, and revolution begins in the thinking mind.'*"

"Very philosophical," I said, with no small measure of sarcasm.

"And not very practical," Sean said with a grin. "And we all know you want practical. But before practice comes theory, so stop depressing Jason with your horrible need for locked-down solutions and systems and finish his butterfly. And I've decided I want a nasturtium on my ankle, just a little orange one, thank you very much, mate."

I bent down and tried to focus on Jason's butterfly. Did theory come before practice when it came to human action? And if the answer was yes, then how could we change politics, businesses, schools, and parenting? It was all too big and, if you asked me, it was a losing battle. But did that mean we shouldn't fight at all? I was exhausted.

And I was getting nowhere with my speech that would change the world. Jason had been right. I was tempted to riff off Martin Luther King, Jr.'s "Now is the time ..." and all that. It was excruciatingly tough, trying to be original. Plus, speech writing had never been one of my strengths. I didn't want to tell Jason, but Margaux wrote all my speeches, even back in my debating days. And she prepped and primed me.

"Jason," I said, reluctantly broaching the unavoidable topic, "you know my speech, the slogan, our mantra, the manifesto...."

"Ah right. I forgot to mention that I had a thought for it," he interrupted me.

I was taken aback. "Yeah?"

"'Be Your Revolution!' What do you think?"

The weight of the world flew off my shoulders. "I love it," I said. "Brilliant. You see, I knew you'd know better than anyone what the message should be. And have you thought about the rest of the speech or do you want me to still write that?" *Please dear God, say you don't want me to do it.*

"I have thought about it, yes," Jason said. "Don't worry, it's done. But you'll have to wait and hear it on the day. I don't want to spoil the surprise."

"I have every faith, mate," Sean chimed in, "that it will be astute and pithy, as only you can be."

"Pithy?" Jason teased him, while I was delirious with relief that I didn't have to write the speech. Flooded by a sense of well-being, the darkness of the future faded from my mind, and for a moment, life was a beautiful thing.

39. MARGAUX

THE BIG DAY APPROACHED. I needed to do two things. The first was get my cards read by Janet, and the second was to loop Adam and Rick in about the protest. I had to remember that they didn't know anything about Jason or that Tim had found Lyndon. I refused to ask Jason about Lyndon, but Tim had brought me up to speed on my estranged husband. From the sounds of it, he was getting along very well without me. He had a whole new look, a shaved head, designer facial stubble, Johnny Cash clothing, and a new career lined up as a tattoo artist.

I was careful to keep my fury at bay when I thought about him—the last thing I needed was another Nancy to come trotting though the open portal of my rage. But in truth, I wasn't angry with Lyndon anymore. I was sad.

Why couldn't we have done all of this together? But realistically, how open would I have been to him shaving his head and growing a designer goatee? While I could imagine it would suit him, in all likelihood, I would have strenuously objected. And wearing all black? I would have mocked him, told him he was having a post mid-life crisis, since mid-life was long gone, and could he please do it less visibly? And a tattoo artist? I wouldn't have given that any credence whatsoever.

I realized that I had been unconsciously restrictive when it came to Lyndon. I had rules of who I needed him to be and what I wanted him to look like. As Trish would say, I needed to widen my sphere of availability when it came to thinking about my husband and who he really was and who he wanted to be. Not that I was sure he was still my husband, at all.

But I couldn't tell Adam any of this. I would just say that I had received word from the leader of the anarchists and that Adam would have to trust me. And I knew he wouldn't be happy about that. Adam, much like me, liked full disclosure. He needed all the facts before he could start processing how he felt or what he thought. So, this would be a good lesson for him.

Practicing new learning experiences while he was still young would help him when he got to Lyndon's and my age. And hopefully his life wouldn't derail as spectacularly as ours had.

I had told Trish and Graham about the protest and they were delighted. They swore they would both be in on the action and that they'd recruit as many people as possible.

I needed to stake out a good viewing point, and my plan was to enlist Rick and Adam into filming the whole thing. I figured if we took up our positions at the railing at the Opera House promenade, right on the edge of the harbour, we'd have a good view. I needed to have Jason in my sight at all times.

He and I emailed and texted and talked daily. My heart broke every time we hung up. I wasn't not sure how I would cope when we had to say our final goodbyes.

This was why I needed Janet to read my cards and he generously obliged. He and Tim knew about the protest and were coming to support it in full drag, along with me and Rick and Adam. At least I hoped Rick and Adam would come.

I decided to tell Adam and Rick what was going on, while I waited for Janet to arrive.

"Mom!" Adam said, meeting me in the kitchen lounge and instantly zoning in on my foot, "you got a tat, wow. *True Love*? Okay. Maybe I should add a tat to my bucket list too."

I was tempted to tell him that his father would be able to do it for him, but I resisted. One thing at a time.

"Here's the thing," I said. "I've got something to tell both of you, but I don't have all the information. You're going to want to know things that I don't have the answers to. In a nutshell, the day after tomorrow, at dawn, your father is going to be part of a massive anarchist protest against capitalism. He's helping set up the protest, the aim of which is to cover the Sydney Harbour Bridge with toilet paper, along with the message 'Stop Shitting On Our World.' The theme of the protest is 'Be Your Revolution!' and it's going to be huge, from what we currently know."

Adam and Rick were speechless. I nodded. "I know, it's a lot to take in."

"It's going to be brilliant!" Tim said, walking into the kitchen. I thanked God for his arrival.

"Tim," I pleaded. "Can you explain the whole thing more clearly?"

And he did.

"But..." Adam opened his line of questioning as I settled back on the sofa. The interrogation had begun. An hour later, I was exhausted. I'd had enough.

"Adam, you now know everything I do, okay? It's up to you. Join us or don't. We're going to get there really early to take up position. I was hoping you that two would film the whole thing."

"Of course we will," Rick drawled. He grabbed Adam's hand. "You can count on us, Margaux. I bought a new camera for the trip, and I'd better figure out how to use it." He got up and pulled Adam to his feet. "Come on, A-man," he said. "Let's go and grapple with technology."

"You've known about this for weeks," Adam said to me accusingly. "That's why we all had to stick around Sydney after the Nancy thing. I wondered why we couldn't leave."

"And go where?" I asked. "I wasn't aware you wanted to go anywhere else. You could have said."

"I was waiting for you to say," he countered. "But then you

didn't and now I know why."

"Moving on," Rick was firm. "Come on, Adam. Give your mother a break."

I expected Adam to look sulky, but he smiled at Rick. "I'm being a needy, whiny kid, aren't I?"

"A bit, but I love you anyway," I heard Rick say as he led Adam away.

"I love that boy," I told Tim.

"Adam?"

"No. Rick." We both laughed. "And Adam," I added.

Tim looked at his phone. "Janet is sorry. He's running a bit late."

"No hurry. I'm happy to sit here for a moment and do nothing."

"*True Love*?" Tim asked, and my eyes welled up with tears.

"Too late," I replied.

He patted my shoulder. "I'll get you a latte. Can't cure a sad heart, but I can warm your belly."

"I love you too," I shouted after him, and I heard him laugh.

Janet arrived, flustered. "I hate being late," he said, and I told him it was quite okay. Tim reassured him by telling him how Adam had questioned me and we got a good laugh out of it.

"He'd have a good career as an interrogator," Tim said, while Janet got the cards ready. I slid off the sofa and we both sat on the floor. Janet noticed my look of apprehension.

"Relax," Janet said. "It will be fine. Remember, the cards are just guides to help your soul find clarity. They're not telling you what your future will be. I like your tat by the way."

I thanked him and started picking out the cards. I felt so responsible for my own future and then I realized that unless I could do this without worry and fear, I shouldn't do it at all.

"Wait, I feel like I contaminated my selection," I said. "Please, can I do it again?"

Janet obligingly reshuffled the deck.

He looked up at me. "This, my darling, is a spectacularly good reading."

"But how can it be good," I asked, and tears rolled down my cheeks and my chest started heaving, "when I am going to lose Jason?" Both he and Tim knew the whole story.

"Margaux, the man was dying before you met him," Tim said. "Your meeting him—and Lyndon's meeting him—was a gift to both of you. I know it's hard, but you can be grateful for that. You'll have true love for the rest of your life, albeit on your foot." He casts a meaningful glance at Janet. "Look at this young buck. I adore him, but soon he will realize he should be with another young buck and not with a wrinkled old dick like me."

"Not true!" Janet protested and jumped to his feet. "I love your wrinkled old dick."

"Settle down, young buck," I told Janet. "Let's get these cards read. Hmm. Homecoming. Does that mean I will reconcile with Lyndon?"

"Were you ever unreconciled?" Tim asked.

"Well, let's see. He ditched me at a ferry stop and disappeared into the night. Since then, the only communication I have had from him is one email that was actually from Jason."

"Classic mid-life crisis," Tim said. "And look at the opportunities it afforded you. You met us, were possessed by a demon, had a surprise visit from your son, banished the demon, fell in love, got a tattoo, and soon, you will be part of a revolutionary protest hosted by a bunch of anarchists who are flying in from all around the world. Quite the adventure, if you ask me. None of which would have happened if you and Lyndon had wandered obliviously around the world, with him in denial and you filling your purse with meaningless souvenirs and trinkets."

"I wouldn't call them meaningless," I protested. "But I get what you are saying. But how does one do that? Genuinely appreciate the good and not focus on the bad?"

"You keep working at it," Tim said. "Persistence wins the day."

"Not sure I agree, but I'll try. For example, young buck here..."

"Please stop calling me that!"

"Okay. Dammit Janet said I have a good deck of cards. Let's focus on that."

Janet looked pleased. "Moving on," he said. "The Four of Wands. Here is the message I'm hearing: I surround myself with the love and support of those around me, knowing that whatever I call home is a source of stability."

"I wish I was taking notes," I said, worried.

"Your soul will remember what messages you need to take with you," Janet said, and he closed his eyes. "Ten of Wands: Only you can decide when you have overcommitted. You must honour your strengths and know when it is time to lighten your load. Ten of Cups: You are ready to live in a way that is fully aligned with your heart's intentions. Three of Cups: Your relationships are a source of abundance. The more you put into them, the more you get back. The Knight of Wands: You trust in the energy available to you now and you move towards your goals with unwavering confidence. Ten of Pentacles: You are getting clearer on what you value most in your life. You work hard and trust that your efforts are paying off. And, The Chariot: You are called upon to create your own path and you will gain confidence in each step you take." He stopped and opened his eyes.

I groaned.

"What's wrong now?" Tim wanted to know. He was looking at his phone.

"I won't remember any of that. And I want to, it was so beautiful. Janet, how do you do that?"

He shrugged. "I just do."

"I recorded him and sent it to your phone," Tim told me. "Check your inbox and stop fretting."

I was as delighted as a kid at Christmas. "Thank you, Tim."

I got up and gave him a hug.

"Are you coming to Dames tonight?" he asked.

"Of course." I sighed. "But I do feel like all I'm doing is waiting for the day after tomorrow."

40. LYNDON

GAME DAY ARRIVED. May 10th: Sid Vicious's birthday. Long live Sid. We were in Wollongong with half of the U-Hauls, while the others, with the porta potties, bottled water, and snacks van were on the other side of the city in Frenchs Forest.

It was three-thirty a.m., and we were all ready. It was time to start rolling slowly towards the city, moving in the darkness. Everyone was jumpy, no one knew what to expect. None of us wanted to fall flat on our faces. We wanted this go off the way we'd planned: the T-shirts, the silence, the toilet paper. We'd even practiced unfurling toilet rolls off the roof of Jason's building, and some had worked better than others.

After our sessions, Jason had issued instructions on how to unfurl the perfect bog roll. "In order to unfurl the roll neatly, you start by making sure that the first sheet is free and loose. Then, with the roll on top, facing away from you, and the sheet at the bottom, curving towards you, you throw the roll away from you. Imagine it's a streamer at a kid's party. The unfurling does not have the same effect if the sheet is on top and the roll faces you. The roll must face away from you for a smooth and fluid movement. Then it flies out like the kid's party streamer. You wouldn't unfurl a streamer towards yourself, right? It's the same with the toilet roll. Practise with one at home."

We had also driven a few hours north and rehearsed the megaphone siren call, measuring the distance that the sound carried on both still and windy days. We had tried to think of everything. By five a.m. the trucks were in position, and the bridge was full of cars. People were moving silently about. The porta-potties were in place, the vans were open for business, and people were gliding around, finding a place to settle.

Jason had two other signs made: "PEACEFUL PROTEST IN PROGRESS UNTIL 7.30 A.M." and "WE WILL NOT MOVE UNTIL 7:30 A.M. SILENT PROTEST IN ACTION." Both of these were fixed at each end of the bridge.

He had a stack of printouts with this message, along with an explanation of what we were doing and when the protest would end. As soon as traffic enforcement got word that cars were stopped on the bridge, they arrived *en masse*. Jason and a bunch of volunteers handed out the explanation leaflets, but the officers were confused and upset and shouted at us to leave. They flicked on the blue-and-red flashing lights and both ends of the bridge lit up like a carnival. The sounds of the officers' anger carried across the bridge from the north and south sides.

This, in turn, attracted a crowd down at the Rocks and over at Kirribilli and before long, the slopes to the North Shore were filled to the maximum with spectators, despite the earliness of the hour. Sean told me afterwards that more people watched than the number who came out for the New Year's Eve bridge fireworks. So the crowd was over a million.

Mark had opened the gates to the bridge climb, and people scampered up the arch. It looked fairly easy and I wondered if I could have given it a go, but my place was next to Jason.

The police were next to arrive, adding to the noise and mayhem. There were dogs barking at full volume, just as Jason had anticipated. The ABC News helicopter arrived, accompanied by three other helicopters, and I was glad Jason had insisted we all remain silent and contained or it would have been overwhelming.

But, to my horror, in spite of my being Jason's second-in-command, and despite of all the preparations and safety measures, I couldn't do my part. I was hit by a panic attack. I was having a complete meltdown. My heart ricocheted like a boxer's speed bag on overdrive, and I couldn't breathe. The world was spinning and I was dizzy. Everything was warped, and my vision came and went like a melting mirage. I was going to let Jason down. I was one of his right-hand men, and I was going to fail him. But it wasn't my fault. He had asked too much of me. I knew what he had planned, and I couldn't face what was going to happen. He had persuaded me that it was what had to happen, but I couldn't face it in reality.

Sweat poured down my scalp, drenching my back and my belly. I closed my eyes, and was about to humiliate myself by falling to the ground and weeping like a baby. Then I felt a hand on my shoulder, a reassuring hand on my soaking wet shoulder. I opened my eyes and there was the frizzy-haired lady, the one who couldn't afford toilet paper, and she was rubbing my back and pointing from my eyes to hers, that I was to look at her and then she mimed breathing, motioning her hand from her belly to her mouth. She pulled something out of her pocket—ear plugs! I jammed them into my ears, and the world immediately slowed down as the picture righted itself. Thank God. The camera lens of my mind found its focus. She handed me a bottle of water, which I glugged half of in one go. And then, I was back to being me.

I mimed, "thank you, thank you," with a Buddhist bow, my hands in prayer. She had saved me. She nodded and grinned, flashing her splayed yellow teeth and then disappeared into the crowd.

I finished the water, crushed the bottle, and put it into my backpack. I had been saved by ear plugs and the frizzy-haired lady, about whom I had harboured only the most ungracious of thoughts.

I looked at my watch. It was 6:25. I was late. I pushed my way to the centre of the bridge, reminding myself that I wasn't allowed to run. I arrived seconds before the scheduled start. Jason gave me a filthy look, as if to say, "Where have you been?" He had no idea how relieved I was that I'd made it at all.

At 6:36, Jason sounded the siren, and the big banner unfurled.

It did not catch and it did not fumble, it rolled out in a perfectly fluid motion. I know, because I watched it later on television. It was perfect. And the sign could be read from miles away—STOP SHITTING ON OUR WORLD, with an anarchy sign on each end.

We let that message soak in for a while. I looked around. At least eight thousand people had swarmed the bridge like a river of black ants, and some of them had climbed to places I hadn't even imagined possible.

Sirens flashed and helicopters whirred and ducked. I looked at the crowds below and on the shoreline. The Opera House pavilion was packed, as were The Rocks, Central Quay, and Kirribilli. As far as the eye could see, people had gathered in their thousands to watch the protest, our protest. Boats and yachts filled the harbour, and the ferries had stopped running because they couldn't squeeze through the unruly waterway. I couldn't help but smile at how annoyed the Australian authorities must be at this disruption. But we'd given them a timeline, we were doing no harm. They simply had to wait it out.

And I could tell that every single one of us on the bridge was affected by the power of what we had achieved. We were singular in our actions; we were indeed the zen warrior army that Jason envisaged. I pulled out my ear plugs and a solid wave of noise crashed into me, but I wasn't pulled into its undertow. Instead, I rode the crest of frenzied sound.

At seven a.m., Jason sounded the next siren, and we were ready. We unfurled the rolls of toilet paper from the top of the arch and the railing, and they fell like a solid white curtain.

While all of this was going on, Jason, miked up and recording, narrated to the live feed on YouTube and ABC News.

We had scheduled thousands of tweets to go out, with a

link to the video. From their phones on the bridge, while they waited for the second siren to sound, the army posted updates on Facebook, Instagram, Twitter, and Snapchat. They fired off emails, text messages, and anything else they could think of to spread the word. Jason had written a script linked to a hashtag, and as long as the hashtag was used, the posts would be deleted after the protest so the cops couldn't trace them.

At the exact moment that the curtain dropped, the police fell eerily silent and even the dogs stopped barking. Afterwards, I realized it was simply coincidental, a command must have been issued for them to quieten down and wait for the protest to be over. But it worked to our benefit because it made the whole thing so much more dramatic.

And then something happened. A groundswell that started slowly. We weren't sure what we were hearing at first, but the crowd started clapping. They clapped and cheered, and the noise grew to the point that I was worried we wouldn't hear the third siren call at 7:15. But we did hear it, and, once again in a single motion, we released the toilet paper. The long white strands fluttered and flew. Some floated down, while others were caught in a breeze and drifted away into the blue sky. Our curtain was a cloud that slowly dissipated. Some of the toilet paper fell onto the boats below, and I saw people eagerly scrambling and grabbing it, souvenirs of what they had just witnessed.

And none of us moved.

At 7:20, Jason made his speech. "Have you forgotten how to think?" Jason began. "I had. Most of us have. We have politicians, teachers, religious leaders, parents, television programs, video games, and enough computer equipment to send us to the moon and back, and all of it is designed to stop us from thinking. I want you to take a moment to think about the fact that you live on a planet. A real planet. Not a virtual planet but a real planet. And we are killing it every single day because we don't know how to think for ourselves anymore. We fill the world with rubbish. Do you need all the things you buy and throw away? Can't we learn to share? Sounds ridiculous, doesn't it? Who on earth shares anything? We want everything to be mine, mine, mine. But I believe we can learn to share. Countries can learn to share. Children and adults can learn to share. We can share jobs, homes, resources, and ideas. We can create communities. We can create financial security because we can look after each other. We look after our own families, we believe in our own countries, so why can't we believe in a global world in the same way? I believe we can learn to find joy in shared societal values that respect human life. Our move to a mechanized future will take us further away from the earth herself and will ultimately lead to our demise.

"We have lost all sense of who we humans are, what we are, and we don't even know what the word 'human' means. We have lost all sense of value. I beg this of you. Think. Think for yourself. See that a robotic existence is not the future for human beings. Be Your Revolution! Steal back your reality. Steal back your life and the world as you would like it to be. If each person tries to live their life with integrity, the world will heal. Steal back moments of being a true human being on planet Earth, not a zombie attached to a device. Take back your world from the thieving corporations, from greed, from the lust of materialism. Be Your Revolution. Steal Back Your World." He paused for a moment.

"I need you to remember this message. And I am willing to take extreme action, to make you all remember this day and this message. You cannot afford to forget."

At 7:26, Jason raised a gun to his temple and shot himself.

He crumpled to the ground. I dropped to his side and cradled him. His aim had been true. The bullet had entered his head cleanly; there was no exit wound. A small pool of blood gathered under his head as his heart continued to pump. When he died, a few seconds later, I closed his eyelids and stroked his head.

I wanted to talk to him, to tell him that he had done it, that he had achieved everything he had set out to do, but I wanted to honour what he had wanted, so I stayed silent and stroked his head.

The crowds around the harbour screamed when they realized what had happened; we heard them clearly over the helicopters.

Sean sounded the final siren, and the army descended from the arches. It turned out that we hadn't accurately calculated the dismantling. It was 8:30 by the time the last anarchist left the bridge. The cars and trucks took longer to leave than we had thought they would. The ground was lined with thousands of T-shirts, the only litter we'd leave. Jason had urged people not to be tempted to take their T-shirts as souvenirs. He had said it was too risky and that if they were caught with them, they'd be arrested. He had asked people to lay the T-shirts down flat to line the road and the pedestrian sidewalks. This blanket would be our final message. It was our way of saying that we would tar the road with our intentions and that even if we were trampled on, we would remain strong.

I had known what Jason was going to do. And Sean had known. Jason had asked Sean to leave me with his body because he didn't want Sean to be arrested, and Sean and I had both agreed to do what he wanted. I had offered to stay with Jason. I had realized that I was ready to end my time as a fugitive and face the music. I would not admit to stealing the car or Queenie. I would simply say that Jason had picked me up when I was hitchhiking out of Sydney the day after I walked off the ferry.

And Jason had said that the blame for the protest would all be on him. And of course, there'd be nothing of value left to find on his hard drive as it was set to implode at 7:26 a.m. And, just to make sure, he had asked one of the fellows at the barber shop to take his laptop and drop it into the bay.

Martha had collected Queenie from me before we left for Sydney and was going to pay some kid to take her to a police

270 LISA DE NIKOLITS

station and say the cat had been found near the Paddington Markets.

"What if the kid steals Queenie?" I had asked.

"I'll watch whoever it is and make sure they carry the box into the police station," Martha had assured me.

I had cried like a kid when I handed Queenie over and I thanked her for being such a great friend to me when I needed one most. She seemed grumpy, but she nestled her head under my chin as if to say she understood. At least I hoped she did. Things were going to change and it was time for Queenie to go home.

And I cried while I stood guard over Jason's body on the empty bridge lined with T-shirts. Police dogs advanced, barking at full volume, and men in combat gear with shields marched heavily towards me. The helicopters hovered, their rotors shuddering like my heartbeat, and a hundred red-and-blue lights flashed.

They were coming at me from the north and south sides of the bridge, and I sat there, guarding the body of my dearest friend.

41. MARGAUX

HE WAS DEAD. My love was dead. I fell to my knees. Janet and Tim rushed to help me. Adam and Rick were in shock. The crowd continued to scream, and it seemed like the whole world was trying to run away.

I pulled myself up and looked up at the bridge through the binoculars I had bought. The police were taking Lyndon away. "They've got him," I said to Janet and Tim. The bridge was curiously empty. It was amazing how the vast crowds had scattered so quickly, like tiny grains of sand blown away by a single gust of wind. The Opera House pavilion was empty. We made our way up to the top of Circular Quay and managed to hail a cab. Adam and Rick were with us, but when we got the cab, I told them I'd meet them back at the hostel, according to the plan.

I could see that Adam was going to argue with me, and I was instantly furious with him. *Don't you dare make this about you.*

"Stick to the plan," Rick told him gently, reading my face. "Come on." He took Adam by the hand. I was angry with Adam for creating a problem at this crucial moment. He knew the plan; he knew I had to go alone. I got into the cab and refused to wave at Adam as I drove off.

I had known the plan too. We all did. But nevertheless, seeing Jason drop like that, hearing that tiny pop that had sounded more like a firecracker than a gunshot in the movies, well, it was terrible.

I forced myself not to cry and choked down the tears. "Follow the plan," I told myself, and the cab dropped me off at the police station. I walked inside and found Sean. I hadn't met him before, but I recognized him. He seemed to know who I was.

"Are you okay?" We both said to each other at the same time. We then we both shook our heads.

"No," Sean said. "But here's the thing. It's what the big man wanted. Did you see the crowds? A hundred million views of the speech on YouTube. He's gone viral. And, all the people there. It was bigger than even he had hoped. And our lot listened to him. They followed the instructions. So, if he was here now, which I know he is, he would be happy."

He was talking to himself more than me, as we were strangers. But we didn't feel like strangers; we felt like a bereaved family.

Sean took Lyndon's passport from me, and we found a police officer and explained who we were and why we were there.

"Lyndon Blaine has committed no offence," Sean said, and his accent changed from lowbrow Westie to highbrow Sydney. "I will not release this passport to you. I need to see Lyndon before I do that."

We were taken to a small room to wait for Lyndon. The room had two plush sofas, a coffee machine, and children's toys in a box in the corner. Sean and I sat down without speaking.

I looked up every time I heard a sound, expecting to see Lyndon appearing at the door.

We waited for two hours. "I should be with him," Sean said, worried. "I am his legal counsel." He got up and I followed him to the front desk.

"I'm his lawyer," Sean told the officer on duty. "I've been here for over two hours. I demand to see my client or there'll be hell to pay. You're not following legal protocol."

The officer spoke into a walkie-talkie on his shoulder. "He'll be right out," he told us, and we weren't sure if he meant Lyndon or another police officer.

But it was Lyndon. They brought him out into the hallway.

I watched him walking towards us. He looked haggard. It was so strange to see him—it felt as if we had never been apart, and yet, we had never been together, all at the same time.

Lyndon was shocked to see me. "Margaux? What are you doing here? Sean?"

"She knows everything," Sean said simply. "We need them to release Jason's body. I'll go and get that going, while you two wait here."

He walked away and I remained silent. I wasn't going to be the one to make this right, if such a thing even existed.

"How did you know?" Lyndon finally asked me, breaking the silence. "How did you know to be here? How do you know Sean?" It was a bit odd, talking to my husband with his flashy new look. He was confident and lean, and I liked that he was no longer the pasty, shrunken, bloated old man who had been shrinking into decrepitude.

"I know Jason," I replied, and it was hard to say his name without crying. "He and I emailed after that first message you sent. After the first message he sent, I should say. And then we met up in Sydney when you came in to plan the protest. I haven't met Sean before."

"You met Jason? When?"

"For God's sake, Lyndon, you sound like Adam. I'm sick and tired of having you both constantly fire questions at me because you need to know the nth detail. And actually, it's none of your business when I saw Jason. You left me, remember? And you wouldn't have messaged me but for Jason. So really, I don't need to tell you anything."

"He meant the world to me," he said, and I looked away. I didn't care about his grief, only mine. I left him and went to sit on one of the chairs that lined the hallway. He joined me and we sat in silence.

Sean appeared, holding a piece of paper. "They're releasing the body to a funeral home. Were they tough on you, mate?" he asked.

Lyndon nodded. "Very. But what could they do? There was a lot of anger, but they couldn't press charges. It wasn't fun, but it went according to plan."

"Let's go and get our man," Sean said, and we walked outside into the warm sunshine of the May day. The whole world was carrying on with its business, and it was like the protest had never happened. It was only noon and Jason was dead.

I stopped on the sidewalk. "You're taking him back to Apollo Bay, right?"

Sean nodded.

"Adam, Rick and I will meet you there," I said. "We're flying to Melbourne and we'll drive from there."

"Adam is here?" Lyndon was astounded. "Who's Rick?"

"Adam's boyfriend. The one you refused to meet."

"But how do you all know all this? I don't understand."

"You're like a broken record, Lyndon," I said. "We'll meet you in Apollo Bay." And I walked away without answering him any further.

42. LYNDON

I STOOD ON THE SIDEWALK, my black jeans and T-shirt covered with blood, and watched Margaux walk away.

"You should know something," Sean said, with clear reluctance. "Jason and your wife were in love."

"What? Don't be ridiculous."

"He was. She was. They were. He came to see her twice in Sydney. They emailed and texted and talked every day."

"Since when?"

"I guess after the first message Jason made you send."

Jason had utterly betrayed me. I couldn't believe what I was hearing. He was my life, my brave new world. I had run away from Margaux. I had wanted to be free of her and the life I had with her. And now, here she was, once again, taking away my pleasure. "She's so controlling," I burst out.

Sean shook his head. "They met because of you. Jason wanted me to tell you. I told him it wouldn't be easy and that you'd be hurt and angry, but he said I had to tell you. And he wanted me to tell you this too. He said that you need be kind to her. Step back and be kind. That's what he said."

"He did not say that." I was taken aback.

"He did. What do you think? I made it up? Why would I do that? It's none of my business. I'm just the messenger."

By now, we were in Sean's BMW, driving to the funeral home. "Why does she get special attention and treatment? We're all grieving but we must be kind to *her*?"

"My God, Lyndon. Listen to yourself, mate. I thought you were better than this. You're like a child whose toy has been taken away. Jason wasn't a toy. He was a man, a good man, a man we lost today. And your little G-string is in a knot because your wife gets special attention? Maybe it's time she did. You weren't very nice to her back there. You treated her like an annoying inconvenience. But listen, like I said, it's none of my business. I don't even want to talk about it. You're not acting like the guy I thought you were, so let's just shut up and get this business done. This isn't about you or your wife and you. It's about Jason."

I heard what he was saying, but the roar of betrayal thudded in my ears. How many emails had they exchanged? When had he texted? When had they talked? Had they talked about me? And finally, sex. They must have slept together. How could he not have told me? Because I would have behaved like this, obviously.

"Wait here," Sean said when we got to the funeral home. I was left alone with my swirling thoughts. I studied the blood on my hands and clothes. Perhaps it was macabre, but I wanted to stay in those clothes forever.

Margaux had looked good. She seemed more confident and she looked younger, less anxious, despite her grief. She looked centred, and I wondered what had happened. But I knew. It was Jason. Jason had happened to both of us. And Adam was here? With his boyfriend? I sighed. I could see that my carefree life had come to an end. It was time to resume the weight of familial obligation.

Jason and I had chatted about what I would do afterwards. He had left the shop to Sean, and he said it was up to Sean if I could stay, but given the mornings' events, I wondered if that was going to pan out. I felt as if I had broken Sean's trust by being so negative about the news about Margaux and Jason. Sean clearly felt like I was being selfish and short-sighted, but how would he have felt? I told myself that it wasn't realistic to expect him to understand, given that his most significant others were botanical variations on a theme. I wondered if I had lost Sean's trust forever? Surely he understood I was grieving? He was, too. The world felt so empty without Jason. I told myself not to take Sean's chilly attitude personally.

Jason had also given me his machine and, as a parting gift, a tattoo of a lemon on the inside of my wrist. After he had finished the last detail on the lemon, he said, "So, when you're reverting to your former self and I'm not around to give you a boxing to the ears, you can look at this and remember your alter ego, Liam Lemon, the guy who changed his life. You've got a good heart, Lyndon, and there's a lot of life and love left for you in the world. I want you to remember that."

"Jason," I said, looking down at my wrist, "I've let you down. Look at me, the only thing I did was whine on about me. No wonder Sean's annoyed. Meanwhile, today was everything you hoped for and more. Did you see the crowds on and off the bridge? I wonder if the toilet paper unfurled like we wanted. I wonder how it looked on the television?"

Sean returned and wordlessly got into the car.

"Did we do it?" I asked him.

"Do what?" He was short with me.

"Was the protest everything we wanted it to be?"

"You were there, mate. What do you think?" But then he relented. "Yeah, it was perfect. Everything happened just like we wanted it to, just like Jason planned. I know that wherever he is, he's a happy man. It's us, the ones left behind who are sad."

"I am sorry Sean," I said. "You lost him too."

"A bunch of us did," Sean replied.

He didn't seem to be in the mood to forgive me, and I realized something. Now that Jason was gone, the dynamic had changed. Sean was the new boss, and this was the start of a new regime. I wasn't sure that Sean liked me very much. I was familiar with this feeling. The sinking in one's gut when new management was brought in, and I had to start ass-licking all over again. Well, no ass-licking this time. I'd leave with dignity, on my terms.

Part of me had known that I wouldn't be able to stay in Apollo Bay once Jason was gone. And that's why I needed to send Queenie home, although it broke my heart. This part of my life was over. "Can I stay at Jason's apartment until the funeral?" I asked.

Sean seemed startled by the question. "Of course you can," he said, without hesitation. "You can stay as long as you like. That's what he would have wanted."

It took us eleven hours to get back to Apollo Bay. Sean even let me drive his treasured car. We both just wanted the trip to be behind us.

Life in Apollo Bay looked exactly the same as when we'd left it. It was as if nothing had happened in the world at all. Our huge statement hadn't had any effect on this little town. It seemed that the ripples from the stone thrown hadn't reached here.

But I was wrong. Sean opened the door to the barber shop and Martha was inside, next to the Mayor of Apollo Bay.

"We're putting a great big funeral on for him," the Mayor said. "We all loved him. The service will be at the RSL Club and anybody who wants to say something, can. It won't be religious as such, but it will be led by a Buddhist priest, which I hope is the correct term. In fact, Jason organized it all. Following that, we will go to the beach to scatter his ashes, and a tent will be set up on the beachfront with cake and English high tea. We will send our man out in style."

Martha outlined some of the finer details, and then we were left with nothing else to say.

"Day after tomorrow then," Martha said. "Have you two even seen it on TV?"

We shook our heads.

"Let's fix that," she said, but Sean told her he was exhausted, and I agreed with him.

"As Jason would say, bollocks to tired," Martha said, flicking the TV on. "Many people recorded the whole thing. There are dozens of versions on YouTube. The newspapers have talked about nothing else. It's on a loop on this channel."

We started watching it and it didn't seem real. But then, it all came back to me: my panic attack, the crowd, Jason's powerful voice, and that sense of being part of something big.

But I felt terribly alone and couldn't watch anymore. "I am going to my room," I said and got up.

I couldn't deal with my grief. I locked myself in my bedroom, but it reminded me of Queenie, a double blow. I didn't even have my cat anymore. I took a quick shower, changed my clothes, and packed my protest clothes carefully into a bag. I put on my running shoes, slipped out the back, and walked for hours. I tried not to think; I just walked. I cried as I walked, sobbing until I had no breath left. I lost track of how long I was gone, and I had no idea what time it was when I returned home. I took another shower and climbed into Jason's bed and everything hit me. Exhaustion hit me like a truck. I was aware of being asleep but it was more like I was anesthetized, dragged to lie in a place of drugged semi-consciousness just below the surface of my mind.

I had no idea how to carry on with my life.

43. MARGAUX

"HE IS SUCH A DICKHEAD," I said to Tim and Janet. "All he wanted to know was why I was there. Like I had no right. Like I was invading his lovely new life. Like I was an annoying inconvenience."

"He was grief-stricken, just like you," Tim said, bluntly. "And after that day, and all the planning that must have gone into it, I bet there was lot going on in his head. And, he was right next to Jason when he killed himself. And then he got locked up in a police station, so it's no surprise he was acting in in a very self-involved way. Plus, he had no idea you were going to be there. What did you expect? Sorrowful recriminations? I don't think that was ever in the cards."

"Why don't you tell me what you really think?" I grumbled, but I knew he was right. Lyndon had behaved as I would have, had I been in his shoes.

"Mom, we're not coming to the funeral, if that's okay?" Adam said.

I nodded my head. "I understand. There's no reason for you to."

"We're going skydiving and scuba diving, and I'm going to learn how to sail a yacht." Adam was excited and happy and why shouldn't he be? He was on holiday, he was in love, he deserved to play and enjoy life.

"Sounds amazing," I told him, trying to sound enthusiastic. "Just be careful. Rick, look after him for me."

Rick assured me that he would, and they left for some adventure or other.

"I'm going to lie down," I said. "Two days until the funeral. More waiting."

And just then, Graham arrived. "I wondered if you might want to come and stay with me until you go to Melbourne," she said, and yes, I did want that.

"It's not that I don't love you," I said to Tim and Janet. "But being here, I'll just wallow in my memories and grief."

"Yes, it's much better that you go and wallow in your memories and grief with Graham," Tim said with a smile.

I collected an overnight bag, hugged the others and left.

Graham drove us away, and I started talking about Lyndon. It wasn't a conversation but a rant, and by the time we reached her house, I noticed that she was quite pale. My hand flew to my mouth.

"Oh God. I'm sorry, Graham. Me, me, me. I'm behaving like a child. I'm sorry. Don't worry, that's it. I'm done shouting about Lyndon."

She looked relieved. "You're angry and you're grieving," she said, excusing me. "I get it."

"Yeah, well, time to stop being so pathetic. Time to woman up and wear the big-girl panties."

We laughed and my heart lifted for a moment. Once inside, Graham poured me a large glass of wine.

"Here's to Jason," I said. "What a man."

Graham clinked her glass against mine. "Do you want to watch it?" she asked. "Or is that too morbid? It was incredible. The whole world talking about us! We don't have to watch the ending."

"I'd love to see it," I said.

We watched it three times in a row. A sense of peace settled upon me. "I was a part of that," I marvelled.

"I know, amazing, isn't it? Trish and I were on the bridge, and it was incredible. I did something Jason wouldn't have wanted though. I kept my T-shirt. A lot of people did. I couldn't bear to part with it."

"I don't think he would have minded. Why don't you come with me to the funeral?"

She shook her head. "I didn't know him, so it wouldn't be right. Will you be okay though?"

"Oh yes, I will be fine." I looked down at my foot. *True Love.* "I won't let him down. He would have wanted me to live life and enjoy it and not use his death as an excuse to sink into depression. That would have disappointed him, I think. Yes, I'll be fine."

44. LYNDON

THE DAY OF THE FUNERAL arrived. My bag was packed. After the beach party, I was going to go back to Sydney. And I hadn't thought further than that.

I had no idea why, but I was looking forward to seeing Margaux. I was surprised by that. I hoped I could make it up to her—my tactless interrogation at such a bad time. She'd been right, I'd been just like Adam, and it was one of the things that always annoyed me about him: his little-boy characteristic of needing to know every tiny thing at the first possible moment. I had done the same thing.

I was the first one at the RSL on Gallipoli Parade, but it soon filled up with bodies packing together. It was standing room only. I kept looking around for Margaux. I had saved her a seat. I finally saw her and I managed to catch her eye. I waved at her to come and sit with me.

She seemed uncertain, but she came and sat down. I didn't know what to say to her. But then, the service started and we couldn't talk anyway.

Margaux was holding it together, but her tears started to fall. I moved closer to her and took her hand, and for a moment, we were together like we had been for all those years: a unit, a couple, a team, a world unto ourselves. Then she had to take her hand back to blow her nose, but I hoped that perhaps we could be that couple again. A part of me would always feel betrayed that she and Jason had been in love but that was my ego talking. I had loved him too, and I had to focus on that when bitterness rose in my heart.

We walked to the beach together. There were hundreds of people. We couldn't get near the front so we stood on the outer edge, in the park where I'd first met Jason. We caught whispers of the ceremony on the breeze. Margaux grabbed my hand, and I held on to it tight.

We didn't go into the tea tent but sat down at the bench with neither of us sure what to do next. We saw a police officer rushing up to people, frantically asking questions. Someone from the barber shop pointed to me. Surely, they couldn't still want me in connection with the protest? And why was there only one officer?

She rushed over to us, asking if we were Margaux and Lyndon Blaine, and we said yes. She told us that our son Adam had been in a terrible accident and was in intensive care at Sydney Hospital.

She said she would drive us to the Apollo Bay airport where a helicopter was waiting to take us to him.

"A helicopter?"

"Your son's boyfriend organized it. You have to get there as soon as you can."

"I was so cruel to him," Margaux said on the way to the airport. "I kept telling him he was too needy, and I was impatient with him." She was sobbing silently, her body shaking, her face a waterfall of tears.

"I was too," I told her. "I always was. It wasn't your fault. We love him. He knows that, right? He knows how much we love him?"

"I don't know," Margaux said, shaking her head. "I really don't. Oh, I hate myself for how I treated him. And I shouldn't have let him go skydiving."

Adam's parachute hadn't opened properly, and the tandem jumper's chute had also malfunctioned. The tandem jumper managed to navigate them to the ground as best he could. He had broken a few bones and would be fine, but Adam had broken his neck and was in a coma. They couldn't say how extensive the damage would be or if he was even going to wake up.

I tried to comfort Margaux as best I could, but I was sick with guilt. I hadn't wanted to return to my old life with my family, but now that it was being taken away from me, it was the only thing in the whole world that I did want.

"He'll be okay," I said to Margaux. "He has to be."

45. MARGAUX

WE WERE SITTING in Adam's room, waiting for him to wake up. Praying for him to wake up. Rick, Lyndon, Tim and Janet, Graham and me. We were all praying. *Wake up Adam, wake up.* The doctor had told us that when he wakes, his neck would heal and there would be no paralysis. Now, all we needed was for him to wake up. But the doctor couldn't say how long it would take.

Two days passed. We fell into a timeless zone of blinding fluorescent lights, bad coffee, and twisted naps in iron-framed chairs. "If it takes longer for him to wake up, is that a bad thing?" I asked the doctor.

He shook his head. "No. It doesn't mean anything. It just means he's healing in his own time."

"What if he dies from the blow to head?" I asked Lyndon. "Of course I am relieved he's not paralyzed, but what if he just never wakes up?" He had no answers. None of us did.

Trish came to visit; she even laid her hands on him. I prayed for her to heal him. Anita popped by and she was restrained and bearable.

"Adam?" Lyndon was talking to him. He was in the chair next to the bed. "Come on, my boy, wake up. We need you to wake up." Lyndon was crying. "I am so sorry I was such a bad father," he said, taking Adam's hand. "I need you to wake up so I can be a better father to you. I want to make you happy. All I ever wanted was for you to be happy. No, that's not true. I didn't want or care about anything, really, except being left alone to live in my head by myself. But I don't want that anymore. I want to have a real relationship with you, and Rick. And Helen's pregnant and she needs you too. We all need you. Please my boy, please, forgive me and come back. Rick needs you and loves you. I need and love you, and your mother does too. Please my boy, come back. It's time to come back. We're a family, and we can't be a family without you."

At this point, we were all in tears. Maybe it was our collective pain and love that jolted Adam back to life because his hand moved, and then he blinked, and then his eyes opened, and when we all broke into a raucous cheer, he was startled but he gave us a cautious smile.

"Hi," he said. "I thought I was dead. I don't want to skydive again."

Rick howled, then laid his head tenderly on Adam's chest.

I found myself in my husband's arms.

"I meant what I said," Lyndon said, holding me close. "And I'm sorry I was such a selfish husband. I want to have a real relationship with you. If you leave me, my life will be all the things I thought I wanted, full of uninterrupted solitude and silence. But I don't want that at all. I miss you so much. I miss your great big laugh and the way you do things. I miss looking at you. Margaux, I am sorry. Please can we try again?"

I answered him in the best way I knew. I kissed him like a teenager and when we finally pulled apart, the whole room applauded.

"Jeez, guys, get a room," Adam said, with a grin. "And can I please have a grilled cheese sandwich and a Coke? A man's dying of hunger here!"

"I am sure we can manage that," Lyndon said and we went to the cafeteria to find a grilled cheese sandwich for our son. While we were waiting for our order, Lyndon looked down at my foot. "Nice tat," he said. "You going to let me do one on you?"

"You never know," I said, smiling. I took his hand in mine. "But I have learned one thing from all of this. Anything's possible if you're willing to take a chance. And I'm willing to take a chance on you and me." He leaned into me, and I knew we were both thinking about the man we loved, the man who would live in our hearts forever.

"We'll do him proud," Lyndon said, and I nodded.

I looked down and my eyes filled with tears. *True Love*. It was all the proof I needed that anything, indeed, was possible.

ACKNOWLEDGEMENTS

Many thanks as always to my beloved Inanna Publications for this and all the books. You make my most important dreams come true. Thank you dear Luciana Ricciutelli, editor-in-chief at Inanna Publications, for your marvellous editing and your constant faith in me, and endless thanks to Renée Knapp, Inanna's tireless and talented publicist.

Thank you to my lovely Bradford Dunlop for eternal patience and support and endless thanks to my family, always.

Thank you Colin Frings for this lovely cover! And to Glenn Larkby for letting us use the artwork.

Thanks to Robert Teixeira, for help with researching anarchism. Robert Teixeira is interested in history, theory and practice of anarchism and is involved in queer community advocacy and politics. Thanks to Toronto Police Services Forensic Specialist, Detective Ed Adach, for his help with the crime scene.

Many thanks to all my early readers for their kindness and loving support of this book: Heather Babcock, Brenda Clews, SK Dyment, James Fisher (*The Miramichi Reader*), Elizabeth Greene, Nate Hendley, Dietrich Kalteis, Fran Lewis, Sylvia Maultash Warsh, Shirley McDaniel, Myna Wallin, and Ruth Zuchter.

Sadly, I lost my Queenie this year, and I say a big thank you to Isabella Creamy Diva, the best furry little friend ever. I will always miss you.

What a great writing community out there too: The Crime Writers of Canada, The Sisters in Crime, Toronto Chapter and National, the Mesdames of Mayhem, The Short Mystery Fiction Society, the International Thriller Writers, Noir at the Bar, the Junction Reading Series, and the Toronto Public Libraries.

And thank you to my patient friends who understand that I need to write above all else and forgive me for missing out on birthdays and dinners and the normal ways that most people hang out!

I acknowledge research from the following:

"Madness" in Australia: Histories, Heritage and the Asylum, edited by Catharine Coleborne and Dolly McKinnon (University of Queensland Press, 2003).

Online research for the following was referenced and fictionalized: transhumanism, eco-eroticism, tattooing older skin, toilet paper as a biodegradable resource ("Littleton TP's its own streets as a way to fill cracks – single-ply only," by John Aguilar, published in the *Denver Post*, November 3, 2016), Callan Park Hospital, Chelmsford Sleep Therapy, eco-erotica, spells (*How and Why to Case a Magical Circle: 6 Simple Steps* by Tess Whitehurst) and "Sydney's Shameful Asylums: The Silent Houses of Pain Where Inmates were Chained and Sadists Reigned" by Ben Pike, *The Daily Telegraph,* in Australia, on March 2, 2015.

Quotes from Mahatma Gandhi and Emma Goldman found

online, various sources. Definition of occult as per Wikipedia and various online medical journals. Thanks also to the Australian Truck Drivers' Memorial for information about the Australian Truck Drivers' Memorial Wall.

Thanks to Liz Worth and her book *Going Beyond the Little White Book: A Contemporary Guide to Tarot,* copyright © Liz Worth (Standard Copyright Licence) (Lulu Publishing Services, 2016). All misinterpretations about tarot are my own.

Photo: Bradford Dunlop

Lisa de Nikolits is the internationally-acclaimed, award-winning author of eight previous novels: *The Hungry Mirror, West of Wawa, A Glittering Chaos, The Witchdoctor's Bones, Between The Cracks She Fell, The Nearly Girl, No Fury Like That,* and *Rotten Peaches. No Fury Like That* was published in Italian in 2019 by Edizioni Le Assassine under the title, *Una furia dell'altro mondo.* Her short fiction and poetry have also been published in various anthologies and journals across the country. She is a member of the Mesdames of Mayhem, the Crime Writers of Canada, Sisters in Crime, and the International Thriller Writers. Originally from South Africa, Lisa de Nikolits came to Canada in 2000. She lives and writes in Toronto.